ALSO BY KAY NOLTE SMITH

Mindspell
Catching Fire
The Watcher

ELEGY
for a
SOPRANO

ELEGY
for a
SOPRANO

Kay Nolte Smith

Villard Books
New York
1985

All rights reserved under International and Pan-American Copyright
Conventions. Published in the United States by Villard Books, a division
of Random House, Inc., New York, and simultaneously in Canada by
Random House of Canada Limited, Toronto.

Library of Congress Cataloging in Publication Data
Smith, Kay Nolte.
Elegy for a soprano.
I. Title.
PS3569.M537554E4   1985   813'.54   85-40188
ISBN 0-394-54667-9

Grateful acknowledgment is made to G. Schirmer, Inc., for
permission to reprint excerpts from *Turandot* by Giacomo Puccini.
Copyright 1926 by G. Ricordi & C. s.p.a., Milan.
Used by arrangement with G. Schirmer, Inc., U.S. agent for
G. Ricordi & C. s.p.a., Milan.

Book design by Amy Lamb

Manufactured in the United States of America

9 8 7 6 5 4 3 2

FIRST EDITION

To my wonderful sister, Judith Nolte Heimer

CONTENTS

PART 1

VICTIM

CHAPTER

1

The voice was like jets of molten silver, arcing and shining above the orchestra. The eyes were half-closed, and the face was lifted in ecstasy, so that the dark hair hung below the woman's shoulders. There was a streak of white at her left temple, like a dagger pointing backward.

Her beautiful hands stretched out, and the long, yearning fingers reached, in imagination, for the head that had been severed and laid on a shield. Although the words were sung in German, their meaning was clear to everyone in the Boston concert hall: "I have kissed thy mouth. There was a bitter taste on thy lips. Was it the taste of blood? . . . Perchance it was the taste of love. They say that love hath a bitter taste. . . ."

The audience sat transfixed by the sight and sound of the dark eroticism, over which youth and beauty lay like a veil.

They forgot that the woman was actually fifty-one years old and had never been beautiful, even when she was young. They forgot that lines had collected in the hollows of her face and the years had darkened her voice. They saw and heard only the Salome of Richard Strauss's opera: the young princess who lusted after John the Baptist, danced to pay for his death, and then demanded his severed head.

Few of them knew by what means the singer made them believe in Salome's youth and beauty. And in her evil. They knew only that whatever she sang, they believed. She gave them no choice; it was as if she willed herself into a role so completely that no one could refuse to accept her. Whatever resistance there might be was conquered by her voice. Despite its darker color it still had a unique combination of purity and sensuousness, and could still move with seamless agility over nearly three octaves or spin out in long, flowing lines that enchained the listeners and permitted them no motion except a quiet inner shattering.

After the final phrase, there was silence. Then the waves of sound began, and crashed up against the stage. The singer held out her arms to receive them, the huge sleeves of her gown swaying like black sails.

Each time she left the stage, the crowd thundered and chanted her name—"Vardis! Vardis! Var-dis! VAR-DIS!"—until she returned and bent in another graceful bow, only to leave once again without an encore. It went on for ten minutes.

Then she came out carrying a guitar.

The crowd sank back into silence. When she strummed the familiar chords, many of them were amazed and delighted. Then came the words they knew so well:

> *See the knives come, see the blood run,*
> *Watch the cutting of all our young flowers . . .*

People smiled with a tinge of sadness or frowned; either way, their minds and memories ran back to the 1960s.

In those days Vardis had temporarily left the operatic stage to appear in the music drama from which the song came: a blistering attack on tyranny in all its forms, written by a fellow Norwegian. She did it first in Oslo and then off Broadway, and its songs became part of the musical vocabulary of protest. Sometimes she appeared at antidraft rallies, along with the folk and popular singers on the platform, to raise the sword of her voice in "The Dead Flower Song."

So when she sang it at the Boston concert, many felt their throats tighten with the anger and sadness, and passion, they had known almost two decades earlier. She ended the song with the famous slicing gesture she always used—"Cut the stems and kill"; somehow the listeners saw not her hands but a young man's falling body.

"Vardis!" they shouted. "VARDIS! VAR-DIS! VAR-DIS!"

But she left the stage and didn't return, and finally they had to accept that she was gone. Many thronged backstage, where they thrust out their programs in mute witness to feelings they could not express. Her presence seemed as large to them as it had been onstage—perhaps even larger, for now they were confronting face to face the power she had over them, which was the power of their own responses.

Afterward, some of them would claim she must have had some kind of premonition, for hadn't everything on the program represented a high point of her career, almost as if she were reliving it and saluting farewell? Salome was the role that had made her a world-class artist, but hadn't she ceased singing it on the operatic stage, and wasn't it rare for her to perform the final aria even in concert, as she did that night in Boston? Wasn't "The Dead Flower Song" something she hadn't sung in public in years? And, most telling of all, hadn't her program included an aria from *Il Trovatore*, which was not only one of her trademark successes but an opera in which her character died by poison?

Two weeks after Boston, home from the tour and rested, Vardis Wolf sat in the dressing room of her house in Manhattan's East Sixties, getting ready for an evening with friends. The room was furnished in the smoky blue color she favored and contained two vases of the white roses she loved, which filled the house whenever she was there.

She sat before a makeup mirror, leaning toward a face that was long, thin, and bony, with a crest of nose she said would have qualified her to sing the witch in *Hansel and Gretel*. Her eyes, even before she painted the black lines above and below them, were huge. In the mirror lights they seemed gray, but they could also look blue or even hazel. Once she had told a reporter that she was too complex a person to have a single eye color. The reporter hadn't been sure she was joking.

From hidden speakers came the voice of a young, new tenor singing "Recondita armonia." When it finished, she glanced be-

hind her in the mirror, at the man who stood in the corner. "He's
the one they want for the Verdi Requiem if I do it in Los An-
geles," she said. "What do you think?"

The man folded his arms. While Vardis applied makeup, her
long fingers moving like a sculptor's, the two of them discussed
the tenor's performance, technically and thoroughly. When they
finished, she was still for a moment, looking at the man in the
mirror. His posture had an unconscious elegance and his face a
harmony of features that she said made her think of Chopin.

Then she wiped her hands on a tissue and threw it among the
blue ceramic pots of makeup, painted with her initials, that were
lined up on the dressing table. "I think I should issue a statement
about Nygaard," she said.

"Nygaard? Why?"

"He died yesterday, that's why."

"That's right. I remember now," the man said.

"No, Conrad. You're just pretending to."

Her voice flicked across his face without leaving a mark.
"Maybe so," he said amiably.

"Nygaard knew how to write for the voice, more than a lot of
the idiots who claim to be writing serious music today. How
many of them could write anything as good as 'The Dead Flower
Song'? None." Vardis applied a dark pencil to her eyebrows. "I'm
going to miss Nygaard."

"But you haven't seen him in years."

She shrugged. "Now there'll be no one to speak Norwegian
with. Except that baritone from Oslo, who's barely civilized in
any language. Nygaard was from a little town up north, not far
from where my mother sent me during the war. Did I ever tell
you?"

"I don't remember."

"Who knows, he could even have seen me then."

"Do you ever think of those days anymore?"

Vardis sat back, her gaze going through the mirror to a farther
distance but gathering no softness as it went. "No," she said in
a moment. "Why should I think of times like those?" She began
to do up her long hair with ornamental pins, arranging the white
streak at her temple to sweep backward and up.

"Do you think of any times at all?"

"What kind of question is that?"

"Don't you ever look back at your life . . . like the time when you first came to New York . . . and remember what you were like? What you did?"

"No. Why should I?"

"I don't know." Conrad's gentle voice was insistent. "I thought perhaps there were events from those days that you would need to think about sometimes."

She turned and looked at him directly. "No. But I gather you do. That would explain where your mind is—in the past."

"Not all the time," he said, still amiable.

She pinned up the last loop of her hair and said, "Get me the dress."

Conrad went into the adjoining room and brought out one of the silk caftans she favored, in a burgundy color. She stood, he slipped it over her head and shoulders, and they went to the small elevator that took them down to the main floor of the house.

In the large, comfortable living room waited the small group of admirers, associates, and friends that Vardis had allowed to enter her private life. Some called them her "disciples," but they preferred the name Vardis herself liked to use: the Wolfpack.

There were nine of them, although there had been more at various times. Some had known her for nearly forty years and some for less than a decade; two had met her by working for her and several by just writing her fan letters; but for all of them, the association with her was one of the most intense experiences in their lives. They liked to gather at her town house, where two of them rented apartments from her, and hear about her tours and concerts and recording sessions and ask her about music in general, or anything else. Once in a while they asked her to sing, but not often. She might oblige, saying there was no greater pleasure than performing for intimates who understood her, but she might also refuse, angrily saying she had given enough of herself already.

They made way for her to sit in the center of the room, on a white couch. She took a glass of the wine Conrad served and listened to them argue about whether the Met's radical new production of *La Bohème* was a disaster or a triumph. She said nothing for a while, only sipped and smiled. Then she put down her glass with a decisive snap and went through the entire production scene by scene, explaining how the stage director's concept had quite overwhelmed the music. When she finished, they all looked at her in a familiar silence of collective awe.

Finally the youngest member of the Pack, Jenny Rostov, asked hesitantly, "Would you sing something tonight, Vardis? Please?"

She leaned back, the hawk lines of her profile aimed at the ceiling. After a pause she said, "All right." The room gave a happy, relieved sigh.

With Conrad accompanying, she stood in the curve of the white baby grand and sang some pieces she liked very much but never performed in public. In the middle of a Schubert lied —afterward they said how poignant it was that her last "performance" should have been his lovely song of tribute to music itself—she lifted her hands, dug her fingers into her temples, and said, "Damn! I'm getting a headache. Get me something, Conrad."

They all stood, ready to help, but she waved them away. After she had taken the capsules and swallowed the glass of water Conrad brought, they watched uneasily while she settled on the couch. Finally the oldest member of the Pack, Hannah Sebastian, said they must leave so she could rest. Within ten minutes they had all gone.

Conrad brought a cold cloth for her forehead, and she stretched out, one hand holding it and the other trailing on the thick gray carpet. He moved about quietly, picking up wineglasses and straightening pillows.

Her hand began to claw on the carpet. After a while she sat upright and threw the cloth across the room. "Where are they? What day is it?"

Conrad stopped and looked at her. "They've all gone home. And it's not day, it's Saturday night."

She nodded, then pressed her elegant hands to her chest. "I feel so . . ."

"What is it?" He saw that she was flushed, almost as if the dusky red of her caftan had seeped into her skin. "Are you all right?"

"I don't know. I don't think so. My heart . . ."

"Are you having chest pains?"

"No. No. But it's beating so fast. . . ." She swung her head wildly, dislodging several strands of hair. "Oh, Conrad, you know I always thought you were . . . Your face, just to look at your face . . ." She stretched out her hands and sang some phrases he couldn't identify; they sounded Norwegian. Then she got to her feet and began to stagger about the room. "Tell them I can't sing tonight. I don't care what they say, I'm not well. Everybody knows I never cancel unless . . . Is Cary here? Was Cary here tonight? . . . No, nobody was. They left me. Merle, too. She wasn't here. . . . I was alone. . . . *Alene* . . . I can't sing tonight, I tell you! But I must . . . All I have is the voice . . . Mother says nobody will care about me unless it's because of my music. *'Du må fortsette så lenge du kan'* . . ."

Conrad didn't move. An empty glass hung from one hand at a forgotten angle. His eyes were frozen wide, and fear tugged at his mouth.

Vardis's words grew even more disjointed, lurching between Norwegian and English and mingling with fragments of arias. Then she gave a loud, strange cry that was muffled by her collapse onto the carpet. Her tall, thin body began to arch and buckle.

At last he threw the glass aside and ran to her. "Vardis!" he cried. He grabbed her shoulders, but they twisted from his grasp.

He stumbled to the telephone. He tried to reach her doctor, who was unavailable, and finally got the police. At first he couldn't make them understand because his voice was as out of control as Vardis's body, but finally he managed: "Vardis Wolf —yes, the singer. Please . . . Something's horribly wrong with her . . . What? Oh . . . Conrad Ashley. Her husband. This is her husband."

Detective Sam Lyons spread out the afternoon tabloid that his partner had just brought in and tossed on his ancient, scarred desk. Lyons scowled and began to read:

SUSPECT POISONING IN VARDIS WOLF DEATH

> (May 1) Despite official Police Department silence on the cause of Vardis Wolf's death, a source close to the investigation has revealed that lethal doses of cyanide were found in the diva's body.
>
> Wolf spent the evening of her death,

April 25, at her Manhattan home with a group of friends, none of whom suffered any ill effects. Police are believed to have tested all the drinks and foodstuffs consumed that evening, with negative results.

Cyanide has been in the news lately because of the recent random poisoning incidents, in which cyanide inserted into the capsules of certain over-the-counter medications has caused the death of five persons. There has been no incident for two weeks, and there is no suggestion that the Wolf death might be another such incident. But when questioned, police department sources . . .

"Damn it!" said Detective Lyons, shoving the newspaper aside. "Where the hell do they get these things? Who in hell is the 'source close to the investigation' who shoots off his mouth to them?"

"Wouldn't be so bad," said Lyons's partner, "if he wasn't telling them the truth."

The two detectives looked at each other wearily. When the autopsy report had come in on Vardis Wolf, the department had been faced with a dilemma.

There was no physical evidence of cyanide in anything they had found in the apartment. But from the interrogations of her husband and the friends who had been there that night, Lyons and his partner learned that she had taken a pain reliever shortly before dying. Immediately they, and everyone else involved in the case, had wondered whether she could be a victim of the random poisonings.

There was no way to be certain. The bottle, which her husband said he had bought for her in Boston several weeks earlier, when she was singing there, had thirty-eight capsules left. But none contained cyanide. Had she taken the only one, or two, that did contain it? Because of the odor and taste, it was difficult to see how else the poison could have been administered.

Sam Lyons drummed a large hand on the newspapers, partly in frustration but also to let out some of the quiet excitement he always felt with a challenging case. "If we confirm this story about the cyanide," he said, "then we've got to say it might be the random killer. Which means another scare for the public. But can we afford not to do it?"

His partner frowned. "If it wasn't for the random killer, we'd be looking for a normal homicide explanation, right? Like probably the husband did it, because they usually do. But nothing we have points to him, except that he bought the stuff. So we haven't got a suspect, and if we haven't got a suspect, don't we have to say it could be the random killer?"

Sam nodded.

"And if it is," his partner went on, "what's going to happen when he hears he didn't get just some average taxpayer? A crazy mind like his, when he hears he got a singer so famous *I* even heard of her, he could go on a real binge. Why the hell couldn't she be Miss Nobody?"

Sam stared into space while his partner watched his face, waiting for a decision that, if Sam's track record held up, would satisfy their lieutenant.

"OK," Sam said at last. "I think we've got to alert the Boston store where the stuff was bought, so every other bottle can be taken off the shelves and checked. But let's try to keep it quiet." He cupped his hand and laid it firmly over the newspaper story, like a big candlesnuffer.

An hour later, when he and his partner were conferring with their superior officers, trying to decide how to word a statement to the press, the desk sergeant came over with a quizzical look. "Sam, Vardis Wolf's husband is here to see you. Says it's urgent. And he looks like he's half ready to pass out."

A surge of excitement carried Sam back to his desk, where Ashley sat as if he had come to the opera instead of a shabby squad room. His bearing was erect, but one hand clutched the edge of the desk, and above the beautifully tailored blue suit his face was a pale, frozen oval.

Sam kept his tone casual. "Is there something I can do for you, Mr. Ashley?"

"I hope so," Ashley said. His voice was flat, but his eyes were haunted. "I came to confess. I poisoned Vardis. I killed her."

But thirty-six hours later, while Sam was thinking the case wouldn't be that much of a challenge after all, Ashley's sister showed up at the station house, asking to make a statement. Her brother was lying, she said. It was she who had poisoned Vardis Wolf.

Within forty-eight hours there were two more statements. The case unraveled completely.

CHAPTER

2

VARDIS WOLF—DEATH OF A DIVA said the legend on the cover of the news magazine. Inside, with the article, was a color spread: photos of Wolf at the Met as Salome, at Covent Garden as Leonora in *Il Trovatore*, at La Scala as Tosca; in Nygaard's *Tyrannus Rex*; at an antidraft rally; with some protesters in front of the United Nations; and at the White House with her husband.

Sam Lyons was reading it at ten o'clock at night, stretched on the couch of the small apartment he had moved into six months earlier, after his divorce. The case was on his mind constantly. He had picked up the magazine on his way home, wondering whether the press had rooted out anything about Vardis Wolf and company that the NYPD hadn't.

According to the article she had no close friends among her operatic colleagues, although it quoted encomiums from some of them: "A superb musician." "A perfectionist." "With her the voice and the acting were of equal power." Et cetera, et cetera. A few people were willing to speak ill of the dead, one critic saying that her voice was "cold and aloof" and her politics "intrusive and wrong." Someone else (nameless) had said that she "ate young singers for breakfast"; and a baritone had huffed, "She sang gloriously. Why did she have to open her mouth to make speeches too?"

There was a sidebar to the article, listing some of her pronouncements:

About the draft: "In the name of freedom, we *force* young men to put on a uniform and die for their country. Are we entitled to kill others with our own contradictions?"

About United States' dealings with certain foreign governments: "Do you think those military dictatorships we call 'friendly' cause any less pain to the people they torture than the Communists cause in Lubyanka Prison? No matter what slogans they use, they're all killers. Blood brothers to the Nazis."

And about the charge that she should stick to singing and quit making speeches: "You think music is above politics? Maybe so. But musicians aren't. They can be tortured and oppressed, like anybody else."

As he read on, Sam grunted in surprise. He hadn't expected to find himself agreeing with her. The only thing he'd known about her before the case was that in his earlier days as a uniform he had worked crowd control after a Central Park rally where she appeared. He had always thought of her as one of the "peaceniks," although an unusual one, but damned if she didn't make sense. Or maybe it was only that the older he got—and he'd just turned forty-eight—the tireder he got of hearing war and global interventionism wrapped in patriotic slogans. As with murder, the dead were just as dead, whatever the motive.

He turned to the section about Wolf's background:

> Vardis herself declined to talk about her early life. "Only my music and my ideas are of interest," she said. The story of her childhood, what happened to her during the Nazi invasion of Norway, didn't surface until the 1960s but quickly became part of the public legend.
>
> Born Hjördis Olafsen—only a few intimates knew her real name, which has come out in the police investigation—she was the child of two music teachers in Oslo. Like most of their colleagues, her parents were

arrested because they refused to obey the Nazi puppet Quisling and join his Teachers Front. After being held in a concentration camp, they did forced labor on the Finnish border. When Quisling finally relented and reopened the schools, Vardis's father, a Jew, was deported—to Germany and Auschwitz. Her mother fell ill and sent the ten-year-old girl to live with an elderly aunt in the far north, who often made her hide. So the child who would grow into an outspoken critic of dictatorships everywhere spent days, even weeks, of her life crouching in barns and sheds lest anyone learn of her existence and tell the Nazis. By the time the British liberated Norway, she knew her mother was dead. Believing herself to be a burden on her elderly aunt, she ran away, traveling alone down the rugged Norwegian coast, subsisting on the scraps she could beg and the fish she could catch, until she found some British troops.

Little is known about her adolescence except that she somehow got to America on a refugee ship and lived in a foster home in New England. Around eighteen she went to New York, to study singing.

Sam put the magazine down. It was pretty much what he had gleaned from the group of friends who called themselves the Pack. To the extent they had been willing to talk about her, they had her on a pedestal so high that she must have had a permanent nosebleed.

Still, he thought, she must have been a hell of a person, to do what she'd done as a child. And then to speak up for what she believed, no matter whom she might have rubbed the wrong way.

He sat up and stretched, unfolding the tall, muscled body that usually slumped on furniture but, in action, was all agility. Despite the sharp angles of his features, his face had a rumpled, comfortable look. He gazed around the apartment and shook his head; a lock of red hair fell in front of one of his very blue eyes. He hadn't cleaned the place in nearly a week. There was nobody to share the picking up, or anything else, and often he just couldn't find the energy. He knew he should hire somebody to do it, but that took energy too. He sank back on the couch and closed his eyes.

He was half-asleep when the phone rang, but his body came alert immediately. He grabbed the receiver and barked, "Yes?"

"Is this Sam? Sam Lyons?" asked a woman's voice that he knew but couldn't place. He said "Yes" again, not so gruffly. "It's Dinah Mitchell, Sam. I know it's been a long time."

"Dinah!" he cried, attaching the husky-sweet voice to a face that made him feel both pleasure and guilt. "Harry Mitchell's Dinah! My God, it's good to hear from you. It must be three years since we saw each other."

"More than that, I think, Sam."

"Ah, it's a damn shame the way people lose touch. Here I worked with Harry for five years, and then I don't even keep in regular contact with his widow to see how she's doing."

"Don't worry about it, Sam. We live in different worlds now. No use pretending we don't, is there?"

"I guess not."

"I called your house, and Peg gave me this number. She says you two are divorced."

"Right."

"I'm really sorry, Sam. I hope it's not too hard on either one of you."

"I wouldn't say it's easy, but it is for the best. Really."

There was a small pause. "I'd like to talk to you about something, Sam. Could we get together and have a drink?"

"I'd love it. Right now, though, I'm kind of in a—"

"It won't take long, I promise. I hate to lean on you, but could you possibly meet me tomorrow?"

"Sounds urgent, Dinah. What's it all about?"

"It's about my mother, Sam. I need help finding her."

"What do you mean? Is she missing?"

"I can't explain on the phone. So is tomorrow OK? Any time you say."

Sam hesitated, thinking of his schedule. Then he recalled the night six years before when Dinah Mitchell had come to meet her husband at the station house. None of them had known she was coming, and when she'd walked in, all dressed up to go somewhere with Harry, her big gray eyes shining, they had just stared at her, their faces numb as masks.

"What's happened?" she had cried. "Tell me, whatever it is. Don't just look at me like that. I want to know!"

"No, you don't," Sam had whispered.

He cleared his throat. "Tell you what, Dinah. I could probably cut out for half an hour or so around five-thirty. Could you come to the old watering hole?" Then he winced; the bar around the corner from the precinct house was a place where she'd probably met Harry dozens of times.

But it was no problem. "Fine," she said. "Five-thirty tomorrow."

He hung up and shook his head. He wasn't part of Missing Persons. What made her think he could help her find her mother?

She came dashing into the bar with the energy he remembered: a nice-looking lady with short, curly, brown hair and shoulders that seemed to belong to a taller, bigger woman. Nothing about her that would knock anybody over, except those huge gray eyes that could look at you as directly as a mirror.

"Dinah!" he said, rising from his seat in a back booth. "My God, it's good to see you again." Before she could do more than smile back, he took both her hands in his and kissed her on the cheek. She smelled faintly of something nice and clean, like roses. "You look great," he said. "Just great."

She stepped back. "You too, Sam. Don't you ever change?"

"I just got a year older. Without getting any wiser." He released her hands. "Here, sit down. A beer OK? Sure, it is." He hollered at the bar, "Bring me two drafts over here!"

Dinah sat down and slipped off a brown cardigan that matched her hair. Under it were a sweater and skirt that showed her figure was as trim as ever.

"If it's still Dinah Mitchell," Sam said, "I guess it means you haven't gotten married again."

"To tell you the truth, I haven't exactly been trying. Too busy. But I'm pretty sure nobody wonderful has showed up. I guess the trouble is I keep thinking there might be another Harry."

He shook his head. "Ah, there'll never be anybody like him."

"No." She smiled. "He loved being a cop, you know. Well, of course you know."

The beers came. She lifted her glass to Sam's and took a sip while he downed half of his at once. "I read in the papers that you're on the Vardis Wolf case." He nodded and sighed. "It must be a tough one," she said. "The papers say you confirm that she died of cyanide poisoning, but it's not one of those random killings, and you haven't charged anybody with her death."

"That's what's in the papers, all right."

She looked at him sharply, but he only smiled and changed the subject: "So tell me how you've been doing."

"Oh . . . OK," she said. "I finally got my master's, so I'm teaching now, up at Tryon Community College. Something called Basic Writing Skills, which means that people who fail their entrance exams have to come and learn things like how to spell and punctuate and what a complete sentence is."

"They teach that in college now?" Sam said.

"They have to. People don't learn it in high school. You see, community colleges can't turn away anybody who wants to attend and lives in the area. But about a third of the people who want to get in haven't got the three Rs, so the college has to try to bring their skills up to par. And that's what I do." She smiled, an action that involved her whole face. "I wanted to teach because I wanted to lead kids by the hand into the splendors of literature. Only I forgot, first they have to be able to read and write. So I'm kind of a glorified tutor. Not exactly the job of my dreams, but it was all I could get. I looked for almost two years."

She lifted her glass like a child with her milk, drank, and set it down carefully. "Were you a Vardis Wolf fan?"

"Me? No. Opera is just something that jams up Lincoln Center traffic."

"You're missing something quite wonderful, Sam. Harry liked it, did you know that? If he was ever off on Saturday afternoons, we'd always listen to the Met broadcasts. And once we got tickets, when Vardis Wolf was singing. But you never heard her?"

"No. Unless you count an antidraft rally where I once did crowd control."

"You were at one of those? Tell me about it. What was she like?"

"Loud. They all were. Why do you want to know?"

"Well, because I . . . Oh, boy." Dinah lifted her hands and ran them through her short, curly hair. "I guess I'm being pretty obvious."

"If you are, I'm thick as hell. I thought you wanted to talk to me about your mother."

"I do." She drank again. "Mother died last summer."

Puzzled, he said, "I'm sorry."

"Did you meet her at our wedding? Short lady wearing a blue dress and hat, and a big smile because she was so proud to have a detective for a son-in-law? Well, you probably don't remember. Anyway!" She put her hands flat on the table. "Get on with it, Dinah. So, Mother died of a stroke. Sudden, quite unexpected. I'm an only child, and my father died years ago, so I had to go through all her effects. That was some job. She'd lived forever in the same Brooklyn apartment, and I don't think she ever threw anything away. She wasn't very organized either. For instance, I found a lot of documents, like her marriage license and my dad's death certificate, in a satin hosiery bag just tucked at the back of a desk drawer. I also found something sewn into the lining of that bag. An envelope. On it she'd written 'Dinah's real b.c.' At first I didn't get what that meant, but inside I found a birth certificate. It said that a girl had been born on my birthdate—March 10, thirty-one years ago. Only she was born in a hospital in the Bronx, not in Brooklyn. And not to Mother and Dad but to a woman aged twenty, who had a foreign name. After the word *father*, there was no name at all. Just a blank."

Dinah lifted her glass but put it back without drinking. "Later on I learned that a lot of people discover they were adopted just the way I did—by going through their parents' papers. But at the time I was in shock. I mean, Mother had even given me a birth certificate to put in my lockbox when I moved into the city, and it said I was born to them, Rose and Dan Leone, in Brooklyn, when they were twenty-nine and thirty-two. So how could I be adopted?"

Sam reached out to pat her hands, clenched on the table. They were cold.

"There wasn't anybody to ask about it," she said. "No living relatives. So I just started making phone calls—to the Bronx hospital named on the certificate, which didn't know anything, and to the doctor who signed it. I managed to track him down in Idaho, but he was dying of cancer. Then I called some adoption agencies. That's where I learned that there's something almost as upsetting as finding out you were adopted."

"What's that?"

"Finding out you weren't. The first agency I called explained it to me: When an adoption is finalized, a new birth certificate is issued, with the names of the adoptive parents. The original is sealed by the Board of Health and is never available again. So, the fact that Mother had my real certificate is virtual proof there was no legal adoption. And the lack of a father's name on the certificate almost certainly meant the mother was unmarried. In other words, whatever happened, it was all outside the law. Probably an unwed mother giving the child away sub rosa or selling it on the black market."

Sam took a long swallow of his beer. "You definitely want to find the woman?"

"At first I thought, well, she gave me away, and if I find her, I'll have to ask her why she did it. And what if she doesn't have a good answer? What if she has a bad one?"

"And what if she didn't want to be found?"

"That too. But then I decided I had to learn who she was, no matter what. I think it's always better to know. I haven't gotten anywhere, though, and lately I haven't been trying that hard."

"Now it's all coming clear," Sam said. "You want to know whether I, or the department, can give you any help in finding her. Right?"

Dinah looked uncomfortable, although she didn't take her eyes from his. "Not exactly."

"Well then, Dinah, what the hell?"

"There's a new factor now." She bent over the purse beside her and took out two things. One was a birth certificate, which she laid on the table. The other was the same news magazine Sam had been reading at home. He felt pressure at the back of his neck, the kind that sometimes came before a lucky hunch on a case.

"Look at the name on this certificate," she said.

He did. "Mother: Hjördis Olafsen."

He knew what she would do next, and she did it: opened the magazine to the article on Vardis Wolf and pointed to a paragraph.

"I read it last night." Sam's voice sounded faraway to him. His eyes moved between the article and the birth certificate three times.

Finally he looked up at Dinah.

"That's how I felt when I saw it," she said. "I read the article two days ago, and I've been telling myself it can't be. The magazine must have got it wrong. Did they? Was her real name Hjördis Olafsen?"

"Yes. According to her husband."

"Oh, my God." Dinah stared into space, then shook her head and went on. "I'd checked out the name, of course, at the beginning. I learned that Hjördis Olafsen wouldn't be unusual in Norway. In fact it would be quite common. But there's nothing like it in the Manhattan phone book. There weren't any Olafsens in the book at all. Isn't that surprising? Except for one in Queens, who knew nothing about a Hjördis." She bit her lip. "If the magazine story is right, Vardis Wolf was living in New York the year I was born. She'd have been twenty then, the age of the mother on the birth certificate."

Sam regarded her without expression.

"Am I cracking up, Sam? You see, she was one of my idols. One of the people who opened doors for me. Doors in the mind, I mean. I'd never heard an opera in my life, before her. Dad drove a cab and Mother was a hosiery saleslady—their idea of classical music was a Strauss waltz." She leaned forward. "In high school I heard a record of 'The Dead Flower Song.' It's hard to describe what happened—the voice seemed to go right through me. No, into me, almost as if my own body was helping to produce the sound. I listened to the song again and again that day, maybe a dozen times, thinking the voice would get less powerful and beautiful. But it didn't. So I went to the library and got some of her opera records. I didn't like all of it, but some was wonderful —melodies that sounded like fire set to music or a sunrise turned into sound. The more I listened, the more I liked. Finally I saved up enough money to go hear Vardis at the Met. I had to get up at four in the morning in the middle of winter and stand on line for eight hours, but I'll never forget that performance. And then the way she stood up for her ideas, no matter . . . She was one of my idols. So it's just not possible that I could be . . . is it?"

Sam's shoulders lifted noncommittally.

"When I learned you were one of the detectives investigating her death, it seemed like a godsend. Because you must have looked into her private life." Dinah locked her hands on her arms. "Could you possibly tell me whether you found anything suggesting that Vardis Wolf ever had a child?"

Sam lifted his glass, and the rest of his beer ran down his throat. He wiped his mouth and said, "No, we didn't find anything like that."

"I see." Dinah nodded. "But that's not proof she didn't have one."

"True." Sam laid his big hands on the certificate. "So you want to find out if Vardis Wolf is your real mother?"

"*Mother* was my real mother. But I have to know if there's any chance at all that Vardis Wolf could have been my birth mother."

"What did you have in mind to do?"

"I know Harry said you had to be careful about involving people outside the department in a case because you might jeopardize it. That's why I wanted to just have a beer and . . . talk."

"So talk," Sam said quietly. But the hunch-pressure at the back of his neck was so strong he put one hand on it.

Carefully she said, "I figure you must have talked to her friends. I wonder if you could tell me who some of them are, the closest ones, and maybe even suggest they talk to me. If I could locate them on my own, I'm afraid they wouldn't even open the door if I approached them cold. So, could you, Sam? Would you?" Her eyes were as wide as a child's, and as demanding.

For a time the two of them regarded each other without moving, the sounds of the bar swirling around their silence.

"I'm going to get another beer," Sam said finally. "You?"

"No, no. I've still got half the first one."

He went to the bar and stood looking back at her, at the curly hair and slant of cheek that were all he could see, thanking God, thanking everybody's gods, that she had called him.

When he returned to the booth and folded himself down into it, he kept his face impassive. He wrapped his hands around the beer glass until it disappeared and said, "About Vardis Wolf's death. We're kind of stuck, and I'm going to do something a little out of line. I'm going to tell you why we're stuck. I'm doing it because you were Harry's lady and Harry was . . . well, you know what he was. Anyway, and nobody knows this outside the department, so you know how far I'm out of line in telling it to you. . . ." He drank deeply of the beer, and hid it inside his hands again. "Wolf's husband has confessed to poisoning her."

Dinah stared. "But you haven't arrested him."

"That's right."

"Why not?"

"Because within seventy-two hours three other people also confessed to doing it."

"But . . . but that's extraordinary."

"Not by itself, it isn't. There's a kind of person who likes to confess to homicides. Harry must have told you that."

"But these people aren't that kind?"

"That's right. All of them—four when you include the husband—had known Vardis Wolf, and each other, for years. Since she first came to New York, I gather."

"You mean they claim they did it together? A collective poisoning?"

"Oh, no. Better than that. Each one of them claims to have done it alone. Each one claims a means and a motive that hold up. And the physical evidence—there really isn't any—doesn't establish which one it was. So we can't discount any of them. Or arrest any of them."

"My God," Dinah whispered.

"That's right." Sam lifted his glass to her.

CHAPTER

3

"If I could live anywheres I wanted I would live in cal. on the
o̶s̶h̶u̶n̶ oshen with a big house and alot of servents to do the work
and look after the kids, I would just lay their all day and lissen
to the oshen and let the sun beat down on me."

The paper was the tenth or eleventh Dinah had graded so far;
she had lost count. She had given the assignment—"Where I'd
Choose to Live"—a week earlier, and now it had to be corrected.
But the words kept melting into a touching, infuriating, ungram-
matical blur, while she stared through them and wondered
things like where would Dinah Mitchell have lived if she could
have chosen "anywheres": with Vardis Wolf?

Her gaze wandered around the place she had in fact chosen to
live: in the heart of the city, not far from Lincoln Center, even
though the rent was so high her mother had gasped and begged
her to come back and live in Brooklyn. There were high ceilings
and white brick walls, one filled with bookshelves, and a tweed
couch and wicker chairs. In one of them her sometime roommate
Cassie was twisted in an improbable position, studying a script.

Dinah's gaze returned to the compositions on the coffee table.

She ran her hands through her hair, then reached into her purse for a scrap of paper.

Before she had left Sam, he had gone to a phone in the bar. When he returned, he said, "I just called Conrad Ashley. I told him you've got some important information about his wife and want to talk to him. He's expecting your call. Here's his address and phone number."

She held the paper. For nearly a year she had hoped to find the woman who was her birth mother, yet now she was hesitating to make the call that could lead her to the truth. It bothered her to be hesitating; it bothered her more not to be sure why. Maybe because if she made the call, she could land in the middle of a murder investigation?

She had realized it while Sam was on the phone. If he introduced her into a group of people he was investigating, she might learn things that would help his bizarre case. She had started to say as much when his eyes had gone an even brighter blue and warned her off. That made her recall things Harry had told her, and she'd realized Sam couldn't ask for her help and she couldn't volunteer it. If she did—or if he did—she could be legally considered an agent of the police department, and whatever she said or did could jeopardize the case if and when it got to court.

So Sam had had to be cautious. All he'd said was, "I'll ask the husband to see you on a matter unrelated to the case. And the rest of the people, the other three—well, maybe you'll run into them. One's a relative and the other two are old friends, but I think that's all I can tell you."

Only the intensity of his look had made her realize what he was hoping: that she would find out who they were . . . and learn something to help him prove which of the four confessors had really poisoned Vardis Wolf.

She too would have to be cautious and not let a soul—even Cassie—know that she was doing anything more than trying to learn about Hjördis Olafsen. Her thumb moved in slow circles on the paper with Ashley's phone and address.

"How's it going?" Cassie looked up from her script a bit too casually.

Dinah tucked the paper in her skirt pocket. "Oh, I'll get the damn grading done, but they might have to take me away in a padded van afterwards."

"What's the big deal if you don't do it tonight? Somebody's going to report you to God?"

"I promised the students I'd return the papers tomorrow, so they have to be done. That's all."

Cassie rolled her eyes. "If those kids spent half as much time on their papers as you do, they'd know how to spell and punctuate."

"Some of them aren't kids. They're in their thirties and forties. And if I was really reaching them, I'd be making them want to learn."

"Want to learn spelling and grammar? You've got to be kidding."

"Why? *I* wanted to learn it. I thought being able to write and speak beautiful English was a key to the kingdom. I used to look at people on the subway and try to guess from their faces which ones could do it."

"Yeah? I used to check for muggers."

Dinah smiled. She had met Cass in a Shakespeare class, when she was working on her master's and Cassie, who hadn't finished college, was picking up some background on the Bard. They hadn't expected to become friends and had been sure that each stage of getting to know each other was as far as it would go. Cassie moved out of the apartment for months at a time, once for nearly a year, to live with some man. She seemed to need to alternate between periods of intense absorption in a man and periods of withdrawal. "Beast or famine" was the way she described it.

"Do you need to be cued on your lines?" Dinah asked her.

"No. It's just a short audition scene. The main thing you have to do is cry."

"How do you prepare for that?"

"Who prepares? You just do it on cue." Cassie put down her script and stared into space. In a moment her eyes filled with tears. "It's practically the first thing they get you to do in acting class."

"How odd. So what do you do when you're really upset, in real life?"

"Eat."

Dinah got halfway into a laugh but stopped. "I don't like that business about the crying. It makes acting seem so calculated."

Cassie shrugged. "A lot of good acting is. You know that."

"I suppose. But . . ." She thought of all the times when she had been moved by Vardis Wolf—and had assumed without putting it into words that Vardis was deeply moved, too. Could one be a performer of such power and do it all by calculation? How did the human being and the performer relate to each other?

She stood up.

"What's the matter?" Cassie asked.

"Nothing. I'm going into the bedroom to make that call."

To her surprise, he answered the phone himself, in a soft, almost gentle voice. "This is he. This is Conrad Ashley."

"My name is Dinah Mitchell. I believe Detective Lyons called you earlier this evening about me?"

"Oh. Yes. He did."

"I guess he told you there's something I'd like to discuss with you. Something about Vardis Wolf." When there was silence, she added, "Your wife," and then grimaced at the foolishness of it.

"Yes? What is it?"

"It's something quite personal. I wonder if I could come and talk to you."

"Personal? About Vardis? You can't tell me on the phone, I suppose?"

"I really don't think so."

After another, longer silence he said, "When do you want to come?"

"Would tomorrow suit you? Three o'clock?"

"Yes. All right. Good-bye, then."

It was over that quickly. She stood listening to the buzz of the dial tone for a moment.

She hung up and walked slowly over to her dresser.

Tucked into the mirror above it were two wedding pictures, her own and her parents'. She held up hers: Harry looked solemn for once, but her face was all eyes and smile. And her hair was as curly as a poodle's coat, despite her best efforts to tame it for that day.

If Harry were alive, maybe he would be on the Vardis Wolf case with Sam. That would be easier in one way, but harder in another. He hadn't believed in bending the rules, even when he thought the rules were stupid. "If we don't play straight," he'd say, "how can we expect anybody else to?" But he would be frustrated by not knowing which of four confessions was real; she could see his eyes sparking, his fist banging into his palm over and over . . . He took it hard when they couldn't crack a case; he took it worse when they did but the perpetrator got off on some legal technicality. "It's not a goddamn game," he would mutter, and be restless and touchy for several days; and she would love him all the more for being unable to accept "the system" with equanimity.

They had met when she was the receptionist for a sportswear manufacturer and he was investigating some thefts in the garment district. She'd had a paperback of a Dickens novel on her desk; he'd seen it, smiled, and said, "I hope it's not one about sweatshops." In minutes they had discovered they were both taking night courses at City College; in a week they were meeting after class. Her desire for an education had been self-evident to him, like his own. He had come to New York from a tiny upstate town; at the wedding his parents, Greek émigrés who spoke little English, were as awed by the city as by the ceremony.

She picked up the other wedding picture, in which her father grinned broadly and held her mother by the waist.

Had they loved each other as she and Harry had? Had her mother run to the door when she heard his key, with that sick-wonderful feeling in the stomach, wonderful because it was only the start of what you would feel when he came in and sick because it was almost too much to bear? Had her father sat in the kitchen, amused and loving while her mother puttered and tried to make dinner?

When her mother died, Dinah had been calm and businesslike. But in the middle of the funeral, during a hymn, she had suddenly found it hard to sing, even to breathe: Guilt had coiled around her like a snake, and didn't lessen its grip for weeks. She had loved her mother but hadn't seen as much of her as she should have. Not for any big reason; for little ones that were petty in retrospect. Just because it was frustrating to watch her mother putter around the kitchen so inefficiently. Just because it was like running a cheese grater on the nerves to hear the dozen detours she made while telling a simple story. What kind of reasons were those not to spend more time with your own mother?

When she found the birth certificate, she had said to Cassie, "Damn it, now I'm mad at her. I'm so damn mad at her for not being here to tell me the truth that if she *was* here, I'd probably scream at her. Pretty ugly, huh? But why didn't she trust me enough to tell me I was adopted?"

Maybe because she'd had to promise Vardis Wolf she would never tell anyone?

But the bargain had been struck with Hjördis Olafsen. Had her mother known who that was?

Dinah tucked the picture back in the mirror, half-angry with her mother once again: Why wasn't she there to explain it all now?

She was getting angry at herself for the anger when her eyes widened; she saw why she had hesitated to make the phone call that could lead to the truth.

Ten minutes later she was in a corner of the couch, nursing a cup of tea and trying to explain it to Cassie.

"You know how guilty I felt after Mother died. It got better when I found the birth certificate because then I could be angry instead. But the guilt never went away completely. In fact I used to feel real twinges every time I did anything to try to locate the Olafsen woman."

"Why?"

"Because that seemed like a betrayal of Mother. Almost as if I was trying to be rid of Rose Leone and put somebody else in her place. But at least the Olafsen woman was a stranger. In my mind, I mean. She had a name, but no real face—like a mannequin before they paint on the features. It was all just a vague, faceless possibility. But now, when the possibility is Vardis Wolf, when she's not a stranger but someone I've admired for half my life . . . now it seems as if I really do want to abandon Mother."

"She's gone, Dinah. You can't abandon somebody who's dead."

"You can't show them you're loyal, either. And Vardis Wolf . . . She's the opposite of everything Mother was. Don't you see what I mean, Cass? I didn't choose to lead the kind of life Mother and Dad had. I got interested in literature and music and went to college. By the time she died we hardly had anything in common. And if it should turn out that Vardis Wolf is my— It'll be as if I wanted to get as far away from them as possible, and got my wish."

"That's silly, Dinah."

"Is it? I remember when I saved up to buy my first opera record—the Vardis *Tosca*. Mother said it was like cats howling. I wanted to cry, but I got mad instead and thought, How can she be my mother and not hear what I hear? Do you know how I feel when I think of that now?" Dinah nested her chin on the rim of her teacup. "Sometimes I'd catch her looking at me, and she'd be so damn proud. I don't think she understood half of what I did, but that didn't keep her from beaming. You should have seen her at my college graduation, wearing a new dress and a hat with a daisy that poked up too high . . . though she never understood why I wanted to go, or what it was all about. And when Harry died, she just opened her arms and let me crawl into them."

"Listen, did you love her?"

Dinah lifted her head. "Yes. I did."

"Did you ever do anything to hurt her?"

"No. Well, never deliberately."

"Did you treat her right?"

"I could have gone to see her more. I—"

"Everybody could go to see her mother more. I mean did you treat her OK?"

"I guess so."

"I know so. So don't beat yourself just because you wanted a better life."

"Is that what I'm doing? Beating myself?"

"Sounds like it to me. Listen," Cassie added lightly, "you don't even know yet if Vardis Wolf is the one. Though if she is, it would explain where you got that million-dollar voice."

"What do you mean?"

"How many times have I told you you've got the kind of speaking voice that makes fortunes in show business?"

Dinah tried to match her tone. "I have to make my fortune in education. I'd better finish those papers."

But ten minutes later she looked up and said, "I don't know if I want it to be Vardis Wolf. Here I've been admiring her for half my life, letting her into my soul, and she didn't give a damn about me. She didn't even want to keep me."

"You don't know that. Maybe she had to give you up, and hated it."

Dinah sighed. "I think it would be easier to look for a stranger."

CHAPTER

4

The town house was located on one of those streets on the East Side of Manhattan where the trees are as beautifully groomed as the buildings and the brass doorplates glow but give little information.

Dinah approached slowly. Black wrought-iron bars, their paint as shiny as patent leather, protected the windows on the first two floors and also on what looked like a basement apartment. Nothing could be seen at any of the windows except drapes and, on the fifth floor, some green leaves reaching for the glass. On the door was a brass plate with the single word *Ashley*; no passerby could tell that one of the most famous singers in the world had lived there. And died there.

She walked slowly up the steps, feeling frozen in time, like a fly in amber.

There was a key in the lock, turned at an angle. A key case hung from it. She stared at the case for a moment, then pressed the bell. Nothing seemed to ring or chime inside. She tried again, but a van with a bad muffler roared through the street and made it hard to hear. After the fourth try she stepped back and looked up at the imperturbable gray brick face of the house. She thought she saw drapes stirring up on the third floor, and tried the bell again. Still nothing.

She looked at the key and the case. Surely their owner wouldn't want them left where they were? She gripped the heavy brass doorknob, which turned easily, and pulled out the keys.

She was in a foyer, with a gray marble floor and a Renaissance mirror that dwarfed the image it sent back to her: a woman with large eyes and shoulders in a pale green dress. To her right was the open-work cage of a small, old-fashioned elevator. The house seemed quiet, carpeted in emptiness, but in a moment she heard voices, both sharp and distant, as if people were shouting in a far room. It didn't take long to locate their source: across the foyer, slightly ajar, was a door that must lead into the first-floor rooms. She shook her head to dismiss a sensation of guilt, then stood quite still listening.

"I told her I never want to see her again!" That was a woman's voice, high and tight with anger and perhaps a touch of sulkiness.

"Jenny, you can't mean that." A man, less agitated. And older?

"I do mean it! I don't know what you're all up to, what game you're playing, but I think Mother *could* have killed her. She's always hated her."

Dinah sucked in her breath.

The man said, "I've never heard her use the word *hate.*"

"She told me to stay away from Vardis! She said Vardis would hurt and disappoint me! Wouldn't you say that was hatred?"

"I'd say it was evidence of how much your mother cares about you."

A disbelieving laugh swelled into the foyer.

The man overrode it. "Don't you know how much she loves you? Don't you know you're more important to her than anything?"

"I don't care!" There was the sound of something banging or slamming.

"Tell Conrad I'll keep coming by till he talks to me." The man's voice came ominously closer. Dinah jerked backward, collected herself, and made her way out the front door.

She got the key back in the lock and was pushing the bell when the door opened and a man emerged.

He was startled by her presence; his body tensed. Or perhaps it was the jangling of the key case in the door, which pulled his eyes to it. His lips tightened. "Is there something you want? Who're you looking for?"

"Conrad Ashley," she said.

"Oh yes?" The man frowned. When she overheard his voice, it had suggested an older, more avuncular person, but he seemed to be only in his early forties.

"Are you Mr. Ashley?" she asked.

He gave her a look as sharp as his tone. "No, I'm not. May I ask what you want with him?"

"Excuse me, but why should I have to explain that to you?"

"I'm a friend of the Ashley family."

One of those who had confessed? "Fine," she said. "And I'm someone who has an appointment with Mr. Ashley."

"As a family friend, I know he's not seeing anybody right now. *Anybody.*"

"Look," she said, "I spoke to him last night and he gave me an appointment for three o'clock. It's now ten after, and I can't see why I have to stand out here and argue about it with someone I don't even know."

"I'm Cary Mathias." He waited. "That was my half of the introductions. How about yours?"

"I'm Dinah Mitchell."

Without taking his eyes from her he pulled the key case from the lock and held it between them, swinging it. She wondered whether he would accuse her in words of using it. But he left that task to his eyes. "Dinah Mitchell of what publication?"

"You think I'm a reporter? That's ridiculous. In fact this whole thing is ridiculous, and I—"

The door swung open behind them.

"Yes? Who— Cary, you're still here? Who was ringing the bell?" The voice was the "Jenny" that Dinah had overheard. Its owner looked the age of many of Dinah's students, barely twenty. She had a lovely, fine-boned face in which swollen red eyes were the only disharmony.

Cary Mathias snapped, "This woman is Dinah Mitchell. She says she has an appointment with your uncle. Can you find out if it's true?"

The young woman pursed her lips in exasperation but went back inside.

Dinah could feel Mathias looking at her, and raised her eyes to the challenge. His were brown, set deeply under black brows, and less hostile than she had expected. The cheekbones were wide, with a small scar high on the right one. There were a few touches of gray in his hair, which was as thick and black as a horse's mane. He was tall and lanky but, in contradiction, gave off an air of restless energy.

"If you're not a reporter," he said, "what kind of business could you have with Conrad?"

"You mean only the press could have a reason to want to see him?"

"Touché," he said sourly.

The young woman named Jenny reappeared. "It's all right," she said. "Conrad says he's expecting her."

Mathias covered his look of surprise with a shrug. He put his hands in his pockets. "OK. I'll go then."

He started to do so but turned back at the last step. "Sorry if I was rude, Ms. Mitchell."

"You were," she said stiffly. "But I suppose you had your reasons."

"I did." He lifted one hand in a mock salute. When he walked away, it was with a slight limp.

Dinah followed the young woman inside and into the elevator. "My uncle's up on the third floor," she said, pushing a brass button set in scrollwork.

She was Ashley's niece, Dinah thought, and she suspected her mother of killing Vardis Wolf. So which side of the family did she belong to?

The elevator moved slowly and grandly, like a royal coach. Dinah looked across its few feet, prepared to smile and start a conversation, but Jenny had turned away. She wore a blouse with huge, dramatic sleeves that overwhelmed her thin shoulders. Suddenly the shoulders began to heave.

The enclosed space of the elevator seemed to fill with her emotion, which was impossible to ignore. Dinah moved to put an arm around her. "What is it? What's wrong? Is there anything I can do . . . Jenny?"

The girl's head collapsed into her hands. "No. There's nothing anybody can do." Tears leaked between her fingers.

"Are you sure of that?" Dinah asked.

"She's dead, isn't she?"

"Do you mean Vardis Wolf?"

"Yes. The most incredible person I've ever— And they're all saying— God, I've got to pull myself together, this is really awful . . ."

"What are they all saying?" Dinah prompted gently.

"That they— they— but I think Mother . . . God, I never want to see her again! I don't care what Cary says! I hope—"

The elevator stopped and so did the words. Jenny lifted her head and stared at Dinah, her swollen eyes struggling with the realization that she was talking to a stranger.

"I didn't know Vardis Wolf, the way you did," Dinah said quietly, "but she meant something important to me."

"What?" Jenny dabbed her eyes with ineffectual fingers.

Dinah opened her purse and handed over a tissue. "Her voice was thrilling to me. But it wasn't just that. It was her ideas, her courage, her . . . She was someone you could look up to."

"Yes!" Jenny clasped her hands below her chin. "You can see that. The whole world can see it. So why can't Mother? And Cary? Why do they say that she's—" She stopped and sighed. "I'm behaving badly. I'm sorry. I just can't seem to keep myself together for more than two minutes. I'll take you in to Conrad, but then I'm going downstairs to my own apartment. Come on." She stepped out of the elevator, toward one of several doors.

"Do you live here, then?" Dinah asked.

"Down in the basement apartment. Vardis always rented it to people in the Pack—to close friends, I mean—and she let me have it last year, when one of them moved to California." Jenny paused at the door without turning around. "I'm a piano student. She believed in me. She said that I was—that I had—oh, damn, I'm starting again." She lifted her hands, made fists, then let them fall back to her thighs. The gesture made her wide sleeves swing; it would have been melodramatic if it hadn't also seemed pathetic.

In a moment she straightened, opened the door, and led Dinah into an elegantly proportioned room dominated by a piano. Shelves occupied two walls, filled with books, photographs, and musical scores. "Here's the woman you were expecting," Jenny said. "Diana Mitchell."

"It's Dinah."

"Sorry. Dinah." Jenny smiled apologetically and left the room.

The man sitting on the piano bench, hands on the closed keyboard, rose formally. As Dinah started toward him, she felt a single panicked beat in her chest.

He had rather short, tapered fingers, which took her hand and shook it firmly but not too strongly. "Miss Mitchell. Won't you sit down?"

She took a deep leather chair, while he returned to the piano bench. She clenched her hands in her lap and stared at them, feeling her pulse pound in her fingers. When she had asked Sam Lyons for advice on how to approach Ashley, Sam had said, "I don't have any. Most of the time he acts like his mind is somewhere else. Personally," Sam had added casually, as if it was irrelevant, "in a homicide I always suspect the husband or wife. They're always the best bet."

Dinah lifted her head and looked at Ashley. He wore casual clothes, slacks and sweater, but the way he sat made her think of velvet jackets. She straightened her shoulders and spoke the words she had thought out in advance. "Before I say anything else, Mr. Ashley, I'd like to tell you that I was a great admirer of your wife and that her death makes my life seem poorer."

He nodded. No reaction stirred his features, but their structure alone gave the impression of sensitivity: the brow was high, like the bridge of the nose, and the mouth was finely curved. His eyes were hazel, as his niece Jenny's were; in fact there was some resemblance between the two of them. He was one of those few men, Dinah thought, for whom the word *beautiful* might have been used. Could still be used, for although she knew from Sam Lyons that Ashley was only four years younger than his wife, his face seemed ageless. Like a statue's, or a portrait's. Like something inanimate.

"You have something to tell me about Vardis?" he said.

"Yes. Or maybe I should say, to ask you."

"Ah." Although he was regarding her attentively, she felt that he wasn't really seeing her. Or rather, that he saw but attached no significance to the perception.

She tried to buy a moment of time by looking around the room. The photographs were all of Vardis Wolf, in costume for various roles. The one in Dinah's direct line of vision was Leonora in *Il Trovatore*, with the long, beautiful hands held out in a heartbreaking gesture. Dinah smoothed the hair above her left ear and said, "I think that my mother and your wife may have known each other. Years ago."

When Ashley didn't react, she added, "About thirty-one years ago. Here in New York. Were . . . Were you here then?"

He looked into the distance, considering. "Not quite yet. Perhaps I came for the occasional visit. I'm not sure."

"If you weren't here in New York then, do you know what your wife was doing? I mean, how and where she lived?"

"She was studying, just getting started with her career, I think. She and my sister had rooms together. It all seems so long ago."

"To me it's a lifetime." Dinah waited, then added, "I'm thirty-one."

"Are you?" he said, as if he wished it mattered.

She clasped her hands. "I believe my mother met Vardis Wolf just before I was born. I believe their meeting had—has—the greatest impact on me."

Again he looked at her attentively, but with no life in his extraordinary face. Had he always been that way? Surely the man Vardis Wolf chose must have been vital. Or perhaps it was the killing of her that had drained him of all vitality.

Dinah felt the panic burgeoning again. She reached into her purse and said harshly, "My mother died last summer. When I was going through some of her effects, I discovered she wasn't my birth mother. That I was actually the daughter of a woman named Hjördis Olafsen." She held out the birth certificate.

Ashley finally took it. He stared at it for a long time.

She had wanted him to show some kind of animation, but she was unprepared for what happened. The motion began in his cheek, where a muscle started to work as steadily as a heart; then it moved to his hands, which released the paper they held and hung between his knees; and finally it lodged in his eyes and became a shivering of tears.

"Then it was true," he said. "It was true."

Dinah froze; the fly was trapped in amber again. She retrieved the certificate. "So you knew about this?"

Ashley pressed one hand against the motion in his cheek as if it hurt. "Why didn't she tell me? Why didn't she trust me enough to tell me?"

Dinah watched him for a long time without speaking, as the

motion receded from his body, leaving only a wet blinking of his eyes. He sighed, then leaned forward and studied her closely. "I don't see anything of her in your face."

"I know," Dinah said. "I'm not positive she's the one. That's why I came to see you. After all, there could be other Hjördis Olafsens in this country."

"She's the one," he said gently. "She did have a child, a daughter, when she first came to New York. There isn't any doubt now, I'm afraid."

Dinah inhaled so sharply that it hurt. "You can be sure? How can you be sure?"

He shook his head as if no answer was possible.

"Will you tell me about it?" she asked. "Will you tell me about her?"

Ashley's gaze was very distant. She couldn't be sure he had heard.

CHAPTER
5

From the beginning he knew Vardis was special. Not like him or his sister or any of them. He knew it as soon as he saw—and heard—her.

She was the same age as his sister Merle, but Merle was like him, part of the world he understood, and her being four years older simply meant that she stood on a higher rung of experience, where he could always reach up and touch her. Vardis, though, had come from some place beyond his world. Beyond his imagining.

She said, in fact, that she came from Norway, and there was no reason to doubt it; she spoke the language, whose sound echoed in her English vowels in the early years and stayed there, to the end, whenever she was angry. But surely her singing voice had been created on some otherworldly mountain, out of snow and honey.

The first time he heard it, it wasn't fully formed, of course, but even then it marked her out from everyone else. That, and the eyes, and an air of confident authority one was used to seeing only in soldiers. She was thin and awkward, but so were many of the others, whose bodies and psyches had been drained by war. With her, though, one knew, somehow, that she had been shaped not by the war but by her own will. One knew it because when she sang, one forgot the war. And everything else.

He wasn't sure whether he turned to the piano for its own sake —its sound seemed always to have been in his life, for his mother had played it and Merle had taken lessons for a while—or as a way to be part of what Vardis did. Both, perhaps. In any case, he took to it eagerly and well and, at the age of thirteen, could accompany her when she practiced and even when she sang the concerts that made her something of a local celebrity. People called her "our Norwegian nightingale." When she and Merle left to go to New York City, his life was twice emptied: of his sister, its comfort, and of Vardis, its challenge.

He filled it as best he could—with Cary and Hannah, of course, and with the piano. In one sense, there was an advantage without Vardis. He no longer had to play and practice for her and could explore more of the literature for solo piano. He had not known how rich and vast it was, or what power it had to insinuate its themes and rhythms into his mind. Once he heard someone play the Chopin Polonaise in C Minor and was unable to hear or think of anything else for days. If one could learn to play such things, then one could banish anything, any memory or sadness or scar, by the power of one's hands. So one grew protective of them, of each finger. One thanked God they had never been hurt. And sometimes one had nightmares about limbs destroyed by grenades and bombs.

Merle and Vardis came back only once to visit. Already they had changed: Merle seemed younger—or perhaps she was just acting her real age for the first time—and told outrageous stories about how they lived in a fifth-floor walk-up with a bathtub in the kitchen and ate nothing but peanut butter and crackers for days at a time. Vardis didn't seem older—she had always been adult—but she was more concentrated than ever, speaking with disdain of the waitressing jobs that financed her lessons, and with cool assurance of the coach who was so impressed with her and of the singing jobs she knew she would soon get. Although she joined in Merle's stories and laughter, there was always a core of seriousness in the sound, a continuo of driving purpose.

By the time he went to New York himself, when he was eighteen, something had altered between the two girls. They no longer lived together, and although they still saw each other, there was a distance between them. When he asked Merle about it, she didn't really explain. Somehow he got the idea that it had something to do with a disagreement over a boyfriend.

He had expected the distance to diminish, because Merle believed as strongly as ever in Vardis's artistry. But an arm's length remained between them; over it their voices would sometimes duel like knives, and Merle began warning him not to get too close to Vardis.

Now, looking back with his new knowledge, he could hypothesize that the distance arose when Vardis had the child. The child who had had such a terrible effect on his life, even though he hadn't known she existed. The child who had grown up and made an appointment to see him and was sitting across from him in a green dress, listening with wide, gray eyes and looking perfectly nice and intelligent. Not like someone sent by a vengeful, malicious God.

Anyway, as he explained to her—because surely she deserved to hear some part of the truth, the part he could tell—she must have been born in the first year or two that his sister and Vardis lived in New York. And perhaps the event had caused some tension between them. Yes, he could tell her that much.

But what she really would want to know, he could see the question forming in her eyes, was what had happened to her after she was born: how Vardis had given her up. And why.

Of that, he could say nothing. Partly because he didn't know the whole story, partly because what he did know couldn't be told. For all their sakes.

So he talked of the way he had seen and experienced things at the time: when his sister's situation with Vardis, whatever its cause, was just one barely heard theme among the many that were forming his life.

Vardis was in and out of New York during his first years there, performing with small opera companies around the country, sometimes going out with a touring group, even taking jobs singing on a luxury liner. Whenever she was in town, they spent hours together, discussing music and performing it. Sometimes they would get standing-room tickets to the Met, and afterward they would go to dissect it at her place, which was nearby. If

Vardis hadn't liked the singing, she could be almost violent about it, striding about her small room as if she carried a whip, crying things like, "Why doesn't the woman look at the score and do what *Verdi* wanted?" Then she would gesture him to the piano and begin to sing some of the arias herself, scrupulously following the composer's notations. And the beauty of the voice would be matched by the soundness of the musicianship. He would look at her and forget she was a woman, if he had ever really known it; she was simply part of what he felt about music and could never put into words. What he didn't need to put into words because she existed.

He was going to Juilliard—the old Juilliard, up near Columbia —and had won a scholarship, so he could cut his hours waiting on tables down to fifteen a week. The Chopin polonaise had long come within his grasp, and he began to think of the possibility of a concert career. But there was much yet to do, including the courses he was taking at Vardis's suggestion, to help him in his work with her: sight-reading and even some singing classes. She had a vocal coach, of course, but said she depended equally on him, on his musical judgment.

Sometimes they couldn't work together. Once, when he'd been chosen to perform a Mozart concerto at a school concert, she got him a short-term job as rehearsal pianist for the touring opera company she worked with. He turned it down because he needed to practice the Mozart, and then she didn't come to the concert —because it was snowing, she said, and she was afraid of catching cold. But he knew it was because she was angry. He couldn't blame her. After all, she was the one who had brought him into music. And when she interrupted the rigorous demands of her own career to find him a job, he refused it. Merle was at the concert, though, and Cary and Hannah, who were in New York by then. Hannah had a gift for him, a pair of fur-lined gloves, and hardly seemed to breathe until he tried them on and said he liked them.

A year or so later, when Vardis was engaged to do some small roles for a summer season in Mexico City, she asked him to come down. While there, he got a frantic wire from some fellow instrumentalists who wanted him to return immediately to replace a member of their chamber-music group, which had festival bookings. But Vardis had just been asked on three-day notice to take over as Leonora in *Il Trovatore*, and how he could think of not staying to hear it? As she said, he had helped her learn the score. He wasn't sorry, as things turned out, for the performance caused a sensation—the president himself went backstage to congratulate her. And when he sat in the audience and for the first time saw and heard her commanding the stage in a real opera house, voice soaring above a full orchestra, he completely forgot the chamber-music group, and everything else.

She had expected that her Mexican triumph would open many doors for her, but American impresarios were uninterested in talent whose training and experience lay on their own side of the Atlantic. One day in his final year at Juilliard she came to find him at the school, in one of the practice rooms that lined the corridors and filled the air with glorious cacophony. "Conrad!" she cried, flinging the door open, "I'm turning down the Met and going to Europe, and you have to come!"

The small room seemed unable to hold her anger and determination. She had finally auditioned for the Met, and that morning they had offered her what she called a beginner's contract. "But I know forty major roles, and I can sing them better than most of their precious European sopranos! Can't they hear what the voice can do? I changed my name so Americans could pronounce it, and now I'm not foreign enough for them!" And then, striding to the window and staring out at the street: "I love this country, Conrad, you know how much I love it. But it is forcing me to go back to Europe and make a name before it will accept me. All right, then, I will go. But you must come with me. You must!"

It was hard to recall, now, just how and when he had agreed. As soon as Merle learned he was considering it, she waged a campaign to stop him. He sat one entire night in the apartment she then shared with Hannah, while she begged him not to subordinate his career to Vardis's. He told her he would be studying in Europe and trying to further his own career. But toward dawn he made a quiet statement he was putting into words for the first time: "Dozens of pianists play as well as I do. But nobody sings like Vardis." Hannah, who had said very little all night, sighed. But she also nodded.

When he finally told Vardis he would go, he was sitting at her piano. She sank down beside him and threw her arms around him. It was the first time she had done anything so personal. He felt two small hardnesses pressed against him and realized they were her breasts.

"Did you go to Europe just to be with her?"

Vardis's child, still seated across from him, asked the question. Her manner was both blunt and gentle, with none of her mother's harshness. But none of the power, either.

"I mean, was Vardis Wolf the reason you went?" she asked.

"Not . . . really. I was still thinking of a concert career myself. Oh, perhaps she was the reason. It's hard to remember after all these years."

"When did you get married, then? Before you went?"

"No. After we got back."

The child cocked her head slightly, wondering.

Oh, they had all wondered, Merle and Cary and Hannah and everybody else who knew them; what happened in Europe to make Vardis Wolf and Conrad Ashley announce, when they got home, that they were getting married. "*Married?*" Merle had cried. "Since when was she anything to you but Music Incarnate?"

Since a night in Paris, although he never told anyone.

They went first to Italy, where she had been engaged to sing several Verdi roles at one of the music festivals. Word of her began to spread through the network of impresarios, and soon she had other bookings in the country. He stayed in Rome, where he had found both an excellent teacher and opportunities for work, largely as an accompanist. But he traveled to hear her as often as he could, and each time he watched an amazing transformation: The brooding woman with cold hands and eyes whom he brought to the theaters' back doors would reappear onstage as someone soft or cruel, statuesque or frail, imperious or girlish, her voice a palette of many colors that shared a common intensity.

Onstage she was desirable, both embodying and inspiring great passion; how odd that offstage he never thought of loving her as a woman.

Yet he was very aware of her physical being—of how her midriff swelled with the controlled power of her breathing, of the subtle lip motions that colored the sounds of the vowels, of the beautiful but spare gestures of her hands. Most of all, he was aware of the line of her throat; he would watch it and know, but not quite believe, that a few strips of muscular tissue inside were the sole physical source of that plenitude of ravishing sound.

When she was in Rome, she shared his flat, and they lived like brother and sister, both tossing money into the blue clay pot that was their household fund and using it to have dinner at one of the neighborhood trattorie. If she had romances, he knew nothing of them. She knew nothing of his affairs, either. Somehow they were always over before she came back into town.

She was asked to sing in Germany but refused—it was years before she could finally bring herself to do that—and at opera houses in Sweden and Norway, which tried to claim her as its own. "I'm American," she would say coldly. He went with her when he could, which was more and more often, for if he didn't, she would behave oddly when she returned, her words and actions normal but devoid of emotion, as if she were merely walking through a role. "Why do you do this?" he asked her once.

"Do what?" she said politely.

"Turn into . . . I don't know, into a stranger, because I couldn't come to hear you last week."

"Because," she said, intensity flooding back into her eyes and voice, "when you don't come, that's what you are treating me like —a stranger!"

Odd that he should have assumed for so long that it was only friendship she felt, and the bond of musical kinship.

They had been in Europe for over two years when a manager who handled some of the most successful pianists on the Continent invited him to Paris to discuss a possible contract. For once it was Vardis who traveled to see him; she had been in England. She came to the little hotel where he was staying, threw off a coat with capelike sleeves—she had begun to dress in the theatrical fashion she never abandoned—pulled a bottle of wine from a capacious handbag, and announced what they were going to celebrate. She had been engaged to sing at the most prestigious music festival in Great Britain. He had never seen her so excited, her gray eyes glittering like sunstruck metal, her face suffusing with color from the wine, which she rarely drank because it affected the voice. The bottle was nearly empty before he told her that he had been offered a contract, which he would sign in a few days and which would take him into Portugal and Spain and possibly to Central America.

She put down her glass slowly and stared at the table like Tosca in the second act, sighting the knife. Then she said softly, "How many hundreds of hours have you spent helping me work on Norma? And now you won't be there when I sing it in public for the first time." When he said nothing, she looked up. "Sometimes when we're working together I feel we become one person. No one understands me musically the way you do. But you don't see me, do you?"

He didn't know what she meant, and said so.

"Nothing reaches you but the voice. You hear me, but you never see me. How can I make you see?"

One hand closed on her throat. Her fingers crawled down to the single large button that fastened the bodice of her dress, clung there, then retreated. The gesture was unlike her, so tentative and unsure that it touched him.

She turned away and went to the window, pushing wide the wooden shutters on a slice of moonlit sky and the sound of a sputtering motorcycle. Then she came back to where he sat, on the foot of the bed, and touched his cheek. "The most beautiful face in the world . . ." she said.

He was unable to move, because if he could move then he could believe and accept what she was doing.

"I need you," she said, bending down to kiss him, and as her eyes and the sharp angles of her nose and chin came closer, he seemed for a moment to stand outside himself and have the power to choose what to feel—pity, or embarrassment, or the desire she wanted him to feel. He realized whichever it was would set the course of their future, and the rest of his life.

When her lips touched his, thin and faintly salty and ready to part, he closed his eyes, and chose.

He opened them, and saw her child looking at him.

He realized that he must have been silent for some moments, thinking and remembering, but she gave no sign of impatience, just regarded him steadily. There was something of Vardis in her after all—the gray eyes. Physiologically they were the same, per- haps, but in the child their gaze was direct and rather gentle. With Vardis, it had been the refracting surface of an inner life no one shared. Not even he. Not even in the days when she used to cling to him and tell him how much she needed him.

"What were you asking me?" he said to the child.

"I was wondering when you got married."

"Ah, that's right. It was after we returned from that first trip to Europe, when she had a success with her first Norma. Afterwards we decided to marry. She . . . we wanted to be married in America. The country that meant so much to her. To both of us."

"I imagine you wanted to be married among your friends, too."

"Yes?"

"Well, your sister. And the others you mentioned, Cary and Hannah. I gather they were old friends."

Had he mentioned them? Perhaps he had. "They were at the wedding, yes." Hannah clutching her purse like a lifeline and looking as pale as he felt himself; and Cary, restless as always, standing in a corner and sizing up everything and everybody; and Merle, smiling because he'd told her he would never forgive her if she didn't smile.

"How did you all come to know each other?"

He looked at the child and reminded himself she was not a child. She was a woman named Dinah Mitchell, and she was intelligent.

"Oh," he said vaguely, "we just ran into each other. You know how it is."

She studied him for a moment, but seemed to accept it. "How long were you married?" she asked.

"Twenty-five years next month."

She folded her hands. "And all that time you worked with her, helped her?"

"That's right."

"Do you mind my asking what happened to your own plans for a concert career?"

"Oh . . . I was ready to sign with a manager in Paris, but he changed his mind. Lost interest or found someone he liked better, I don't know . . ." He lifted his hands, looked at them, let them fall back to his thighs. "I did do some things, but they just never worked out. I don't think I had what it takes to build a solo career. The drive, the ambition, the single-mindedness . . . You can't imagine the work that goes into it. The way she had to work, the hours and weeks and years of practicing . . . Besides, the world is full of good pianists. Overfull. Dozens of them play as well as I do. As I did." After a moment he added, "But nobody ever sang like Vardis Wolf."

"I know."

"You heard her?"

"Hundreds of times on records. And three times at the Met. I'll never forget them."

"No," he said. "One doesn't."

She crossed her arms, gripped each shoulder with the opposite hand, and leaned forward in her chair. "I can't think of a subtle way to ask this, so I'll just blurt it out. Do you know who my father was?"

She was so intent that he hated to say no. But he said it.

"Do you know anything at all about the circumstances of my birth?"

Very carefully, that was the way to answer. "She never told me anything about it."

"So how do you know? When you saw the birth certificate, you said, 'Then it was true.' And you said there wasn't any doubt I was her daughter."

Had he said those things, without thinking? Or was she trying to trick him into answering? He leaned forward, matching her posture. "I can't talk about things that were private between us. You understand that. But I can't have you thinking she was . . ." He watched his hands clench. "Vardis was a great artist. Very great. If she did things . . . Maybe she did things . . . maybe I don't like it that she had a child she . . . gave away, maybe I don't like it that she didn't tell me about having that child, about you, but she . . . She wasn't like me, or you, or anyone else. The power she had, the artistry—that sets her apart from the rest of us. Whatever she might have done, it doesn't matter. How can we know what it took out of her, what it required of her, to produce the kind of art she was capable of? God touches people like her, maybe only a handful in a century, if the human race is lucky. He lifts them to a place the rest of us can never go. We can only hope to know about it through them, through their art. Their magnificent art. And then we repay them by . . ."

"By what?"

"Destroying them."

CHAPTER
6

Dinah watched the man's head sink into his hands.

He made her think of a Greek statue, beaten by time, sitting among ruins. Whatever he was feeling, she thought, she had seen only a part of it; his disjointed answers to her questions—his picture of a woman who depended on him heavily—were just the flotsam and jetsam of his inner visions.

Carefully she said, "Why do you say 'destroy'? Who is it that's been destroyed?"

His shoulders lifted once, slowly. "Vardis."

"How was she destroyed?" No answer. Dinah took a short, deep breath. "You tell me I'm Vardis Wolf's daughter. Then don't I deserve to know what happened to her?"

He raised his head. Then he turned away and pressed his hands on the closed keyboard as if he could feel the notes beneath the cover.

At length he said, "Yes, you deserve to know. But it's not easy to tell." He stood. "Excuse me," he said and crossed the room with easy grace to a walnut sideboard. "Would you like a drink?"

When she shook her head, he took out a decanter and poured

half a glass of Scotch. In a moment the glass was empty. He didn't react, merely lifted the glass, looked at it, poured it half-full again. The urgency of his movements didn't destroy their elegance.

"We were on tour," he said, still facing away from the room and from Dinah. "Two months we'd been out, all over the country. San Francisco, Chicago, Denver, Philadelphia . . . they blur together after a while. The whole country seems like one big city. In a way it's easier to tour Europe. At least the language changes. She could speak them all, by the way, all the languages." He drank half the glass, put it on the sideboard, and turned into the room. "She always got tired toward the end of a tour. Giving so much to every performance, having to educate the conductor half the time . . . There are a lot of mediocre conductors in the world. She knew how to get her way in the end, but it took a lot out of her. 'Why do I do these tours?' she'd say. 'Why do I keep doing them?' I'd tell her I didn't know why." He refilled the glass and took it with him to the far end of the room, where the volumes of Grove's musical dictionary filled an étagère. "Anyway, when we got to Boston, the last stop, she was very tired and having a lot of headaches. I bought something for them—I took care of all her medications, everything she needed for the voice. And after we got home . . ."

He paused for a long time, staring inward, then shuddered and drained his glass. "She had a headache one night when everybody was here, the whole Wolfpack, so I gave her some of the capsules I'd bought. She took them as trustingly as a baby. Everybody went home. She was lying on the couch with a cloth over her eyes. She started to talk . . . oddly. She got up and kind of staggered around the room. Her face was very red. Then she collapsed, and her body started to . . . And I just stood there. Watching. Letting her die. It was hours before I finally called the doctor."

"Do you mean that literally? You waited for hours?"

"Whatever it was," he said, "it was too long."

"But you were probably in shock. Numb. People don't react normally in a state like that. Maybe that gives you a kind of technical culpability, but it doesn't mean you were responsible for her death."

Her words didn't alter his inward gaze. "I just stood there," he said. "Watching. I couldn't believe it was finally happening. For so long I'd been waiting, dreading . . . wondering if and when it would . . ." His words trailed into silence.

If he confessed to her, Dinah thought, she would have to accept the burden of his confession—even if it turned out to be false. Perhaps even more, in that case. Accepting people's confidences obligated you—either to feel or to act. Sometimes both. "Are you saying," she asked more loudly than she intended, "that you deliberately poisoned her?"

He lifted his head. His eyes cleared and fixed on her. "Yes. I thought perhaps Detective Lyons had told you."

She didn't know what she had expected: anything but that gentle admission. She heard herself say "But" and then repeat it twice before other words came to the rescue. "You thought she was a great artist. Magnificent, you called her."

"Yes. She was."

"Then . . . why would you poison her?"

He sighed, as if she were a child wanting answers beyond her capacity to understand.

"What did she do—what was she like—that you decided she should die?"

"None of that matters," he said. "I did it, that's all. So I deserve to die too." He stared into his glass as if it would never be full again.

Outside on the stoop, Dinah inhaled deeply and realized only after several moments that it wasn't fresh air she needed so much as the act of breathing without caution.

She started down the steps but stopped midway, clutching the wrought-iron railing: Vardis Wolf was her mother. However he knew it, Ashley had said it was so.

She stood waiting for some inner corroboration. Surely some sightless memory should be shaking loose, something to make her nod and say, "I always knew a thing like this might be true." But there'd never been such thoughts. She was, and had always been, Dinah Leone Mitchell: a girl, and then a woman, with nothing out of the ordinary in her name, her face, or her life. Except possibly her determination to leave her blue-collar background, and millions of other people had done that.

She thought of a girl in her high-school class, a strange girl with a wispy voice and eyes that never quite looked at anything, who dreamed of being the secret love child of Marilyn Monroe. The kids had called her "Bubblehead," but Dinah had felt sorry for her: She must have been really insecure to dream of a glory that was only reflected.

But what if the dream, and the glory, were real?

She turned and looked up at the house. The drapes were still closed on the third floor, where the music room was, and everywhere else, even Jenny's basement apartment. A blindfolded house. Or perhaps the drapes were there not to keep out light but to hold in sound—to preserve all the years of echoes of Vardis Wolf's singing.

It hit her then, starting in her spine and sweeping down to her toes and up along the back of her neck: the tingling realization that she was the child of greatness. Not of the genetic mainstream but of one of its extraordinary exceptions. She was the daughter of Awe.

Her life could have been so different: exposed to great music from infancy instead of discovering it in adolescence ("Turn that down, Dinah, for God's sake!") Exposed to great artists, and to all the world's great cities, not just New York ("I don't see why you have to go live in Manhattan.") Expected as a matter of course to graduate from college, not just high school. ("But *college*, Dinah honey, where on earth will you get the money?")

She felt her mother standing there on the steps with her, Rose Leone, the mother who was real, smiling and fussing and demanding her rightful place.

Hadn't Rose Leone's life been dominated by love for her, by worry or joy or pain, but all of them rooted in whatever was happening to "Dinah honey"? Had Rose Leone ever been unkind? Had she committed any sin except not sharing her adult daughter's values? How could she be compared in any way with a woman who gave up her child?

Dinah went slowly down the rest of the steps. At the bottom she turned and looked at the house once more. *Why* hadn't she had the kind of life Conrad Ashley described? Why had Vardis Wolf decided she shouldn't have it?

"Excuse me," said a voice, "but are you coming down that walk or not?"

She swung around, feeling she'd been spied on. Cary Mathias

sat in a car at the curb, his expression wavering between impatience and a smile.

She cleared her throat. "What are you doing? Waiting for me?"

"Forty minutes so far."

"What for?"

A group of schoolchildren in uniforms came chattering along the street, making a barrier between her and him. When they passed, he said, "I'd like to talk to you. Will you get in?" He swung the car door open.

"Meaning you want a long conversation?"

"Long or short, I'd like it private."

She didn't want to talk to anyone, even Cassie. She wanted to be alone and shake out the kaleidoscope of her impressions and reactions. But for Sam's sake if not her own, she couldn't pass up a chance to talk to someone associated with the Ashley household.

She shifted her purse, walked to the car, and got in. It was small and sleek, with leather upholstery and a dashboard like a cockpit. Mathias held out a pack of cigarettes, but she shook her head.

"Mind if I do?" he asked.

"As a matter of fact, yes."

"Disgusting habit? Yes, I agree." The pack slid into the side pocket of his white coat-sweater. The shirt beneath was expensive, and so was the boot she could see restlessly tapping the carpeted floorboard. "I need to talk to you," he said. He was facing straight ahead. In profile his eyes seemed even more deep-set than before.

"Are you still trying to find out what business I had with Conrad Ashley?" she asked.

"Right. Are you still refusing to tell me?"

"I haven't heard a good reason why I should."

"I told you I'm an old friend. I mean a close one. Con and I have known each other for donkey's years. I don't want anything to upset him right now."

"Are you a member of the Wolfpack?"

Mathias turned to her. "Who told you about them?"

"Is it supposed to be a secret?"

"No, of course not. They're Vardis's inner circle, that's all. That is, they were. But usually they're the only ones who use that name. It's kind of an inside reference." His eyes glittered beneath their overhanging black brows. "So how come you know an inside reference?"

"How come you won't say whether you belong to the Wolf-pack?" She wondered why she was sparring with him. Why she was enjoying it.

Mathias turned away and beat a fist on the steering wheel. "When Vardis was alive," he said finally, "strangers used to come and hang around the house. Groupies, trying to see her or talk to her, or God knows what some of them wanted. Now that she's dead, there's another kind of person coming around as well. You said you're not a reporter and I believe you. I guess. But then who are you? Because there are a lot of damn curious people who'd try almost anything to get into the house and see who or what they could find. I'm concerned for my friends who live there. Is that so hard to understand?"

She started to reply, but he added, "And I'm not part of the Pack, by the way. Not anymore."

"That's provocative. Care to tell me why?"

"No." The muscles in his jaw bunched like a fist and then released. He turned to her and said, "I find someone on the front step when I've left the keys in the door. The person could have used them, how do I know? Could have been inside the house, eavesdropping. I figure it's my responsibility to try to find out since I'm the one who was stupid enough to leave the keys. So why can't you just tell me who in hell you are?"

For a moment she considered confessing about the keys. But he didn't look as if he would find that amusing, or tolerable. "I'm not a reporter or a groupie," she said, "or anything remotely dangerous. I'm just a teacher—Basic Writing Skills at Tryon Community College on the Upper West Side. A friend in the police department arranged for me to see Conrad Ashley."

His fingers did a drumroll on the wheel. "The police? Why would they do that?"

She could break it gently, she thought, as she had with Ashley. But something about Cary Mathias made her want not to be gentle. "I asked my friend for an introduction because I had good reason to think Vardis Wolf might be my natural mother."

He took only a beat. "That's a new one, I admit. Most people who wangled their way in wanted to sing for her or play something they'd composed."

"Sorry, no musical talent at all. But it did turn out that I was right."

"What do you mean?"

She took the birth certificate from her purse and handed it to him.

Mathias read it, twice, with no change of expression, then gave it back. "I don't see what it proves, except that a woman with the same name as Vardis's, which isn't a very unusual Norwegian name, had a child."

"On the day, in the year, I was born."

"Coincidences happen."

"Conrad Ashley says it's true. I'm her child."

"Does he, by God?"

"Yes."

All motion in the man stopped, all the surface restlessness she had seen and the subterranean energies she had only felt. The crescent-shaped scar on his right cheekbone emerged white against his dark skin, like a tiny moon suddenly rising.

After a moment he ran his hands through his thick black hair. "I don't see how Vardis could have had a child. I would have known."

"Were you that close to her?"

Some private memory registered in his eyes, over which one brow made ironic comment. "I mean," he said, "that somebody would have known about it. Some of us who knew her well."

"Apparently someone did—her husband."

Mathias looked at her with a gaze that made her want to move but made moving difficult. "A daughter of Vardis's," he said wonderingly. Then he added, "What do you propose to do about it?"

"For one thing, try to find out what she was like."

"Why?"

"Because I . . . What do you mean?"

"Why do you care what she was like?"

"Are you serious? If you had just found out your mother wasn't the woman you'd always thought, but someone else, wouldn't you be curious about her?"

"I doubt it. She wouldn't have had anything to do with my life, so there'd be no reason to be curious." He smiled, for the first time. "From the look on your face, I guess you don't agree."

"I'll say. Wait till it happens to you. Then you'll know."

"I'm already speaking from experience. It just so happens that I know nothing about my own mother, except that she's dead. And if I could know, what would it matter? The reality is the person who took over for her." He looked beyond Dinah for a moment, into a private distance.

"But if you learned your dead mother was someone like Vardis Wolf? If you knew something about the kind of life you might have had?"

"But I didn't have it, that's the point."

"Why not? Why did she decide you shouldn't? Wouldn't you want to know?"

Mathias shrugged. "I just told you. Believe it or not, as you like. Who else knows about your being her daughter, by the way?"

"Well . . . nobody. I mean, my friend in the police department knew it was a possibility. And so did my roommate. But I certainly haven't been telling it around."

"Are you going to give it to the press?"

"I'm not thinking about them. I haven't even taken it in yet." She considered. "I think I'll be keeping it to myself. I'm not interested in publicity, if that's worrying you."

"Fine. Excellent. What are you interested in?"

"Talking to people who knew Vardis Wolf, like you. Finding out what kind of person she was. How long did you know her?"

"Oh . . . since after the war sometime."

"Tell me about her. Please."

He put both hands on the steering wheel, fingers tightening and relaxing, over and over. "She was a great artist," he said finally. "And a brilliant woman."

"Tell me the things that aren't in every magazine article."

"Oh. Those things." He smiled as if nothing was amusing, took the pack of cigarettes from his sweater pocket, and lit one. His eyes narrowed against the smoke until they focused on her disapproval. "Sorry," he said, and took one more deep pull before stubbing it out in the ashtray. "Well, for one thing, she hated smoking. Anyone who smoked in her house or in one of her dressing rooms was never allowed back. With one or two exceptions."

"Like you?"

He shrugged. "And if she went to a party, the host had to keep a no-smoking section clear for her, in effect."

"She must have had an allergy."

"No. She just hated smoking. And she liked to have things her own way."

Dinah shifted in the seat. "Smoke can't have been good for her voice."

"Ah, the voice. The voice that ruled everyone's life."

"You don't sound as if you liked it."

"I didn't." He gripped the wheel again. "I loved it. The first time I heard it, I remember I had a funny sensation all over, a kind of tingling. I didn't know what was the matter. Thought I was sick, maybe. It took a while to realize it was happening because I was hearing something beautiful."

"How old were you?"

He started to tell her, Dinah was positive of that. But he checked himself and said, "Oh, I don't know. Young, I guess."

"But you knew her before she was famous?"

"Oh yes."

"Did she change after she got successful?"

She watched him consider the question. Fine lines spread out from the corners of his eyes and mouth. He was, she decided, at least ten years older than she, if not more. "I think Vardis was always the same," he said slowly. "It just took me a long time to realize what she was."

"And what was she?"

She thought he was deciding whether to tell her the truth or a lie. After he told it, she wasn't sure which it had been.

"She was a great artist, a brilliant woman, and a terrible human being. Quite monstrous, actually. I'm sorry the voice is gone, but I don't think she deserved to live." He turned to her, his eyes so dark they looked black. "Your friend at the police department. Didn't he tell you that I killed her?"

"I . . . He . . . No, he didn't."

"Ah. Then I should have kept my mouth shut. But it's true. And the police know it. Pretty soon they're going to have to do something about it." He started the car and pulled out so quickly that she had to reach for the grab bar.

"Where are you taking me?"

"I don't know." He sounded puzzled. Then he smiled. "Wherever you want to go, I guess. This isn't an abduction."

She told him where she lived, and he headed toward the West Side.

"*Monstrous?*" she said. "You can't mean that."

"Oh? You're the English teacher. You tell me. A person who is cruel to others, indifferent to their needs, egocentric to the point of—"

"Please! Look, it's probably true that one can't be a great artist without having some abrasive qualities. I'm sure Mencken was right—'The great artists of the world are never Puritans, and seldom even ordinarily respectable.'"

"Don't confuse the artist with the work of art."

"But a monster . . . That's impossible."

IIe shrugged. "Whatever you say. You told me you wanted to know about the woman who was your mother, but if you'd rather get it from Mencken than me . . ."

"I want the truth," she said. "I think you have to have the truth, even if you choke on it while it's going down."

He didn't answer.

A block later she said, "If you killed Vardis Wolf, you're the one who's monstrous."

There was no response, except for his fingers working the wheel.

"If you did kill her," she said, "why tell me?"

"There's something about you that makes me want to throw the truth at you."

It almost sounded as if he was smiling again, but when she glanced over at him, his lips were tight and straight. "As a matter of fact," he added, "I was afraid Con might have said something to you about being the guilty one himself."

"As a matter of fact, he did."

"I knew it! Dammit. Dammit! He has this crazy idea of taking the blame himself. Which I can't let him do."

"Why not?"

"He's an old friend. And he's innocent. It's a good thing I waited to see you, then. So you could hear the truth."

"I'm not sure it is the truth."

"That I killed Vardis? Or that she deserved to die?"

"Both." In a moment she added, "The police will find whoever is guilty."

"You have a lot of faith in them."

"Yes." Not sure why she wanted him to know, she added, "My husband was a policeman. A detective. Killed six years ago in the line of duty."

"That's rotten," he said. "I'm sorry." The feeling in his voice surprised her.

He drove fast, snaking through the traffic more expertly than a cabdriver. She felt that whatever he did for a living, it must involve something physical.

In front of her building he braked the car, dug into the white coat-sweater for his cigarettes, and let one play through his fingers unlit while he looked at her. His gaze was so intense that she felt he had touched her.

Finally he said, "I just can't believe it. You're Vardis's daughter?"

In the same tone she said, "You're her killer?"

A moment later she was out of the car, staring after it as it pulled away.

PART 2

IDOL

CHAPTER
7

Outside was the colorful bustle of Lincoln Center on a spring evening. Inside, the quiet was deep, shared, peaceful. The several dozen heads bent over the long tables were not bowed in prayer, but Dinah sometimes thought of the room's activity as the academics' form of praying—doing research.

She was in a reading room at the Library and Museum for the Performing Arts, facing a pile of material on "Wolf, Vardis" that she doubted she could get through in one sitting. There were articles from both music and general magazines, folders of reviews, some dating back to the 1950s, and dozens of newspaper stories, many flaking at the edges and turning the color of tea:

NEW NORMA THRILLS BRITISH
SOPRANO STEPS OVERNIGHT INTO "SALOME"
    AND STARDOM
WOLF IN MET "MACBETH"
WOLF TO LEAVE OPERA FOR NORWEGIAN MUSICAL?
50 ARRESTED AT PEACE RALLY WHERE
    MET SOPRANO SINGS

In all the photographs, she noticed, even the earliest ones, Vardis had the streak of white hair at her left temple. Had she been born with it?

She got out her notebook and began to read.

An item in a tabloid:

> Operatic superstar Vardis Wolf last week dismissed the fifth person to serve as her personal manager, Henry Larsen. Officially Larsen had no comment, but they say he mutters *'Impossibile'* in his sleep . . .

From a magazine spread titled "Backstage with Vardis Wolf":

> On the day of a performance she sleeps late and has a very light brunch of tea, an orange, and Norwegian *flatbröd* with her husband. He is, she says, "the only one I can talk to on a day that belongs to music." She spends the afternoon alone in her music room—not using her voice, however—eats a steak around five o'clock, and arrives at the opera house an hour later, where she vocalizes for twenty or thirty minutes. . . . The woman who has been her dresser, dressmaker, and hair stylist for over twenty years, and who speaks of her with obvious affection, says, "Of course Madame is afraid. Who wouldn't be afraid, to go out and fill the whole opera house with the sound from just two little cords in your throat? I give her juice to drink, with egg and a little wheat germ, and talk about how well everything will go and how splendid she will be" . . .

Another tabloid item:

> Ranting backstage after a performance of *Il Trovatore* in which she said that the tenor, making his debut, had sung off pitch throughout their big duets, Vardis Wolf heaved a plate at her dressing room door and narrowly missed a fan who was trying to enter . . .

From an interview with Vardis Wolf, on the occasion of her turning fifty:

> I have given everything I have to music. I don't think it is possible to give more. To the composers, and to the audiences. And sometimes I feel, Why am I doing this? Why am I making these extraordinary demands on myself? After all, the composers are dead. And the audience, they are not experts. There are only half a dozen other singers in the world who could truly understand what it is that I do. But, shall I tell you, the public is harder to please than the composer, or even than one's fellow artists. Much harder. Because they come to see whether you can still do it. Whether the thing they cheered in March is as good in April—no, better. They want each time to be better, so each time will be "Vardis Wolf sang tonight as never before." It is like a bullring or cockfight—they cheer for you, but if you are defeated, that is just as exciting. Maybe more. You cannot please the public enough, but you must keep trying. And when you have given them everything of yourself, then what, eh? Then what?

Dinah put the clipping down. The woman had been difficult, demanding, afraid. And what else? Agonized by giving up her child?

Of course. She must have been.

Cary Mathias couldn't be right about her, Dinah thought. In the little more than twenty-four hours since he drove her home, he had taken up residence in her mind: making impossible statements, glowering, moving restlessly, then becoming quite still and turning his gaze on her as if it were a pin and she were something quite small.

An upsetting, agitating man.

Just the opposite of Sam Lyons, whom she'd be meeting the next night. There were things to tell him; that's all she'd said on the phone. "That's great," he'd said softly. But what would she say to him about Cary Mathias?

No one, she thought, would tell a virtual stranger he had committed murder. Not if he really had. Didn't that almost prove that Mathias's confession—and the motive he gave for it—was false?

She thought of Harry and knew what he'd say: "Assume the worst. Ninety percent of the time it'll be true."

But hadn't he always believed in the other ten percent as well? She picked up another clipping.

"The library?" Cassie said when she got home. "Doing research? My God, I've got it. You're going to write a book about her."

"Of course not. I wouldn't dream of doing that."

Cassie flung her straight blond hair over her shoulders and sank back into the couch. "I don't see why not. Then you could give up that teaching job."

"Don't be silly, Cass."

"What's silly? I see how it affects you. And you said it could be years before you get to teach anything more advanced and interesting."

"Then I guess it'll have to be years."

Cassie shrugged and stretched. "Bet you're hungry. How about some food?"

"You can't be thinking about eating again."

"Why not? Food is the one thing you can count on. A career will frustrate you, a man will deceive you, but pasta will never disappoint you."

"We haven't got any pasta."

"Yeah, well, we haven't got any men either." Cassie went into the minuscule kitchenette and peered into a cupboard. "I mean it, Dinah. Now's a perfect time to think about quitting teaching."

"Didn't you just have dinner?" Dinah asked. "And how can I quit teaching when I worked so hard to be able to do it?"

"You know when we ate, and I know when we ate," Cassie said, "but what does my stomach know? Dinah, don't act like a prisoner of your upbringing. Especially now. You working-class types, you think just because you came up via the bootstraps, you have to stick with whatever you struggled for."

"You don't understand how I feel. College helped me turn my life around, and if I can help others to— Cass, those things are lethal. A hundred and fifty calories apiece."

"Why do you think they taste so good? And *you're* the one who doesn't understand, because nothing on you is too big except your shoulders." Cassie came from the kitchenette licking chocolate from her fingers. "Seriously, Dinah, if you're not getting the satisfaction you expected from the job, why not get out?"

"Get out and do what?"

Cassie sank into a chair. "Have a nice long affair."

"Please, don't start on that again."

"But you don't even try. You haven't had a serious relationship since your husband died. You've barely had any *superficial* relationships—two or three, maybe? That's not right. That's a condition against Nature."

"Against your nature, not mine." Cassie opened her mouth to argue, but Dinah said, "I just don't want to talk about it. OK?"

"Yeah, well, sure. OK, here's another thing you could do instead of teaching. If you don't want to write a book, at least you could sell your story to the newspapers: 'How I Went Looking for My Mother and Found Vardis Wolf.' "

"I couldn't do that."

"Why not?"

Dinah hesitated. For one reason, she was trying to learn who had poisoned Vardis. But if that couldn't even be spoken between her and Sam Lyons, it could hardly be told to Cassie. Let alone to the press. "I don't want to," she said.

"Look, you're trying to find out what Vardis was really like because she was your mother. And already you've got conflicting versions, right?"

"Yes."

"Well, my God, it's a perfect story. 'Wolf's Unknown Daughter Seeks Mother's True Nature.' Magazines would jump at it."

"Not if they don't know about it. And Cass, you promised not to tell anybody. I'm counting on that."

"Not to worry. Everything else aside, Dinah, it would be a hell of a valuable story. Think of all the fans and students and scholars who'd love to know what Vardis was really like. You'd be doing a service to the musical world."

"Are you sure?"

"Why are there so many biographies of the famous? Because we want to know about them as people. It's important to hear about the human being behind the achievement. God, think if we could know what Shakespeare really was like!"

"Do you hear the assumption buried in your wish? That whatever quirks he might have had, Shakespeare was a basically decent man. But suppose he wasn't? What if he was a real bastard? A monster?"

She saw Cassie blink at her vehemence.

"That would be a hell of a story," Cassie said. She added slowly, "I guess I'd read it. But I'm not sure I'd believe it."

"Why not?"

"It wouldn't jibe with what's in the plays and sonnets. And it would make me feel . . ."

"What? Different about the plays?"

"Not really. I guess that's the point. I'd think, Why are we hearing all this about him? He was a great poet, so who cares what he was like in person?"

"I thought it was important to hear about the human being behind the achievement. Isn't that what you said?"

"Yeah, well, but . . . this is *Shakespeare*, for God's sake."

"Special rules for the great ones, you mean?"

"I mean, I'm sure he got drunk sometimes and didn't always pay his bills on time and he probably could hand out a damn good lie when he needed to. But if somebody was suggesting something major, not just normal human peccadilloes, I wouldn't believe it. Not about a person who wrote what Shakespeare did."

Dinah suddenly felt more cheerful. "I'm sure you're right," she said. "It couldn't be true."

Sam was late. When he got to the bar, Dinah was already there in the back, ready with her notebook. She watched him get a beer at the bar and head toward her. "Hey," he said, lowering himself into the booth, "we've got to stop meeting like this." She laughed.

"It's nice, the way you laugh," he said. "With your whole face. Some people, it's like their mouth and eyes are on separate circuits."

"Thank you, Sam."

"You're kind of a cheerful lady, I think. Harry used to say that. Dinah's got her feet on the ground, he'd say, but it doesn't give her a long face. And boy, is the world full of long faces. And short tempers."

"And short memories."

"And short beers," Sam said, draining half his glass.

She laughed again. "How long have you been on the force, Sam?"

"Twenty-three years in June."

"I guess you've seen everything."

"Twice."

"How about four separate and convincing confessions to the same crime?"

"Ah, well, no. That's a new one."

"Suppose you can never prove which of them did it?"

"Then it's an unsolved homicide. Like most of them. Once in a while the press will mention it, and people will talk about it for a day and say the cops never solve anything." He spoke without bitterness; in fact he was smiling, and even in the dimness of the bar she knew his eyes were very blue. And warm.

She pushed aside her notebook, revealing the scar of a cigarette burn in the table. "Conrad Ashley confirmed it, Sam. She was my mother."

His right hand came down over hers. "Is that the answer you wanted?"

"I don't know. It's the truth. And I always say I want the truth."

"All the good guys want it. But there's no law says we have to like it."

"My mother, Sam! Now I have to find out what she was like, and why she . . . But how can I? I don't even understand the mother I knew all my life. She and Dad were just . . . my parents. Do you realize that in every other important relationship, you try to learn as much as you can about the person, and try to be sensitive to their context? But parents, you don't see them as human beings. You just take them for granted. It's unfair but you do it. Parents are just . . . there, taking care of you and loving you. Until you learn they've kept a hell of a secret from you, and then they aren't there anymore to explain it."

She heard her voice trembling and looked down at Sam's hand, still covering hers. She sighed. "What a dumb thing to say to the father of two boys."

"No, there's a lot of truth in it. The kind we have to know but don't have to like." His hand squeezed hers and went back to enclose his glass. "I gather Ashley didn't tell you how Vardis came to give you up?"

"He didn't tell me anything except that I was her daughter. I asked how he could be sure, but he didn't answer. I didn't push. He seemed . . . breakable."

"How do you mean?"

She swung her head, to shake off the mood Sam's eyes had induced. "It was as if he'd known about me but hoped it wasn't true. Prayed it wasn't. And when I came with the birth certificate, he looked like someone who suspected he had a fatal illness and had just gotten the confirming diagnosis."

"Sounds like a pretty strong reaction. Too strong, maybe?"

Dinah frowned. "Maybe. It would be upsetting if your wife had a child she never told you about, but would it be that shattering?"

"Wait a minute. Wolf hadn't told him about the child?"

She hunted in the notebook. "I wrote down as much as I could remember when I got home. Yes, here it is—he said why couldn't she have trusted him enough to tell him. And later he said she never told him anything about the birth. But he must have suspected, because when I told him and showed him the certificate, he said, 'Then it was true.' "

"He suspected? Or somebody else told him? Or what?"

"I don't know. But I want to find out." She pushed up the sleeves of her blouse. "Sam, let me just talk for a while. Don't say anything unless you want to." Checking the notebook, she summarized her conversations with Ashley, Mathias, and Jenny. When she looked up, Sam was staring at his glass, but his rumpled face was sharp with attention. "So," she said, "both Ashley and Mathias told me they killed her, Ashley in response to my question and Mathias volunteering it. Neither one said how he did it or why." She hesitated. "Ashley says she was magnificent while Mathias says she was . . . monstrous. Why would two people with such opposite views both say they killed her?" No answer. "So, which one did I believe? Neither one convinced me. But I don't think real murderers go around volunteering their guilt."

Sam nodded, but so imperceptibly it could have meant anything.

She locked her hands. "Have you learned anything to back up Mathias's view of Vardis Wolf?" No answer. "Would you tell me if you had?" Still silence.

She sighed. "A friend at the college who's a big admirer of Saul
Bellow's wouldn't go to a party where she could meet him. She
says people never live up to their achievements and she didn't
want an idol toppled. Maybe she's right."

Sam's hand covered hers again. "Maybe you'd rather not go on
with this."

After a moment she said lightly, "But I'm going to. Now Sam,
you told me that the other two confessions besides Ashley's came
from a relative and two old friends. Cary Mathias is obviously
one of those friends. I think the other confessions must come
from two people Ashley mentioned a lot when he was talking
about the past: his sister, Merle, and a woman named Hannah."
She looked a challenge at Sam. "But I'm not positive I'm right."

He said nothing, but his hand left hers.

She went on. "I'd like to talk to them. They might know
something about the child's birth. My birth, I mean. It sounded
as if the sister, Merle, was living with Vardis Wolf around the
time it happened."

"Hey, Sammy," cried the bartender, swooping by, "ready for
another round?"

Sam nodded, but Dinah shook her head.

He looked at her, started to say something, but instead blew up
at a curl of red hair hanging over his forehead. "Never have time
to get it cut."

She leaned across the table. "It doesn't make sense unless all
four of them are trying to cover up for the one of them who did
it. Isn't that so?"

Almost idly, he said, "You're a smart lady, Dinah. I'm not
surprised you went on to college."

"Last time you told me they've known each other since Vardis's early years in New York. Do you know how they all met?"

"No. We've been concentrating our efforts on the, ah, the
present."

The bartender returned with a fresh glass and put it on the
table with a wet smack. It foamed up to meet Sam's lips.

He relaxed into the corner again. "If you're looking for more
information about your birth and adoption, the two people who
could probably help are Ashley's sister, Merle Rostov, who lives
on an estate up by Chappaqua, and a Hannah Sebastian, who's
with the Dolan Company somewhere in the Seventies."

She scribbled in the notebook. "I understand, Sam. Thanks."
He lifted his glass. "Thank *you.* And by the way, we didn't find anything very awful in Wolf's life. Nothing that would interest the law, anyway."

She felt herself grinning at him. "You're terrific, Sam."

For a moment, he looked at her with an intensity that reminded her of Cary Mathias. But then he relaxed and smiled back.

CHAPTER
8

When Dinah left, Sam stayed and had dinner. Afterward he thought of heading home, but the apartment was still one of the lonelier places in Manhattan. So he walked back to the station house, thinking of Dinah and becoming aware that he wasn't thinking of her as a lucky break in the case or even as Harry's widow. He was just thinking—of hair always shiny, like she'd just washed it, and eyes that looked right at you. Not to mention the voice, which had that sexy scratch in it. And the way she talked—brisk and to the point, but never cold . . .

She was thirty-one and he had turned forty-eight. Did that matter? Not really. Except it was a gap as long as his older boy's lifetime. Probably she thought of him as Harry's very senior partner. If she thought of him at all.

He was in pretty good shape, though, considering the battering the body had taken, and his hair was going to be like his father's, red till the day he died. But there was nothing good to say about forty-eight, except that it was better than being dead, or forty-nine. His ex-wife had sent him one of those cute birthday cards that weren't really funny, and over the verse she'd written, "to the old war-horse." About as funny as the verse. Still, it was better than being with her, fighting and hearing how anybody who marries a cop should have her head examined. Just because she had a point hadn't made it any easier.

He went through the heavy glass doors of the station house. The building was only three years old, but it felt middle-aged. He took the stairs down to the basement, where the videotaping facilities were, and asked to see the Conrad Ashley confession. Again. If you were stuck, you had to keep combing through what you had, hoping something would strike you differently and send your mind in a new direction.

Sam and his partner, and the ADA they called in, had decided to tape the confession, not only because the victim's fame would put the case on the front pages but because Ashley had waived his right to have a lawyer present. The original tape was at the DA's office, but Sam had prevailed on them to give him a copy to study at his convenience.

He wished he could show it to Dinah Mitchell, but that would certainly be involving her in the case and endangering it by, in effect, making her an agent of law enforcement. Which could blow the whole thing out of court, if it ever got that far. So they'd go on as they were: She could keep calling him up and saying, "Let's have a beer" and telling him whatever she wanted to, and he could sit and listen and nudge her in the right ways to go because she was too sharp to need more than a nudge. And if she came up with something to show which of the four was guilty —and what kind of goddamn game they were playing—he'd deal with that when it happened.

After he'd given her a hell of a kiss.

He told them to turn down the sound on the tape; he wanted to focus on the body language. He pulled out a straight chair, sat on it backward, and rested his hands and chin on it.

On the tape Ashley looked even paler than he had been in reality. He sat at the table in an interrogation room, wearing the blue suit that whispered Money and a silk shirt and tie. He wasn't nervous or hostile, just kind of frozen. Like that old movie where aristocrats waited for the guillotine.

"My name is Conrad Ashley. I make this statement voluntarily. No one has suggested it to me or threatened or coerced me into it. What? Oh yes. Yes. I have been apprised of my right to have a lawyer present, several times in fact, and I have declined to do so. My statement is that I am guilty of the death of my wife, Vardis Wolf. Vardis Wolf Ashley. I poisoned her." He lifted his hands to the table, folded them, and looked at them. "I got the idea from the stories that were in the papers, about cyanide being put in pain-reliever capsules and the bottles put back on drugstore shelves. I thought if I killed her that way, it would seem to be another of those killings." He looked up, right into the camera, and then back at his hands. "Some friends were with us that night, April twenty-fifth. She was singing. She stopped and said she had a headache and asked me to get her something. I had the capsule hidden in my bathroom. I got it, along with a normal one from the bottle, and gave them both to her. She took them. Everybody went home. After a while she started to behave oddly. I knew why, of course. I waited to call the doctor, to make sure she would die. But I couldn't reach the doctor. I called the police. I didn't tell them I'd done it. But now I have to tell. Because I can't live with it any longer."

He looked up as the ADA asked a question. "Oh, yes. I got the cyanide from my sister's place. My sister Merle. She's a gardener, and in the potting shed on her estate there are some old tins of weed killer, the kind with cyanide in it. She mentioned the tins, sometime last winter. She said she should throw them out because they were so old and nobody was allowed to make weed killer with cyanide in it anymore. The day after Vardis and I got home from the tour, I drove up to Merle's. I talked to her for a while, and when she was busy with something, I went to the shed and took one of the tins. When I got home, I got the bottle I'd bought for Vardis in Boston and fixed one of the capsules. The next day I put the tin of weed killer out with the garbage."

The ADA asked, "Why did you choose to do it that night? April 25?"

"I really didn't choose it. When she asked me to get something for her headache that night, I just felt . . . that I couldn't stand to wait any longer. And I thought everybody, all the Wolfpack, would stay and be there with me, and it would be easier. But they all went." The first sign of feeling crossed his face: pain. "I loved her. Revered her. She was a great artist. Very great."

"If you loved her," Sam's voice prompted, "why did you kill her?"

Ashley blinked. "Oh. Yes. I killed her because . . . because it had to be done. That's all I can say. There were reasons it had to be done. Private reasons, between me and God. But I . . . whatever you do to me now, I deserve."

Nothing could make him expand on those "private reasons." Not that they had to know why he had killed her; in court there was no need to prove motive. As a young officer Sam hadn't seen the wisdom of that principle, but he had learned. People could have reasons so crazy nobody would believe them—like the man who said he killed his wife because she cracked her boiled eggs on the wrong end. But whatever the reasons, or lack of them, the dead were just as dead.

Sam sighed. The tape had strengthened his early impression about Ashley to some extent: The man wasn't stubborn or hostile. It was more like he was close to empty and was giving them everything he had. In a way, that was the most convincing part; Sam had seen quite a few people who had killed their spouses, and often they had that numb, drained look. As if they'd just cut off an arm or a leg, and even though they thought it had been full of poison, they hadn't yet figured how to get around without it.

But this time, with Ashley's words in the background, there had been another impression: The whole thing seemed rehearsed. Not in the usual way, with every phrase too pat; more as if Ashley had put himself deep inside the story and had to stay there or he'd lose it. He didn't dare let himself look or feel or think outside of it. Because if he did, everything would fall apart. Because the story was all that stood between him and . . . reality?

Meaning the story was a lie?

But if Ashley's story was a lie, then why in hell had the other three come in and confessed? Wasn't it logical that the first confession was the real one and the rest were trying to cover up for him?

Sam stood up and told them to put the videotape away again.

He took the two flights of stairs up to the detectives' squad room. A colleague who was hunched over a typewriter looked up and said, "Thought you went off at five, Sam."

"Just came back to check a few things."

He went to his desk, pushed a path through the papers that nearly covered it, tossed his jacket on a chair, and set out his file on the Vardis Wolf death.

The other confessions hadn't been videotaped. Once the second one came in and it became clear that the husband couldn't be booked, at least not yet, they had gone back to normal procedures. And procedures were the only normal thing about it.

The day after Ashley confessed, Sam and his partner had gone up to the sister's estate and found some old tins of weed killer in the potting shed, six altogether. The sister, Merle Rostov, claimed she couldn't tell whether any of them were missing, but she confirmed Ashley's story that he had driven up to see her shortly after returning from the tour.

She had been rattled by their visit; she had one of those heavy-cream complexions, and by the time they left it had looked more like skim milk. The next day, May 3, she had shown up at the station house, around three o'clock, and the merry-go-round had begun.

Like her brother, she had good bones and a way of wearing classy clothes as if they were everyday stuff—but her face was older and harder around the edges. In spite of her earlier agitation, something about her seemed numb, the way it was with the brother. Only different—as if she had done it to herself.

They had questioned her for a couple of hours, and after dinner the ADA came back. At 8:42 they sat her down to write out her statement. She took out a pen that looked like a family heirloom, pure gold or something, and wrote in a small, neat hand that kept sloping off to the right. All the while her lips were pressed together tightly.

"I am Merle Ashley Rostov, the sister-in-law of Vardis Wolf, and I am the one who killed her. I did this because I know what she truly was like. For almost thirty years I watched her destroy my brother Conrad, who was a magnificent pianist, but she kept him from having the career he should have, always making sure he did what she wanted instead. I know that Vardis Wolf was a great artist. But I deeply love my brother, who is the most important person in the world to me next to my daughter. All those years while Vardis was working her poison I had the desire to kill her. So it is fitting that when I finally got the chance to do it, the chance was poison. *The punishment suited the crime.*

"I cannot allow my brother to take the blame for my act. The fact that he has tried to do so is merely proof of her influence over him. I know that deep within him he hated her, too, for what she had done to him, and he felt guilt over that. When she died, I am sure his guilt increased, so much so that he tried to take the blame for her death. But I cannot allow that to happen. *I* am the one who killed Vardis Wolf. I planned for it to be taken as one of the random killings in the newspapers, but now that he has claimed to do it I must come forward. I do this willingly and freely. No one is forcing me.

"I took the cyanide out of one of the old weed killer tins in my potting shed. The tins were there when I got married and started to do gardening and landscaping. I believe my husband's mother had bought them. I forgot about them until one day I saw them in the back of a cupboard I hadn't looked in for years. Conrad was there shortly afterward and I think I mentioned it to him, but if he says he got cyanide from one of the tins, he is lying. I myself lied to the police yesterday when they came up. I said I didn't know if any of the tins were missing, but I do know. One is missing because I used it to fill a pain-reliever capsule and then threw it out. I got the idea from a conversation I had with Cary Mathias, when we said how easy it would be for somebody to poison someone and hide behind the public killings.

"I knew what kind of medication Vardis used, so I got a bottle and fixed a capsule, just as the newspapers said it was done. I went to see Conrad about a week before Vardis died, on a day when she wasn't there, because my hatred for her is so strong that I cannot control it and we fight. While I was at the house I went into Vardis's bathroom and put my capsule into her bottle. I knew she was the only one who would take it because Conrad uses regular aspirin, but she is allergic to it and uses the nonaspirin kind.

"I did not know if it would work, but it did. I have no remorse for my action, only for my brother trying to take the blame. But *I* was the one.

"There is no lawyer with me because I know he would try to prevent me from making this statement. He has been my lawyer for many years, and he would not allow me to do this. But many times I have been told by the police and the man from the District

Attorney that I could have a lawyer. After they arrest me I will call him, but I do not want him here now.

"(Signed) Merle Ashley Rostov."

But they couldn't arrest her. The physical evidence didn't support her story any more strongly than it did her brother's. That was the trouble with the goddamn case: no physical evidence, except for the presence of cyanide in Vardis Wolf's body.

"You're only doing this to save your brother's skin," Sam had said to Merle Rostov. She'd looked at him, smiled so briefly it seemed like a mistake, and answered: "He has to be saved, since he is innocent."

Even though a lot of what she said checked out, her statement rang false to Sam. For starters there was the obvious flaw: saying she had thrown out only the one tin of weed killer, when, if she was guilty, she would have destroyed all evidence of possession by throwing out all the tins. And why in hell did they call them tins instead of cans?

Ashley had to be released, of course. When he heard why, he had gone three shades paler and tried to argue, with a kind of sick desperation. If only, Sam thought, he could have been a fly in the cab in which the two of them had ridden away from the station house. Did they congratulate each other? Or did one of them tell the other what the truth was?

The phone on his desk rang. He frowned at it but ignored it. "Hey, Sam," someone yelled from across the room. "Call on three."

He shrugged and picked up. It was a reporter. "No," he said, "there's no new developments. When and if they come, headquarters will announce them. You know that, pal." He listened, tracing lines with his fingers across Merle Rostov's statement. "Yes, the investigation is continuing, yes, we still think this isn't one of the random poisonings, and yes, that's all I've got to say."

He hung up. If the department didn't say something more pretty soon, the press would turn into hornets instead of just gadflies. God forbid they should hear about the confessions and tell the world how four people were jerking the NYPD around. God forbid Dinah should somehow let it out, without meaning to . . . No, he told himself, she wouldn't do that. A smile flicked across his face.

He held Merle Rostov's statement at a distance and squinted, hoping some new insight would rise from the blur. It appeared to be true that she and Wolf didn't see much of each other, and fought when they did. That group called "the Pack" had confirmed that Wolf and Merle Rostov were "estranged," as one of them put it. And some of them had been eager to say that Cary Mathias was persona non grata. None of them knew exactly why, except that he had "insulted Vardis and shown a complete lack of understanding of her art and her character."

Sam tossed Merle's statement aside and picked up Mathias's. Short and sweet.

He had come in the morning after Rostov: a man who seemed used to taking charge, who wore expensive but casual clothes and limped a bit in one leg. He brought a lawyer who looked like he thought he had a fool for a client. Mathias had himself on a tight rein. He told his story quickly and answered questions as briefly as possible. They kept at him for several hours, and Sam had gotten pretty tough, but Mathias kept his cool. It wasn't until he stood up after signing his statement that they noticed the back of his shirt. It was soaking.

"I am Cary Mathias. I own Demeter, Inc., a computer software company at Forty-sixth and First. I live in the building. I know Conrad Ashley has confessed to killing Vardis Wolf. I know his sister plans to do the same. Both are old and dear friends. That is why they are both trying to cover up for me.

"I poisoned Vardis Wolf Ashley. I've wanted for years to kill her because she is an evil woman, despite her artistry. She brings people under the spell of her personality, which is powerful, and turns them into blind worshipers who stop living for themselves. Her husband is a prime example.

"I could never see a foolproof way to kill her. But one day Merle Rostov and I were talking about the random poisonings, and one of us, I honestly can't remember which, pointed out they would make a good screen for a deliberate poisoning. Right then I decided to do it. I got the cyanide from Master Plastics, a Long Island City industrial plastics firm owned by a friend of mine. I went there to see him on April 5 and stole a small quantity from the factory's supply. When Con and Vardis got back from their tour, I called her and said I wanted to see her, to patch up a bad quarrel we had about four years ago, when she kicked me out of her house and her life. I've hardly seen her since. She told me to come the next day, when Con was going out to his sister's. I got her to take me up to her room. I faked a bout of indigestion, so I could get into her bathroom. I found a bottle of her pain-reliever capsules—I knew she was allergic to aspirin—took one out, and filled it with the cyanide powder I had brought, using the tweezers and little paper funnel I had also brought. I wiped away all my fingerprints. I told Vardis I felt too ill to stay, and left.

"I have been advised of my rights. I state for the record that I make this statement against the strong advice of my attorney. But I cannot allow either of two valued friends to be charged with a crime I committed.

"(Signed) Cary M. Mathias."

Mathias's story checked out: He had gone to the industrial plastics place on the date he said, and it was possible that he'd lifted a small quantity of cyanide, although they couldn't be sure —which had started a flap about their security procedures.

And when Sam asked him how he got Wolf to take him up to her bedroom, the dark eyes had been stone cold and mocking, and the answer—which he refused to expand on—had been, "I know how to get a woman into a bedroom."

Sam blew upward at the lock of hair falling on his forehead. Mathias was his second choice, if it turned out Ashley hadn't done it.

Mathias had had to be released, of course, like the other two. When the fourth one came in, it would have been almost like a farce except that she was so agitated—crying most of the time. The only one of the four to show any real emotion. They had had to keep feeding her tea and tissues.

"I am Hannah Sebastian. I am forty-six years old. I have never married. I am a biochemist with the Dolan Company at 631 East Seventy-fifth Street. I was close for many years to Vardis Wolf, who is the finest human being I have been privileged to know and whose memory I revere. The only person who means more to me than she did is the person for whom I had to kill her: Conrad Ashley.

"It is harder than anyone can imagine for me to make these

confessions, to say that I killed her and that I am in love with Conrad. I have been in love with him as long as I can remember, but I have never told it to anyone. Even to those who knew. It was obvious to me that I could never be more than a friend to Conrad while Vardis was alive. She was the sun in the firmament, blotting out everyone else. She was the sun for me, too, but Conrad was the moon. The sweet moon that inspires a scene of horror, as in *Salome*. I have always felt that Conrad could love me as I want him to, if she were not alive.

"So when the stories appeared about the cyanide placed in capsules of medicine, I thought I had found a way. One day when Vardis and Conrad were back and I was talking with her in her bedroom, I went into her bath and got two capsules from the bottle in the medicine chest. One was for a backup, but the first one worked very well when I filled it with cyanide at my lab. The next day I took it to Vardis's and put it back in the bottle.

"That night when we were all there, she got a headache and asked Conrad to get something. I watched her take the capsules, and then I couldn't bear to stay and see whether anything would happen, so I urged everybody to leave.

"When Conrad called to tell me she had died, I couldn't believe it. I couldn't accept that I had done it. But I had. And it is all dry as ashes in my mouth because I cannot bear what I have done. I loathe myself for doing it. Even though I had to.

"I do not know why Conrad is trying to take the blame, but if I had dreamed he would try, I never would have done it.

"I am the most wretched human being on earth. I should have been left to die as a child.

"(Signed) Hannah Sebastian."

No, Sam thought, she hadn't done it. When she said she did, she had looked ready to faint. And when he asked her why, if she loved Vardis Wolf so much, she had killed her in such a painful manner, Hannah Sebastian had put her head in her thin hands and bent over, shaking, as if she was in a high wind. They had been thinking of sending for the nurse when she finally looked up and said, "I had to do it that way, to make it look like the newspaper killings."

It had been about as convincing as somebody saying he liked death and taxes.

Except on one score; she might really be in love with Conrad Ashley. If so, Sam had argued, it was another reason to figure Ashley was the guilty one: Why would she confess to killing a woman she idolized, except to save the neck of the man she loved? The man she must therefore know to be guilty?

But the ADA wouldn't buy it. He said no matter how much she loved Ashley, she wouldn't forgive him for killing her idol, let alone try to get him off.

So then why had she confessed? Who *was* she trying to shield: Merle Rostov? Cary Mathias? But why would she try to shield either of two people who both said they hated her idol? Was she really unaware, as she had claimed at the time, that Rostov and Mathias had also confessed?

Sam tossed her statement on top of the others and rubbed his eyes. The quiet undertow of excitement he usually felt was turning into a nagging headache. How the hell was he going to make sense out of the case? The frozen husband; the hard, cool sister-in-law; and the two friends, one a cocky sonofabitch and the other drowning in grief.

Sam's headache suddenly got worse. Suppose his review of the Ashley confession tape had hinted at the right idea and the man was innocent. Suppose *none* of them had poisoned Vardis Wolf and they were *all* lying, for some reason Sam couldn't begin to imagine.

CHAPTER 9

There wasn't much color in the laboratory: white coats, equipment made of metal and glass, beige tiles on the floor.

There wasn't much color in the woman either. Her hair was a very white blond—long, baby-fine, held in a tail by a rubber band—and her skin and mouth were pale and free of makeup. The light blue of her eyes was made even lighter by her glasses, which magnified them to loom out of scale with her face.

In her lab coat, with several inches of gray skirt showing, she moved among the people working at the benches. Her face was grave, but not particularly because of the questions she asked or the answers she got. She was grave and serious about most things and had been since childhood. Laughter and joy seemed to have been bleached out of her.

She went into her small office off the lab, where books filled the shelves in orderly ranks and the desk held no papers except the rough draft of a report she was preparing. She sat and began to read it through.

The phone rang, but she finished a paragraph before picking it up.

"Hannah! Finally. I've been leaving messages for you for two days."

"I know," she said quietly.

"And last night I tried to call you at home a couple of times."

"I wasn't answering the phone last night."

"Hannah, please don't go incommunicado. Not at a time like this. It's not fair."

"I suppose you're right. I'm sorry. What is it? Is something wrong?"

"I don't know. Yet. There's a woman who's been to see Con. I talked to her too."

"Someone from the police?"

"No, I don't think they sent her. She came around because— This is going to surprise the hell out of you. Are you sitting down?"

"Just tell me," she said evenly.

"All right. When Vardis was about twenty years old, she apparently had a child. But she gave it up. A daughter. The woman is that daughter. That's why she came around."

Out in the hall voices crescendoed in a laugh, then faded.

"Hannah? Hannah! Are you still there?"

"No," she said. "Vardis can't have had a child."

"Yes, that's what I said too, at first, but it seems to be true. The woman—her name is Dinah Mitchell, by the way—has a birth certificate to prove it. She found it recently, after her mother died. That is, the woman she'd always thought was her mother."

"Papers can be faked. She's only trying to establish a false claim to Vardis's estate."

"I don't think so. Con confirms that Vardis had a child."

There was a pause. "Conrad says it?"

"Yes."

Hannah clutched the receiver more tightly. "Was he the father?"

"No. It happened before he came to New York."

"I don't believe it happened at all. How could she have had a child and not told *me*?"

"I knew it would be a shock. That's why I had to get to you before Dinah Mitchell could."

"You mean she's coming to see me?"

"I think it's a possibility. I have a feeling she might try to talk to all of us."

"Merle? Does Merle know?"

"I told her."

"I mean, did she know there was a child?"

"She says she's stunned by the news."

"That's because there wasn't a child!"

"Hannah, I'm sorry, but you'll have to come to grips with it. And I know you will. After all, you're the one—"

"How old is this Dinah Mitchell?"

"Born thirty-one years ago, according to the certificate."

"What does she look like?"

"Not like Vardis, if that's what you're getting at."

"Like what, then?"

"I don't know! Big eyes. Dark hair that's curly and shiny. Good figure. A voice that makes you— What difference does it make?"

"Is she a singer?"

"No, no. Teaches English up at Tryon Community College. So, if she comes around, be careful what you say. OK?"

"Of course."

There was a pause. "Are you all right, then?"

Softly and bitterly, she said, "I'll never be all right again. You know that, Cary."

"Yes. Well . . . *Buď opatrný.*"

She hesitated. "*Ahoj.*"

She hung up and removed her glasses. Her eyes sank back into scale with the rest of her face. The delicate skin around them trembled. She picked up the report she had been reading and looked at it, unseeing and, without the glasses, unable to see. When the papers began to shake in her hands, she put them down and arranged them neatly. After a few moments she dug the heels of her hands into her eyes, replaced her glasses, and rose.

She went down the hall. Outside the tissue culture room she collided with one of the research assistants, who gave a little shriek of apology. "Dr. Sebastian, I'm so sorry! Are you all right?"

"Yes, certainly. Yes." But it seemed to her that she had been badly jarred. She turned away, toward the tissue culture room, where the dishes sitting beneath the sterile hoods were bathed in ultraviolet rays. After a while the cold, bluish light began to throb against her eyes.

She went on down the hall, quickly, lab coat flapping, and told her secretary she was leaving for the day.

Dinah was giving her late afternoon class a test, to find out which areas they needed to work on most. The term would be over in three weeks, and she had to know what to concentrate on to be able to pass the students.

Not that there was such a thing as failing them. A student got a grade of C, at least—or else got no grade at all and was allowed to keep redoing the work until he could get a C. The college regarded Ds and Fs as "punitive," having an adverse effect on the students' psychologies and motivations. If no one was labeled a "failure," he wouldn't experience himself as one, and would be more psychologically able to master the work. At least that was the theory.

Privately Dinah thought it was a crock. If students couldn't do acceptable work, expunging their Ds and Fs was simply adjusting reality for them. Which no one was going to do out in the real world. Besides, why should those who couldn't meet the standards be entitled to a special privilege?

She knew hers was the minority view among the faculty, and maybe in the whole world, but the issue mattered to her deeply. "I pulled myself up out of my background," she would say when arguing with colleagues, "so why can't the students?" The answer would be some form of "Don't be elitist. Just because you could do it doesn't mean everybody else can." Of course that was true. But a college was supposed to safeguard intellectual standards, not keep lowering them so everybody could get in. Where could it end, the granting of special privilege to the poorly qualified, except by enshrining mediocrity?

Then, said her mind's nagging voice, what about those who *exceed* all standards? If you want the disadvantaged to be judged by the same rules as everybody else, what about those at the opposite end of the scale? Like Vardis Wolf. Didn't she have to live by the same codes as the rest of us?

One of the students, who usually finished first, got up to hand in his test and leave. Dinah smiled at him. "How'd you do?"

He shrugged. "OK. I guess. But sometimes commas get me crazy."

"I know," she said. "They can be devils. We'll work on it some more next time. Have a good weekend."

She touched his arm affectionately and watched him leave. The paradox was that the more dissatisfied she grew with her job, even to the point of listening when Cassie suggested she ought to leave it, the more determined she was to pull the students through all her four sections of the course with at least a C. A C they had earned.

Three more students brought up their papers and left. She checked her watch; perhaps she'd be finished early and could get back to the library before dinner.

Another student left without closing the classroom door. She turned around to do it herself, but a woman was standing in the doorway. The woman hesitated, then shut the door, and walked to a seat in the rear. In a moment Dinah went back to her and asked, "Are you waiting for someone?"

The woman nodded.

"They'll all be finished soon."

But when the last student had gone, the woman was still there.

Dinah smiled. "Are you sure you're in the right room? This is Basic Writing Skills, Section 4."

"Are you Dinah Mitchell?"

"Yes."

"Then the room is right. But you're not. You're not who you claim to be."

Dinah stopped with one arm halfway into the sleeve of a green velvet blazer. "I beg your pardon?"

"They say you claim to be the daughter of Vardis Wolf."

Dinah finished putting on the jacket and tugged out the cuffs of her white shirt. "And who do you claim to be?"

The woman took a sharp little breath, but when she answered, her voice was soft and precise. "I was close to Vardis Wolf. Very close. I dispute that she ever had a child."

Dinah studied the woman: thin wrists protruding from a bulky beige sweater, long pale hair half in and half out of the collar, large glasses. She was obviously in her mid-forties, if not older, but she had the gravity of a child. A child who had been bundled into her clothes by an uncaring adult.

"If you knew Vardis so well, you must be part of her family," Dinah said. "Are you her sister-in-law?"

"No, no. Perhaps Merle was the closest to her at one time, but that was years ago. And why do you call her Vardis? You didn't know her, did you?"

"I was an admirer. I'm sure you know that that's what her admirers usually called her."

Irrelevantly the woman said, "You do have an unusual voice. Cary said so. But it's nothing like Vardis's."

Dinah gave up all thought of the library. She came around the desk and perched on its edge, as she often did while teaching. "You must be Hannah Sebastian."

"Well, yes. Of course."

"Good. I wanted to talk to you."

"No doubt you hope to make me believe you're Vardis's child. The way you've made Conrad and Cary believe it."

"I don't have it with me, but there's a document proving that on my birthdate—March 10, thirty-one years ago—a daughter was born to a woman named Hjördis Olafsen."

"I'm not concerned with documents. They can be faked. I'm concerned with the truth of character. People," Hannah Sebastian added calmly, "do not behave in ways that violate their basic characters."

"Excuse me, but why would it violate Vardis Wolf's character to have had a child?"

The woman's eyebrows lifted above the frame of her glasses, but her voice did not rise. "Because she didn't *want* a child. I've heard her say, oh, more than once, that a child would be as emotionally demanding as music was and since she couldn't do justice to both, she couldn't have both in her life. So of course she wouldn't have had a child."

"Maybe you won't believe this," Dinah said, "but it's hard for me, too, to accept that she's my mother. It was a great shock. Wouldn't it shock you to learn that your mother wasn't your birth mother at all?"

The woman shook her head, neither to agree nor disagree but only to shake off the question as irrelevant.

"Among other things that are equally hard to accept," Dinah said, "I have to face the fact that she gave me away."

"If she did, she would have had a good reason."

"Obviously—she didn't want me."

"No, no. If Vardis had a child, it would be because she *wanted* one. So why would she give it away? She always got what she wanted. And she wanted what she got."

"But . . . but look, it must have been a situation in which she made a mistake. Many women do, especially when they're that young. Remember that when it happened, Vardis was only—"

"Vardis doesn't make mistakes." It was said pleasantly, as if Hannah Sebastian were announcing a fact, like the temperature of the room.

Dinah pushed her hands into her skirt pockets and stood. "I can't believe you mean that literally. I've never met a person who didn't make at least a few mistakes."

"You didn't know Vardis Wolf."

"Are you saying she was never wrong, that—" Dinah stopped, and tamed her expression and voice. It would be pointless to argue. After all, her purpose was to get information about Vardis's character, not to debate it. "True," she said, "I didn't know her. But maybe you'll tell me about her. Her work has meant a lot to me for many years, so I'd love to hear about her." She walked to the back of the room and sat a few chairs away from Hannah Sebastian, altering the physical relationship between them from teacher-student to that of colleagues. "How long did you know Vardis?"

There was no hesitation. "It seems like all my life. It's hard to remember, sometimes, what things were like before I met her."

"But when did that happen? When did you actually meet her?"

"Oh, she was already there when we got to the—" Hannah Sebastian stopped abruptly. She blinked, took a deep breath, and ran her hands along the collar of her sweater. "When I got to New York, Vardis was already here."

"Where did you come from?"

"Oh . . . Connecticut. A small town. I was glad to leave it and come here."

"Why did you come?"

"We all—" She stopped. "It was time to come. I was eighteen."

"Was Vardis already well known when you met her?"

"Not really. But you knew she would be. There was always something about her, from the start. Wherever she was, she just took over. Your eyes kept going to her, even if she wasn't singing. Even when she went to somebody else's concert, people would notice her, just sitting in the audience."

Dinah asked, "How exactly did you get to know her? You came to New York and just met her, or what?"

"I don't . . . remember, exactly."

"That seems odd, if I may say so. I remember very clearly the first time I heard her sing, even though it was just a record. 'The Dead Flower Song.' "

"Ah!" Hannah seemed to sit up straighter, although her posture had been erect before. "Do you know the whole score? Of *Tyrannus Rex,* I mean. I was at the rehearsals. Yes, in Oslo. I arranged to take my vacation during the time they were putting the production together. I was so curious—Vardis doing something that wasn't really opera, and in her native country, too. Of course she'd been back a number of times since the war, giving concerts, but she'd never stayed in Norway for an extended period. And there she was, committed to at least three months, rehearsals and a limited run. Of course it turned out to be longer than that, what with bringing the production back to New York. The rehearsals were exciting, even though I couldn't understand much Norwegian. They were all in awe of Vardis, of course, all except Nygaard. I thought he was rather vulgar, actually, but she didn't seem to mind. And Conrad said not to worry, she was having a good time. But the cast—"

"Conrad Ashley was there?"

"Of course. He went everywhere with her. He and I sat out in front watching. Occasionally she'd call him and they'd go into a corner to discuss something, but most of the time he and I were together watching. Then at night the three of us would have dinner and she'd explain everything that had gone on, that we couldn't get because of the language. She had a lot of private meetings with Nygaard, though, so then it would be just Conrad and me at dinner. 'Go, go,' she'd tell me, if I felt that maybe I . . . 'I think you and Conrad *should* be together,' she'd say."

Hannah removed her glasses and laid them on the table; her eyes grew smaller but brighter. "Anyway, the cast was shy of her until they saw she really was there to work, harder than anybody. Then most of them started to relax, but there was one girl . . . well, I should call her a woman because she was in her twenties, but she was so pretty and petite that you kept thinking of her as a girl, almost a doll. She got to be afraid of Vardis, I don't know why. I suppose it started when Vardis was helping her with her big number. She only had the one, and she seemed to do it fine at first, but the more she worked on it, trying to do what Vardis said, the worse it got, until she was so tied in knots they had to let her go. Vardis told me she never did much work after that.

Isn't it sad? But if she couldn't handle working with a true genius, perhaps it was just as well. Except that the one who took over her part wasn't nearly as attractive . . . The rest of the cast was fine. Any suggestions Vardis made, they took. Nygaard didn't always like it that much, though." Hannah smiled, slowly, as if her lips had to move against a downward pull. "The two of them had arguments, right onstage, and it was like a clash of Titans. He was taller and bigger than she, and he would shout words at her that certainly sounded like swearing, but she gave as good as she got, better actually, and afterwards they'd laugh and throw their arms around each other. He wasn't in awe of her at all. He reminded me of Cary. And she—"

"Do you mean Cary Mathias?"

"Yes."

"Did he treat Vardis as an equal?"

"He tried to. Not as a singer, of course. But as a person, he thought she should behave like the rest of us. He said artistry and humanity were separate accounts and you couldn't transfer credit between them. Vardis was very patient with him, but finally he went too far and she had to put him out."

"Out of what?"

"Her life."

"What exactly did he do?"

"She said he insulted her in a way she could never discuss or forgive."

"You don't actually know what he did?"

"There was no need. And I still love Cary, in spite of everything. I always will. But if Vardis said so . . ."

"Couldn't she be wrong?"

"I knew her nearly forty years, and she was always right."

Dinah's shoulders heaved, as the price of keeping her face expressionless. "I've heard she could be selfish and cruel."

Hannah's nostrils flared. "Don't listen to such talk! She knew what had to be done, and she did it, that's all. She had to fight for her place in the operatic world. Everybody who gets to the top has to do that. But cruel . . . Oh, no. No! She could be so gentle, sometimes, so comforting . . . And look how she treated the Pack—sharing her triumphs with us, converting two floors of her house into apartments so some of us could live there, letting us share her life and her career . . . She used to tell us about the roles she was offered and what she decided, like going anywhere to work with Zeffirelli or never doing *Aida* with a certain conductor or never doing *Medea* under any circumstances or making sure that the tenor in *Macbeth* was— Oh! Once she took us through the score of *Macbeth*, telling us exactly how she prepared the role. It was . . . extraordinary. That's the only word for it. I'm a scientist and I don't use such words lightly, but that's what it was. She began with the musical totality, getting the sweep of the work. Then she analyzed each act, and then each scene, and finally each phrase. By the end, she said, she usually knew the whole score by heart, all the roles. Oh, and she paid the most scrupulous attention to Verdi's markings—for example, a place where he had written *Senza voce*. No voice. How do you sing with no voice? She showed us. . . . The relationship of word to sound was crucial, she said. You couldn't think in either musical or verbal terms. You had to think in a way that combined both. *Cherchez le fond,* she'd say. Find the core. Then, she said, when you'd analyzed the score as completely as possible, you had to put the analysis behind you and let the role come alive. Come to life in your blood and bones, that's how she put it."

Hannah had come to life herself; color had washed up into her cheeks and voice. "All the while Vardis was explaining, she was showing us, too. Singing phrases half a dozen ways, so we could hear the effect of the differences in attack and coloration and where the vowels were placed. And when she sang a passage, you felt, there in her living room with the white couch and Manhattan outside the windows, you felt the cold of a castle in your bones, and Lady Macbeth's power loose in the room like some kind of animal."

"I never saw her Lady Macbeth," Dinah said. "Or her Salome."

"Oh!" Hannah cried. "I saw the Paris Salome!" She appeared to have forgotten who Dinah was, and claimed to be; she seemed absorbed in an inner monologue that was called up into speech by a listener's comments without really addressing them. "Conrad sent a wire to tell us she was going to do Salome on twenty-four hours' notice at the Paris Opera, and I had a feeling it would be extraordinary. I couldn't get away for the first night—there was a meeting I just couldn't bow out of—but I did get there to hear the second performance. It was everything I'd known it would be. No one has ever touched her in that role. And what a reception she got! The papers were full of her. Everybody in Paris wanted to interview her or ask her to parties. It was like . . . Oh, I can't say what it was like. I don't have the words. If I had a gram of artistic talent, perhaps I could express it, but I don't. I can only say that everything was beautiful: the city, the people, the air, the trees. . . . I felt as if I were lit up, like the chandeliers at the Opera. Vardis took me to some of the parties, and the homes were so elegant and the women so stunningly dressed. . . . One of them was a marquise, who owned a fifteenth-century château just outside the city. There were peacocks on the lawn and real gold on the china. Vardis loved it. She loved beautiful things. I don't know why she took me with her. I asked her to help me pick out a dress for the marquise's dinner, but she laughed and said I was just fine and it would do the snooty French good to entertain someone like me. And of course everyone was very polite to me, because I was with her. From then on, you know, she was an international star. She'd been well known before, since the Norma in England, but after the Salome in Paris, every door in the world was open to her. And she took me with her . . . I don't know why, but she liked to have me with her. Of course I could do little things for her—arrange the white roses in her dressing room, keep strangers from trying to barge in, make coffee if anybody wanted it. Things like that, to help out her dresser. She liked to have me with her. Even in the early years. When she was shopping for her wedding lingerie, for example, she wanted me along. I said no, because I know nothing about clothes. But she insisted. So I went, even though I felt . . . Of course I was glad that she asked me. . . . She loved to have beautiful things next to her body. Even at Cross of Glory she talked about it. She said if you didn't do everything possible to make yourself feel physically attractive, how could other people feel you were? And of course she was right. Anyway, there we were in Saks while she was looking at nightgowns, and she'd take one and hold it up against herself and move in front of the mirror and ask how did I think Conrad would like it, and of course that was hard because I felt . . . Pretty soon the other customers stopped what they were doing and watched her. People always watched her, wherever she went. It was as if . . . Oh, it's hard to explain . . . As if those women in Saks were experiencing it themselves, or wishing they could, or . . . I don't know. But I remember it clearly, and that was twenty-five years ago. Just before they got married."

Dinah was leaning back, head cocked, watching the play of color and light in Hannah's cheeks and eyes. "You were at the wedding, then?"

"Yes. I saw it." She folded her small hands, with the nails cut short and square. "Of course there was never a doubt that he would want to marry her. She *was* music to all of us, and to him most of all. Obviously. There really was never any doubt."

"You're a good friend of Conrad Ashley's?"

"Oh, yes." A smile tugged at Hannah's lips but failed.

"I've heard that you were part of a group and all of you were close to each other as well as to Vardis Wolf. Is that true? That you and Conrad and his sister Merle and Cary Mathias are all close friends?"

Quietly Hannah said, "We know each other very well."

"And Vardis?"

"Some of us have been better friends to her than the others have. I mean, I . . . Once she said to me, 'You'd do anything for me, wouldn't you, Hannah?' And when I said of course, she started to tease me: Would I give up chocolate forever? Eat worms? Quit my job? Cut off my tongue? Kiss her feet? When she said that, she took off her shoe, but she was just teasing, of course. She had a wonderful sense of humor. Although I would have done *almost* anything, and she knew it."

"You'd never harm her deliberately, then?"

"Of course not!"

Softly Dinah said, "But the others would?"

"I'd never do anything to hurt her, and whoever says—" Hannah's voice cut off like a bird shot in flight.

Dinah ignored the frightened plea in her eyes and pressed on. "Why do you think the others would harm her?"

"I didn't say they had! I only said that I— It doesn't matter what I said!" Hannah reached for her glasses and put them on. Her eyes grew larger, yet seemed to shrink back.

"But surely you know what the others feel, what they would do. Haven't you all been friends for many years?"

"Yes." She stood up. "I have to leave now. I only came to tell you that Vardis couldn't have had a child. If she had, she would have told me."

"Then why do Conrad Ashley and Cary Mathias accept it?"

Hannah shook her head, a tense little motion, as if an insect had flown too near. "I don't know."

"But I thought you were all such good friends, for so long. Wait, that's it!" Dinah cried. Something that had been nagging at her for fifteen minutes, refusing to surrender to words, had just done so. "You said you'd known Vardis nearly forty years. You must have known her before she came to New York. You must have been a child when you met her. Have you all known her since childhood?"

"No, no, I didn't say . . . I didn't mean that. I meant that we . . ." She clutched her sweater collar. "We didn't meet Vardis till later."

"Ah. Would that have been . . . at Cross of Glory?"

Hannah's stare told Dinah she had been right to fix on that name.

"I suppose Cross of Glory was a school?"

There was no response.

"In that small town you mentioned? Yes, that must be it. You all grew up and went to school in the same small town in Connecticut."

"No, that's just where the orphanage—I mean, we didn't grow up together in Connecticut. We didn't!" Hannah let go of her sweater and pushed futilely at her hair. "I'm afraid I have to leave now. Thank you for your time."

She lifted her head and walked to the front of the room, stiffly, as if she expected Dinah to rush from behind and stop her.

But Dinah stood where she was, eyes wide.

In front of the college Hannah managed to flag down a cab. She gave her address and sank into a corner.

"Hey, lady," the driver said after a while, as he approached the park entrance on Sixty-sixth Street, "you feeling all right?"

"Yes," she said. "Yes."

But of course she wasn't. For weeks, it seemed, she had been making that same reassurance to people. Why were they always asking her whether she was all right? Why did Hannah Sebastian's state seem to matter now, when it never had before?

She sat through the whole crosstown trip with her arms locked across her chest, even though sunlight was pouring into the cab. She had been warm while talking to the Mitchell woman, but now she was shaking inside the sweater, with a cold that emanated from her stomach and pelvis.

When the cab reached her apartment building, she got out and managed to pay the driver. He looked at her oddly, so she supposed the tip wasn't big enough, but before she could do anything about it, he pulled away.

She wanted to talk to someone. To go upstairs and call one of the Pack and simply talk, normally, the way they used to before Vardis died. But she had had to avoid them ever since her confession. How could she possibly talk to any of them and tell them what she had done? She couldn't, that was that. So she had to stay away from all of them. Not answer her telephone or doorbell. But it had been so lonely. So quiet. As if she had gone deaf while the world gibbered around her, mouths working without sound.

She had walked halfway to the house before she realized where she was heading. She stopped, in the middle of an intersection, and when the cars made their soundless honking at her, she moved ahead and went the rest of the way.

The curtains were drawn on Jenny's basement apartment, and on the first two floors. But a window was open on the third.

There was music coming from it, faintly. She took a deep, sweet breath. Lovely. The Brahms Sonata in F-sharp Minor.

Conrad? No, a recording. Rubinstein, perhaps. Conrad didn't bring out the inner voices in quite that way.

In any case, he hadn't played in years, except to work with Vardis.

But when he had started playing, at the orphanage, it had been lovely. Everything had been lovely then. At the orphanage.

CHAPTER 10

Sixty heads were bent over sixty thick white plates, each holding two pieces of roast chicken, a scoop of mashed potatoes cratered with pale gravy, and a little pile of carrots and peas. The plates sat on long refectory tables, and the heads waited for the director of the home to finish the blessing.

She was a small, kindly woman who liked to be called Mother Louise but whose round face was crosshatched with so many lines that the children sometimes called her Tic-Tac-Toes behind her back. She stood at the head table, beneath the picture of Martin Luther, beseeching the Lord to let His face shine upon children all over the world, to admit to His favor those who were in the care of the Cross of Glory Home, as well as the staff who taught and cared for them, and to bless the Sunday dinner they were all about to enjoy.

When she said "Amen," sixty pairs of shoulders heaved expectantly. She smiled at the rows of bent heads, sat down, and lifted the little copper bell beside her water glass. Its tinkle had barely begun before it was drowned in rising chatter and clattering forks. Some homes had a strict rule that meals were to be taken in silence, but Mother Louise believed that conversation aided digestion, so she never rang the larger bell beside her napkin ring, the one that called for quiet, unless the children's noise impeded the talk at her own table. Which rarely happened; they had gauged her level of tolerance expertly.

She was a devout, unmarried woman who had started as a teacher at Cross of Glory and gradually poured more and more of her energy and emotion into it, until the outside world began to seem as far away as the Kingdom of Heaven, and much less desirable. When the war came, the main thing it meant to her was shortages: of manpower, which helped her promotion to director, and of food and materials, which made it more difficult to feed and care for her charges.

When the war ended, her practical problems eased; her inner one did not. Always she had to struggle with it—liking some of the children more than others. Doctrine decreed that all her charges, indeed all people, should be loved equally. But she could not force her heart to measure itself out in prescribed doses. By way of compensation, she was harsher to those she liked best and made pets of those she didn't much care for.

Originally the home had been designed to accommodate fifty girls, but with the war the board of governors had decided to admit some boys as well, and Mother Louise had somehow managed to stretch its resources over sixty children. The youngest was four and the oldest ones, who would leave when the school year was finished and they had graduated, were eighteen. The forty-six girls and fourteen boys slept in separate dormitory wings, but otherwise shared all the home's facilities. They even shared its uniform: a brown print that looked rather like muddy paws on a white carpet. It was made at the textile mill owned by one of the home's benefactors and was turned into dresses for the girls and shirts for the boys, who also wore brown trousers. Inside each dress, shirt, and pair of pants a number was printed in indelible ink, the number each child was assigned on entering Cross of Glory, to be carried till the day of departure.

Although the staff tried hard to create an atmosphere of one big family, the children's sense of community came from the opposite—having no family at all. To them, the lucky ones were those with at least one parent, who presumably would be able to take them back someday.

Mother Louise nibbled the last meat from her chicken bones, wiped her lips, and reached for the handbell that commanded silence. It was obeyed immediately. She stood and looked around the large room, noting who was sitting next to whom.

The children liked to eat with their particular friends, usually of their own age and sex. Little girls giggling together, bigger boys boasting to one another. There was the usual exception: The Five, as the staff privately called them, aged nine to seventeen. Vardis Wolf and her bosom friend Merle, and the three younger ones. A strange group, in Mother Louise's view. Vardis seemed to be the leader, yet there were times when she looked more like an intruder. Whatever the internal workings of The Five, they were bonded together, almost as if the group were an island unto itself, even though others tried to build bridges to it. Why they clung together was not clear to Mother Louise. Their personalities were so different. There had been some trouble soon after they arrived—an apparent theft that couldn't be solved. Although she had had her strong suspicions, she had had to forget the incident.

Everyone was looking at her in obedient quiet. She cleared her throat and said, in a voice lower and lighter than the one she had used to address the Lord, "I have an announcement. A special announcement. As you know, on Friday night our own Norwegian nightingale, Vardis Wolf, will sing in town, at the spring concert sponsored by the Women's Guild. This afternoon at four o'clock Vardis will give that performance just for us at Cross of Glory, in the small auditorium. Conrad Ashley will accompany her in several of the songs. All of you will attend, of course. The rest of your Sunday schedule is the same. There will be free hours all day except for the concert, the library will open right after dinner, and supper is, as usual, at six."

Mother Louise reached for the copper bell that would call Dismissal, but, before she could pick it up, a voice called her name. She looked up, startled. No one addressed the director at meals, or any other group meeting, unless Permission for Questions was in force.

The words "Mother Louise" sounded again. The speaker stood —tall, bony, rising above the sea of brown clothing like its captain: Vardis Wolf. The director's instinct was simply to reprimand her and then ring Dismissal, but she checked it. "This is not normally permitted, as you know, Vardis. But because of the concert, you may speak."

"Thank you, Mother Louise." The voice was not deferential, nor was it arrogant. "You said everyone *will* attend my concert. That means attendance is mandatory. Couldn't they be free to come or not come? I would feel odd singing when the audience has no choice about listening. I'm sure you know why."

The staff at the head table took a collective breath, and beyond them the rest of the children were as immobile as startled birds. Mother Louise colored and knew it. Her abdomen stiffened against her corset. She was facing a trap: either agree and lose authority or refuse and be aligned with the enemies of freedom. But one didn't become director without knowing how to manage youngsters. "That thought does you credit, Vardis. I'm sure all those who didn't suffer as you did in the war will profit by the example of your concern with freedom. But I never meant to suggest that attendance was mandatory. I'm well aware of how eager everyone is to hear you, and I simply can't conceive that they won't all be there." She smiled, picked up the bell, and rang Dismissal.

Vardis Wolf stood, with the rest of The Five. She took young Conrad's hand, and they all made for the door. Why were they almost always together? Mother Louise wondered. She watched them go: two of them lovable—one very much so, in fact; two of them pleasant enough; and, God forgive her, one she could hardly bear.

Hannah crept along the hall. The door to the room where the piano was kept was closed, but sounds came faint from behind it.

She stood, shifting from one foot to the other, the flesh plumping up around the strap of her shoes under her lisle stockings as the pressure changed. Finally she put both hands on the knob, looked up and down the hall so quickly that her hair swung out like white sticks, and opened the door.

Conrad didn't hear her. His eyes were on the keys and on his hands moving over them. His tongue protruded a little, the tip twitching with his efforts. Hannah didn't know what the music was—perhaps one of the songs he would do with Vardis that afternoon—but it didn't matter. She slid down to the floor behind two of the chairs in the back, so he wouldn't see her. That was how she liked it best: to be invisible while he practiced. To imagine they were alone in a great rich house, just the two of them, with beds as fat and soft as geese. And food any time they wanted it. White rolls that pulled apart in feathery pieces and sweet, heavy chocolate that turned into lovely puddles on your tongue, and eggs every day for breakfast, eggs no one cared if you took. And a huge piano just for Conrad. And Vardis and the others coming to see them all the time.

After a while they would have a baby, which she would take care of and love so dearly. That was how she always said it to herself: "I will love it so dearly."

She leaned back, closed her eyes, and listened to Conrad's playing. It was hard to hold on to the dream the rest of the time, when she was going to classes and doing her assigned chores and being sent here and there by the bells that rang eternally at Cross of Glory and ruled all their lives. And night, which should have been a good time for the dream, was the worst of all because that was when the nightmares often came, the nightmares about the Bad Times.

But when Conrad played and she was alone to listen, then the dream seemed real.

Dreams could come true; she knew that now. Being at Cross of Glory was in itself a dream come true, because it was so much more wonderful than anything she had thought possible during the Bad Times. Arms thin inside the sleeves of her brown uniform-dress, she hugged herself with the pleasure of the dream and listened to the playing.

But it stopped. The room was silent. Cautiously she lifted her head and peered between the slats of the chair in front of her. Conrad was still on the piano bench, his head in his hands. His whole body looked unhappy, as if he'd been beaten. He started to mutter something, which Hannah couldn't catch.

She came out from behind the chairs and, still crouching, rocked from one foot to the other. Slowly she began creeping toward the piano, until she could catch what Conrad was saying: "I can't do it, I can't, it's no use."

"Oh yes, you can," she whispered. She kept whispering it, without realizing, and gradually it got louder.

Conrad's head snapped up, and he saw her. His face flushed, but he didn't say anything. Just held out his hand. She got to her feet and ran to him. He tucked her on the bench beside him and put his left arm around her. They sat that way for ten minutes, not talking, just rocking with a slight motion that one of them started, although neither knew which.

Twenty minutes later she went upstairs to the room Merle and Vardis shared with six others. They were the only ones there. Hannah sensed she had walked in on a private conversation. Perhaps they had been talking about adult things, for they were both seventeen and had periods and globes of breasts, Merle especially, whereas she had nothing but a body like a slat. Merle said not to worry, she was only twelve: "I was very late, and you could be too."

Merle was on her narrow bed, propped on the pillow, arms behind her head. She asked, "Isn't Cary with you?"

"He's outside playing ball."

"Oh. All right."

"And Conrad is practicing?" Vardis said. She stood by the room's one window. Her uniform draped on a chair, she was in the ugly regulation cotton slip, which hung on her hipbones, but her long hair shifted with every move she made, like a dark brown river in the sun. A barber came in monthly to give all the girls short haircuts with bangs, but Mother Louise allowed Vardis to keep hers long.

"Yes, he's in the piano room," Hannah said. "Vardis, he's going to do just fine. Isn't he?"

"Let's hope to God." Vardis's words were distorted because she was chewing on her lower lip.

Merle turned over on her stomach. "Don't worry about Conrad."

"*You* don't worry," Vardis said. "You're not the one who is going to sing with him. He's never played for anyone before. Who knows what kind of nerves he'll have before an audience?"

"I'm telling you, he'll be fine." Merle used her lazy voice that seemed to have a smile in it, buried deep. "And it's not Carnegie Hall. It's not even the Women's Guild in town. It's only the auditorium at little old Cross of Glory."

Vardis swung around. "The size of the audience doesn't matter. You give the same performance whether it's ten people or ten thousand. And you go through the same agonies."

In some obscure way Hannah felt that Vardis had been threatened. "You don't have nerves," she said stoutly.

"No? Why do you think I'm standing here shivering?" She thrust out one of her bare arms.

Hannah saw that it was indeed full of little whitecaps. "I don't know," she said wonderingly. "What are you afraid of?"

Vardis gathered her hair in one hand and pulled it over her right shoulder. "That I'll forget the words. That a string will snap on the guitar, or the piano. Or in my throat. That somebody will send me back to Norway. A million things."

Hannah sat on Merle's bed and tucked up one foot. "But why would anybody here send you back to Norway?"

Merle reached over and stroked her arm. "They won't," she said, still in the lazy voice. "Vardis means that when she has to sing in public, she gets nervous about everything. Even silly things."

It was a sober thought. Vardis, who always seemed to know just what to do, who never had nightmares. "But you never look afraid to me," Hannah said.

Vardis came over and patted her hair, and she felt both wonderful and uncomfortable, with one of them stroking her arm and the other her head. But in a moment Vardis moved away, saying, "It's time for me to dress."

Hannah cried, "Can I get the dress out? Please?"

"All right. But be careful! If anything happens to it, I won't sing."

Merle sat up. "Nothing will happen to it."

Hannah ran to the end of the room, feeling their gazes on her back like reins. She opened the big closet, divided into eight sections. In Vardis's, with tissue paper stuffed up its sleeves, hung the dress: blue and silky, inches longer than her uniforms, with lace on the low, square-cut front and the cuffs. And beneath it, shining expectantly, the black patent, midheel shoes. She took them all out with care and walked back with them.

"Put them on the bed," Vardis said.

She did. The three of them stared. The outfit was vibrantly unlike anything at Cross of Glory—even the smell, which was like new pennies. "Mother Louise really likes you a lot, I guess," Hannah said.

"Does she?" Vardis said, with an odd sound in her voice.

"Well, sure. To buy you all that. You must be her top favorite. Don't you think she is, Merle?"

Merle didn't answer.

"I'm not her favorite," Vardis said. "I don't think she likes me at all."

She didn't seem to be joking. But she had to be. Mother Louise liked girls who were talented, or pretty, like Merle. Why shouldn't she? The ones she didn't like at all were the ones like Hannah Sebastian.

"But I don't mind," Vardis said, "because she's afraid of me."

Hannah was so surprised that her jaw fell like a trapdoor. She knew a lot about being afraid, but obviously Vardis knew things she didn't.

Merle squeezed her hand and said, "Don't worry about it, Han." Merle was beautiful, even with her dress scrunched up from lying all over the bed. The Cross of Glory haircut even looked good on her. As if it fit her face.

Vardis laughed. With one hand she lifted her hair high behind her head and struck a pose. "I will be splendid," she said. "Magnificent. And when I am in New York and have become a world-famous singer, I will have a thousand dresses, each one different —and no numbers on any of them—and people will fall at my feet and declare that my singing and my dresses are incomparable!"

Hannah laughed and clapped.

"And today," Vardis said, "I will not wear this ugly Cross of Glory slip, not with this beautiful dress." She pulled it over her head violently and stood there in her panties and brassiere. "Nor will I wear these damn Cross of Glory stockings!" She tore them off too and tossed them on the bed, where they lay like cast-off snakeskins.

She looked at Hannah and Merle and stalked to the row of dressers along one wall. She opened the top drawer of the third one—which was not hers—and took out a tissue-wrapped bundle. A pair of nylon stockings slid out of the paper.

"Vardis," Merle said, no longer lazy, "those are Mary Susan's. For graduation. Her father sent them."

"Yes. And I'm wearing them this afternoon."

"Did Mary Susan say you could?"

"I won't look like a fool just because old Tic-Tac-Toes was too cheap to buy me nylons!" Her voice lifted into a deadly, accurate imitation of Mother Louise. " 'You don't need them, my dear. Your regular hose will do quite well. Besides, no one will be looking at your legs.' What does she know about what I need? And who is going to be the most famous alumna of this orphanage? Who's already got the trustees talking about an extraordinary young musical talent? Before I leave here, the whole town —the whole state—is going to be talking about Cross of Glory. And she wouldn't buy me a decent pair of stockings!"

"She bought you the dress and shoes," Merle said. "And she got the board to pay for special lessons for you, and now for Conrad, too."

"But that's the point! She does what she knows she has to do. She can't leave a voice like mine to the music teacher she's got. She can't have me wearing that ugly uniform and shoes while I'm out representing Cross of Glory. But she makes sure I never get anything more than is absolutely necessary—so she can keep reminding me I'm a charity case and she's only doing her *duty*."

Merle frowned. "I don't think that's it, Vardis."

"Well, it is, and I know it. I've met her before. She's just like my Aunt Inge. The one they sent me to live with up north when the Nazis came. She fed me and hid me because she had to. She talked sweet enough, like Mother Louise, but I knew what she thought of me: an ugly, skinny nuisance she couldn't wait to get rid of."

"OK," Merle said. "But I think you're wrong about Mother Louise. And anyway, what does any of it have to do with Mary Susan?"

"She's one of my fans."

"Yes, but did she say you could wear her nylons?"

Vardis said nothing. She smiled and let the stockings unfold from her hands and hang in the air like streamers.

"I don't believe she told you to wear them," Merle said. "I think you'd better put them back."

"It's three-thirty," Vardis said. "I have to get ready." She sat on the bed and began to put on one of the stockings.

Merle got up and went to stand over her.

Hannah slid from her own perch and headed for the door. Neither of them paid her any attention. They were locked in the kind of struggle she had witnessed before. It seemed to her, although she couldn't explain why, that they both enjoyed it. Sometimes Vardis won, but not always.

She went along the dark hall, lined with bedroom doors, and down the stairs to the classroom floor. But Conrad had left the piano room, and all the other rooms were deserted as well. Moving faster, she went to the main floor and looked in all the places where the children could conceivably be spending their Sunday free hours: library, game room, common room. . . . There were children everywhere, but no Mary Susan. At last she dashed out the back door.

She saw Cary playing stickball. Despite all the brown-and-white shirts and Buster Brown haircuts, she could have easily picked him out, even if he hadn't limped. His thin shoulders were more stubborn than anybody else's, and his coal-colored hair flapped more wildly. She ran on, by the gardens and sheds, along the side of the house, up on the huge front porch with its swings. No Mary Susan.

She started around the other side of the house toward the little woods, her bangs growing damp and her breathing harder. Before she had gone a hundred yards, the bell sounded for Assembly. She came to a thudding halt, whimpering in her distress. There was no escaping the tyranny of the bells; one had to obey them immediately or face extra chores, at the least.

When she got back inside, lines of children were already converging on the auditorium. By now, Vardis would be backstage with Conrad. She saw Merle coming down the stairs and ran to her. Together they waited for Cary, who dashed in the front door, slicking his hair down with his hands.

The three of them joined the line into the auditorium.

Vardis's teacher, who lived in town and had once belonged to the Metropolitan Opera Chorus, accompanied her in the first part of the program, which consisted of songs by Schubert, Brahms, and Mozart. The audience was quiet and appreciative, although some of the youngest children shifted in their chairs and one, who was only four, listened with her head on the chair arm and her fingers in her mouth.

Hannah was so nervous waiting for Conrad that her heart was louder than Vardis's voice, and for the first time she didn't really listen to it. At last he came out, looking pale in a white shirt instead of the omnipresent brown. The three of them clapped the moment he appeared, as they had for Vardis—she had explained how that was always done for the artists—and the others joined right in. Conrad looked out and bowed deeply, as if it was a normal thing and he had done it all his life.

He played "Für Elise"—perfectly, it seemed to Hannah—with his head bent slightly over the keyboard. The light shining on his pale brown hair turned it into silk. The notes came from his fingers in trills and swoops that she had heard often while he practiced but that seemed different now, somehow, because everybody else was listening too, and looking at him. She turned her head and saw that Merle was smiling. Cary had a fiercely grown-up look on his nine-year-old face, which made her want to hug him. She turned back to the stage and closed her eyes, pretending she was in the back of the piano room, hidden.

Then the two of them were up there together, Vardis standing imperiously by the piano and nodding to Conrad to start. Hannah didn't recognize the music, for Vardis wouldn't let anyone listen when the two of them practiced. It was quite beautiful, with the notes from the piano like oars going smoothly through the water—and her voice like the water: so clear and cool and pure it made you thirsty and at the same time took your thirst away. As she listened, the two of them up on the stage began to seem like one person—Vardis-Conrad, joined at the waist and hands by the piano, which would hold them together forever.

It held them for three songs; even when they split apart, they came together again with their hands, and bowed. Conrad was no longer thirteen years old; he was nearly grown up, like Vardis.

They walked off the little stage together, and then Vardis came back with her guitar. All around Hannah the children rustled with pleasure.

She sang in Norwegian and no one knew the words, but before each song she explained a bit: "This is about a shepherd boy up in the mountains tending goats," and you could see them leaping on the rocks and hear their bells clanking in frosty air. Another was about fishing for herring, and you could smell the salt and feel the spray stinging your cheeks. Then there was a lullaby so beautiful it hurt because while it lasted you had a mother holding you. And the nightmare was gone, far gone.

Beside her, she felt Cary reach for her hand.

The children listened, as still as wax figures.

Mother Louise, sitting in the back with her staff, looked up at Vardis over the rows of identical haircuts. Fifty-eight of them, God be thanked—fifty-eight plus Vardis and Conrad Ashley made sixty. No one had taken advantage of the scene in the dining hall about "freedom" and stayed away.

When the clapping started, she shook off the spell of the songs, which had made her forget almost everything else about Vardis: that she was teenaged, rather coltish, and unattractive, except for her hair. Should she have been allowed to keep it long? And to have the special singing lessons? And the clothes? How did God mean one to act, when He placed such a truly gifted child in one's care? It was rather frightening to see that kind of talent, with its power over others, in one still so young. Would it be well used? God, in Mother Louise's experience, did not usually give personal power to those with the kindest hearts. Perhaps He reasoned that they didn't need it.

She sighed and descended from that lofty level of speculation to look once more at Vardis's legs, which would require some attention because they clearly were not clad in Cross of Glory lisle.

The applause ended. Some of the children left the auditorium quickly, but a number clustered around Vardis and Conrad as soon as they came down the steps from the stage, holding hands. Conrad's sister kissed them both. So did Hannah Sebastian, with an adult formality. Little Cary Mathias held Merle's hand and looked on. Vardis's singing teacher was still in her front-row seat, beaming.

They all fell silent as Mother Louise came close, and parted to leave a path between her and Vardis.

"It was lovely. Quite beautiful." Mother Louise smiled. "More than that. Exceptional. We're so fortunate that God sent you to us."

"I'm glad you think so." Vardis's color was high and her speaking voice a bit breathless.

"Yes. Well. I'll speak to you privately tomorrow. Come to my office before your first class. And Conrad—step out so I may shake your hand."

He did. Conrad was too pretty for a boy and not as awkward

as most of them, either. Masking her feelings, as always with any of The Five, she said, "How well you did! I see you're going to be a gifted musician, too."

"Thank you." His manner was grave. Vardis wasn't smiling either. If only they would smile more. All of them.

"Well," Mother Louise said brightly, after a pause, "enjoy yourselves till the supper bell. All of you."

She moved away. When the singing teacher joined her, she asked the woman, "Are you pleased?"

"Beyond all my hopes. The girl has always said that she was going to be a great singer one day. I believe she's right."

"Oh dear," said Mother Louise.

The two of them went slowly up the aisle discussing what to do for the year and a half remaining before the girl graduated and left Cross of Glory.

At the door Mother Louise frowned and stopped. Her ear, attuned to every shade of her charges' behavior, detected something in the chatter behind them. She turned. There was some kind of argument in the group by the stage.

By the time she got to it, she knew Vardis was at its center.

"All right," she said in the sternest voice she could muster. "What is the trouble here?"

Silence and frozen expressions.

"Fighting is never a way to settle a dispute. And on the Lord's day, it is a sin." She hesitated, decided not to start with any of The Five, and turned to a little girl who had clung adoringly to Vardis's skirt. "Lucy, what is the problem here?"

The child gasped but knew she had to answer. Twisting her hands, she stared at the floor and mumbled something that Mother Louise made her repeat three times before it was intelligible. "Stockings."

"Ah. Yes. What about stockings?"

The child's head hung lower, but she lifted one hand like a chubby periscope and aimed her index finger in the general direction of Vardis's legs.

"You mean that Vardis is wearing nylon stockings? I have already noted that. Is that what the quarrel is about?" No answer. Mother Louise turned to Vardis. "I had intended to ask you privately, so as not to intrude on your time of success, but perhaps I should put the question to you now: How did you get nylon stockings to wear?"

Vardis regarded her calmly. There was none of the normal girlish squirming and reddening. There never was. "I got them on my own," she said.

"On your own? How?" The children at Cross of Glory had no money unless a parent or relative sent it to them. No one ever sent Vardis anything.

"I don't see why it matters how I got them," she said.

Despite the quiet voice, she was being insubordinate, and everyone knew it.

Mother Louise fastened on the girl she knew was closest to Vardis. "Merle, how did Vardis come by the stockings?"

Merle Ashley, almost as tall as Vardis and with such a lovely face, hesitated for a long moment. "I really don't know."

Mother Louise sent her fiercest gaze rolling among the children, knocking aside their own stares like ninepins. But no one spoke.

Finally a choked voice announced, "The stockings are mine."

It was one of the oldest girls. Normally she had a sugary voice and worked into every conversation the fact that her father would come to get her soon, although there was absolutely no evidence to that effect.

"Ah. Mary Susan. Vardis is wearing your nylon stockings?" The girl nodded. "Did you lend them to her?"

"Yes, she did," Vardis said, still calm.

Little Lucy gasped and then stuffed her fist in her mouth like a cork.

"If Mary Susan lent you the stockings," Mother Louise asked, "then what were you fighting about?"

Vardis shrugged. "Nothing."

Mother Louise shivered inwardly. Lying and stealing were not only sins before God, they were a disease that could be contagious. Earlier, with that apparent but unsolved theft, she had been able to keep it secret. But if this was a theft, it was already public.

Praying silently, she turned to Mary Susan. "Is that true? You gave Vardis permission to borrow your stockings?"

The girl, turning red in agony, shook her head in a way that could have meant either yes or no.

"I want an answer," Mother Louise said firmly.

There was silence, until a desperate voice broke it by calling her name.

"Yes? Who is it?" Then she saw who. "Hannah," she said sharply. "Do you know something about this? Come forward at once."

The girl did. She was still much too thin, already too tall for the dress she had been issued only months before. "I know how it happened," she said. "It's really my fault, Mother Louise. Honest. See, I was up in Vardis's room when she was getting ready, and she was wishing she could borrow Mary Susan's nylons, and she asked me would I run and find Mary Susan and ask her. She said, 'Tell her I'll be real careful and afterwards I'll wash them out for her.' So I went, but I didn't go fast enough or look hard enough and I couldn't find Mary Susan, and then the bell rang for Assembly, and I had to come in. But Vardis didn't know that. She probably thought I got Mary Susan's permission and it was OK to borrow them. Because we all know Mary Susan thinks Vardis is wonderful and would want her to borrow them, even if they are from her father. Who's coming to get her soon." Words had tumbled from Hannah's mouth faster than her breath could support them. She drew in a gust of air and rocked from one foot to the other. "Maybe Vardis should have waited to make sure, but she gets nervous before she sings. We should understand that and not get mad if she doesn't always act like the rest of us. And if I were Mary Susan I'd be proud that she wore my stockings. I'd want her to wear them every time she sang. I wouldn't think stockings were as important as having Vardis sing the way she does. Some day we'll all have nice stockings, but none of us will ever sing like Vardis."

She took another deep breath and looked around as if she couldn't believe she had spoken. Merle Ashley put a hand on her shoulder, and Hannah stepped back quickly and stood against her.

The children shifted as if they were one body, and the motion conveyed a subtle, unmistakable change. They had withdrawn to the safety of childhood, leaving the issue to be decided by the adult world.

Mother Louise devoutly wished she too could leave it to another world. Or at least turn to the singing teacher for help. Her instincts told her Vardis was lying, a sin one had to punish. She knew she could take Mary Susan to her office and get the truth. But what the child Hannah said was true. Vardis was not like the rest of them. God must have extracted some price for the wonderful talent He had bestowed on her. Perhaps she had to suffer spiritually—with a loss of spiritual grace—to pay for it. But wasn't that all the more reason to punish her when she transgressed? To help save her soul?

But how to punish such a girl? Mightn't one scar her in some way, psychologically, and mar her talent?

"Mother Louise," said a tentative voice. It was Mary Susan's. "Yes?"

"It's all right about the stockings. We just had a misunderstanding, I guess. It's OK that Vardis wore them."

"Lying," said Mother Louise sternly, "is a sin before God. Do you swear you are not lying?"

"I am not lying, Mother Louise."

"Very well, then. Vardis will remove the stockings as soon as she gets up to her room. She will wash them and return them to you. And all of you will be ready promptly at six-thirty, when the supper bell rings."

She turned and went slowly back up the aisle. The singing teacher came behind her and said, when they were out of earshot, "Thank God. How awful if Vardis had been lying! I don't see how you could have punished her."

Mother Louise nodded, and thought of the consideration she hadn't allowed into her mind. If Vardis had lied, then so had Hannah Sebastian. And it would have been very hard to have to punish the child who was her favorite.

At ten o'clock, Lights Out rang. Everyone was in bed, fourteen in the two big rooms in the boys' wing and forty-six in the six girls' rooms.

Wearing a cotton gown just like her neighbors' except that each was mended in different places, Hannah lay in the dark and hugged the day to herself. She could barely remember what she had told Mother Louise, for she had been numb while saying it. Numb, with the strangest feeling that Vardis was willing her to do it.

Afterward had seemed like a dream too. Vardis took her hand and walked upstairs with her and sat talking till Supper rang. "You were clever, Han," she said. "I could have handled it myself, but you were very clever." Hannah decided not to ask Vardis how she had given her the power to do it. Then after supper, when Merle took one of the big chairs in the common room and tucked Cary beside her to read him a story, she and Conrad sat close and listened too.

She fell asleep remembering the warmth of all of them.

Three hours later she sat up as if she'd been jerked on a lead. Her hair and nightgown were damp, her heart was pounding on her ribs, trying to get out, and her staring eyes held the images of the nightmare.

She pushed the covers aside and slid out of bed. Shivering, she got to the door, opened it, and ran down the hall, which seemed endless and full of things with no heads that tried to grab her.

By the time she reached her destination, she was gasping. Inside the room, the dark was thick, but she felt her way to Merle's bed. When she finally slid into its haven, she whimpered with relief.

But the body she fastened herself to wasn't Merle's. She knew right away that the scent and feel were different. She started to pull away, but a voice whispered, "Is that Hannah?"

Afterward she could wonder whether she had crawled into Vardis's bed truly by mistake, but at the time she could only shiver and gasp that she was scared.

"Poor Han," Vardis whispered. She put an arm around her. Then, so very softly that at first it seemed to be the wind and not really a voice, she began to sing, right up against Hannah's ear.

Gradually the shivering stopped, and, slowly, tumbling through a space in her mind, she fell into sleep.

The next thing she knew was Vardis shaking her gently, with the sun starting to rise, and telling her she'd better get back to her own room before the first bell.

For weeks afterward, there was no nightmare. In fact, when Hannah was grown and looked back on it, she could date the diminution of the nightmare to the Sunday when Conrad had played in public for the first time and she had been comforted by Vardis.

When Conrad left Cross of Glory and followed Vardis and Merle to New York, the image of him she carried deepest in her heart was from that Sunday: the boy bent slightly over the keyboard, his hair silky in the light, his beautiful face intent, and the piano joining him to Vardis.

Later she followed them all to New York, leaving only Cary behind at Cross of Glory, and tried to develop the one meager talent she could find in herself—for science, which was a cold, pale companion next to the glory of music.

When she stood at their wedding, the image that came into her mind again was of that long-ago first concert at Cross of Glory. Who should be envied more? Conrad, for being able to share the magnificence of music with Vardis? Or Vardis, for being joined to him?

CHAPTER
11

The phone rang five times before Dinah heard a pickup and a gruff "Yes?"

"Sam, it's me."

"Oh." His voice softened. "Hi, sweetheart."

For a moment she stared at the phone. "Did I wake you?"

"No, it's OK."

"I know it's early, but I tried to get you last night until about eleven."

"I was out on a case. What's up?"

"Hannah Sebastian came to see me yesterday." Sam was silent, but Dinah could imagine his face sharpening to attention. "She knows nothing about my birth. She won't even accept that Vardis had a child. But she talked about her and got so carried away she let something slip. Something you should know."

"Oh?"

"Sam, those four people may have known one another longer than you thought. It sounded as if they were together before New York, in some small town in Connecticut. In a school, or maybe an orphanage, called Cross of Glory."

"Could you tell me exactly what Hannah Sebastian said?"

"Sure." Notebook in front of her, Dinah went through the conversation.

"It's interesting," Sam said noncommittally. "I'll look into it. Thanks."

She waited. When he said nothing more, she said, "Sam, I have a strong impression that Sebastian didn't kill Vardis. In fact I asked her if she could have harmed Vardis deliberately, and before she realized, she blurted out a big negative. I think she's innocent and the only question is what could make her confess to killing a woman she obviously worshiped."

"I guess I can tell you," he said slowly. "She claims to be in love with Ashley. Says she killed Wolf so she could finally have a chance with him."

Dinah thought for a moment. "Well . . . Yes, I could believe she loves him. But there's something peculiar about her."

"You could say that about all four of them."

"But Hannah Sebastian makes me uneasy. The way she talked about Vardis like a kind of sacred idol."

"When you and I first talked about Vardis, didn't you call her an idol?"

"Yes. And don't think I haven't wondered if there's a touch of Sebastian's attitude in me. She was so intense and yet so . . . blind. Yes, that's it, blind. I hope to God I'm not that way."

"I think it's like being crazy—if you can worry about it, you're not."

She laughed. "You're such a comfort to me. Sam, do you have any heroes?"

"Well . . . sure, I guess. When I was a kid."

"I think all kids do. It's important to feel there are people in the world to admire. You don't put it into words, but it's what you feel. But when some kids grow up, they want to attack that feeling. I had a professor once who'd practically sneer at the idea that anybody could have real stature of character. He'd give a cynical smile and quote something I'll never forget. 'Heroes,' he'd say, 'are created by popular demand, sometimes out of the scantiest materials.' "

Sam chuckled. "Maybe he had a point. The media's always coming up with instant celebrities."

"Yes, but why do people want them? That's the question. Do

they fill some basic need? Do we maybe need heroes as role models? Sam, are you still there?"

"Mmmm," he said. "I was thinking of my uncle the cop."

"You wanted to grow up and be like him?"

"Yeah," he said softly.

"If he was a good cop, then you did. But I think there's more to it than needing role models. I'm sure there is."

"That isn't what Wolf meant to you?"

"It's true she set an example, in a way. If she could escape the Nazis and grow up to denounce oppression, then I could stand up for what I believe in. But there's something deeper. Some response to her artistry, and other people's too, like Shakespeare's and Mozart's and Verdi's. Part of me is responding to what they created, but part is just kind of standing back and thinking, Isn't it wonderful that my species is capable of such greatness? And the lower the species sinks, the more important it is to see some heads rising above it."

Into the silence Sam said, "And you don't think Sebastian feels that?"

She frowned. "Probably. But with her there's something else, too. Something I can't put my finger on. Sam, tell me, do you still believe in heroes? Or did you grow up and turn into a cynic?"

She had thought he might laugh, but he said gravely, "I don't know if I'm a cynic or a realist. You can't be a cop in this town and not realize how subhuman people can be. But I guess I still believe in a few heads rising, too."

"I think that's what makes you a good cop. And you know what else I think? That cynics are only people whose heroes have betrayed them. Oh my God!" she cried, suddenly focusing on her watch. "It's after eight and I've got to get to school and this is a crazy conversation to be having so early, anyway."

"I liked it," he said simply. "I like talking to you."

After she hung up, she thought that she had liked it too. Sam was such a . . . sweetheart.

Lives of great men all remind us
We can make our lives sublime,
And, departing, leave behind us
Footprints on the sands of time. . . .

Somehow the verse had gotten stuck in Dinah's mind. It stayed with her all day—through a divisive faculty meeting, two hard classes, and a session with a student who tried but couldn't grasp the difference between a sentence and a fragment of one.

At five-thirty, when she went out running, her feet pounded the rhythm all through Central Park. She kept trying to focus on something else—trees uncurling into green, a child tugging at a nursemaid as if she were a giant toy, pigeons rising from a rock and carrying its colors with them. But when she made three miles at the western edge of the park and slowed to a walk, there it was:

> LIVES of GREAT men ALL reMIND us
> WE can MAKE our—

She swung her head, squared her shoulders, and started toward home. What about the lives of great *women?* Damn Longfellow, anyway. She had never liked either his sentiments or their expression. And damn Hannah Sebastian, who had started the whole thing.

That morning she had asked her class to talk about the people they admired most. The result was a very mixed bag: John Kennedy, Martin Luther King, John Lennon, several rock superstars, two superstar comedians who relevantly or not were black, and—surprisingly—the rich, powerful villains from several TV series.

So the kids admired two kinds of people: the idealistic and the successful. And if a person struck both chords, he had a hold on them that seemed unshakable. Like Kennedy's and Lennon's.

Like Vardis's hold on Hannah Sebastian? No, some other element was involved. Something desperate—her insistence that Vardis be perfect. Why? Because if she wasn't . . . Hannah couldn't function? Couldn't see? Couldn't live?

Dinah shivered as she turned onto her street. Could somebody fix her existence, literally, on another human being?

In a moment she grimaced at her naïveté. History was full of tales of people who surrendered their will to charismatic figures —for whom they slaughtered their Jewish neighbors, drank Kool-Aid laced with cyanide . . .

But Vardis Wolf hadn't poured out cyanide for others. She'd

been the one to drink it. And she hadn't been a messianic political or religious leader; she had been an artist.

Couldn't art be one of the great carriers of idealism, though? Hadn't Vardis, through her art, offered a view of a better world, based on beauty? And hadn't she had material success, as well?

Dinah stopped short; a doorman running to hail a taxi almost crashed into her. She saw that she was in front of the building where John Lennon had been assassinated. By a devout fan.

She was still thinking about that, Longfellow finally driven from her head, when she got back to the apartment.

Cassie was there, stomach-down on the couch, head hanging over the side. She waved, then moved to rest her chin on her arm and watch as Dinah sat down to unlace her running shoes. "What do you get out of that?" she asked. "Running?"

Dinah considered. "It feels good, physically, when you're finished. But I guess the main thing is psychological: the feeling you've done something with your body that you didn't expect to be able to do."

"Mmmm. Like sex."

Dinah was ready to retort, but the ring of the phone cut her off.

"It's probably for you," Cassie said. "Some guy called for you about an hour ago. Wouldn't leave his name. I said you'd be back by now."

Could it be Sam? Dinah wondered. When she was just getting ready to call him again? She smiled and said, "I'll take it in the bedroom."

But it wasn't Sam. "Dinah Mitchell?"

"Yes."

"The one who quotes Mencken?"

"Oh." She sat abruptly on the bed. "I wasn't expecting to hear from you."

"I hope you like the unexpected."

"As long as it's pleasant."

"Me too. Frankly I expected you might hang up on me, but here we are talking. Pleasant."

She reached to pull the sock from her left foot.

"What are you doing?" he said.

"This minute? Taking off my running socks. I just came in."

"Do you run every day?"

"If I can."

"My game is tennis. Do you play?"

"No. But I've sure been wondering what your game is."

He laughed. "Fair enough. My game is I want you to have dinner with me."

"When?"

"Tonight?"

"I can't, I'm afraid. I've got papers to grade that have to be handed back tomorrow morning."

"Tomorrow night, then?"

She pulled off her other sock. "Why?"

"Because you can't do it tonight."

She smiled. "Why should we do it at all?"

"Maybe because I've been thinking about you. Hearing your voice. Wanting to see you again."

She leaned against the pillows. "Or maybe because you want to find out what I've been up to?"

"What a good idea," he said. "Will you tell me?"

"I doubt it. Unless you tell me a few things in return."

"Why don't we both expect the best, then. May I pick you up at seven?"

"Yes. All right."

She hung up and lay staring at the high ceiling, listening to traffic gearing up for Lincoln Center. Eventually she realized she was still smiling.

She sat up, undressed, and got into an old terry robe. As she cut through the living room to the shower, Cassie, still prone on the couch, said, "Child, there's a look about you, which says your gentleman caller wasn't just the butcher. Are you by any chance about to embark on a relationship, capital *R*?"

She stopped. "And what if I was?"

"I'd send up flares into the night."

"Why make such a big deal of it?"

"Because it is a big deal. Sex makes the world go around and all that."

"I wish you wouldn't harp on sex so much. What's the point of it?"

Cassie sat up. "Does everything have to have a point?"

"Does everything have to lead into sex?"

Cassie's laugh was forced. "Only if you're still alive."

"Meaning that if I don't feel like sleeping with every man I meet, it's a character flaw?"

"Don't tell me I'm sharing the place with Little Miss Moral Majority."

"You don't *share* it," Dinah heard herself say loudly. "You only move in when you're tired of a man."

"Dammit!" Cassie scrambled to a standing position on the couch, blond hair angry on her shoulders. "I pay a quarter of the rent when I'm not here. How many other people would do that? Not very damn many. But I guess you figure you don't need me, now you're Vardis Wolf's daughter. You've got it made, so you can cut loose from your old ties."

"Cassie! I never had any such thoughts! What are you talking about?"

They stared at each other. Dinah's heart pounded as if she were still running. How in hell had this happened in fewer than five minutes?

Cassie lurched off the couch and reached under it for her shoes. "I'm going out." She grabbed a sweater from the closet and shoved a fist into one sleeve. "If my service calls, I'll be at the Show Bar."

The door slammed behind her.

Dinah stared at it. No, she thought, she wasn't trying to displace her mother with Vardis Wolf. Or drown her mixed feelings for her mother, and her guilt, in a new relationship. She swung her head and went into the small bathroom and started the water. Her hands shook as she turned the tap. Once in the shower, she told herself it was only the shocks of the past week that had made her so short-tempered. Although she had always wished Cassie would be more . . . fastidious, that was how she thought of it. But it had never seemed very important. Now, somehow, it had taken center stage.

Part of the reason was Cary Mathias. Whom she couldn't tell Cassie about. Because if she shared the way she felt, that would be admitting it. Because Cassie would talk about it as if it were nothing but a sexual urge. Because, dammit, part of it *was* a sexual urge.

For a man who claimed to have committed murder.

She lifted her face to punish it with needles of water.

. . .

The day was warm, the traffic wasn't bad, and Sam felt pretty good.

He had made it to the Connecticut Turnpike in less than an hour, so even if his trip was in the wild-goose category, it wouldn't take too much time. He was off-duty but had to be in by four. He leaned his arm on the open window, took one of the New Haven exits, and headed north.

If the four friends had a longer history than he'd thought, there might be a perfectly innocent reason they hadn't mentioned it, like just not volunteering anything they didn't have to. But it was worth looking into.

Dinah had called him again, right after supper. "I've been thinking all day about Hannah. And the more I do, the more I wonder whether she isn't guilty after all. Maybe she killed Vardis in order to have total and permanent identification with her idol. Remember the man who killed John Lennon? Didn't he want to be linked with Lennon forever? As in fact he now is?"

It was a hell of an interesting idea: that Hannah Sebastian could have killed Vardis out of a pathological hero worship.

They had talked about it for a while. He noted how easily they had slipped into a fairly open discussion of the case, which wasn't what he had planned. But then he hadn't planned to have the feelings about her that he had, either.

He had finally told her he didn't accept her Lennon idea. But in fact it wasn't that much harder to believe than Sebastian's confession. And if his own view was right, he should be able to explain why Sebastian had confessed if she was innocent—why she was lying about poisoning Vardis Wolf. But he couldn't.

Maybe some kind of clue was buried in the past. In that hope, and because he had no other, he was driving to see an old woman named Louise Solberg.

In half a dozen calls he had learned that something called the Cross of Glory Home had existed from 1920 until the mid-1960s. Someone at a Lutheran social services headquarters was still working on locating and checking its records, but had been able to give Sam the name of the home's last director, who had been there during the time in question. When he called the police in the small Hartford County town where Cross of Glory had been located, someone had come up with the fact that the Solberg woman was still alive, in a nursing home not far away.

At about eleven-thirty he reached the home, a huge colonial house well provided with trees and lawn. Inside, though, was that faintly sour smell that often accompanies old age, although he'd never been sure what caused it. When he was old himself— that would be time enough to learn. He stood straighter than usual and walked briskly behind the nurse who took him upstairs.

"Like I told you on the phone," the nurse said, "you never can tell whether she'll know what you're talking about or not. Some days she's not too bad, some days it's hopeless." She took him down a hall, opened a door, and spoke with mechanical brightness to the woman sitting by the window in a wheelchair. "Miss Solberg, here's the man I told you was coming. Detective Sam Lyons of the New York City Police. He's come all this way just to talk to you, isn't that nice?"

The woman was as wrinkled as a newborn, and tiny. She had little claw hands, hooked over a shawl as white and wispy as her hair, and eyes that didn't open even when Sam said her name three times. The nurse told him to sit and wait a bit, so he folded himself down into a chair, feeling big and noisy and not very hopeful.

He thought about Dinah, and wondered whether his kids would like her.

He was holding an imaginary conversation with his oldest boy, who said Dinah was neat, so when there was a faint "Hello," it didn't register for a beat.

The woman's head was upright, eyes fixed on him. "Hello. Are you one of my children?"

It took him a moment to get it. "No, ma'am. But I came to talk to you about them—your children at Cross of Glory."

She sighed. "I suppose it's the Eiselman twins. I've been thinking about them, but I don't see the answer. They were difficult from the start. Didn't take discipline well. Always wanted to sleep together, boy and girl, when we had separate dormitory wings." She went on, voice shaking its way through a long story Sam was afraid to interrupt for fear he might stop her permanently. It was like listening to his children when they were babies. They always wanted to tell long involved stories you could only half understand, and you had to let them or they got frustrated and cried. Why did God arrange it so you babbled on both ends of your life span? The woman, they had told him, was eighty-eight.

When she wound down he said, "You have a good memory, Miss Solberg. I wonder if you remember a girl who was at Cross of Glory in the late 1940s, a girl from Norway who was probably a pretty good singer?"

"Ah," the old woman said. "Our Norwegian nightingale."

"So you do remember her?"

"Vardis Wolf."

Sam didn't let his voice reflect any excitement at all. "Is that the name you knew her by?"

"From Norway, she was. Such talent. I saw to it that she had special lessons. I always tried to do my best for the children."

"And I'll bet they appreciated you for it. Miss Solberg, I don't know if the nurse explained it to you, but—"

"Mother Louise, that's what they all called me."

"That's nice. I hope the nurse told you why I came. It's because I—"

"I was never married but I had hundreds of children. What do you think of that, young man?"

Sam chuckled, which seemed to satisfy her. "I'm trying to find out something about Vardis Wolf's early life," he said. "I wonder if you remember some of the other children who were at Cross of Glory at the same time she was. Four in particular. I wonder if they were there, at least some of them. There were a brother and sister named Merle and Conrad Ashley, a girl named Hannah Sebas—"

"The Five," she said.

"I beg your pardon?"

"We called them The Five. Always together. Came together and stayed together. Vardis and Merle, and little Hannah, and a younger boy, Carl."

"Carl? Are you sure it wasn't Cary?"

"Well, perhaps it was. A quiet boy."

"Let's see. You said Vardis and Merle, Hannah and Cary. But that's only four. Wasn't Merle Ashley's brother there too? A boy named Conrad?"

"Conrad!" she said with surprising sharpness. "Yes. Conrad was there."

"Let's start with him. What do you remember about him?"

"Not a boy you could trust."

"Why not, Miss Solberg?"

"Mother Louise," she said fretfully. "The children call me Mother Louise."

"That's right, you told me. Well, Mother Louise, I'd really like to know why you couldn't trust Conrad Ashley."

She sighed. There was a silence so long he thought she had dropped off to sleep, although her eyes were still open. At length she said, "The ten dollars. I don't care what they said. He was the one who took it."

"Conrad Ashley stole some money?"

"He had a pretty face. Too pretty. More than some of the girls. Why does God distribute his gifts so unequally? I know we mustn't question His wisdom, but why should He allow a boy to look like something from a picture book?"

"What made you think he stole money?"

"Who else?" Her head and voice shook angrily. "It was in my desk drawer, a ten-dollar bill, put there in the morning to give to the gardener at lunch. But by lunch it was gone. And all morning, who had been in my office but staff people and Conrad Ashley? Stealing and lying are terrible sins to countenance in children, but it wasn't in his room or anywhere we could find, so I couldn't do anything. You can't punish a child without proof. That would also be a sin. And I couldn't be too hard on him, or any of them, even if they were trying to play some kind of trick on me. Not after what they'd been through. But I knew it was him. No matter what they said. Why does God give such a face to a boy?"

She went on chewing over the story without adding to it, and Sam had the sudden perception that the words had replaced the experience. Maybe at that age there was only one thing you could still control: your past, by reducing it to repetition.

"Mother Louise," he said gently, "what about the rest of The Five? Can you tell me something about them?"

"Oh . . . well . . ." She looked disoriented. "What is it you want to know?"

"How old were they when came to you? Can you remember that?" There was no answer. "Take Vardis. How old was she?"

"I'm not sure. Around fifteen, I think."

"How about the others? Hannah Sebastian?"

"Ah. She came on her tenth birthday. She could barely tell us because her English was so bad. They all had trouble with English at first, except Vardis."

Sam felt pressure at the back of his neck. "You said they came together. Do you mean they all arrived at the orphanage at the same time?"

"All five at once."

"I want to be sure I get this right. They were all orphans, and they all came together?"

The woman nodded, but she seemed to be running out of energy. She started to sink back into the wheelchair like a doll being slowly deflated.

"Were they all from the same family?" Sam asked.

She frowned, and made a small sound of distress.

"Not from the same family? Where did they come from?"

"The war." Her voice was quite faint.

"All of them? Not just Vardis?" She nodded. Sam gripped the arm of her wheelchair as if he could transfuse some of his own energy to her. "Do you mean they all came from Norway?"

"From the war," she whispered.

"All five of them?"

It was clear that she nodded yes, but beyond that he couldn't get, although he stayed for another forty minutes, long after the nurse told him it was useless to wait and he'd have to come back another day.

PART 3

DOUBTER

CHAPTER
12

In questa Reggia, or son mill'anni e mille,
un grido disperato risuonò . . .
From this palace, thousands of years ago,
a cry of despair went out . . .

Vardis Wolf was singing the famous aria from *Turandot* in a voice
like the title character herself: cold, remote, and dazzling. Ice on
a sunlit peak.

The voice flooded the whole apartment, even the bathroom,
where Dinah was sunk in the tub, chin resting on a blanket of
bubbles. She had got home at six, with an hour to spare before
Cary Mathias arrived, and found the apartment empty, no sign
that Cassie had come and gone. She had put on the record of
"Vardis Sings Verdi and Puccini" and run a bath as hot as she
could bear. Her body had protested, reddened, then accepted,
until there was no feeling left and she was bodiless, reduced to
the capacity to hear and to react to what she heard.

. . . nel tempo che ciascun ricorda,
fu sgomento e terrore e rombo d'armi . . .
In that time all recall,
of the horror and rumbling weapons of war . . .

A major critic had said Vardis was the only soprano who could handle the role of Turandot not only vocally but histrionically. She completely became the virginal Oriental princess who loathes men. Who makes all suitors try to answer three difficult riddles, and executes them for failing. Whose motive is revenge for a virgin ancestress dragged from her palace during wartime and killed by a man. Perhaps only at the end of the opera, when Turandot surrenders ardently to the one suitor who solves the riddles, was Vardis less than convincing. But, as the critic had noted, Turandot was one of the more improbable heroines in the operatic canon.

. . . notte atroce,
dove si spense la sua fresca voce . . .
. . . cruel night,
when her sweet voice was stilled. . . .

Vardis's voice grew darker as Turandot sang of war and her ancestress's death, and Dinah shivered at the sound, thinking that she had never known anyone who didn't respond to music of some kind. Whatever music did, it did almost universally. But what exactly was it that music did? Certain sounds were arranged in a certain way, and somehow the result struck people in the viscera. She had a fuzzy idea that it all worked something like a piano, where a key made a hammer strike a string. Music, the key, hit the hammer of one's hearing mechanism, which sent the message to the "strings" in the brain where feelings and emotions were stored. But that didn't explain why certain sounds produced certain emotions. Or for that matter, why sound should produce any emotion at all.

She thought of the omnipresent rock music she'd grown up on. The pounding beat and the melodies like barely contained ecstasies and furies seemed to be an expression of adolescence itself: everything felt with first-time intensity, nothing quite within one's control. But which came first, the music or the emotions?

Did you like a certain kind of music because it expressed feelings you already had, or could music make you feel something before you had experienced it?

> . . . *io vendico su voi quella purezza.*
> . . . I take revenge on you for her innocence.

Dinah remembered standing in a ticket line to hear Vardis for the first time. All around her were people who seemed to know everything about opera and argued passionately over various conductors and singers. She had been amazed, but the more she listened to opera, the more like them she became. Adamant about her favorites ("*Nobody* does that more beautifully than Björling!"), she was violent on her side of the eternal debate about what the highest value in opera should be, beautiful sound or convincing drama. ("Yes, the voice is glorious, but he's the size of a house and has about as much acting ability.")

One of her college professors had said, "Opera was created for the rich, and it's still the most elitist art form. It's the most expensive and the furthest removed from reality." She had told Harry it was a slam at the working classes to say that grandeur and passion were elitist and unrealistic. Harry had laughed and said he thought passion was realistic as hell. Especially at their house.

> . . . *Mai nessun m' avrà!*
> No man shall ever possess me!

Why she had gotten interested in opera, the only one of her high-school crowd to do so, Dinah had no idea. When she tried to involve her friends, they had said it was silly—people taking poison and falling on swords just for love or honor, or announcing they were going to die and then singing for ten minutes. It was true that people in real life didn't act like opera characters. For openers, they didn't sing instead of talking. But, as she had tried to explain, singing was more beautiful than speech, and opera characters cared more deeply about things than most people she knew. If they loved each other, it was blazing and forever, not just in and out of the sack. If they died, it was with grandeur, not gore.

And if they broke the law, as Harry once said, they never got away with it.

>*Gli enigmi sono tre, la morte è una!*
>There are three riddles but only one Death!

Dinah opened her eyes. Suddenly she focused on who the singer was and the fact that her death was a riddle, involving at least three liars.

Why would those who worshipped Vardis and those who hated her be willing to lie for one another about killing her?

The bubbles stirred around Dinah, disappearing with tiny popping sounds.

She reached an arm over the side of the tub and picked up her watch from the floor. Six-forty. She sat erect, sloshing water, and climbed out.

When the phone rang, she was half-dressed. She ran to turn down the music and picked up the kitchen phone, half-expecting to hear Cary Mathias, canceling the date. If it was a real date and not just a pretext for checking up on her.

But it wasn't Mathias. "Sam!"

"Glad I finally caught you. I called a couple of times before."

"I had a class till five-thirty." He had never called her before. He must have discovered something. But he didn't sound like business as usual.

"I thought teachers kept bankers' hours. What are you doing now?"

"I'm . . . Actually, I was listening to a record of Vardis."

"Wouldn't you rather come out for a beer?"

She leaned on the kitchen counter. "I'm sorry, Sam. I'm going to dinner."

"Oh. I guess you wouldn't be free later on tonight?"

"I don't think so." She moved the salt shaker in arcs on the counter, circling around the fact that she didn't want to tell him she was going to dinner with Cary Mathias. "Was there . . . Is there something you wanted me to know?"

She could hear him hesitating, see the blue eyes narrow. "What the hell," he said. "Today I saw the former director of the Cross of Glory orphanage."

"Sam!"

"They were there. Vardis Wolf and the other four you're interested in."

"They've known each other since childhood, then?"

"Sounds like."

She put the salt shaker back. "What do you think it means?"

Again he hesitated. Something he'd learned but felt he couldn't tell her? "They all got to the orphanage at the same time," he said. "From the war."

"What are you saying? That they all came from Norway? With Vardis?"

"The woman got kind of incoherent, but I think it's a real possibility."

Dinah stared blankly at the stove. If the four friends had known Vardis that long, then they must know about the child. Who its father was, why it was given up. At least one of them must know something. But it wasn't "the child"; it was her. Why couldn't she think of it—of herself—that way?

"Dinah? You still there?"

"Just taking it all in. Do you think . . . they're all from the same family?"

"I asked that. I couldn't get a clear answer."

She frowned. "But Sam, when Hannah Sebastian told me about going to Norway as an adult, she said Vardis was the only one of them who spoke the language."

"So? It's not exactly like none of them ever told a lie. By the way, Cross of Glory was a Lutheran orphanage. We know Vardis was part Jewish. Maybe the rest of them are too. Makes you wonder how Jewish kids got to a Lutheran orphanage, doesn't it?"

"Yes. It does."

"Right. Well . . . I'll see you then, I guess."

"Wait, Sam, don't hang up. Sam!"

"I'm here."

"I haven't thanked you. For finding out, and for telling me. You're being very good to me."

"It's easy," he said.

After they said good-bye, she stood for a moment with her hand on the phone, eyes closed, thinking, Sam, don't ask me for more than friendship. Not yet.

She was in the bedroom struggling with the back zipper on

her dress when she took in the other implication of Sam's news. If the four had grown up with Vardis in Norway, then the roots of their relationship to her—and the reason they were all confessing?—could go back for decades and into another culture. And if that was the case, how would she, or Sam, find the truth?

By being ingenious, tenacious, devious, and whatever else it took, she thought. She started brushing her hair and then stopped and looked at herself in the dresser mirror, face framed by the two wedding pictures, her own and her parents', tucked one on each side. You're enjoying this, she thought. Whatever else is going on, in some way you enjoy acting like a detective and trying to find out who's guilty and who's lying and why.

She raised her eyebrows at her image and nodded in surprised agreement. Then her gaze went to Harry, in the picture. She thought of how keyed up he had been during an investigation, how she had felt his frustration and excitement and determination. She smiled at him.

Ten minutes later she buzzed to let Cary Mathias in. Waiting in the living room, she took a deep breath, as if she were going to enter some kind of ring.

When he took her arm as they walked into the restaurant, she felt the pressure of his hand, through her jacket, and a slight imbalance in his walk, as he favored his right side. She wouldn't have mentioned it, but after they ordered drinks, he surprised her by saying, "You noticed the leg?"

"Yes. I did."

"Good. You admit it. A lot of people pretend they don't. Silly."

"Maybe not. Maybe they're just trying not to embarrass or upset you."

"It wouldn't do either of those things."

"That's good. But how is somebody supposed to know it?" He started to answer, but she went on quickly. "It takes time to learn which things people are willing to talk about and which ones they want to keep private."

He smiled but said nothing.

"Well, since you say it doesn't embarrass you, can I ask if it happened during the war?"

The look he gave her, speculative and appraising, made tension rise between them. After their drinks came, he said, "What gives you the idea that I was in a war?"

"Just a guess. A lot of men have lived through two or three wars by now."

"Which one did you have in mind for me? Not that it matters. All the goddamn wars are alike."

"I don't know," she said. "You might have been too young for Korea."

"And too old for Vietnam, thank God."

She waited until he lifted his glass and took a swallow before she said. "And of course in World War Two you'd still have been a child."

She watched his throat, as the liquid ran inside it smoothly. The skin was tanned and rather rough, and disappeared into the V of an open white shirt collar. He put the glass down. "That's right."

"But children can get hurt during wars, so maybe it could have happened during World War Two after all."

He rattled his fingernails on the glass. "The boring truth is that the leg is the result of an accident. I fell and broke it when I was a child. It never healed properly, so the left is a bit shorter than the right."

"I see. I'm sorry."

"Don't be. I'm quite used to it."

She took a sip of her wine, crisp and dry, and decided to go further still. "If it happened when you were a child, then I suppose it was in Norway."

"What on earth are you talking about?" he said. He looked so startled that it startled her.

"But I thought . . . Aren't you from Norway? Like Vardis? I thought you knew her over there."

"I assure you I've never set foot in Norway and probably never will. Not if I can help it."

"I see. Then I guess you can't . . . I was hoping you could tell me something about Vardis's early life."

"Sorry. She said very little about it. Didn't like to talk about it. Where in hell did you get the idea that I was from Norway?"

His reaction seemed so natural, a little indignant, a little amused. As natural as Hannah Sebastian had seemed when she talked of Norway as a strange country. "Oh, I heard it somewhere," Dinah said. "Maybe it was something Hannah Sebastian said. She came to see me the other day."

"So she says. But she couldn't have told you I was from Norway."

"I don't know, then. Maybe I read it somewhere."

"Not possible. The press has written a lot of stuff, but never that. For one thing it's just not true. Not that that always stops the press, but in this case it has."

She must have been searching his face, because he said, "What's the matter? Do you think I'm lying?"

"I have no idea. I barely know you. It takes time to learn what things people lie about, and even longer to learn why."

"But eventually you can find out?"

"I think so. If you're determined enough."

He looked at her over the rim of his glass. "And I think you are very determined."

"Yes."

"But the question is, what exactly are you determined to do?"

"I've told you. Find out as much as I can about Vardis Wolf."

He drank again, and when he put his glass down, tension flared between them once more.

She lifted her shoulders and said, "If Hannah Sebastian told you she'd been to see me, I guess that means the two of you are in close touch."

"I didn't say that."

"What did you say, then? I can never be sure."

He smiled. "I say as much as I want you to know. You try to turn it into more."

She resisted the desire to smile back. "On the other hand, sometimes you tell me more than I ask."

"When do I do that?"

"When you say you killed Vardis Wolf."

He sat back slowly against the dark red of the banquette, smile fading as he moved.

"And I ask myself," she went on, "why you should want me to know it."

"I told you. I was afraid Con might have said that he was the one."

"Even so, why should you confess to a stranger? It doesn't make any sense. Unless . . ."

"Unless what?"

"Unless you know you can't be arrested and convicted. Because you know you're innocent."

She tried to decipher his expression, but it was both fleeting and contradictory: Something like hope flashed in his eyes, but in the next instant it was more like fear—afraid she had guessed the truth?—and before she could be sure of either, his face had closed again, leaving only a hint of irony—or perhaps it was mockery—in the mouth. The little scar on his right cheekbone stood out whitely.

"Why," he asked, "would I claim to be guilty if I'm not?"

"That's the question, all right." She leaned forward. "And asking it rhetorically is a just a way of evading it."

A waiter sailed to their table, destroying her attack as effectively as if Cary Mathias had signaled him to do it.

"We'll order now," Mathias said, taking one of the red-suede-covered menus. "I'm starving. Aren't you?"

For the next half-hour he gave her no chance to ask anything. He was the one with questions, capping each answer with a new query. He didn't seem to have a hidden purpose, although she knew he must. Just as she did. She answered as if he really wanted to know and gradually it began to seem that he did.

She told him about teaching: the high hopes, the desire to open for others the same doors she had found, the frustration of dealing with subliterate students who often seemed indifferent to learning. "I know it's hard to come to college and have to take courses in the rudiments of English, but damn it, they don't seem to have any questions in their souls. They're too willing to accept their own inadequacies. To accept everything the way they find it—including themselves, and the whole world. I try to ignite them, but they're green wood."

"Wouldn't it make a difference if you had a couple of students who really responded? Or even just one?"

"Sure. But I'm starting to think the problem isn't just the students, or the fact that I'm teaching Basic Skills. I'm not sure I really like the process of teaching." She raised her eyebrows; the words had come unbidden, but they rang true. Slowly she added, "Maybe I should leave teaching." She looked at him. "That's the first time I've said that. Or seriously thought it."

"What would you do instead?" he asked, eyes intent on hers.

"I don't know. That's the trouble. It would have to be something I could care about. I don't see myself just putting in time to earn a living. It would help if I could find something my education was right for. Otherwise there'd be the expense of training for something new. . . . My God, I never thought I'd be in the position of not being sure what I want to do. I've always known. Always."

She swung her head and took a bite of some excellent crab-stuffed flounder, and then he asked about Harry, how he had been killed. It was strange, talking about Harry with another man's gaze touching her face like a hand. "He was proud to be a cop," she said. "He got frustrated by things that happened, and angry, but never cynical. He liked to read history—he said it proved the law is all that stands between us and the barbarians. It was one of the barbarians who killed him. A kid stealing TV sets on Avenue C shot him in the chest."

"How long did it take you to put your life back together?" Cary asked.

"There's a way in which I never will. But if you mean how long before I felt halfway human again . . . about a year, I think." She pushed her plate aside. "They caught his killer and put him away. Three years later he was out. What kept me from going crazy was knowing that Harry wouldn't have. He'd have been mad and frustrated, but he'd still have believed in the law."

After a long silence Cary said, "I marvel at the things people live with. The disasters and tragedies. They stay with us forever, yet we have to go on as if they hadn't happened."

She looked at him, a question forming, but abruptly he shifted his position and his mood, and asked how she had gotten the birth certificate linking her to "Hjördis Olafsen."

When he asked what her mother had been like, an image leaped into her mind—her mother, wearing the old red cardigan that had candy for Dinah hidden in the pockets, bent over the sewing machine in her bedroom, squinting as she fed in fabric. ("I saw a lovely dress in the children's-wear department, honey, and I found a pattern that's close. Oh, you're going to look nice!") One day her hand had slipped and the needle plunged into her finger. She had had to go to the emergency room at the hospital and stay home from work, in bed. It had been strange to have a mother who was sick. The apartment had felt and looked different, as if the furniture had grown and squeezed out some of the air.

She looked up at Cary Mathias. "Mother sold hosiery in a Brooklyn department store. She was hard-working, not all that efficient, proud as hell of me though she didn't quite understand me. And she was a good human being."

For once he didn't respond with a question. They sat looking at each other. The tension had not dissolved but had become darker, and sensual. Questions were ways of asking for something that words could not, and answers, of granting it.

"Cary . . ." She realized it was the first time she had used his name.

"Yes?"

"I don't know anything about you. Anything at all. Where do you come from, if it's not Norway? What do you do?"

He looked at her as if she had issued a challenge and it amused him in some way. Then he shrugged and leaned back, one hand around his neck. "I spent too many years doing nothing in particular. Came to New York when I was eighteen and drifted from one job to another. Stock boy, cabdriver, bartender, you name it. The kinds of things people do to put themselves through college, except I didn't stay in college. Worked my way across the country one summer, and came back two years later. Worked in a record store down in the Village. Even became the assistant manager. One morning I woke up and decided it was time to think a little further ahead than the next day. I'd started to hear people talk about computers, and they interested me, so I went to work for a place out on the Island that made components, and started taking whatever courses I could find. There weren't too many at the time. It was the software that intrigued me, and, to shorten a long story, I eventually started a small software firm of my own. We were lucky or smart enough to come up with some good programs for small businesses at a time when there wasn't much competition yet, and now we're doing pretty well. I call it Demeter, Inc."

"Demeter? The Greek goddess of agriculture?"

"Yes. Not many people know who she is."

"At the end of every summer her daughter, the goddess of spring, has to go live in the underworld for several months, and while Demeter mourns for her child, she neglects her duties, so we have winter. Or something to that effect."

"You've got it just right."

"But why Demeter? What does she have to do with computer software?"

"Nothing. She's for me." He looked away, and, when he spoke again, Dinah felt that whatever guard he usually posted over himself had been allowed to relax, that she was hearing from the man, not the sentinel. "It's wonderful," he said, "to see things green and growing. After winter has killed the land, after you've walked for months over something scarred and dead, when life comes back stronger and greener than ever . . . Once I was hitchhiking out in the Midwest somewhere, and for three whole days I stopped lifting my thumb and just walked and walked. Miles and miles of newly plowed land and green shoots and buds. I felt drunk on it. Oh, I've no desire to be a farmer—I'm sure I'd hate the life and be rotten at it. The city's for me. But . . ." His eyes returned to Dinah's. "Five years ago I bought the building where Demeter, Inc., is located. Way over on East Forty-sixth. I live on the top floor. The whole roof is a garden, maintained and monitored by computer. Software written by me, for me. Right now the season is getting under way up there. I'd like you to come see it sometime. Soon."

She knew she was staring. He was different from the man she had expected to find beneath the restless exterior and the terse, almost antagonistic manner. But even as she thought it, that man was back. The one who was familiar, and guarded. Who claimed he had poisoned Vardis Wolf.

What was wrong with her, she thought, that she was too attracted to the man who said he was a killer, and not enough to the man on the side of the law?

A little moon of wine remained in her glass. She finished it. "Why didn't you answer the rest of the question, I wonder? I asked where you came from, if it wasn't Norway. Is there something secret about your childhood?"

His expression didn't change, but she felt he was weighing some decision. At last he said, "I was born in Czechoslovakia, during the war. It's not a secret. It's just not something I like to talk about."

Someone came to clear away their plates, and then the waiter wanted their dessert orders. "Just coffee," she said.

"Me too."

She leaned forward. "I gather from Hannah Sebastian that you and the others met Vardis at a place called Cross of Glory. Is that a town or a school or what?"

Once again he seemed to be weighing something. "A foster home," he said.

Her hand, which had been clutching the empty wineglass, relaxed. "May I ask you about Vardis?"

"What do you want to know?"

She thought of the memory that had jumped into her mind from nowhere when he asked about her mother. "If I just ask you to tell me about her, what's the first thing that comes into your mind? No editing or censoring. Just tell me the first thing you think of."

He tilted his head to one side, looking inward. His fingers played on the heavy white cloth, then stopped. "Now why would I think of that?"

"What is it?"

"Oh . . . something that happened six or seven years ago. At a rehearsal. Do you remember that she once sang the *Kindertotenlieder?*"

"Vaguely."

"Do you know the music?"

"Not really. Just that it's a song cycle by Mahler."

"*Songs on the Death of Children.* Five of them, based on poems by Rückert. Heartbreaking, especially if you know German and can get the words. Damn unusual thing for her to sing, because they're written for a lower voice, but she got this bug about it. She said she had plenty of power in the lower register and she was already famous for doing things sopranos weren't supposed to do and, dammit, she wanted to do it. Well, they weren't about to turn down Vardis Wolf at the box office, especially doing something so unexpected. So, she did it, with the Philharmonic. I went to a rehearsal with some of the Pack. We weren't going to be able to make the performance, for some reason. She'd let us come to a rehearsal in that case, but you had to be as quiet as death because she wouldn't permit any kind of distraction. At all. Anyway, she and the Maestro kept disagreeing about some of the tempos. She was in her usual rehearsal outfit—black slacks, black top, some kind of turban thing on her head—and if you knew her the way we did, you could tell she was getting edgy. She had a

way of, I don't know, starting to look taller and even thinner, and
her eyes would glitter. We were all expecting trouble—Con sat
there looking down at his hands, I remember. But when they did
the last song, they went straight through without a hitch. She
was using full voice, with that dark, creamy sound she could get
in the lower registers, and the words . . . Something like 'In this
weather, in this storm, I'd never have sent the children out. I'd
be afraid they might fall ill and die. But now there's no reason
for such a fear. Because they've been taken. Now, in this weather,
they rest, protected by God's hand.' Well, it doesn't sound like
much when I say it, but the melody is so haunting, and her voice
was . . . Anyway, I became aware that a woman was coming down
the aisle, as if the music was pulling her. In her sixties, I'd guess,
a handkerchief pressed to her mouth and her face running with
tears. We all stared while she went right down to the edge of the
stage. After the last notes, which are very hushed and beautiful,
her head fell on her chest and she started to sob. Vardis's eyes
snapped down to the sound like two searchlights, and we expected gunfire. She asked what was the matter, very sharply, and
the woman answered in German, which made it worse because
Vardis wasn't fond of anything German except music. The
woman said she worked for a messenger service that had sent her
to pick up tickets at the box office but she sneaked into the
auditorium because she'd never seen it before. The songs made
her think of her daughter, she said, who had died in childhood,
twenty years before."

Cary paused. His eyes cleared. "How do you think the story
ends?" When Dinah shook her head, he asked, "How do you *want*
it to end?"

"What do you mean? It ends the way it ends. I have nothing
to do with it."

"But wouldn't you like it to end with Vardis doing something
nice?"

"No doubt you're telling it to me because she did something
rotten."

He sighed and leaned back. "She came down, took the woman's
hand, and led her out, to the dressing rooms, probably. The
maestro waited a few minutes and then, what else could he do,
started working on something else. After half an hour Vardis
came back. She said she'd talked to the woman and would see she

got house seats to the concert. And she trusted the orchestra members would keep the incident to themselves. That was all. She wouldn't discuss it with any of us, either."

He stopped and pushed his hands through the mane of his hair. "You asked what came into my mind. God knows why it was that, which was hardly a typical event in Vardis's life. Neither what she sang nor the way she behaved."

"Maybe that's why. Maybe you wanted to come up with something atypical, for my sake." Cary looked at Dinah sharply, but there had been no sarcasm in her tone. "Do you think the incident had some special meaning to Vardis?"

"At the time I thought she was just being unpredictable. And now, looking back . . . Ah, I don't know." His fingers drumrolled on the cloth.

"You didn't think the old woman's reaction had touched her in some way?"

"The truth is, I'd be tempted to say she did it for the publicity. Except for one thing. Her manager found out about it somehow and was ready to feed the item to the press. But she threatened to fire him if he did."

Dinah said softly, "I want to know why you hate her so much."

"Not here," he said finally.

"All right. Not here."

"Let's go to my apartment. I want you to see it."

"No," she said, "not now," instinctively certain they shouldn't go there, not to a place where she would have the disadvantage of unfamiliarity. "We can go back to my place."

He nodded and called for the check.

All the way across town he drove without saying a word, his eyes fixed only partly on the streets.

CHAPTER
13

On the tiny stove in Merle's apartment a large pan of spaghetti sauce grew slowly thicker and more pungent. Merle tasted it frequently, tossing in another pinch of herbs and trickling in more wine. Hannah, who was living with Merle while she went to the university, had provided a bag of greens for salad and a pound of butter. Cary, who had the least money because he had been in New York for only two weeks and had just gotten work at a bakery, brought two long Italian loaves with hard crusts over fat, soft bodies.

They hadn't let Conrad bring anything—"No, no, it's your bachelor party"—and of course the bride-to-be wasn't allowed.

Hannah had put on the ruffled white blouse and long black skirt in which she ushered at Carnegie Hall. "Why're you dressed like that?" asked Merle, who wore jeans and a faded sweater but looked quite beautiful.

"Because it's the best I have," Hannah said, in her quiet, measured way. "And this is such a special occasion."

"The special occasion is tomorrow!" Conrad cried. He had had three glasses of wine already, and his color and spirits were high.

"Yes. But tonight is special, too. It's the first time in years that the four of us are together. Just the four of us."

They all stopped for a moment and looked at one another, realizing that she was right: Cary had been at Cross of Glory until just two weeks before, and for a long time Con had always been with Vardis, not only while they were in Europe but ever since their return. Three of them had been together, and five of them, but not just the four.

Con put his arm around Hannah.

"It doesn't matter if we're not always physically together," Cary said. He spoke rather fiercely, to hide his pleasure at being with them again. He was the youngest, and they had all left Cross of Glory before he did. When Hannah had followed the others to New York, he had been left alone for three years.

"Of course it doesn't matter," Merle said. "But Han's right. Tonight is special." She poured wine from her glass into the spaghetti sauce and tasted the result. "I think it's ready. Hannah, please drain the— No, never mind, stay there with Con. Cary, get me that platter on top of the icebox and set out your bread." She had everything ready in so few motions that it seemed to happen by itself.

They all went to the table, set with a new blue cloth and lit by two candles. Merle had gotten a good job at an importer's office and was trying to fix up the apartment. When they were seated, Hannah lifted her glass. "To Conrad. May he be very happy. Always."

"May he never stop making music," Merle said.

Cary thought for a moment. "May he never be hungry or poor again."

The glasses were emptied.

Con refilled them and then raised his. There seemed to be chips of melting light in his hazel eyes. He looked at each of them in turn—Merle, Cary, Hannah. "*Jeden za všechny a všichni za jednoho,*" he said. They nodded and drank.

"Even after we're all married," Con said, "we'll still get together often like this. Just the four of us." Their glances locked like hands.

Finally Merle said, "The food will get cold." The other three smiled at her and they all began, eating with complete absorption. No one said a word except Hannah. When she pulled off a chunk of the Italian loaf, she murmured, "Oh dear, I do love white bread and butter."

And a little later—as if she was answering someone although nobody had spoken, "But if Vardis was here, that would be nice, too."

Con smiled but Merle stared straight ahead, eating her salad. Suddenly they all seemed like separate beings, not four-as-one, and Cary realized he had felt the same awkwardness several times since arriving in New York. He'd been too busy taking in the city to pay attention, but now certain things swirled through his mind and fell together, like kaleidoscope pieces. On the one visit Merle and Vardis made back to Cross of Glory after they had gone to New York, they had laughed all the time, telling about their apartment with a pull-chain toilet and an old stove that got so hot on the outside they couldn't touch it while they cooked. But later Merle wrote that they had gotten separate apartments, and when they called on Christmas and for everybody's birthday, they called separately. And since coming to the city, Cary realized, he hadn't seen them laughing together at all.

He leaned across the table to Merle. "Has something happened between you and Vardis?"

She didn't answer right away, and as he waited, another thought slotted into place. Merle wasn't happy. Not that she'd ever gone around glowing and humming—none of them had, God knew—but he had always felt that she was only waiting to go into the world on her own, when she would lead a normal life and learn to be happy. But she had been in the world for eight years and still seemed to be waiting and watching, with a kind of dark patience. Into his mind came the image of a cypress at the edge of a lake, forever yearning down toward the water but never able to trail its branches. He clenched his teeth. If Vardis had kept Merle from being happy, he would kill her. Yes, even Vardis.

But the moment he thought it, he knew Vardis wasn't the reason for Merle's detachment. Whatever it was came from something within Merle herself.

"Well?" he said to her. Con and Hannah were staring at their plates.

Merle put down her fork and reached over to touch his hand. "I knew you'd ask sooner or later. We're not as close as we used to be, that's all."

"OK. But why not?"

"Oh, things happen, baby. People change."

Con looked up. "Merle thinks I'm subordinating my career to Vardis's."

"Oh. Well . . . are you?"

Con lifted the bottle of wine and let a thin stream trickle into his glass. "I'm doing exactly what I want to do."

"What Vardis wants you to do," Merle said quietly.

"I think we want the same thing."

"You think what Vardis wants you to think."

"I'm nearly twenty-three years old, Merle. I make my own decisions. Try to remember that you're not my mother."

Hannah's eyes jerked up from her plate, and they all looked at Merle, waiting for her response.

"That's right," she said. "I'm not your mother." She smiled, but so painfully. As if her mouth were full of broken glass.

"Don't let's do this," Hannah whispered. "Please. Vardis loves Conrad, I know she does. They love each other, and tomorrow they're getting married, so don't let's do this."

"We're not doing anything!" Cary's voice was too loud. "I just asked a dumb question, that's all. Forget it."

"Yes, forget it." Con lifted his glass. "Tomorrow's my wedding day, and you're all going to be there, smiling. Isn't that right, Merle?"

She nodded, but it didn't look as if she ever wanted to smile again.

"Yes, yes!" Hannah cried.

"I'm counting on you," Con said. "*Jeden za všechny a všichni za jednoho.*"

At the wedding—a civil ceremony, held in a hotel—Vardis looked different than Cary had ever seen her. He couldn't exactly say why, but it was more than her dress, pale blue with ruffles at the high neck, or her hair, trained into long curls but still showing the jagged white streak that had appeared sometime after she left Cross of Glory.

After the ceremony she embraced each of them: "Hannah, dearest girl in the world . . . Cary, the little brother I didn't have . . . Merle, my sister in spirit and now in fact . . . I feel closer than ever to you all." Hannah, very pale, was crying. Cary gripped Vardis's hands. Merle was expressionless until she looked at Conrad. Then her lips lifted into a smile as if it was heavy.

There were about twenty others there, mostly from the music world—singers, some of Con's former fellow students from Juilliard, Vardis's manager, her first New York vocal coach, the woman who later became her dresser, and a press agent. Holding Con's hand, Vardis moved among them weightlessly, smiling at whatever was said to her, her gray eyes large with light. Cary watched her, and realized what was different about her. She looked beautiful.

The knowledge was oddly upsetting.

He had always found her unattractive, almost ugly. But he had liked it. Not because he had bad feelings toward her—quite the opposite—but because the way she looked was part of the wonder of her singing. The first time he heard it, it had pierced him, not only because it was beautiful but because it came from a gawky girl with a bony face. Most of her life, and theirs, had been ugliness. Yet she could produce those sounds. It was reassuring, inspiring that out of ugliness could come great beauty.

He stood in a corner of the room, sipping punch and watching while a photographer took pictures of Con and Vardis. They cut the first piece from the three-tiered cake and fed bites to each other. She tossed her head and smiled. Suddenly Cary was reminded of one of the little girls at Cross of Glory who had sailed through the halls with a stuffed animal her father had sent her for Christmas, grinning and showing it off to everyone.

After the newlyweds left to spend a week at an upstate resort, Cary walked to the apartment with Merle and Hannah. They told him to stay over, as he sometimes did, instead of going back to the Y.

He curled up in blankets on the living room rug, near Merle, who slept on the couch. Before she turned the lights out, the two of them sat talking. "Do you think you'll get married, too?" he asked her.

"I don't know, baby." She sat cross-legged, a long nightgown pulled tight over her knees. "I've met a lot of men since we came here, but none of them make me feel . . . The one I work for, who owns Rostov Importing, he asks me out a lot. About half the time I go because I don't have any reason not to. He's nice, but . . . I don't even know what it is I wish he could make me feel."

Cary hesitated. "Happy? Isn't that what everybody wants?"

"Ah yes. Happy." Merle pulled her fingers through her cap of auburn hair. "Americans talk about happiness as if it's the answer to everything. Didn't you hear people at the reception? All saying, 'I know you'll both be very happy.' As if they could know. I bet they don't even know what the word means."

She spoke without bitterness or resignation, but with something worse than either: indifference, which Cary didn't know how to answer. "Con says he's happy, Merle."

"Yes, but he can't be."

"Don't you think he ought to know?"

"I know him better than he does. I know everything he thinks and feels."

"Even about Vardis?"

She looked away, lamplight clinging to the fine lines of her nose and mouth. "Vardis will be one of the great singers, but not because of her voice. Yes, the voice has to be there, but she'll be great because she wants it above everything else. Above friendship or happiness or peace of mind or love or anything else you can think of." She gazed down at him, eyes fiercer than he had seen them in years. "Never forget that, my sweet boy. And never trust her."

"You mean she doesn't love Con, then?"

Merle sat back. "I don't know what Vardis means by love. I only know what I mean—the way I feel about Conrad and you and Hannah. I don't think she feels that. She does need Conrad, though. In a lot of ways. That much I know. But what does it mean to have Vardis Wolf need you? I don't know that. Not yet."

In the first years of the marriage, whenever Vardis and Con were in town and she wasn't singing the next day, they made a Sunday ritual of having everybody come to their apartment on Central Park West from midafternoon until God knew when. Cary and Hannah were always there, and sometimes Merle, because Con would beg her to come. Gradually others were added. The woman who wrote Vardis "the most touching fan letter I've had." The doctor who looked after her voice. The mezzo who had sung with her in a small opera company but gave up singing and became her secretary. And a Hungarian refugee, formerly a count, who worked as a translator but cared only for opera in general and Vardis Wolf performances in particular. Because Vardis despised cooking and was terrible at it, people took turns bringing food, but she and Con provided drinks, coffee, and dessert.

One Sunday, when they were talking about going to hear her sing in Philadelphia, Laszlo, the Hungarian, said they should call themselves her claque. She was angry—"Even as a joke, never suggest that Vardis Wolf has to pay people to applaud!" Frances, the secretary, tried to lighten things: "I think we're more like a pack. Vardis Wolf's pack." There was a tense moment, until Vardis threw back her head and laughed. "I like that," she said. "The Wolfpack."

Often on Sundays the whole time would be spent on music. They would analyze scores or recorded performances, discuss approaches and responses, or hear about Vardis's career. In one mood, she would imitate various colleagues and managers with deadly, hilarious accuracy. In another, she would sing for the group. Or she might talk about her voice: "Yes, I do feel that the voice is part of me, the essential me. But also I feel it is a separate thing, which I resent sometimes or even hate—like some kind of animal, a lion, which I have had to train. Or it can seem like a child, needing all your attention and strength, making you worry all the time that it will get sick. . . . I can never hear the voice as you do, because I am always inside it. Sometimes I have dreams about this—that I am able to be another person and listen to the voice of Vardis Wolf. But the dream will never come true."

Sometimes the talk ranged more widely, to include all the arts, or it might center on politics. But wherever it went, Vardis was in dazzling control. Not only had she acquired a thorough knowledge of music history and practice, she had read widely in other fields. No one would guess that her formal education had ended with Cross of Glory.

Wearing something with flowing sleeves or big collars or draped scarves, she would stand by the fireplace, raise an issue, and listen as everyone groped for answers. Soon she would begin pacing back and forth before the fire, throwing out observations and new questions. Finally she would swing around and make a concise, often brilliant statement that summed up the group's ideas but went beyond them. "I think we are saying that people respond to art because art is a way of experiencing our own thoughts and feelings, refracted through an outside sensibility. And if that's true, then music does so on the most physiological level. With music we experience our selves on the level of pure sensation. Music lets us know directly *that* we feel and *what* we feel—without the intermediary of all the life experiences and thoughts that lead us to those feelings."

As she talked her huge eyes glittered, and in the motions of her hands and the angle of her head authority spoke clearly. Perhaps people responded less to her ideas than to the strength with which they were held. Perhaps her brilliance was simply the force of her personality. Even as a child, she had been able to command attention, and now she was becoming a mesmerizing figure.

For a while Cary was mesmerized.

Then one afternoon he stopped by the apartment, not on a Sunday but just to see Con. After a long wait Vardis came to the door, wearing something shapeless and dark, quite unlike her usual outfits, her hair held back by a towel. She gave him a look that stuck pins into his smile and said, in a stranger's voice, "What do you want?"

He was so surprised he could barely get out, "To talk to Con."

"He's not here. I'm alone, so I've had to answer the door. Do you know what that means?"

"No." In barely a minute she had made him forget he was twenty years old. He felt half that age.

"I go to Italy in two weeks for my first Leonora in *Forza*. Since ten this morning I've been working on it, seeking the core, going deeper and deeper. I cannot do that without immense concentration. Which the sound of the buzzer has just broken. How dare you come by without permission?"

"I'm sorry," he said stupidly.

"What use is that? Does it put me back into the proper state to work?"

"I *am* sorry, Vardis. I didn't realize you—"

"You realize nothing. Do you realize what is required for me to become the singer that I am? The days and weeks and months of study and practice? Do you realize that to perform opera one has to have an athlete's strength and a poet's sensitivity? Do you ever ask yourself where I get that strength and sensitivity, what they take from my spirit and my body? No one asks! No one realizes! Only half a dozen people in the history of singing are capable of understanding what I do and what I am!"

On and on she went, eyes and voice afire. Cary had seen her angry before—more than once at Cross of Glory—but never with that messianic intensity. Even though he was its object, he felt she wasn't really talking to, or looking at, him but rather at some audience of which he was only the symbol.

In a few moments his mind cleared and his sense of himself returned. "I've apologized, Vardis," he said into the torrent of words, "and there isn't a hell of a lot else I can do."

The torrent didn't stop. He turned and walked away from it.

"Cary! Cary Mathias!" she shouted. "Come back here!" He stepped into the elevator and the doors closed.

He stayed away from the next Sunday, and didn't see her again until she and Con returned from Italy. She acted as if nothing had happened, so he brought up the incident. "Oh heavens, Cary," she said, "don't let it worry you. It happened because of the pressure I work under. When something disturbs or blocks me, it can be psychologically necessary for me to explode. If I didn't, the result could be disastrous."

Con, who was there, said nothing.

Cary tried to talk to Hannah about it, but she said only, "Yes, that happens sometimes. You don't expect her to behave like the rest of us, do you?"

Everything had become complicated. Nothing was as it had been when they were children.

He tried to understand, and began to look at Vardis the person, apart from the voice.

He watched her with Con. She seemed to dote on him, touching and kissing him, saying things like "This is a Renaissance face, a Michelangelo face." But in conversations she would dominate or ignore him, just as she did with the others.

He noted that she had no real friends among her musical colleagues, although musicians, in his experience, were a warm, close-knit group. She had only the Pack. As he sat with them on Sundays, he looked at them with new eyes. He saw that Frances, the secretary, had no life apart from Vardis's concerns. That Martha, the fan, tried to model herself after Vardis in every way —dress, speech, ideas. That Harvey, the throat doctor, had some liking for contemporary music, but once Vardis denounced it he quickly adopted her contempt for anything later than Richard Strauss as well as the rest of her musical opinions.

He saw that Vardis asked the Pack to run menial errands for her ("Be a dear and pick up my shoes, would you?"). She assumed they would adjust their schedules to hers and was irritated if they couldn't. He learned that she sometimes called Hannah, who had to get up early, at three or four in the morning although she could easily have done it earlier in the evening.

"I don't mind," Hannah told him. "It's kind of exciting. And I don't know what you mean by being more independent of her. You mean, disagree with her sometimes, just for the sake of disagreeing? Why should we, when she knows more than we do? Well, not about science, that's true. But it's not the same. Science deals with simpler kinds of issues than art does."

He thought that if they were all mesmerized by Vardis, they had to *want* to be. Her artistry was the precondition, but they wanted, or needed, something else too. They all wanted to be taken out of themselves, to be part of a life that was better than theirs. Maybe "better" was the wrong word. More exciting? More certain of itself? More "alive"? It was as if they could experience themselves more deeply through the medium of her attitudes and actions. Of her existence.

Did she need to be needed in such a way? Certainly she did nothing to discourage the Pack's uncritical admiration. In fact, she praised them for their response to her. One Sunday she played an advance pressing of her first major recording, *Norma*, and said to Laszlo afterward, "The look on your face during the 'Casta Diva'—that is exactly the way a sensitive, intelligent listener should feel."

He wondered what was the source of her hypnotic intensity, what made her so much larger than the life around her that only the operatic stage seemed to be the right scale for her.

There was only one possible explanation, he decided—an extraordinary degree of self-confidence.

But then why did she suffer agonies of doubt and fear before going onstage? And suffer them every time? Why did she worry so greatly, and usually needlessly, about her voice that Harvey had to go by at least three mornings a week to examine her and assure her it was all right? Why did she get angry out of all proportion over any negative comment in her reviews, denouncing the writers sometimes for months afterward?

Cary could not make all the pieces he saw fall into a neat pattern that would explain the phenomenon of Vardis Wolf.

One piece was oddest of all. She knew he no longer admired her uncritically—he was sure of that—but his detachment seemed to make her more interested in him than she had ever been. "Cary, come have dinner with us," she would say, "just the three of us." Or, on Sundays, she would solicit his opinion on everything that was discussed. Or she would sing favorite pieces of his. Sometimes when she looked at him, her gaze would be intense but speculative, as if she was trying to understand him. Just as he was trying with her.

He couldn't talk to anyone about his thoughts. When the four of them got together, as Con had promised they would still do, Vardis was often mentioned but never discussed. If he was alone with one of them, especially Hannah, he couldn't raise the issue. Or with Con—if Con shared his questions about Vardis, why had he married her? And if he didn't, how could you plant them in his mind? No matter how much you loved him.

Only Merle was left to ask, but she had married the owner of the importing firm, Frank Rostov, and moved up into the country. Cary hoped that Frank had finally made her feel happy, but she seemed the same as before. Like someone watching her own life from the wings. The two of them rarely came to the Sunday affairs. In fact, Merle was hardly ever in the city. The first time Cary went up to their place alone to see her, she said, "I'd really rather not talk about Vardis. Do you mind, baby?" He agreed. He would always do whatever she asked.

While Merle was pregnant, she and Frank came to only one of the Sundays. For the entire visit, something was going on between her and Vardis that Cary couldn't decipher—not words or looks, but a kind of edgy, mutual awareness that seemed to be focused on the pregnancy itself. It was as if Merle carried not only a child but a secret, which the two of them shared. Unwillingly.

By coincidence Jenny was born the night Vardis made her debut at the Met. They all went backstage to see her, surrounded by white roses, triumphant in Lady Macbeth's nightdress, her eyes, ringed with black, like huge coals in the pale makeup of her face. Before anyone could say anything else, Hannah cried out, "Vardis, we just called Frank and the baby came about an hour ago and it's a girl! And Merle is fine."

Daggers glittered in Lady Macbeth's eyes. "That is the first thing you say to me? After the performance I just sang, and thirty minutes of curtain calls?"

Hannah gave a little moan.

"But of course," Vardis went on, "the news is wonderful, so I suppose I must forgive you."

At the celebration party, however, she hardly said a word to Hannah. Cary stayed by Hannah's side through all of it, took her home, and then lay awake for what remained of the night, trying to understand.

During Cary's travels outside New York, while he explored both the country and himself, he read about Vardis wherever he went. Not only had she become a superstar of the opera, but she had also done *Tyrannus Rex*, and many jukeboxes played "The Dead Flower Song." He got news of her directly as well because he phoned Merle and Hannah every week during that two-year period, no matter where he was. Merle was full of Jenny's doings ("She prints her name by herself now!") and sounded so good that he asked her once, long-distance from Missoula, Montana, if she was happy. There was a startled pause, a laugh, and then, "If I'm not, this sure will do."

She or Hannah would tell him where Con and Vardis were. If they were in America, he'd try to reach Con. Sometimes Vardis got on the phone too. Her presence came through the receiver so strongly that it seemed she had squeezed into the booth with him. Although her questions were usually innocuous—"How long will you stay in Minnesota?" "You're sure you don't need any money?"—he sometimes felt they had a hidden meaning, which he could never figure out.

He got to San Francisco just as she was arriving to do her first *Salome* in the United States. She laughed with pleasure, embraced him, and sat talking with him for two hours. She was warm and caring, and interested in a way that might have meant something different if it had been any other woman.

He and Con got to spend several afternoons alone. Being to-gether again was so good that it almost dispelled the shock of the change he saw. Con had turned thirty-three in March, but it wasn't that he was a little older. There seemed to be less of him than before, not physically, but less of his personality. His self. As if he had a slow leak in his soul. He wasn't different, just less.

But Vardis was more.

She dazzled the San Francisco press, which gave her wonderful coverage ("The way to be news," she said, laughing, "is to act as if you are news"). She had a ten-decibel fight over her *Salome* costume with the designer, who finally was fired ("I don't care if he designs robes for God—I know what is best for the dance of the seven veils!"). She spent hours advising the young tenor who would make his debut in the Narraboth role ("We who reach the top have the obligation to pass on what we have learned"). He became as devoted to her as his character was to Princess Salome. She ran the dress rehearsal into hours of overtime by insisting on changes in the lighting. Then she gave everybody on the crews a handsome piece of jewelry as a gift on opening night, at which her performance, vocally and otherwise, was stunning.

To Cary's surprise, several of the Pack flew out for the event. "She calls me her best fan," Martha said. "What would she think if I missed it?" Martha really couldn't afford such trips, so he assumed Vardis had paid her fare. But when he told Vardis it was a nice gesture, she laughed and said, "Don't be silly. Why would I do such a thing?" He noted that she paid almost no attention to Martha during the three days of her visit, and that Martha seemed not to mind: "She's so busy. I wouldn't expect her to have time for me."

"I would," he said. "I think you should remind her you've flown all the way out here. Tell her she should at least have lunch or dinner with you."

"I couldn't do that!" Martha was shocked. "No, no. I came. I'll hear her Salome. That's all that matters."

As he stared at Martha, she seemed to change before his eyes from a plump and pleasant woman into a creature bound in medieval chains and covered with sores. Glorying in the mortification of her flesh because it proved her love of God.

He could shake the image from his mind, but not the idea it led him to. Vardis knew she had Martha's uncritical admiration and devotion, but nonetheless wanted, or needed, to test her. Just as she "tested" people by asking them to run menial errands. By attacking things they liked but she didn't. By constantly asserting her needs and wishes over theirs.

If she was in fact testing the Pack, he seemed to be exempt—at least since the day he had walked away from her tirade. So was Merle. No doubt she'd made clear that she wouldn't put up with any such thing. And, of course, Con was exempt because he was her husband.

But what if Con's whole life with Vardis was her test of him?

She made an amazing announcement just as they were due to leave San Francisco. She was planning to stay over a few days to join an upcoming rally protesting the war in Vietnam.

Cary went, of course, along with the thousands of others who jammed one of the city's biggest parks, moving and shouting to the rock music and the speeches interspersed with it. When Vardis walked out, her clothes seemed to come from another universe. She was wearing not jeans and a headband but pants and a tunic of some shiny, pale blue fabric, and a silver-mesh scarf to hold back her hair. The crowd didn't really know who she was, but she carried a guitar, so they murmured expectantly. She played the few simple opening chords and began, her voice pure and sweet like a child's but mournful as a widow's:

> *Stand here, my friend, with me*
> *And help me look at death.*
> *That is where our flowers*
> *Sprung from the earth, to live in the sun,*
> *And there is the wall where they stand to die.*

The crowd knew the song, if not the singer:

> *See the knives come, see the blood run,*
> *Watch the cutting of all our young flowers . . .*

Some of them started swaying, their motion spreading until the whole lawn was like a field of human wheat moving in the wind. After the last words—"Cut the stems and kill"—they were silent for a moment. Then their approval roared up to the stage.

She held up her hands and finally restored quiet. "I am Vardis

Wolf, the opera singer," she said. "I join you because I do not want to see you die." People gaped, and then whistled, at the directness and simplicity of it.

"I do not think America should be in Vietnam. But that is not why I am here. Vietnam doesn't matter. What matters is your right not to be forced to go to war."

Again she raised her hands to silence a roar. "I grew up in the midst of a war. I saw the Nazis occupy my country, Norway. The Nazi war, people say, was worth fighting, where this one isn't. I don't know if this war is worth fighting. But I do know that if a country can't convince its young men to fight a war willingly, it has no moral right to be involved in such a war." Another wave of sound crashed toward the stage.

Finally, she could continue, "They say we must fight in Vietnam in order to stop Communism." There were some groans from the audience, and a few hisses. "No!" she cried. "I didn't come here to tell you that Communism is good! Are you too young to remember Hungary? You are? Can you at least remember a month ago, in August, when Russia invaded Czechoslovakia because the Czechs had dared to experiment with freedom? Do you know that men and women stood in the center of Prague battling with Soviet tanks, trying to keep their radio station— their voice—from being captured? Do you know that young people like you pried cobblestones from the streets to hurl at the invaders? If you don't know these things, learn them! And do not try to claim that the reason you shouldn't have to go to Vietnam is that there's nothing wrong with Communism! The reason you shouldn't have to go is that they give you no chance to refuse. They take away your freedom by ordering you to fight for freedom." The crowd was silent.

"The greatest evil in the world is tyranny. And when America tells you, 'Go to war or else go to jail,' then to that extent America is a tyrant herself. She accepts the most terrible idea in the world —that the state controls the life of each individual citizen. That is an idea that kills. The world is piled high with its corpses. Yours mustn't be thrown on the pile!"

Cary stared up at her, thrilled by her, proud of knowing her, yet remembering how, just that morning, he had heard her on the phone with her manager, ordering him to drop all other business and fly to Europe on her behalf, threatening to fire him if he didn't. The woman speaking so passionately in public for political freedom had become an autocrat in her private life.

After he returned to New York, he came to believe that that double vision of her was accurate. It contained the explanation he had been seeking: Vardis was a creature of irreconcilable contradictions. Commandingly in control onstage, yet shaking with terror in the wings beforehand. Caring for nothing but music and her own greatness as a singer, yet needing to be surrounded by a circle of friends. Idolized by that circle, yet constantly testing its loyalty—she threw several people out of the Pack for somehow "failing" and "disappointing" her. Intellectually brilliant and curious, yet intolerant of all views but her own. Sensitive to the smallest nuance in music, yet oblivious of the needs of people around her, unless they served her own.

But what did it really explain to say that everything about her was contradicted by something else?

He would have liked to talk to Hannah about it, but that was more hopeless than ever. Although Hannah's eyes now peered through strong glasses, they saw Vardis even more blindly.

It was Con, the last person Cary expected to say something, who finally did.

They were in Cary's apartment, the semidecent place he'd finally gotten while he worked at the record store and took computer classes on the side. Con had taken to dropping by in the evenings if he and Vardis were in town. "Just to relax a bit," he'd say, settling on the couch, then, "How about a drink?" Cary would watch Scotch slide down Con's throat more easily and more often, gradually coating his eyes with glass and turning his gestures into a painful slow motion.

He always left while he still had some control—except one night when he just kept settling deeper into the couch and the Scotch. With every inch of the descent Cary felt more like crying, but he hadn't allowed himself to do that since childhood. So he just twisted his fingers until they ached. But finally he blurted out, "Don't, Con. Please don't do this. . . ."

Con blinked. "Do what?"

"You know what I mean."

"Do I?"

"Yes. Don't destroy yourself this way."

Con gave his sweet, rare smile. "What way should I do it, then?"

"Don't do it at all!"

"Why not?" Con lifted his glass as if it were heavy.

"Because I love you."

"I know."

They looked at each other long and painfully.

"You were going to be a great pianist, Con. What happened?"

"Nothing." Con drank, stared into space for a while. "Everything."

"Can you tell me about it?"

"No." But then he set the glass on the table, slowly and crookedly, and said, "I'm not me anymore, Cary."

"What are you saying?"

"I don't feel most of the things I used to feel. Some stranger lives inside me. And I don't like him."

"Why not?"

"He's not a man."

"Con, I don't think—"

"She wants him to be. But she can't let him be. Not a man. In any sense of the word."

Frozen, Cary asked, "What do you mean?"

The answer came harshly, like someone else's voice. "You know damn well what I mean."

The next day, thank God, Con didn't remember any of it.

Cary could never forget it.

CHAPTER
14

Intent on Cary's face, Dinah reached for her cup, sipped, and then looked down in surprise. The coffee was cold, although it seemed as if she had made it only minutes earlier.

He had been as preoccupied coming up in the elevator as on the drive across town. Once inside the apartment, she had offered to make coffee. "Fine," he'd said, "thank you." He had taken off his jacket, laid it on one of the wicker chairs, wandered over to the wall of books, and stood there studying titles like one of her students pretending to be interested in library research. She had been looking at the breadth of his shoulders and the way his thick hair sloped down toward his collar, when he turned around and began to talk about Vardis Wolf—just like that, abruptly, sometimes pacing, his hands clenching and unclenching as if truth were sliding in and out of their grasp. When the coffee was ready, she'd poured it, set cups on the coffee table, and tucked into a corner of the couch. He had stopped to drink several times. His dark eyes narrowed above the warmth but saw only their own visions.

Dinah hadn't been able to stop watching him. Cary Mathias

and what he was telling became inseparable; she couldn't take her mind from the stories, or her eyes from the face. It wasn't until he stopped that she finally drank some coffee and found it cold.

When he didn't go on, she said, "I'm not sure I understand exactly what Conrad Ashley told you."

His laugh was brief and unamused. "I didn't want to understand, either. But of course I did. And so do you."

"He talked about their sex life?"

"Yes."

"I don't want to hear it," Dinah said.

"I thought you wanted the truth."

"I do. I accept that he was having trouble, but I don't want the details of his sex life. Of anybody's, for that matter."

"I don't intend to give details. Not that Con gave me that many, actually. And it wasn't even the details. It was seeing him like that. Hunched over like an old man, Con, who always looked like the model for a Greek statue. Crying, and ashamed. Ashamed of the crying and of what he was telling me. Not a man, he kept saying. And he meant more than sex. He meant everything about himself. God! Con who used to write me letters when he was at Juilliard, about how he loved it, even the practicing when he was too tired to practice, about the concerts he'd go to or the music he'd discover—one whole letter was about hearing Horowitz, nothing else, and sometimes there were pages on Mozart or Chopin, and then I'd go crazy trying to find a way to hear the music for myself. He'd write about being a concert pianist when he got good enough. He *expected* to be, that's the point. And he was, damn it." Cary started pacing again. The room was too small for his stride, and his feeling. "The first time they went to Europe —together, but just as friends, they weren't married yet—he'd mention women in his letters sometimes. Like one Italian piano student I know he cared about because he wrote about her a lot. Maria, her name was, and they used to pack up bread and cheese and wine and go on bicycles out to the country, and it all sounded so right, so . . . normal. Aaaah, God damn it. Damn it all to hell."

Dinah said gently, "Why don't you sit down? I'll get us some hot coffee." She rose and started to the kitchen. As she passed by him, he reached out and caught one of her hands. They stood looking at each other, her eyes wide, his growing narrower.

"I can't," he said, and released her hand as abruptly as he had taken it. After a moment he added, "I can't have any more coffee."

Dinah went into the kitchen alcove and poured herself some milk. When she came out, he was sitting in a wicker chair, which seemed too small for him. She held up her glass. "Want some?"

"No. You look like a little girl sometimes, you know that?"

"I promise you I don't feel like one." He smiled.

She went back to the couch. "Some of what you've been telling me isn't very nice, I grant you. Conrad Ashley is a sad, pathetic man. I thought it as soon as I met him. But are you suggesting Vardis was the cause of what happened to him, or to the others you mentioned? She ruined them?"

"I think so."

"I can't quite accept that. I think maybe some people aren't complete personalities in themselves, so they'd be awed by someone with as incredible a power of personality as she apparently had. But however much they changed, whatever they gave up, they had to *want* to do it. Unless they're drugged or something, I don't think people are just passive victims of someone else's will."

"Maybe not. But when you're young, you're very vulnerable, and if you meet Vardis Wolf at a time—"

"Which one of you was younger when you met Vardis? You or Conrad Ashley?"

Cary hesitated. "I was."

"But you weren't ruined by her. So that means it was something in *you*. Not in her."

"Now you look triumphant," Cary said.

"I'm not. Just confused." Dinah kicked off a shoe and tucked up that leg. "I'm sure you don't get to be Vardis Wolf without being monomaniacal. But she had to be, didn't she? How can you be a great artist, or a great anything, without driving yourself and focusing on your work to the exclusion of a lot of other things? So you *can't* be a nice, normal person. By definition."

"If you only knew how many times Hannah Sebastian has said that to me."

"But she's right! Look at Beethoven—slovenly, sour, almost paranoid. Always flying into rages. Mozart was irresponsible and childish. Richard Wagner was a megalomaniac and a racist. Jenny Lind was cold and ruthless and unpredictable. And it isn't just music—I've read that Freud demanded obedience from his followers. Maria Montessori was authoritarian."

"Sounds like you've been reading up on the issue."

"I have. And I just read something about Jed Harris, that theatrical producer who was such a genius—he was horrible to his actors, his friends, and his family. But all those people did magnificent things. Maybe to become great you have to put on blinders and screen out things the rest of us work at—like being a good friend or parent or lover. Otherwise you won't have the mental and emotional energy to achieve the greatness you're capable of."

"How about someone like Verdi? Or Mendelssohn? Great artists who were also decent human beings?"

"Yes, well . . . I think they're exceptions. I think the normal price of greatness may be losing some of your humanity."

"Which means, translated, that Vardis could get away with anything because she was such a great artist."

"No, wait, don't put words in—"

"What can you get away with if you're just a *good* artist or a *semi* genius?"

"That's not what I'm saying. I don't mean—"

"Dammit!" He stood up. "What do you think I've been talking about? Peccadilloes? Being eccentric? A little rude and insensitive sometimes? I'm talking about her unforgivable treatment of people who were devoted to her."

He was pacing again. "I wasn't going to tell you this story—for Con's sake—but I guess I'll have to. To make you understand. One night, about five years ago, I think. . . . But if you ever let on to Con or anybody else that you know, I won't be able to face my mirror again." He headed toward the bookcase wall as if he might ram into it but swung around instead. "All right. Five years ago. I'd kind of pulled away from the Pack by then. Once in a while I'd go by if there was a special occasion, but basically I went my own way, except for seeing Con and the— I was too busy with Demeter to have much time for anything else, except some of Vardis's performances. No matter what I was thinking about her in private life, she could always rivet me to a seat in the Met or Philharmonic Hall. One day she called up and invited me to dinner. Called personally, I mean, didn't have Frances do it. Said she and Con hadn't seen me for ages and we had to get together. So I went. A Friday in April, I'll never forget. Nobody else was there, just the three of us. She'd actually cooked the dinner herself, beef stroganoff, and it wasn't as bad as I expected. I remember she laughed about not being able to keep it from curdling. Afterwards she started talking about old times, at Cross of Glory and on the ship—talking about things we'd been through together. Con really perked up for a while."

He stopped and was quiet for a moment. "God, how I'd love a cigarette."

"You haven't been smoking tonight."

"No. It bothers you."

Dinah looked at him wonderingly, but he swung his head and began moving again, more slowly. "Vardis even put out an ash-tray for me that night. That should have clued me she was up to something. But she was being wonderful. Witty, warm, brilliant. She asked me a lot about the business, things some of my own people aren't clever enough to see. When she wanted to, she could charm the feathers off the birds. So I was enjoying myself, which I hadn't expected to do. Then she said she felt like singing. Con headed for the piano, as usual, but she said she'd play for herself because he'd drunk too much. Which he had. For an hour I had an exclusive concert by Vardis Wolf. It was, well, mesmer-izing. The full force of that voice and personality directed at me, singing whatever I asked for. Even a couple of Norwegian songs she used to sing when we were all— A shepherd boy's song and a lullaby. I got very relaxed and nostalgic. But when she was finished, she . . . dammit, I shouldn't be telling this."

"But you are," Dinah said softly.

Cary sat at the other end of the couch, leaned against the back, and stared at the ceiling. Dinah watched his profile.

"When she was finished, she came and sat beside me, close, and started telling me how she admired me because I was sensitive to music but I had ambition and drive, I wasn't weak. I tried to laugh it off, but she leaned closer and kissed me. On the mouth. Not like a friend. I was so surprised that it took me a minute to grab her arms and push her back. She said, 'Don't you know how long I've wanted to do that?' OK, over the years she'd paid me a kind of special attention, ever since the day she screamed at me and I walked away from her. But I never really knew why, and I never wanted to think she was after anything more than my unqualified admiration. But that night I had to think it. She leaned into me again and started whispering that she— Never mind what she whispered, but I didn't worry any more about hurting her, I just shoved her away again, hard, and got up. Con was glued to his Scotch, but he'd seen what happened. I'll never forget the way he looked at me, like his nails were being pulled out or something but he was determined to smile instead of scream. I asked Vardis what the hell was the matter with her. She pointed one of those long fingers at Con and said, 'What do you think it's like for me, with a husband like him?' I told her to shut up, but she wouldn't. She started talking about Con as if he wasn't there, how he understood all about her music but nothing about her as a woman, how they were in separate bedrooms, how I was a real man and she needed . . . Jesus, it was awful. Con sitting there with that horrible smile. Finally I grabbed her and shook her and told her she was disgusting, and that shut her up. For a minute. Then she pulled herself together and got that Queen of the World look on her face and started laying into me. She said things like I was no more a man than Con and if I had any understanding of her artistry I would have known how to respond to her. And if I didn't respond, in spite of everything she had tried to do for me, if I could humiliate her the way I'd just done, then I couldn't go on being part of her life. I said I didn't want to be in her life *or* her body, and she damn near went up in smoke. I knew I had to leave, before one or both of us got violent. I tried to get Con to go with me, at least for that night, but he said no, he just wanted to go to bed."

The words had come in a torrent; they stopped. Cary lifted his hands to cover his eyes. "So, I went over to Con and told him I loved him. And kissed him. And left."

Dinah, still watching his face, said nothing.

"To do it in front of Con, that's what I couldn't forgive. OK, the marriage wasn't good, and even if it was her doing, she was unhappy. I could understand that. But to want Con to hear and see what she . . . Jesus."

"Did it harm your friendship?" Dinah's voice was flat.

"Nothing will ever keep Con and me apart. Nothing. But we've never discussed that night. Never even mentioned it. It just lies between us like a corpse we pretend isn't there." He added, "I've never told anyone, till now."

There was a long silence. Dinah said, "She must have been bitterly unhappy to behave like that. But there's no way to defend it."

"But you wish there were."

"Yes. I won't lie to you. Don't you understand? She was important to me. Because her greatness mattered to me, personally. Because, dammit, I was her child, but I never had the chance to know her."

"She mattered to me, too. The sound of beauty in a world of screaming." Although Cary's hands left his face, he kept staring at the ceiling. "But she wanted power over people."

"That's not possible. How can she have loved and served music the way she did, and wanted power over people?"

"I don't know. Maybe because deep down in that cold heart of hers, she was insecure and scared." He turned to Dinah. "There are certain careers nobody goes into except to gain power. Like politics—politicians try to control the economy, which means controlling our lives, so power *has* to be what they're after. I figured Vardis couldn't be like that because how could art give you power over people? But then I realized it could give you power over something more important than their livelihoods. It could give you power over their souls.

"I think," he added in a moment, "that she was a killer."

"You can't be serious." He said nothing. "I don't believe that. I won't believe it. Tell me whom she killed."

"Con, for one. Some of the others, she could only disable." He held up both hands to stop Dinah from interrupting. "OK, maybe the people had strains of weakness in them, maybe they *let* her do it to them—long ago I decided that could be true. But if she hadn't walked into their lives, they'd have gone after what *they* wanted, instead of acting as if all her ideas and wishes were sacred. They'd be living for themselves, not for her."

"You can't know that. They might have found someone else to live for."

"Is that what you'd say if a person was hit by a car? That if it hadn't happened, he'd have gotten in some other driver's way?"

"That's a specious analogy! I'm saying there may be a kind of person who goes looking for somebody else to live for. Who needs to surrender his or her personality to a stronger one."

"An interesting question, but it's not the one that matters to me. What I care about is, why should Vardis be allowed to get away with it? I tell you she was a killer, and some day you'll know I'm right. She came into our lives like a goddamn cancer and ate them away!"

"So you killed her?"

The little scar on Cary's cheekbone pulsed white. "That's right," he finally said.

"I believe you wanted to kill her. But I don't want to believe you did."

He got up and walked away, to the bookcases. He lifted his arms above his head and leaned on them, the muscles of his back shifting under the white shirt. "I gave the police a statement," he said, "and I stand by it."

After a long silence Dinah said, "I'll tell you what I think is going on."

He turned around. "Yes?"

"You say you did it. So does Conrad. I think his sister Merle and Hannah Sebastian have made the same confession. I think the four of you are in this together, all confessing in order to cover up for the one who really did it."

"Why would we do that?"

"Maybe because you've been friends for so long."

"It would have to be a hell of a friendship to make us all willing to risk a murder charge."

"Isn't it a hell of a friendship?"

He didn't answer.

"The problem is you have such opposite views of the victim. You hated Vardis, so why would you lie for Hannah Sebastian, who idolized her? Or vice versa, which is even harder to accept?" Dinah waited until Cary finally looked at her. "When you called, you said you'd been thinking about me, wanting to see me. I felt the same way. You must know that. So how can you want me to believe you're a murderer?"

"I can't answer you." He looked away. "I'm thirsty. No, no, stay there. I just want some water." He went into the kitchen alcove. She watched him fill a glass and drink it all at once. He rinsed it out, set it upside down on the sink towel, and said, without turning around, "Suppose I told you I'm innocent but have a powerful reason to do what I'm doing. Would you believe me?"

"I told you, it takes time to learn which things people lie about."

His shoulders lifted. "Fair enough."

Laughter, a man's and a woman's, welled up outside the apartment door, then faded happily down the hall.

"*Are* you telling me you're innocent?" She couldn't breathe, waiting for the answer.

He came out from the kitchen. "I'm not telling you anything. I can't."

Her fingers dug into the couch. "If you're guilty, you've broken the law. If you're innocent, you're mocking it. I don't see much choice between them."

"I suppose you have to choose?"

"Can't you understand how I would feel about someone trying to get away with *murder?*"

Cary crossed to her and took her face in both hands.

She lifted her arms and gripped his wrists.

There was the sound of a key in the lock. Dinah's gaze moved to the door, and she shifted away from him.

The door opened several feet, and Cassie's head peered around it. "Oh!" she cried. "Dinah, I figured you'd be in bed. Alone. I mean, I figured you'd be alone. I mean, I'll just get— I'll be out of your way in a minute."

"Never mind," Cary said. "I'm leaving."

"Don't let me break up any parties."

He picked up his jacket. "I think this party is over."

Dinah stood, unevenly, one shoe still off. "Cary, this is my— the woman who shares the apartment, sometimes. Cary Mathias, Cassandra Barber."

"Hello. I don't think I've met anyone named Cassandra before."

"Don't worry, I never make prophecies."

"Good. I'd have to disbelieve them anyway."

"What do you know, somebody who reads the old Greek legends. A hell of a lot of people never even heard of Cassandra, you know."

Dinah said, "Mr. Mathias owns a computer software company named after Demeter."

"Who?"

Cary smiled and pulled on his jacket.

Dinah said to him, "Thanks very much for dinner," and proffered her hand.

He took it but held it in both his own. "I'm not telling you anything," he said softly, "because I can't."

"I accept that. But I hate it."

"Will you believe that I feel the same way?"

She didn't answer.

He released her hand. "Good night, Cassandra," he said, giving her a little salute. The door closed behind him.

Cassie cleared her throat. "Sorry my timing was bad. I just came by to pick up some things."

"At one in the morning?"

"I was sure you'd be asleep. Don't you have an early class tomorrow?"

"Yes. I worried when you didn't come home last night."

Cassie's chin lifted. "I was with somebody I met last week. At an audition. A stage manager. Terrific guy."

For the first time the two women looked directly at each other, their glances identical: hopeful but defensive.

"So who is Cary Mathias?" Cassie asked.

"A longtime friend of Vardis Wolf's."

"I see. If I tell you he's attractive, I suppose you'll say I always harp on sex."

"No." Dinah sighed. "I'll tell you you're right."

"My timing really was lousy, then."

"Maybe not. Maybe you saved me from having regrets in the morning."

Cassie's eyes rolled and she bit her lip. She went to the closet, singing "Je Ne Regrette Rien."

Dinah couldn't help smiling.

Cassie backed out of the closet with a jacket and a suitcase. She set it down and asked plaintively, "Dinah, you really think all I do is sleep around?"

"No. Of course not. Do you really think I want to cut off my old friends because I'm Vardis Wolf's daughter?"

"No. I don't. But I do see it's twisting you up in some way."

Dinah sighed again. "Several ways. Look, Cass, about the other thing . . . I just can't be casual about going to bed with people."

"The way I am, you mean? No, no, it's true. I am. I go to bed with somebody if I like him. Because it's fun. I don't know what you think it is—some kind of holy ritual? Aha!" Cassie cried. "I see the look on your face! That *is* what you think! So here comes this attractive Cary what's-his-name that you probably could have a great time with, and you won't because you don't know whether he's a saint!"

After a silence Dinah said, "I don't know why it matters to us that we don't agree about this, but obviously it does."

"It matters because you think the way I act is wrong. Not just dumb, but *wrong*. And that bugs me."

"I'm sorry." Dinah sank back onto the couch. "But I won't pretend I'm not different from you. I won't apologize for it, either. And I wish you'd stop trying to change me. You always talk as if, if I'd just come to my senses, I'd be like you."

"Oh hell." Cassie began to fold up her jacket. "Look, maybe I *am* wrong. Maybe I'd be a better human being if I didn't have so many men. But it doesn't change the fact that we've been good friends to each other, does it?"

Dinah shook her head.

"So what do you say we live and let live? Only I'll be living somewhere else for a couple days, so I'll just go get some of my stuff. OK?"

"Sure."

As Cassie was leaving, she stopped by the door and turned back. "I think you're doing the same thing with Vardis—wanting her to be perfect, afraid to hear if she wasn't."

Dinah didn't answer. The door closed.

Cary Mathias stopped at the traffic light at Sixty-fifth and the park drive. When the dashboard lighter clicked, he reached down for it and lit his second cigarette since leaving Dinah. He exhaled deeply and through the smoke watched the red circle give way to amber. A moment before the light changed, his foot touched the accelerator.

Driving through Central Park, he decided his mission had been accomplished.

When Hannah had called to tell him there might be a problem, her quiet voice was pulled thin by panic. "Cary, I went to see that Mitchell woman. I know I shouldn't have, but I had to see her. If she was claiming to be Vardis's child. It was . . . I was upset, you know I can't sleep anymore, and I haven't been able to go into the lab for days, and she was asking so many questions, and I let something slip." It had taken him time to find out what it was: "I mentioned Cross of Glory. And I think I probably said 'orphanage.' I know that's bad, but she was asking so many things, all at once, and I was . . . Somehow she knew about Connecticut. She asked if we all grew up there together, but I said no. At least I did that."

Cary had had to go to her apartment and soothe her. He took some of the pastries she loved and sat on the couch with her, drinking tea and telling her everything would be all right, even though he wasn't at all sure. When she was composed again, she looked much better, and he suddenly realized that, plain and pale as she was, she could have been attractive, perhaps even striking. She had the bones, the hair, the features. Everything but the will.

It had been odd to see her that way—as others might, instead of as one of the fixtures of his life.

The two of them had called Merle, and all three agreed that someone had to find out what Dinah Mitchell might have learned, or guessed. He had volunteered; he was the logical one. But Merle could always tell what was in his mind, even on the phone. She had said, "Be careful. I think maybe you like the woman."

Right on both counts. Dinah had been much too interested in his childhood and his war experience. He had had to navigate with caution around the land mines of her questions. He thought he had landed safely, but there was a good deal of intelligence in her gray eyes. She had guessed about the four confessions—or been told by the friend in the police department she had mentioned the first time he met her—so it had been necessary to tell her a lot about Vardis, always being careful not to refer to things she mustn't learn. Had it been smart to tell her about the "seduction"? Maybe not. But he had wanted her to understand, for her own sake.

He had told her only one outright lie, but there had been sins of omission. Including not saying how lovely she was, how appealing. A face with character, and confidence, and humor. A manner straightforward as a child's, even when she tried to trick him into revealing something. A voice that made him think of being in bed with her.

As he turned onto Third Avenue and headed south, he passed

by a familiar building. One of the best programmers at Demeter lived there. They had gone together for nearly two years, until the previous fall. She was funny and sharp, and he'd been quite attached to her, but when it was over, he couldn't honestly say there was a black hole in his life. Before her there had been several others in the serious-relationship category. He had memories of them he wanted to keep, but no wounds that wouldn't heal. He wasn't sure why nothing had ever become permanent, although one of the women had said, just before she left him, "I can't stay, Cary. There's just too much of you marked 'Private.' " Looking back, he thought perhaps she was right, even though he didn't know exactly what she meant. If he was a man with closed doors, they led to rooms he rarely used. At forty-three, or however old he really was, he had decided he probably wasn't going to marry, and the realization had bothered him more than he expected. He didn't miss the formality of marriage —who cared about that—but he regretted the verdict of impermanence hanging over his life.

Could there be reprieve with Dinah Mitchell?

With Vardis's daughter? He shook his head, amazed, as he was every time he thought of it. She didn't look or sound—or behave —like Vardis, except, perhaps, in her tenacity. But she had reached him, somehow. Behind some door marked "Private."

And so had Vardis.

He turned onto Forty-sixth Street, hearing Dinah's voice again, seeing her curled up on her tweed couch, eyes fixed on him and his story. If only it were possible to tell her he was innocent. To see the relief that would flood her face and animate her touch.

But he couldn't do that to the others. Couldn't.

He pulled into the garage next to his building, where he kept his car.

"Hey, how you doin', Mr. Mathias?" asked the attendant. "You have yourself a good time tonight?"

"You bet," Cary said mechanically. But he didn't know whether it had been good or disastrous.

CHAPTER
15

From his table on the glassed-in porch of an Upper West Side restaurant, Sam saw Dinah hurrying down the sidewalk, briefcase swinging in rhythm with her stride. She was wearing something yellow, and a sweater was tied by its arms around her shoulders. Breaking into a smile, he watched her come closer, until a row of hanging plants blotted her from view and made him admit that a world in which he could look at her was a lot nicer than one in which he couldn't.

Minutes later she emerged from inside the restaurant onto the porch. The sun and air seemed to come in with her. "Hi," she said. "It's only six blocks from the college, so I walked over."

Sam stood and found himself taking her hand and bending down to peck at her cheek. She smelled of some nice, clean cologne, but did she pull away a little bit? She sat and looked around at dark wood, Art Nouveau posters, and bright glass lamps. "How nice, Sam. We could have done it all on the phone, but I hardly ever go out to lunch. This is a treat."

"I'd have suggested dinner if I didn't have to go on duty at four."

She cocked her head. "You seem awfully pleased. Is there some good news?"

"I think I'm just glad to see you." He reached over to touch her hand.

"Oh," she said, a shade too brightly. After a pause, a shade too long, she added, "I'm glad to see you, too."

Sam withdrew his hand. He studied her face, then pushed his chair nearly back into the one behind him. "I don't have any news but what's in the papers."

Dinah looked puzzled. "Oh, do you mean the new random poisoning? The one yesterday in Delaware?"

"That woman makes a total of six victims. And no leads. Not one."

"What a vicious business. The police must be ready to— Just a minute. Does this have any bearing on Vardis's death?" Sam shrugged. "Wait, now. At first you thought Vardis might have been one of the random poisoner's victims, but after the confessions, you decided not. So now . . ." Dinah's eyes widened. "Good God, you don't think she was poisoned by the random killer after all? And none of the four people did it? Is that it, Sam?"

"No. But you look like you'd be real pleased if it were."

"Pleased? No, why should I be?" Dinah's gaze dropped to the linen napkin in front of her, and she smoothed its fold with her left hand.

"We haven't changed our view of how Wolf died."

"Then why did you bring up the new victim?"

"No reason, really."

"I didn't think you ever did things for no reason."

Sam snorted. "That makes me sound dull as hell." He picked up a menu. "Why don't we order? Then you can tell me whatever it is you called me about." He smiled at her, his sharp features settling down again.

After they ordered, Dinah propped her notebook against the salt cellar. "About those four good friends of my mother's. I don't think they all came from Norway with Vardis."

"Why not?"

"I saw Cary Mathias again. I put the Norway business to him as if it were a fact. He denied it, with that kind of half-surprised, half-amused reaction you have when somebody gets some fact wrong about your life. He swore he's never been to Norway. He was born in Czechoslovakia, he says."

"And you believe him?"

"About that, yes, I do."

"How about his telling you he poisoned Wolf?"

Dinah turned to the window. Outside, the May sun struck sparks on the cans spilling from a trash basket. "I don't think he's guilty. But I can't be sure."

Sam said nothing.

"Well," she said briskly after a moment. "I've now talked to three of those four friends, and I've noticed a couple things. One, they all love music and know a lot about it. And two, the more I go over my conversations with them, the more it strikes me that they don't want to talk about their early lives. When I ask about those years, they say, 'Oh, I don't remember' or they slide off the subject. Ashley did, even though I wasn't especially trying to probe that far back. Hannah Sebastian did, though she let a few things slip because she was agitated. And Cary Mathias just tried to do it, too."

The French onion soup arrived in a small earthenware crock. Sam watched Dinah taste it, dipping delicately around a rich crust of melted cheese. "I can't reach Merle Rostov, so I don't know what she'd say. I've left a message for her three times. When I call back, the maid says she delivered it, but so far, no luck. Still, three out of the four friends . . . . I think I'm on to something."

"I don't want to rain on your parade, but it could be nothing, you know. Even if they are keeping some secret from childhood, it may not have anything to do with the, ah, present situation."

Dinah smiled. "Harry used to say he had wonderful hunches, it was just the facts that were lousy. I'm going to keep on, though. I just have a feeling it could be important. And isn't it the case that the more you know about them, the better chance you have to learn the truth?"

"Sure." And the four of them knew that too, Sam thought. That's why they had volunteered as little as possible.

"Is there some way of finding out where they all came from, besides waiting for the orphanage records to be found?"

"Unfortunately, people don't usually put their birthplace on documents." Sam paused as the waiter brought him a huge chef's salad and Dinah a quiche. "If they all came from the war, we assume they were naturalized. There might be records in Washington or maybe in the state where it was done. But even if somebody would release the information to me, it'd just be the date they came and the country of origin. What could that tell us that we don't already know? Namely, that they're four old friends who are in this thing together?"

"But Sam, if they lied about when and where they met Vardis Wolf . . ."

She was bloody right, of course—it was a wedge, provided he could figure out how to use it—and she knew it as well as he did. But discussing the case so explicitly was making him uncomfortable.

She got it right away. "I'm talking too much," she said.

He plunged his fork into half a hard-boiled egg. "How did you get to see Mathias again?"

She smoothed her hair above her ears. "He asked me to dinner."

"Ah. When I called the other night, were you going out with him?"

She hesitated. "Yes."

Sam lifted the impaled egg and pushed it into his mouth to keep himself silent.

"I think," she said, "that he just wanted to find out what I knew."

Sam chewed hard. "And you say you believe what he tells you?"

Dinah looked at him defensively. "He told me the truth about some things. I asked what Cross of Glory was, and he said it was a foster home."

Sam shrugged. In a moment he said, "You still think Hannah Sebastian is like John Lennon's killer?"

"I still think there's something unhealthy in her feeling for Vardis." Dinah pushed aside her half-eaten quiche. "But I don't think she's a killer. I've decided Conrad Ashley probably told me the truth when he said he was responsible for Vardis's death."

Sam leaned back. "Why do you say that?"

"For one thing there were problems in the marriage. Personal, not musical, problems. I understand that sometimes she . . . humiliated him."

"Who told you that?"

She lifted her chin. "Cary Mathias." Quickly she went on. "But besides that, Ashley is the one they all love enough to put themselves in jeopardy for. He's the love of Sebastian's life, according to you. Cary loves him deeply, I saw that. Merle Rostov has the strongest tie—he's her brother. Besides, if I posit anybody else as the poisoner, there's trouble. Say Hannah Sebastian did it, for some private, pathological reason. I don't think Cary would cover for her. He disapproves too much of the way she submerged her life in Vardis's. Or say Cary did it. Hannah knows he hated Vardis, her idol, so why would she lie for him? Or for Merle Rostov, who was also apparently quite critical of Vardis. So I keep coming back to Ashley. Of course I could be all wrong. Maybe the others are lying for him because he's got some kind of hold over them. Maybe that's what they're all trying to hide by not talking about their early years."

Sam poured cream in his coffee and watched the slow swirls. "The director at Cross of Glory didn't like Ashley. Said he stole some money from her."

"You never told me that."

"I didn't want to influence your perception of him."

"Which you share, don't you?" Dinah leaned toward him. "I don't like the idea, Sam. I hate that Vardis was killed by her own husband, that he's the one to keep me from knowing her. But if . . ." She shrugged with her hands. "I don't know how he did it, but isn't that in his confession? Oh, you can't tell me, of course. Forget I asked. I'll have to see Ashley again. I meant to anyway." She jotted something in her notebook, then looked up, gray eyes intense. "We both understand my visits have nothing to do with your investigation. I'm trying to find out what Vardis was like. And why she gave me up."

Sam nodded. "You want dessert?"

"No. I've got a class at three-thirty, so I should be going soon."

"I'll walk you back."

"You don't have to do that."

"I know," Sam said firmly. "I want to."

They had the same argument about the check.

They headed up Broadway, Sam discoursing on the people sitting on benches in the traffic islands. Welfare clients, winos, elderly widows and widowers, some holding their faces up for sun, others staring at the pigeons strutting among them. Sam called them "peacocks of the poor." Dinah smiled.

"Those are the saddest people in town," he said, "I hope I die before I get like that—lonely in a crowd, cold even if the sun is out. Poor bastards."

When they reached Tryon Community College, housed in two buildings that had once been a warehouse and a grade school, he put a hand on Dinah's arm, above her elbow. "How about we play some tennis this weekend?"

"Oh, Sam, I haven't played for years. I don't think I'd be much good."

"Sounds like my speed. How about Sunday morning?"

She hesitated, but he kept holding her arm and looking at her. Finally she said, "I . . . well, OK, if I can find my racket. And remember how it works."

"Good. I'll call you Saturday."

He watched her go, smiling at her arrow-straight posture and the way the sun coaxed red out of her curly brown hair. But as he headed back to Broadway, thinking, the smile went flat. Her reasons for fixing on Ashley as the poisoner were shaky. What was really going on, he'd bet, was a desire not to have it be Mathias. That cocky damn Mathias, who at worst was a killer and at best was deeply involved in a weird, unhealthy situation. Who was too old for her, too.

Damn near his own age. He sighed.

The green was thicker on the beautifully groomed trees, but nothing else had changed on the block where Vardis had once lived. The buildings were just as remote and elegant, the walks as freshly swept.

Dinah had no reason to expect change, but it didn't seem right for the house to be just as she had left it—even the drapes still guarded all its windows—when what she had learned in that house had altered her whole world. Not even her career was safe. She was thinking of leaving not only her job but the whole profession. And unthinkable as that had once been, it was practically the least of her concerns. She had a murder to solve, whose solution mattered more than she could explain. She had let friction develop with one good friend. With another, something was developing that she wasn't ready to handle. And she was attracted to a man she was afraid to trust—a man who was defying the law.

The law that had been Harry's life. And still was Sam's.

She stared up at the house where she had met him, remembering how they had sparred at the door. She hadn't known whether he was rudely calculating or just preoccupied, and still didn't. For everything he said and did, she could see two explanations, one of which made her a fool. But it didn't seem to matter.

The basement apartment had a separate entrance, which Jenny Rostov had told her to use—"So I don't have to tell Conrad you're here. Just walk down the side steps and ring."

She had called Jenny after still another failure to reach her mother. "I'm sure you know by now who I am and why I came to see your uncle. I'm Vardis's daughter, and I'd like to talk to you about her."

The door to the basement apartment opened and Jenny said, "Hello."

Fine-boned, with delicate coloring, she was even lovelier than Dinah remembered. This time she hadn't been crying, so her thickly fringed hazel eyes were clear. "I'm incredibly glad that you called. Please come in," she added with a gesture that sent the wide sleeves of her blouse sailing like a cape. She led the way in on platform shoes that brought her height up to average.

The living room was larger than it seemed from outside—it held a white piano and a huge white couch—and was furnished to reflect a single personality. But not Jenny Rostov's.

One wall, covered with posters of Vardis's appearances, held in its center a life-size photo taken during a curtain call, one arm lifted, the other cradling a bouquet of white roses. An étagère displayed photos of her in numerous costumes. On the piano, in front of stacked scores and exercise books, was a framed close-up inscribed, "To darling Jenny with all my love, Aunt Vardis."

Jenny brought in two cups of tea, put them on the coffee table, and looked at Dinah as if the room were a test and she wanted her grade.

Dinah merely smiled. "How long have you been studying piano?"

"I took lessons as a child, but working on it seriously, about two years."

"Are you good?"

"Not good enough. Yet. But Vardis said I could be. She thought I had real musical sensitivity."

"I see." Dinah sat on the couch and looked at a montage of snapshots beneath the coffee-table glass: picnics, parties, and holiday gatherings. Vardis was in many of them. "I recognize Cary Mathias here, and Hannah Sebastian and your uncle. But I don't know your mother yet. Is she in any of these shots?"

Jenny's chin lifted. "I took out a lot of early ones, but she's still in some. Down in the left corner, where I'm in my high-school graduation outfit."

Dinah bent closer and saw a face like Conrad Ashley's, with a cap of auburn hair. "She's very beautiful."

Jenny hesitated, said "Yes," and silenced herself by drinking tea.

Next to that photo was one of Cary holding a two- or three-year-old, presumably Jenny. He had to be in his twenties, but his face looked very much as she had seen it last. The years had drawn their lines on him early, she thought, and then had left him alone.

"I've noticed that Cary Mathias has a slight limp. Do you know why?"

"Something that happened during the war, I think. He hates talking about the war, so I never really asked. They all hate it. Vardis did too. Oh gosh, would you like anything with the tea? There's no cake or cookies, they're not healthy, but I've got wheat or rice crackers or Norwegian flatbread."

"No, thanks."

Jenny put down her cup, lifted her elbows to shake out her wide sleeves, and leaned forward. "You're her *daughter*. God. What does it feel like?"

After a moment Dinah said, "Jenny, I think you and I have something in common. It's one of the reasons I wanted to talk to you. The day we met, I saw you were in a real conflict over your mother. Struggling with contradictory feelings about her. And I'm doing the same over Vardis."

"What do you mean? Why do you have a conflict?"

"Apparently Vardis was my natural mother. That's wonderful. But she gave me away. She didn't want me."

Jenny sat back slowly. "I didn't think of that."

"I have to find out why she did it."

"Sure. God. Of course you do."

Dinah stared into her cup. She had planned to establish a "bond" just to make Jenny talk, but the girl's sympathy suddenly made the bond seem real, and she felt a great need to tell someone. Someone who might understand.

She lifted her gaze to the photo on the piano. "It's like being offered a new identity. Only the identity begins with rejection, so you don't know whether to take it or not. Why should I want to be Vardis's daughter, why should I give her a place beside the woman who really *was* my mother, if she didn't want me to be her child? Why should I let her into my life when she kept me out of hers? Ever since I learned of our . . . relationship, I've been waiting to know what to feel. Holding off feeling anything, really, until I know what she was like, and why she didn't keep me. I can't . . . surrender emotionally to being her daughter until I find the answer." In a moment she added, "And what if I never find it?"

Jenny sighed deeply.

"I don't suppose you know, do you?" Dinah asked. "Why she gave me away?"

"No. How could I? She never even told us she'd had a baby. All I can remember her saying about children was she didn't want any. She used to say why did she need a child when she had a niece like me."

"I thought your mother might know something about the circumstances of my birth. I hear she and Vardis were great friends at the time."

"Not anymore." The answer came with sudden, adult bitterness.

"Do you know why?"

Jenny looked at the wall of posters. "Because of me."

"I'm so sorry. It must be hard when two people you love don't get along."

"Yes. And when one of them— Yes. It's hard."

Dinah rocked the tea in her cup. "Would you like to talk about it?"

At first it seemed Jenny would. But then, with a look as suddenly adult as the bitterness had been, she said, "Didn't you come here to try to learn the truth about Vardis?"

"That's right," Dinah said smoothly. "Do you think there's such a thing as *the* truth?"

"Of course there is."

"I'd like to know it. I've been hearing confusing things. Your uncle and Hannah Sebastian say Vardis was wonderful, magnificent, but Cary Mathias claims she treated people badly. Exploited them, threw temper tantrums, tried to—"

"Please! I know what people say and I know why they say it. But you've got to understand that they're *wrong*. I mean maybe she did get angry sometimes, but she was *alive* the way most people never are. She cared about everything, got involved in everything, and that meant she wasn't always polite. Especially if people did things that kept her work from being as good as she knew it could be. She was a *perfectionist*. She wouldn't put up with halfway measures. If she was hurt or disappointed, she didn't bottle it up—she let it come out, and that way it couldn't hurt her over the long haul. Once it was out, she was free of it."

"Did she explain that to you?" Dinah asked, when Jenny paused for breath.

"Yes. Once after I saw her get furious at Con— Yes, she did. She said she wouldn't be as good an artist if she tried to hold things in."

Dinah put down her cup and leaned back. "Did she spend a lot of time with you?"

"As much as she could. Especially when I got a little older. She was so good to me—she'd do *anything* for me."

Dinah felt a knot beneath her heart: Why had Vardis lavished her time and love on this child? Why had she chosen Jenny Rostov—and given up the child she could have spent her whole life with?

"What's the matter?" Jenny said.

"Nothing." Dinah swung her head and said, "Tell me about her."

Jenny sighed. "She just made everything . . . come alive. Like once when I was in the eighth grade she came to talk to my class. I mentioned that one of the other girls had a brother on a soap opera who came and talked to us about TV—I just mentioned it, that's all—and she offered to come too. The class went nuts over her. God. She was there a whole afternoon, talking about Mozart and Verdi and how she had to work as a waitress and things when she first got to New York. She had Liza, her dresser, bring some wigs and costumes, and she explained things like how they helped her get into the roles and how a lot of theaters want you to wear their wigs to be sure they're fireproof but she always used her own that somebody made for her in Paris. At the end she showed a sketch I'd made of her as Turandot and told everybody she thought I really had talent. Oh, and then when I finished high school, she offered to take me with her and Conrad to Europe in the fall as a graduation present. Mother said no—Dad was dead by then—and we had a real fight. I knew Mother would never take me herself because she's sworn never to set foot in Europe again, but why did that mean I had to stay away? Finally I got her to go see Vardis about it, and I think they had a fight, too, but the upshot was that Mother quit saying no and arguing and I went."

Jenny got up, rocking a bit with the height of her heels. "What a trip that was," she said, moving to the piano and lifting her arms in a gesture sized for the opera house. "London, Paris, Venice, and Vienna. God. Vardis had performances in all of them, and she took me to all her rehearsals and meetings and everything. There were always dukes and counts and princes and God knows who all giving parties and receptions for her. In Venice I met the son of some friends of hers, Pier Andrea Vianello, isn't that a gorgeous name? And she let me go with him to a weekend party. Mother would have had a stroke, but Vardis trusted me. She treated me like an adult. 'Just remember, Italian men are to be enjoyed, not believed'—that's all she said. And in Vienna . . . Well, you don't care about things like that."

Dinah smiled. "You liked Vienna?"

"Yes. God. Vardis did too. She said the Viennese knew more than anybody else about the two most important things in the world—pastry and opera. She said the Staatsoper was the most beautiful house in the world but they never gave enough rehearsal time, so she was always arguing with people. Trying to get everything perfect. Once she had to do *Trovatore* with a tenor who didn't get there till the morning of the performance, and it made her so angry and nervous she couldn't eat for two days before. Then afterwards at a party she had so much Sacher torte she got sick." Jenny grinned. "She said she waited to throw up till she found the tenor's hat, but I don't think I believed that."

"Was she an amusing woman?" Dinah asked. "Did she have a sense of humor?"

"I never thought of it that way, exactly. But she could make me laugh. Like in London there was a pretty fat soprano doing Tosca, and Vardis said she could kill Scarpia just by sitting on his lap. Or sometimes I'd laugh just to hear her talk—she'd put on a kind of grand, exaggerated manner and say things like 'Please pass the salt to the world's greatest living soprano.' But she wouldn't tolerate any kind of breaking up or joking onstage. Once during a *Norma* the mezzo's costume split up the back and the tenor was smiling, almost laughing. Vardis said she'd never sing with him again." Jenny looked at Dinah uncertainly. "That's probably not the kind of thing you came to find out."

"It's all interesting. But I admit I most want to hear about your relationship with her. She encouraged you to study piano?"

"Ah." Jenny swung around and sat on the piano bench, facing out. "If only I could have been a singer, think what she could have taught me! But I have a really stupid voice. She used to tease me about it. She said I couldn't even sing Trouble in *Butterfly*."

"Didn't you say she thought you had a talent for drawing?"

"Oh, that's just something I did when I was young. I certainly wasn't any Leonardo." Belligerently Jenny added, "And why would you go into something like design if you had the chance to be in music?"

There, Dinah thought, was a place to probe. "Were you planning a career in design for a while?"

"Oh . . . I guess I used to think it would be fun. But you grow out of your high-school ideas. People have got to realize that. And when you find what you really want to do— People have to accept it."

"Did Vardis make you change your mind about your career?"

"No! She didn't!" Jenny smacked the arm of the piano. "It was my idea, and don't let my mother tell you any differently! She doesn't think I have any future as a pianist, but how does she know? Is she a musician? Vardis says I'm very sensitive musically, and Vardis should know. I switched to piano because I *wanted* to. If you have musical talent, it would be a *crime* to waste your life on something like being a designer. But Mother won't accept that. She's always tried to keep me away from Vardis, but she could never give me any *reasons*. She thinks Vardis has got me under some kind of spell. You can't talk to her about it. She thinks Vardis is the only reason I'm studying music, and that's why she hated her, hated her enough to poison her, I think she could be the one who—"

Jenny's voice skidded to a halt. She swallowed hard and turned away to the wall of posters, her throat still working.

Dinah wanted to rock her in her arms. She walked over, touched her shoulder, and felt it shiver. "Poor kid," she said. "I bet you're going through hell."

Without looking, Jenny reached up to clutch Dinah's hand.

"Maybe you'd feel better if you told me—"

"No," Jenny said fiercely. "I've already told you too much. I think you better go."

After a while Dinah realized she would have to. The girl was determined to be silent.

"Well, thanks for the tea," Dinah said. "And for what you told me about Vardis."

Jenny nodded.

Dinah was nearly out in the entry hall when she turned and said, "Oh, I did want to know one other thing. I don't imagine you'll mind telling me."

"What?" Jenny said guardedly.

"Somebody told me your mother came to this country from Norway. Is that true?"

Jenny looked relieved. "Oh, no."

"But she did come from somewhere in Europe, didn't she? Like the others?"

"Yes, Czechoslovakia. They all got out after the war."

CHAPTER
16

Cary Mathias stopped pacing his living room and checked his watch again. He had told Merle and Hannah eight o'clock, and they were fifteen minutes late. Merle hadn't wanted to come at all—"Cary, you know I hate the city"—but he had persuaded her they all had to talk face to face. If for no other reason, she needed to see what bad shape Hannah was in. But there were other reasons.

He stood motionless until the digits on the watch changed to 8:16. Then he shrugged and went abruptly toward the stairs that led to the roof and his garden. The apartment, which covered the top floor of the building, was divided into three huge rooms: bedroom, living room, kitchen. He had wanted to live among space and greenery, so there were many windows and plants. One wall of his bedroom was all glass, a virtual solarium. He went up the stairs two at a time. At the push of a button a door slid open to reveal a potting shed that was also the control room for the computers that monitored the garden.

Out on the roof the air was pleasantly cool. He turned on the lights, letting his gaze sweep from the fruit trees espaliered against a low wall to the birches and laceleaf maples in their heavy, ornamental tubs, from the rose garden just beginning to bloom to the greenhouse at one end, where orchids and begonias led their delicate, brilliant existence. As always, the sight raised in him a pleasure that came from his earliest years. It was not a re-creation of anything he had known, but rather the wiping out, again and again, of a dark, charred landscape.

He never discussed that pleasure with Merle, but he was certain she shared it. Their conversations about things such as seeds, fertilizers, and pruning techniques never rose above the practical level, but he always felt she was gripped by the same underlying emotion, and for the same reason.

He checked his watch again—8:21—and turned off the lights. It was just as nice without them. He seemed to stand on a carpet of illumination formed by the city, with the garden a comforting, shadowy presence around him. The birch leaves rustled with a soft metal sound, and the wind brought him a faint scent of roses. He smiled and let himself imagine that he was showing it all to Dinah Mitchell. To the enemy.

"I think the Mitchell woman suspects something about us," he had told Merle on the phone. "Did you tell her anything?" Merle had cried. "My God, did you tell her about the Pact?" He assured her that of course he hadn't.

He stared out at the city. Dinah wouldn't be the enemy if it weren't for Vardis. But if it weren't for Vardis, he wouldn't know Dinah at all. Even in death, Vardis could create and destroy with the same action. His hands clenched as if her neck were between them. He wished to God he had the power to go backward in time and wipe her out of his life, to erase the day he had met her.

But then he would also be erasing his journey to America.

They got on the ship because of Major Dan.

None of them knew his full name; he was just Major Dan—a giant with a big, deep voice and hair almost the color of his khaki uniform, who was one of the Americans in charge at the refugee center. From the time the four children were brought in, by a patrol that had found them nearly thirty miles away, he took a special interest in them.

He was the only one who could understand them at first.

Afraid to believe they were really among friends, they refused to say anything, either in their own language or in the German they knew. Major Dan overheard them talking among themselves. He understood, and began to speak to them quietly until Mila started to relax a bit. When she did, the other three could, too. He took them into the mess hall and sat with them while they ate. "*Jez pomalu!*" he cautioned, but how could they eat slowly when there were hot soup and hot meat? And soft, white slices of something Hana thought was cake but Major Dan told her was bread. He took them to have their rags of clothes burned and to bathe, and saw that some Army things were cut up until they more or less fit. He took them to a doctor, who frowned and spent a long time examining Karel's leg before he sighed and said it would be best to leave it alone. For a while after that, no one could find Karel. At last he was discovered in a bathroom, flushing the toilet over and over, staring at it in wonder.

Major Dan let them all stay in the same room, instead of splitting up the boys and girls. The first night, he brought in two oranges for them. Karel, who had never seen one before, smelled it, turned it all around in his hand, and stuck his nail into the rind. Then he did what Major Dan said, peeled it and pulled it apart. He bit into one of the sections, and gasped with pleasure as the sweet juice ran down into his throat.

Major Dan made sure they went to the English classes one of the women held regularly. He tried to spend some time with them every day, asking questions, wanting to hear their story over and over, and in return telling them about America.

After they had been in the camp for over six months, Major Dan said he had arranged for them to go to America and to live in the same place where he had grown up himself, a home for orphans in something called Connecticut. He said he didn't have a family of his own to send them to, but they would be well looked after in the place they were going, which was run by the Lutheran Church. "Now look, people might say it's odd for all of you to go there, but I figure the Lutherans owe it to any Jewish children who come their way to take them in, after some of the things Martin Luther said about Jews."

He said their journey would start in a few weeks, and the first thing to do was to find some nice, easy, new names for America. Karel Matyáš and Hana Šebesta were simple to fix, and so was

Konrád. But Mila—short for Miroslava—was a problem. "Not Millie," Major Dan said, "she's too pretty for a name like Millie. And too special." The next day he came back smiling. "Merle!" he said. "She kind of looks like Merle Oberon, anyway. And Háša—that can be Ashley, like in *Gone with the Wind*. So that makes you two Merle and Conrad Ashley. And, say, let's have the little one here be Cary instead of Carl. For Cary Grant. That way there's some Hollywood in everybody's name but Hannah's." He made them practice the new names until their pronunciation was American enough to suit him. (Later, at Cross of Glory, some of the girls had movie magazines, and Hannah pored through them, hoping to find a star or starlet with her name. But she couldn't. "I didn't really think I would," she said gravely.)

It was wrenching to leave Major Dan, who was an island of solidity in their world. (He wrote to them at Cross of Glory for almost a year, but then he died, of a heart attack, Mother Louise said. Cary hadn't realized that people died in ways other than being killed in war.) After a long, bewildering journey by jeep and train, they got to the ship. A Liberty Ship, they were told: a huge thing, with so many ropes and cranes and cables that it seemed to have a net of snakes thrown over it. When it groaned out of the harbor, they all stood on deck, holding one another's hands. "*Sbohem,*" Merle said. Then she searched for a rough equivalent in English: "Good-bye forever. From now," she added, "we speak English only."

All refugees were quartered in the forward holds; wounded soldiers filled the stern. Everywhere things were crowded and noisy, with a Babel of languages and emotions. People would tell each other their stories, weeping softly or moaning, but sometimes they would laugh and embrace each other with fierce joy. When a clanging bell announced mealtimes, everyone rushed into the galleys, held out aluminum mess kits, and pointed to whatever they wanted the soldiers to dish out. There were goulash, frankfurters, potatoes, macaroni and cheese, and huge bowls of mysteriously shivering color, called Jell-O, which Conrad spat out at first but soon acquired a passion for. Hannah always took more white bread and cookies than she could possibly eat, hid them in her clothes, and carried them back to her bunk. She said they kept the nightmares away, and put them under her pillow. Sometimes when the ship rocked or lurched, crumbs would fall down on Merle.

They had not been at sea long when word spread that the refugees were going to give a concert. After a day of preparation, during which a stage was hastily built over one of the hatches on the main deck, everyone gathered—wounded soldiers, off-duty crew and officers, and refugees. Merle found a place for the four of them to squeeze in, between a soldier in a wheelchair and a Yugoslavian family.

The sea was as green and calm as a painted plate, and the sun had gone behind clouds but left its warmth. Everyone was excited. There were shrill whistles after three young women danced, roars after a comedian, and loud applause after a juggler. Then out came a girl with a guitar. They had noticed her at mealtimes, always alone, never speaking to anybody but the soldiers who dished out the food. "Now here's Hjördis Olafsen," the MC said. "She's from Oslo, Norway, and we don't know how she got all the way down to join the ship. But we're glad she did. She'll give us a few songs and arias." The Yugoslavian man next to Cary muttered something that he thought meant "a scarecrow can sing?"

When the girl opened her mouth, she disappeared. The dress that hung on her as if she were a hanger, the nose that was too sharp, the legs too long and thin—all were forgotten, replaced by a pair of eyes you couldn't escape and a voice that ran into your throat like the taste of your first orange.

She sang one song, then another, then two more. Throughout the crowd people had strange looks on their faces, as if they had grown younger and older at the same time. Some of them were crying, including Merle. Merle, who in Cary's whole memory had never cried. Afterward she said, "It made me think of the times before the Germans." Merle, who had always told them never to look back.

That night the four of them were huddled on the deck, where the air was cool but not cold and didn't smell of diesel fuel, gazing at the star patterns without talking but all of them thinking of the strange girl and her singing, when they suddenly looked down from the sky and saw that she was standing before them. "Hello," she said in an ordinary voice that startled them. "I notice you four because you are together always. Will you tell me of yourselves?"

She sat with them for a long time, telling her story after hearing theirs. The next morning she joined them in the breakfast line. Soon she was with them constantly, as fascinated by their closeness as they were by her singing, which she would do whenever they asked. She seemed to want both to join and to test that closeness. Frequently she would try to get one of them, any one, to leave the others and come with her for a while.

They felt odd at first. They were four parts that fitted into one, but gradually the spell of the singing, and of her personality, worked among them like a solvent and made room for her.

She was going to America, she said, because she had convinced her British rescuers that her dead mother had relatives in the States, although she didn't know where. "Is that true?" Merle asked. "It could be," she said. The British had somehow managed to get her into a group sponsored by a Jewish relief organization in Chicago. "But now," she announced when the ship was nearing New York, "I have decided to go with you four instead."

They smiled sadly, sure she wouldn't be able to.

Two days later the ship sailed into harbor, past a green statue that made most people on the crowded decks weep. They all hung around their necks cardboard tags bearing their identification numbers, and soon they were lined up in a huge, drafty hall to be examined by a battery of officials and doctors.

Hjördis began her campaign right away. "I must go with my friends to the Cross of Glory Home," she told a government representative, who consulted various papers and said in a kind but firm way that she was mistaken, that someone from the Jewish relief organization would be there soon to prepare his group for its journey to Chicago.

"I do not make a mistake," she said. "I must go with my friends, and if you do not arrange it, I will do myself an injury." The authority in her gray eyes was adult enough to make the man hesitate.

Within half an hour she was facing a circle of perspiring, frustrated officials. "I gave concerts on the ship," she said. "Ask anyone, they all heard, they will tell you. I am going to be a great singer. But if you do not send me with my four friends, I will do myself an injury so I will never again be able to sing."

The men tried to coax her, explaining that special arrangements had been made for the four children she wanted to go with. Their jaws tightened in frustration, and finally they got two nurses to come and take her away with them.

"I don't think we will see Hjördis again," Merle whispered to
the other three. They were sad, but not surprised. They had no
concept of a permanence of relationships, except their own.

That evening one of the nurses came running to fetch a doctor.
"The Norwegian girl," she panted to him. "You have to come
and do some stitches. We had no idea she would— We were
trying to help her!"

A day or so later Hjördis suddenly reappeared. "I will go with
you," she announced to the four children. "I knew I could make
them permit it."

As if nothing had happened, she started talking about the name
she had found for herself: One of the nurses had had an American
magazine, and in it had been the name *Vardis*. "I think it will be
excellent for an opera singer," she said. "And now, before we get
to your Cross of Glory, I must decide what name to use instead
of Olafsen."

"Why do you sound funny?" Cary asked. "What's wrong with
your mouth?" But she wouldn't explain that, or anything else.

They were at the home for several months before Merle finally
learned what had happened. When the nurses had refused to
believe that Vardis would injure herself, she had quietly done it:
closed her mouth and slowly bitten a quarter-inch into her
tongue before they saw the blood leaking between her lips and
stopped her.

Up on the roof, Cary heard the doorbell ring.

He started, swung his head so his gaze swept over half of
Manhattan, and went to the intercom in the potting shed. "We're
here," Merle's voice said tinnily.

He activated the switch that let them into the small elevator on
the ground floor, and went back down to the living room. By the
time they rang the apartment bell, his watch read 8:31.

Merle came in first. As she hugged him, she whispered, "Hannah's not good. That's why we're late."

He saw what she meant: The skin around Hannah's pale blue
eyes, magnified by her glasses, twitched with a life of its own, and
her hands, when he took them, were as cold and thin as twigs in
winter. "How about some brandy?" he asked her.

"All right," she said, freeing her hands.

He made a Scotch and water for himself and poured sherry for

Merle, who abhorred hard liquor. She asked about the garden, and the two of them sat discussing new varieties of lilies while Hannah, sitting on a couch across from them, took birdlike sips of brandy without looking at it. Merle spoke with her usual calm, but in both her eyes, which she kept rubbing with her fingertips, were tiny red threads.

"I'd like to see the roof before we go," she said.

"Sure. I was up there when you rang."

"Working?"

"No. Thinking."

"About what we're going to do?"

"About what we did, a long time ago." Merle frowned. "I was thinking of the ship," he added, "and meeting Vardis."

"Why?" None of them liked to think or talk about the early years, but Merle disliked it the most.

"I don't know. Maybe I've been thinking about the past because Dinah Mitchell's been asking questions about it." He went on before Merle could say anything. "I just realized there's something I never thought about. Why was Vardis so damned anxious to come with us? We weren't the only kids on the ship. Far from it. So why us?"

"We were a group," Merle said. "She wanted to belong to one."

Hannah had finished the brandy and was rolling the glass between her palms. "And we didn't have any adults to watch her or keep her from being the leader."

Cary looked at her in surprise, but she seemed unaware that she had said something unusual.

"Do you remember how Conrad loved the Jell-O on the ship?" she said. "But I haven't seen him eat any for years and years now. Oh dear, I'd like to talk to him. Why does he shut himself up in that house?"

More sharply than usual, Merle said, "You know why." She turned to Cary. "Let's hear everything about the Mitchell woman."

"She has gray eyes," Hannah said.

"You told me that before, Hanička. Let's listen to what Cary has to tell us about her."

He put down his glass, put the gray eyes out of his mind, and began to list things. "She knows we've all confessed, and she told me she suspects we're doing it to cover up for the one of us who did it. She knows about Cross of Glory. She knows, or suspects, that we have a common childhood past. She thought it might have been in Norway, with Vardis, but I assured her it wasn't. In fact when she asked me outright what country I was from, I told her."

"Why?" Merle asked urgently. "Why didn't you lie?"

"What's the difference where she thinks I came from? That's not what has to be kept secret. The damn country isn't what matters. Besides, I have to answer at least some of her questions to make sure she keeps talking to me. The more I refuse to answer, the worse it'll look."

Merle rubbed her eyes. "What else does she know?"

"Maybe she's just on a fishing trip for information about her dead mother. But I don't think so. My guess is that she suspects our early history is important in some way. Maybe even has some connection to the confessions."

"Damn it," Merle said flatly. "God damn it."

"But I'm not going to tell her about the Pact, Merle. Neither are you. Neither is Hannah. So how could she possibly find out?"

"I don't like it. It opens a door. Publicly our position has to be that each one of us is telling the truth about having acted alone. The police must know that can't be so, but we can't afford any hint or suggestion or evidence that we're doing this together. That it's our plan. And the more they know about us, the more they—"

"I'm cold." Hannah pulled her coat-sweater more tightly around her.

"I'll get some more brandy," Cary offered, but she shook her head so violently that her pale hair sprayed around her shoulders.

"Is the Mitchell woman trying to find out which one of us did it?" Merle asked.

Cary kept his voice expressionless. "That's my guess."

They were all silent.

"I don't think," Hannah said quietly, "that we can go on with it." She got to her feet. "I don't think we *should* go on with it."

"We can't back out," Merle said. "Not after what we've told the police. You know that."

Hannah began to walk back and forth, arms locked, her whole body sinking toward its center.

"Come sit down, Hanička," Merle coaxed.

Instead she gave a retching sob. "Why does he say he did it? *Did* he do it, Merle? How could he do it?"

"Darling, you know I can't believe he really did it. I think she was one of the random poisoner's victims. But he confessed to the police. He seems determined to destroy himself, and we can't let him."

"He must know what we're doing. Why won't he talk to us? Why?"

"I don't know. Perhaps he's afraid to."

"Why would he be afraid of *us?*"

Merle lifted her shoulders helplessly.

Hannah's pacing began to slow. "I don't know whether I can keep on, Merle. I said in the beginning I didn't know whether I could do it. Don't ask me anymore. Please."

Merle went to her and took her by the shoulders. "Do you want Conrad to be convicted of killing her? Do you want him to spend the rest of his life in prison? Or even be executed?"

Hannah's head rolled back. Her "No" was more of a howl than a word.

"Then we have no choice. You know that, don't you?"

Hannah nodded. Merle took her in her arms and rocked her like a baby.

Over her limp form she looked at Cary. "You didn't want to go along, either. From the beginning."

He said nothing.

"Do you want to back out now, too?"

He answered quietly. "Yes, I do. Very much. But I won't. I'm doing it for you, Merle. And I guess I have to keep on doing it, for you."

"As long as the Mitchell woman doesn't learn any more, we'll be all right."

"I hope so."

"Yes," Merle said. "I am telling you, *we are going to be all right.*"

PART 4

KILLER

CHAPTER
17

Merle Rostov opened the back door of her handsome country house and took a deep breath—freshly cut grass, a faint, pleasant hint of horse, a wash of sweetness from new leaves and buds.

She took down the old cardigan she usually wore on her morning tour of the property. She needed the sweater not for warmth —the eight o'clock sun was already heating up the day—but for the comfort of habit in a world where so many things had suddenly changed.

She was still beautiful at fifty-one—a tall woman who shared the features that made her brother handsome, although her face was both harder and softer than his. The nose and mouth were carved at sharper angles but the skin was smooth and delicate, except for a strong crosshatching under and around the eyes.

She pulled on the sweater and started off authoritatively. The tour usually took two hours, for she liked to go along the south edge of the estate, past the orchard and the pasture, then back beside the stream that wriggled through the woods, into a final circle around the garden.

In a way, she had more feeling for the place than for the man who had left it to her. Not that she had married Frank Rostov for his money. It had been his kindness and gentleness, and perseverance, that finally had made her decide to accept the warmth he offered. Affection, she had thought, was all she'd ever be able to give, and safety and contentment all she could be made to feel. But she had been a good wife to Frank. If there was something lacking at the core of her, if she was hollow where she should have been most alive, he hadn't seemed to know. Or perhaps he had known and hadn't cared. She had marveled at him: a self-contained, self-sufficient man who ran on his own emotional fuel yet seemed to need her in his life.

Before they married, she had tried to explain herself to him. She said sometimes she felt as if she had been resurrected after the war, but with some pieces missing, the ones that would have enabled her to care deeply about things. But Frank had been unable, or unwilling, to grasp what she said. He had told her not to worry because he wasn't an emotional person either. That answer had revealed how little he understood, but it had also freed her to marry him. And she had liked Frank. They had gotten along splendidly.

She hadn't always been hollow at the core. She could remember being excited as a child by school, friends, piano lessons. Everything. The streets of Prague had promised a hundred adventures, and she had assumed they always would. Along with breasts and lipstick and the other accoutrements of growing up, new things would come to keep her absorbed. It wasn't a matter of planning ahead. It was just that confidence in her future was part of the furniture of her mind.

Even in the worst of the war, she had believed it would end someday and when it did, she would be as she had been before.

But the childhood sense of pleasure and involvement didn't return. Instead she felt old. Like an old woman remembering her life—without having lived it. Sadly but gratefully, she saw that the others didn't share her loss. Conrad talked eagerly of becoming a pianist, Hannah was interested in science, and even though Cary was restless and confused, things mattered to him in a way they didn't to Merle. Except for her feeling about the three of them, and about music. Music had the power, while one was hearing it, to make the world right again.

She had first learned that from Vardis. When she heard the

strange Norwegian girl sing at the refugees' concert, it had seemed as if torn edges inside her were coming together, connecting her again to what she had felt when life held singing and piano lessons and parents' love. In the years after, no matter what Vardis did, no matter what occurred between them, the voice could always give her that sense of connecting again with her true and deepest self.

In the beginning it wasn't only the singing. There was the intensity behind it, and behind everything else. Whenever Merle was with Vardis—listening, talking, arguing—she would watch the gray eyes flash and probe, and wonder what was the secret of such passion, which she herself had lost.

How could she blame Jenny for responding to that vitality, when she had too?

But to have found herself again, through Jenny, and then to watch Jenny succumb in the same way she had done . . . That was hard. Unbearable.

Frank had wanted children badly, and to please him, she had been willing to try. After five years and several infertility clinics, she had conceived.

In the delivery room, in the final rush of pain and tearing and blood that sent the child sliding out of her, she had had the unearthly, exhilarating sense that she had created herself over again, able to regain all she had lost.

Later, when they said she couldn't have another child, Frank had been unhappy, but Merle hadn't minded. Jenny was enough.

Jenny was everything, and everywhere. Every corner of the house, every foot of the grounds held her presence. The pasture where she had gaped at the horses and been lifted onto the backs of the gentler ones, the trees she had climbed for fun and apples, the stream where she had splashed and made mud pies, the woods where she'd had a hideaway to read and think. One year she had grown gourds in a corner of the garden. There still were boxes of them in the attic.

Merle stood staring at that empty corner. She had taken off the old cardigan and tied it around her waist. The sun beat on her bare arms and turned her auburn hair into a red cap. Some gray had crept into it; she used to touch it up, but since Jenny had moved into the city, she hadn't bothered.

After a while she shook her head and started back to the house, which had so many windows that the first floor almost seemed made of glass.

As she neared it, she heard the outside bell for the phone. She started running and pulled the back door open just as the ringing cut off. The maid had picked up. "I'm back," she called, and got to the kitchen phone, her heart wild with more than the exertion of running. She closed her eyes, touched the receiver, then picked it up. But the voice wasn't Jenny's.

The man asking the maid for Merle Rostov was the private detective she had hired, after two weeks of resisting the idea, to find out about Jenny's doings. Not to spy, she told herself; she would never spy on her daughter. But what else could she do, when Jenny refused to talk to her? How else could she know where and how Jenny was? And how could she stand not to know?

She interrupted the maid: "I'll take it."

When the extension clicked off, she said, "This is Merle Rostov. Is there some news?"

"You'll have to decide if it's news, Mrs. Rostov. Yesterday morning she spent two hours at the apartment of one of the people on the list you gave us, a Martha Foley."

"That's all right," Merle said; Martha was one of the Pack.

"In the afternoon she had a visitor, female, thirtyish. Stayed sixty-five minutes. We've ascertained that her name is Dinah Mitchell, address 464 West—"

"Damn it! Not her!"

"Excuse me, please?"

"I was swearing, that's all. Don't your clients ever swear when they hear your reports?"

"All the time, Mrs. Rostov. Do you want what we have on Dinah Mitchell?"

"Yes, all right."

"Address 464 West Seventieth. Widow of a police officer killed about six years ago. Has a roommate named Cassandra Barber. Teaches at Tryon Community College. Been there two years." The man paused. "You want us to dig for more?"

"No." Merle stared across the kitchen at a bank of windows, her hazel eyes translucent in the sunlight. "Not yet, anyway."

For some reason she didn't try to name, and couldn't have if she had tried, she dressed very expensively, in a suit of raw beige silk. She felt almost like an impostor because she hadn't worn anything but pants and sweaters for so long.

The traffic on Sundays was usually sparse, so she took the car and got into the city by one, for a three o'clock appointment. Plenty of time to go by Jenny's, she thought, pretending it was just an impulse and not the reason she had left an hour and a half early.

In the East Sixties she drove past the house. No life was visible. The street looked like an empty set waiting for actors. She drove to the end of the block, pretending she wasn't going to go back. But she made a left turn, went around the block, and drove back slowly. The car slid to a halt. She double-parked and went up the walk and down the side steps to the basement apartment.

She rang the bell once. Twice. Three times. She kept herself from pressing her face against the door's single, small window, but not from ringing two more times.

There was a blur of motion behind the window. Then it held part of a face.

"Jenny!" she cried. "Jen! Please let me talk to you!"

There were only the forehead and nose, and the two beautiful eyes regarding her dispassionately, as if they had been cut from the living Jenny and pasted to the window. As if there were nothing left of her daughter but pieces.

"Please, baby. Please!"

The disembodied face hung there, so near. Then it disappeared.

"Please," Merle whispered.

After a while she turned and went back up the steps. She stopped for a moment and looked up at the windows of the music room on the third floor, standing as motionless as a decoration. Finally she went back to the car.

She got to West Seventieth Street over an hour early. She found the building, parked a few doors away, and sat listening to a Mahler symphony on the car radio, trying not to think or feel. Her hands were folded and her face composed. One of the things she knew how to do best was to wait.

At ten past two, a couple in tennis clothes, carrying rackets, came along the block. The male half looked familiar: tall, big, red-haired. He was listening to the woman, smiling, but as they neared the car, he asked a question and frowned at the answer. Merle recognized him then, for he had frowned at her in the station house while she was telling him she had poisoned Vardis.

She was startled. Coincidences did occur, and after all, policemen had private lives. But then the couple stopped at Number 464, and the woman was in her thirties with short curly hair and a trim figure, and it was worse than coincidence. Detective Lyons was playing tennis with Dinah Mitchell.

Merle watched. They stood before the building, the Mitchell woman talking earnestly. Lyons didn't seem to like what she was saying, but he didn't argue, just nodded once in a while, as if he had to, and swung his racket. Finally she put a hand on his arm and peered up into his face. He nodded again, stepped back, and said something. Then he walked away, back in the direction of Merle's car. Merle turned her head away. When she looked again, Dinah Mitchell was still staring after Lyons. Eventually she swung her head and went inside.

The clock on the dash showed Merle she still had forty minutes to wait. She turned the radio dial until Mahler was exchanged for Beethoven, refolded her hands, and leaned against the high back of the seat, trying to decide what she had witnessed. They could have been arguing about what tactic Dinah Mitchell should use with Merle Rostov. Or the detective could have been saying the police believed Conrad was the killer and Mitchell, for some reason, was trying to convince him otherwise.

Or it could have been a personal argument. A lovers' quarrel?

But even if they were just friends, they seemed on close enough terms to be discussing the case. So it would be safest to assume that everything Mitchell knew or learned would get to Lyons.

Merle closed her eyes. She opened them just as the dashboard clock showed 2:55. She looked at herself in the rearview mirror, pressed her lips together tightly, and got out of the car.

The apartment door opened. Dinah Mitchell, out of tennis clothes and into slacks and a loose-knit cotton sweater, said, "Mrs. Rostov? Please come in."

She had the kind of scratchy voice that Cary would like.

She offered something to drink and Merle refused, both of them polite and stiff. If only there wasn't such a thing as manners and one could just take her by the shoulders and shake her and say, "Go, go, get out of our lives!"

They sat down and looked at each other. It was even odder than Merle had expected to be face to face with her. There was nothing of the child in her; she was definitely a woman. Attractive in a kind of healthy-American way. And she looked nothing like Vardis.

"When you didn't return my calls," she said, "I thought maybe you didn't want to see me."

"That's right," Merle said. "I didn't."

"Why not?"

"I had my reasons."

The woman's eyebrows rose, but not her voice. "Then what made you call me now?"

"You talked to my daughter, Jenny."

"Yes, I did."

"What do you want with her? Why are you bothering her? Can't you leave her out of this?"

"Out of what?"

Merle didn't answer.

"I talked to her," Dinah Mitchell said, "for the same reason I want to talk to you: to learn about Vardis Wolf."

"Jenny can't give you an objective picture of Vardis."

"Can you? Can any of you?"

"More than Jenny. We knew her longer and better. From the beginning."

"Mrs. Rostov, why are you defensive? Do you disapprove of what I'm doing?"

"I don't know what you're doing."

"But I told you! I'm not hiding it. I'm trying to find out about the woman who was my mother."

"If she wanted you to know about her, don't you think she'd have kept you?"

Mitchell gave her a cool, level look. "Did you mean that to hurt? I won't let it. I'll assume you're just talking as a mother who would never give up her child, and can't understand how anyone else could."

"You're clever," Merle said, admiring it in an abstract way.

"Not clever enough to know why you don't like me."

Merle laughed.

"And I'm certainly not clever enough to know what's so amusing."

"I'm not amused." Merle compressed her lips for a moment. "What did my daughter tell you?"

Dinah Mitchell tented her hands, stared at them, looked up. "Jenny's very beautiful. It's too bad she works so hard to copy Vardis—dressing like her, even gesturing like her. Thinking like her. It must be upsetting to you. But Jenny's barely twenty, isn't she? Sometimes young girls do get these worshiping crushes, but eventually they grow out of them. As Jenny will, I'm sure."

"Oh? Who are you to be sure?"

"I only mean that I've seen girls her age . . . I've taught, and I—"

"You haven't seen anything like this."

"So you think Jenny's attachment to Vardis is more than just a phase?"

"Dear God." The words came out flat and hard, like a knife blade slapped against wood.

"Jenny told me about Vardis, of course—how she came to her school, how she took her to Europe, things like that. It's easy to see why Jenny was so smitten. It sounds as though Vardis treated her wonderfully."

"Oh, yes." Merle's hands were resting on her bag, a small leather clutch that matched her suit; they pushed into it as if it were dough. "It's wonderful to make a child think music is better than any other career, isn't it? More worthwhile? The only thing to do? To convince her she has real musical ability when she doesn't?"

"Surely Vardis would know whether someone has talent."

"Who could know better?"

"Well, then?"

"She knew perfectly well Jenny was just an ordinary piano student. But she convinced her she was special anyway."

"Why?"

"Isn't it obvious? To take Jenny away from me."

"Mrs. Rostov, it's not obvious to me why Vardis would want your daughter."

There was a burning sourness in Merle's throat. She said nothing.

"Was there jealousy between the two of you? Did you have a fight?"

"Many."

"Over what?"

"My brother. Her marrying him. When she destroyed his career, I told her I never wanted to see her again."

"But you did keep on seeing her."

"For his sake. Only for that." Again the knife blade slapped wood.

"And you think she wanted to destroy Jenny the same way?"

"No. A different way."

Dinah Mitchell stood up, locked her hands on her arms, walked to the wall of books. "Mrs. Rostov, don't you think Vardis regretted giving up her own daughter?" She turned back. "Isn't it possible that with Jenny, Vardis was trying to make amends for having given me up?"

For a moment Merle could only stare, breath leaking from the little round O of her mouth. Then her reaction welled out.

"This time," Dinah said stiffly, "you do think something's funny."

"Funny," Merle echoed. "Oh yes." She shook off the rest of the laughter; it was irrelevant. "What did Jenny tell you about me?"

"I'm afraid she thinks you could be the one who poisoned Vardis."

"Ah." The sourness burned in Merle's throat again. She choked it down. "I knew that, of course. I know what she thinks. Was there . . . anything else?"

"She said you wanted her to go into design."

"Because that's what she's good at! If you'd seen some of her sketches, heard her ideas . . . Was that all she said about me?"

"I'm afraid so. We talked mostly about Vardis."

"Why don't you leave her alone? Why don't you leave us all alone, instead of poking and prying into things that don't concern you?"

"Because they do concern me."

"No, they don't. She put you out of her life. That's where you should stay."

Dinah Mitchell came toward her. "You know about it, don't you? How I was born, who my father was, why she gave me up —you know it all."

Merle sighed. "Yes."

"Tell me, Mrs. Rostov. Please tell me."

"You don't want to know."

"Damn it, don't say that. I do want to know! Why didn't she keep me? Did somebody force her to give me up? I *have* to know."

"It's easy to be for the truth before you hear it. But once you've got it, you can't get away from it except by dying."

"I want to hear it," Dinah Mitchell said.

"If I tell you, will you leave us alone? All of us? Even Cary?"

"I can't promise that. No. Why should I?"

"Because otherwise I won't tell you."

"But if you don't tell me," Dinah Mitchell said, "I won't leave any of you alone. Cary or your brother or Hannah Sebastian. Or your daughter. Ever."

Merle closed her eyes. There was something of Vardis in the woman, after all: strength. "Damn you," she whispered. "Why did you have to come back?"

CHAPTER
18

The hallway smelled like a trunkful of old clothes, and all five flights of the stairs creaked (in the key of G, Vardis said). Halfway up the last one, coming home from a day of clerking at Macy's, Merle could hear her practicing. Not at the piano, which she had recently bought secondhand for ten dollars and then paid five more to have some NYU students haul up the stairs. She was doing solfège—scales, arpeggios, and other exercises, all sung to a vowel. Her new teacher said the one at Cross of Glory had allowed her to spend too much time on songs and arias, so it was back to hours of solfège. Scraps of *ah, ee,* and *oo* seemed to linger permanently, like dust, in the corners of the apartment.

As Merle approached the door, the solfège gave way to a full-throated rendition of "Oh, What a Beautiful Mornin'." Once inside, Merle could see all the way to the back of the railroad-style flat, and there was Vardis in the kitchen: Long hair tied up in a towel, she was singing and soaping herself in the old bathtub they turned into a counter by putting on its wooden cover.

Merle walked back and flopped on one of the two kitchen chairs. "Hi."

Vardis smiled and went on singing. There was high color in her cheeks, and excitement came from her like the flower scent of the soap. "What's happened?" Merle asked. "You look like the Met offered you a lifetime contract."

Vardis finished a triumphant "Everything's going my way" and sat upright in the tub. "I have a date tonight."

That was only slightly less incredible than if the Met had called. In the ten months the two of them had been in New York, Merle had gone out many times—with assistant buyers, salesmen, customers—but Vardis, never. Except with some fellow music students, in a group. Merle tried to arrange blind dates, but Vardis always refused. "A man who needs to be fixed up isn't a man I want to be with." You couldn't argue with her; she wouldn't discuss it. She simply turned away and went back to her Italian or her solfège or any of the other things she studied. Sometimes she would add, "I'm too busy anyway." That did seem to be true, for she had lessons five days a week and waited on tables at least thirty hours to pay for them.

"Well, hallelujah," Merle said. "Who is it?"

"Someone you've met. Just wait. You'll see."

In a moment Vardis was out of the tub, drying herself with one of their Army-surplus towels. Then she made a comic-opera scene out of which of her two decent dresses to wear and finally asked to borrow Merle's black patent purse.

"By the way," she said, half embarrassed, half defiant, "don't mention anything to him about my singing opera. Please."

Merle recognized him as soon as he came in: one of the NYU students who had hauled the piano upstairs. Vardis had taken an imperious tone with him, and he had laughed, called her "Duchess," and done things his own way. She had subsided, but stared at him the whole time. His name was Lou Roberts and he was very, if conventionally, handsome—tall, big, and blond, like the midwestern football players pictured in the sports pages. He had been in the Army and was going to school on the GI Bill, although with no particular career in mind. It didn't seem that he and Vardis would have much in common.

But soon they were going out two or three times a week.

They went to a lot of movies, Vardis said, and to some jazz clubs in the West Village. Apparently he thought Vardis was studying to be a nightclub singer: "He thinks opera is high-brow," she said. "He wouldn't understand it."

"Then what do you talk about?" Merle wanted to know.

"Oh . . . we laugh a lot," Vardis said. "He's funny. He makes me laugh."

She didn't want to talk about him but couldn't be silent. In the middle of other things she would blurt out, "Lou can recognize good singing, you know—he likes Frank Sinatra." Or "Lou might like to go into some kind of business." Or once, quite sharply, "Lou says you're beautiful but you're not his type." The one thing she never said was how she felt about him, although it was pretty obvious. When he came to pick her up, her eyes would lock on him, and when she got home, she would seem dazed. Like someone headed for a certain destination who had somehow been shunted to another.

Merle was sure Vardis was a virgin, of spirit as well as body. It wasn't just that she had no experience with men; she hadn't allowed them into her awareness, except as part of the world of music. Music gave them reality and then superseded them. But now there was someone outside music, in competition with it. Vardis never missed her lessons and practiced as much as ever. But often Merle saw her staring into space, looking puzzled, as if she couldn't believe what was happening to her. Any more than she could stop it.

And Merle—yawning after evenings with men who took her out and begged her to say where she wanted to go, any place she named, but she could never make it matter where they went—Merle watched Vardis's eyes and envied their hunger. As well as their satiety.

She watched Lou, too, wondering what he really felt. "Come on, Duchess," he would say to Vardis, laughing, "let's go." He didn't seem to take anything seriously, including her. She should have hated that quality in anybody, but, perversely, she seemed unable to resist it in him. When she finally told him the truth about what kind of singer she was, he started calling her "Lily," for Lily Pons, even though she explained over and over that she wasn't a coloratura like Pons. "Hey, Lily," he would say anyway. Laughing. She would lock her eyes on him and go.

It went on for one whole summer.

At the end of September, Merle realized that he hadn't been around for over a week. "Where's Lou?" she asked.

Vardis was at the piano, working on a score. "Gone." She didn't look up.

"What do you mean, gone? Left New York?"

"I mean that I don't know where he is anymore." She sang a phrase over three times.

Merle hesitated. Although they shared many things—a calendar age, the fate of being pushed years ahead of it by war, and the toughness to survive that push—each of them was still a private person, although perhaps for different reasons. But Vardis was suffering. Merle went to her, put a hand on her shoulder, and said, "I'm sorry. Really sorry. You want to tell me about it?"

Vardis stared at her hands, in place on the keys. "He didn't care for me the way I cared for him. I know that now."

Merle couldn't say what she thought: that they had been a real mismatch—the conventionally handsome lightweight and the serious ugly duckling; that Vardis had fallen for his looks because what else did he have; that he'd probably made her feel she was a "normal girl," for the first time. So all she said was, "I think you're right. He didn't care the way you do."

"The way I *did!*" Vardis said fiercely.

"OK. Good." Merle squeezed her shoulder. "Hey, why don't we try to save some money and go out to Cross of Glory to spend Thanksgiving with the kids?"

"No."

"But we've only gone out once since we left. It'll be good for you to get away from New York and your lessons and all your worr—"

"I'm pregnant," Vardis said.

"Oh, my God." Merle sank beside her on the piano bench. "Are you sure?"

"Yes. Almost three months. I went to a doctor yesterday. I've been having morning sickness."

"Have you told Lou?"

"Two weeks ago."

"What did he say?"

"Not much. He said he had assumed I knew how to . . . be careful. He said he had to think. But I haven't heard from him." She swallowed. "I've left messages for him. Three times. He doesn't answer them." She fell against Merle's shoulder.

Merle put her arms around her, and looked down at the head

of dark hair and the spectacle of Vardis Wolf reduced to tears.
She felt two emotions collide within her: sympathy, and a hollow
envy that once again, whatever she did, Vardis did at peak intensity. Life lived *con fuoco*.

Voice muffled against Merle's blouse, Vardis said, "Why do
you have all the luck? You're so goddamn beautiful they all want
you, you don't care about a career, and you don't get pregnant."

Merle would have laughed if she hadn't been so taken aback.
Vardis thought *she* was lucky? But all she said, mildly, was "I
don't get pregnant because I don't sleep with them."

Vardis raised her head; her eyes were muddy and her nose red,
and for once she looked helpless. "He said he'd never met anybody like me."

"Mmmm. I'll bet."

"I thought he loved me, Merle."

"Did you? And here I kind of thought you knew better."

"Yes? How could any man love me?"

"I don't mean that. I—"

"Only a mother could love my face? I'll tell you something. She
didn't love it either. She always said to me, 'You must practice
as hard as you can, because your voice will have to be your
fortune.' "

"Stop talking as if you're ugly. You're not. You could be stunning if you tried. When you take care of yourself and get really
fixed up—"

"You don't know what it's like to be me," Vardis said harshly.
"You can never know." She sat erect. Merle could almost see her
shove the pain aside. "I was a fool to believe anyone like Lou
could love me. One must pay for being a fool. But I won't let it
ruin my life. No. I will not have this baby."

She meant it. If she cried at night, on her side of the lumpy,
secondhand bed they shared—and she must have, for sometimes
Merle could feel the bed shake—there was no sign during the
day. Calmly she announced she had learned that Lou had gone
back permanently to his home in Ohio. Calmly she called the
doctor whose name Merle had managed to get after two weeks
by asking around at the store ("for a friend . . . can't be a quack
. . . somebody who's a doctor . . .") Calmly she took her hundred-
dollar savings out of the bank and accepted another hundred

from Merle. The doctor's office was in Queens, and they were to go there on a Saturday morning, on the subway. Merle was very worried. Vardis was calm.

The night before, Merle brought home one of the tabloid papers and pointed wordlessly to a second-page story. ABORTIONIST DISMEMBERS DEAD PATIENT. A twenty-year-old had died during an abortion, and the doctor, terrified of discovery, had dissected her body and fed the pieces into the sewer system. After weeks of investigating, the police had finally arrested him. He was the doctor in Queens.

"All right," Vardis said grimly, "I have to have it. But I won't go away. I'll stay right here. We'll tell people I'm sick, something that needs a long time of rest, or we can say I've gone away for a while. The minute it's born, I'll give it away. Will you help me do it, Merle? And swear you'll never tell anyone, not even the three. Especially not the three. Will you swear it?"

Merle swore. She didn't much like the whole business—she had never lied to the kids before, even though she agreed it was probably for the best, and she thought lying to people in New York would be awkward—but she finally did swear. To have an illegitimate child was a terrible stigma. Even Vardis wasn't willing, or perhaps able, to go about her business and brazen it out. So how could she be a friend to Vardis and not do what she asked?

In November, her fifth month, Vardis told everybody—voice teacher, language teachers, musicians she'd met on the singing jobs she got (mostly at churches)—that she had infectious mononucleosis and would have to stay very quiet, maybe in bed, for at least several months.

"They'll want to come see you," Merle objected. "They'll be concerned."

"No, they won't," Vardis said. She was right.

It was all much easier than Merle expected. Vardis stayed in touch with her voice teacher by phone, and there were almost no other calls.

Vardis gritted her teeth and her spirit and accepted the new life: six hours a day of practice and study on her own, and, to keep from going crazy, a long daily walk, for as many weeks as she could still hide her condition under the shapeless, bulky winter coat Merle found at a church rummage sale. By the end of January, Vardis was apartment-bound, but she still didn't complain. She seemed to will herself to feel nothing about her shrunken life and her swelling body. Perversely, although Merle should have been sympathetic to such detachment, she wasn't. If you carried life, shouldn't you feel more alive?

Early in March, the month Vardis was due, her singing teacher phoned. Merle heard her telling him that the mononucleosis was almost under control and she expected to be back to normal soon. Then, as she listened to him, her color rose and her eyes fixed on space as if it held miracles. "I'll be there," she cried. "I promise I'll be there."

She put down the phone and said to Merle wonderingly, "Paul wants to recommend me to a conductor friend of his who'll be in New York in ten days. Casting for some summer opera productions in the Midwest. Paul wants me to audition, at least for some smaller roles." She looked down at herself. "In ten days." She raised her hands as if trying to reach God, or threaten him. "This baby has to come soon. I order it to come! Now!" Her hands pulled into fists and smashed down on the mound of her pregnancy.

Merle jumped up. "Don't do that!"

But she did, and had her fists raised once more when Merle got to her and grabbed her hands. "Let me go!" she cried, but Merle wouldn't. She hung there, her wrists in Merle's grip while the fear and pain and anger she had been walling off for months finally broke out, twisting her face as they came.

The next day her labor started.

Vardis had gotten a midwife's name, but Merle refused to let her call. They fought, struggling with the phone, but Merle had reserves of strength, little used but still there. She threatened to pull out the phone and leave Vardis to give birth alone. For an hour or so she feared Vardis might try to do just that, but when the pains got bad, she finally said she would go to a hospital as long as it wasn't one in the neighborhood. "Go up to the Bronx," she pleaded, and Merle decided to pacify her. She got her down the five flights and into a cab, and they headed for the Bronx, Vardis groaning so much that the driver glanced over his shoulder apprehensively whenever he stopped at a light.

After twelve more difficult hours, the child was born—to Hjördis Olafsen, as she signed herself in.

The doctors said she should stay at least a week, but on the fifth
day she signed herself out. When Merle got home from work, she
was lying on the couch, so pale that her eyes looked black. On the
floor, in an orange crate lined with blankets, was the child.

Tossing aside her coat and purse, Merle knelt beside it. The
tiny face was red, eyes staring earnestly, mouth working without
sound. One hand waved in the air, fingers incredible in their size
and perfection. When Merle put out her own finger, they closed
around it.

"I'm giving it up tomorrow," Vardis said.

Merle compressed her lips. Nothing that had happened during
the pregnancy had given her any reason to think Vardis would
change her mind, but somehow, she realized, she had expected
her to. "Where are you taking it?" she said. "I mean, where are
you taking *her?*"

"To a home."

"You're sure that's what you want?"

"Of course. Do you think I would give up my career for a
child? Never. So don't try to argue with me."

"All right. Which home?"

"I'm not going to talk about it, Merle. I'm just going to do it."
There was no sign of hesitation in her face. Or of anything else.

The evening passed in chunks of uncomfortable silence. If the
child cried, Vardis gave it her breast. Otherwise, she barely
looked at it. Once Merle tried to hold it, but Vardis told her
forbiddingly not to.

"Have you given her a name?" Merle asked, but she knew the
answer.

Vardis said she would sleep on the couch so that the child
would not disturb Merle. "I don't mind at all," Merle protested,
but she was ignored.

Merle slept little. The moon, which had never before kept her
awake, lay on her eyelids like a searchlight and kept jerking them
awake. She heard the child cry, the couch creak, the building
utter sighs of age. Around four in the morning she woke once
again and found she heard nothing. Even the street outside
seemed to be holding its breath.

The preternatural quiet set her heart racing, and she couldn't
lie still any longer. She rose, looked out the window, blinked up

into the moon, and went to open the bedroom door cautiously.

She knew she must be seeing wrong. She blinked again and shook her head.

But the sight remained, blazoned by moonlight: Vardis on the couch, looking down at the orange crate beside her, holding a pillow about a foot above it.

She didn't move for a long time.

Nor did Merle. She ordered her brain to find some different meaning for the image, and when it refused, she kept staring, paralyzed by a thought she knew was crazy but couldn't shake: that she couldn't speak what she saw, because then Vardis would have to realize what she was doing.

Vardis lifted the pillow inches higher, ready to strike.

But it stayed there, until at last she brought it down, on her lap. She fell back against the couch as if someone strong had shoved her.

Merle's muscles returned to life. She rattled the doorknob to which her hand had been glued, stepped into the room, and said, as sleepily as she could manage, "Just going to the bathroom. Are you all right?"

"Yes," Vardis whispered.

Merle left the bedroom door ajar and got up a dozen times, responding to the smallest sound from the living room, but each time she peered out, Vardis was lying quietly, with the makeshift crib on the floor beside her.

In the morning Merle said, "Today I'm supposed to work from noon till nine, but I'll take off and go to the home with you, shall I?"

Vardis shook her head. "Anyway, I'm not going until tonight. My appointment is for nine o'clock."

It didn't seem right to Merle, nor did anything else, all day long. Even her body. At work her heart raced for minutes on end, her head kept throbbing and then stopping, perspiration ran down her midriff and just as suddenly dried up. A little before eight she told her supervisor she was ill and left.

She approached the apartment building from the other side of the street. Instead of crossing over and getting out her keys, she huddled against the opposite building. Light shone from the fifth-floor living room windows, where she thought she caught Vardis's shadow. The night was raw and the street, a commercial one, had shucked off its daytime constraints. Noise and people swelled from the pool hall on the corner, cats pawed through garbage cans at the curb, and a man staggered by, sucking on a bottle, to collapse three doors away. Although cold crawled beneath Merle's coat and causeless heat surged into her cheeks, she waited quietly and stoically. She was good at waiting.

Not until she saw Vardis emerge from their building, carrying the infant, did she realize that she had been planning all along to follow her.

She expected Vardis to hail a cab, but three went by and were ignored. The subway then, she thought, but Vardis went off in another direction, moving slowly, as if she hurt. Once Merle thought she heard the infant cry, but the tiny mewing sounds could have been a cat.

Vardis headed west, into the river smells blowing from the Hudson. Each time a car passed, she turned her face away and moved close to the buildings. On the corner of Tenth Avenue was a vacant lot. She moved out of the streetlight spill and stopped, staring into the lot. She walked into it and disappeared.

Watching, Merle ran soundlessly across the street and spotted her picking her way across some discarded lumber. The lot smelled of cheap liquor, urine, and rotting vegetables. Toward its center, behind a pile of bricks, were some trash cans.

Vardis went to them. She looked down into each of them. Then she stopped before one and lowered her blanketed bundle into it. Gently.

She turned to the pile of bricks and took one. She stood over the trash can and lifted the brick the way she had lifted the pillow the night before.

Crouched behind what smelled like rusting oil drums, Merle couldn't make any of her muscles move, even the ones in her throat. They would move if she could believe what she saw, but how could she believe it?

At last the brick came down, but slowly, still in Vardis's hands. She put it back on the pile.

She retraced her steps without once looking behind her.

Merle got up and ran to the trash can. Where people put dead things. She reached down into it, for the evidence she would take to the police.

But when she lifted out the bundle, it gave a tiny mewing sound.

. . .

She sat holding it in a coffee shop on Ninth Avenue. She had ordered coffee and a glass of milk, but when she dipped her finger into the milk and tried to get the tiny mouth to suck, the baby wasn't hungry. Vardis must have fed her before taking her out. To make sure she was quiet.

There was no time to feel, or think, about Vardis. Everything must wait until Merle could decide where to take the baby. The most logical place was the one she positively couldn't consider— Cross of Glory. So that left the police. Or a foundling home. She could locate the nearest one in the dog-eared directory at the back of the coffee shop.

No matter which she did, the child would end up living the regimented, artificial life of some kind of institution. An orphan hoping for an adoption that might not come. Thinking a "mother" was someone like Mother Louise.

Merle looked down. The tiny girl, who was dressed only in a diaper and a flannel gown, kicked a bare foot out of her blanket. Merle held the foot, then tucked it in. Although she had done her best to brush the baby off, she saw a shard of eggshell in the dark fuzz of hair. She picked it off and saw her hands begin to shake with the anger she had been denying.

When it receded, there was an idea in its wake.

The week before, one of the assistant buyers she dated had mentioned some neighbors of his, a couple devastated by losing their two-day-old daughter.

She didn't get back to the apartment until after one. Her buyer friend had been at home, thank God, and so had his neighbors, Rose and Dan Leone, but it had taken them time to get ready and come into Manhattan. Then they had asked many questions about the infant's mother and father. Merle told what little she knew about Lou Roberts, except his name, but almost nothing about Vardis, only that she was young and in good health. The Leones had hesitated, but briefly. Once they heard the infant had been born on the same day as their own, the woman took the baby in her arms, and it was clear what their decision would be.

Merle climbed the five musty flights of stairs thinking of Vardis and what she would do to her: strike her, scream at her, sink fingers into her long hair and pull her to the nearest police station.

She opened the apartment door. A light was on, and Vardis was sleeping on the couch in her pajamas. Her head lolled to one side but her fingers clutched a score—*Il Trovatore.*

Merle stared down at her. How could she have done what she had, and then come home to work on her music?

There was no answer. No way to answer.

And there was another question, which Merle's rage had swept aside. How could she turn Vardis in, when arrest could lead to conviction for attempted murder and conviction would lead to prison—and to the end of the voice? The voice that teachers said could be one of the great ones. Should there never have been a Galli-Curci, or a Pons, or a Flagstad, if one of them had left her child to die?

Never mind the teachers. What did Merle Rostov say? Could she silence the voice that could reach through her private wall of deadness . . . could she bear to do that?

She had no idea how long she stood there, in spite of her exhaustion, unable either to answer or to swallow her rage.

At length Vardis opened her eyes. "Merle," she said slowly, her head still at a crooked angle. "What time is it? Where were you?"

"I . . . With one of the assistant buyers. And some friends of his." Merle cleared her throat, compressing the rage into a piece of metal in her voice. "I know what you did tonight."

Vardis blinked and sat up. "Of course you know. I told you what I was going to do, and I did it."

Her calmness and self-assurance took Merle's breath away. In spite of everything she knew about Vardis—from the time she had nearly bitten through her tongue to get what she wanted—it still took her breath away.

"It's over," Vardis said. "And I don't want to discuss it, or even mention it. Ever again. Will you promise me that?"

"I don't think I can ever promise you anything again."

Vardis's eyes turned muddy. "Oh, Merle," she whispered, clutching the *Trovatore* score to her chest as if to plug some kind of leak. "I can't sing right, Merle. I tried all yesterday and today, but I can't. Something's not . . . My throat muscles don't . . . work." She collapsed into the couch. "What will happen to me if I can't sing? Merle? How can I live if my voice is gone?"

Merle exhaled slowly. She was not superstitious or religious—Cross of Glory had been her only experience of religion, and it had bored her—but there must be gods somewhere, for they had devised a punishment more awful than any she had contemplated. They had taken away the voice.

She looked down at the figure on the couch—not Vardis Wolf any longer but a huddle of pain and panic—and said, "I'm exhausted. I'm going to bed."

"Merle," the thing whimpered.

She shook her head and went into the bathroom.

In the next weeks Merle stayed away from the apartment whenever she could, putting in overtime at Macy's, going out afterward on dates or with female co-workers, getting home as late as possible. And she no longer shared the double bed with Vardis. She used the couch.

One night when she came in, she found bottles of peroxide and other chemicals on the kitchen sink. Vardis came out of the bedroom, with a white streak in her dark hair, at the left temple. Despite herself, Merle asked, "What have you done? What's that for?"

"To remind me of what I have lost," Vardis said.

Did she mean the voice? Or the child? Was it a flamboyant, self-dramatizing gesture? Or the only acknowledgment she permitted to seep from a buried well of guilt? Merle couldn't decide, and wouldn't ask.

Occasionally she heard Vardis practicing, desperately. The sound had little power. One day, though, it seemed a bit stronger. Merle made no comment.

Two weeks later, when she came into the apartment, Vardis swung around at the piano. "The voice is back!" she cried. "Completely!" And breaking the silence that had prevailed for six weeks on the subject of the child, she added, "It must have been because of the birth. Why didn't one of those idiot doctors at the hospital tell me? Obviously childbirth weakened the muscles. They needed time to regain enough strength to support the voice properly. If only I'd known! If only I hadn't had to miss that audition Paul set up for me! Oh, isn't it wonderful that the voice is back?"

"Yes," Merle said. But she felt sick. Mocked by the gods.

Three days later, on a Sunday morning, she announced, "I'm moving out. I found a new place, closer to Macy's. I'm leaving today."

Vardis put down the book she'd been reading on the history of singing.

"I can't live with you any longer. I know what you did with the baby. I saw you do it. I followed you that night."

If the answer had been "Thank God! Is she safe?" if the blood had rushed to Vardis's face in guilt and relief, Merle might have forgiven her, even then.

But she said nothing. She turned white, an absence of color so total that Merle had never before seen it in a living face.

"I saw you lift the brick," Merle said. "I saw you leave her to die."

If only Vardis had cried, "Where is she? What did you do with her?" But the response was a slow shake of her head. And then, clasping her long fingers together: "But I didn't use the brick, Merle. I couldn't."

"You tried to! Just the way you tried to smother her with a pillow the night before. You left her in that trash can to die!"

"But I went back. The next morning."

"I don't believe you. You're lying."

"I'm not. Merle, I'm not! I went back the next morning, and she was gone. I've been sick about it ever since. I wanted to tell you a hundred times, but I couldn't." The gray eyes flashed with passionate sincerity.

Merle waited until the silence was awkward. "I think you're going to be the best actress in all of opera. But you don't convince me. You might have, if you'd cared enough to ask where the baby is, and how she is."

The pause was tiny but fatal. "Of course I want to know those things."

"You never will. I took her, I saved her, and I'll never tell you how."

"In the circumstances," Vardis said stiffly, "perhaps I shouldn't know."

"Why in God's name didn't you take her to a foundling home? That's all you had to do. Or leave her at the door of some hospital, or even some apartment building, where somebody would find her. Why did you leave her to die? Why did you want to *kill* her?"

"I didn't Merle, I . . . wasn't myself. You know what I've been through! Months of hiding away, of not being able to get any singing jobs. And then when it finally was over, I still couldn't sing!"

"Oh, Christ," Merle whispered. She saw a scrap of eggshell caught in fine, dark hair. "Now I understand. You wanted to punish her. You wanted to kill her because you thought she had destroyed the voice."

Vardis was silent. The chasm between the two of them widened to an unbridgeable distance.

"I'd like to put you in prison," Merle said.

"But you can't. How can you? There's no evidence I did what you claim." Vardis's color, and her confidence, were seeping back. "And I will deny it. It will be your word against mine."

She was using the arguments Merle had recited to herself dozens of times, but leaving out the most potent one. Going to the police would reveal and perhaps ruin the arrangements Merle had made for the child, which were illegal.

"I'll say the child died of natural causes," Vardis added.

"The police will ask to see the death certificate."

"I'll say I didn't get one. I'll say I threw the body into the river."

Merle understood, finally, that she was defeated. Whatever strength she possessed, and once it had been great, she was no match for Vardis Wolf and never could be. Vardis had a passion and a monomania that lay outside the range of her experience. Almost of her belief.

She did do one thing. She went up to the Bronx hospital where the child was born, told several complicated lies, and managed to get a copy of the birth certificate, which she sent without explanation to the Leones. She couldn't explain her need to do it, but once she had, she felt as if some kind of justice had been done. To herself? To the baby? She had no answer.

She finally accepted that there was nothing else she could do. The acceptance left her more hollow than ever, but she could sometimes console herself by reflecting that, after all, two things had been saved which would otherwise have been lost—the child and the voice.

· · ·

She warned the others about Vardis, in general terms. But she tried to use the weapon of her knowledge only once, six years later, when Conrad and Vardis returned from Europe and said they were going to marry.

She went to see Vardis in a rage so cold that her teeth kept knocking together. "If you try to go through with this marriage," she said, "I'll tell Conrad about the child. That you had her, and that you tried to kill her!"

Vardis looked at her calmly. In those six years she had begun to use makeup skillfully and to dress dramatically, but there was another change, deeper than cosmetic, which Merle identified, even through her anger: a newly sharpened edge of imperiousness. Vardis had never been good at dealing with people as equals; now she wasn't even trying.

"Tell Conrad if you like," she said. "I'll deny every word. He already thinks your dislike of me is 'irrational'—that's his word —so you'd simply be giving him further proof. I'll say you're jealous of me because he loves me—so jealous you've stooped to telling a revolting lie. Then he'll ask you something you can't answer. He'll want to know why, if your story is true, you never went to the police. He'll ask why you've waited six years to say something."

She was right. Merle knew it.

And a new fear gripped her: Even if Conrad believed what she told him, Vardis might be able to convince him, somehow, that what she had done was justified. That it had been necessary, to save the voice.

The next day she went to the wedding, where Vardis took Conrad away forever, smiling, laughing, wearing her hair in curls but still flaunting the jagged white streak. . . .

"You abandoned your own daughter!" she cried to the bony face in her memory. "You left her to die. I saved her! And now you want to take *my* daughter away from me. To destroy her the way you destroyed Conrad. But I won't let you do it. I'll kill you before I let you do it!"

It took her a moment to realize what she had just said. When she did, she blinked and looked around slowly and saw Vardis's daughter sitting across the room, her face like crumpled paper.

CHAPTER
19

"And did you kill her?"

After a moment Dinah realized she hadn't asked the question. She had only thought it.

It didn't matter whether she asked it or not. Or even what the answer was. Nothing mattered but the fact that she couldn't get enough air into her lungs to breathe right.

Across from her in the wicker chair Merle Rostov sat quietly. The hate had drained out of her face, which was once again as smooth and composed as the silk suit she wore. "I've never told it to anyone before," she said, and sighed, the sound falling in relief. "Do you think I should have gone to the police?"

"I . . . can't say."

"No? And all these years I've wondered what somebody would say if I ever asked that question. Because I let her get away with murder. Didn't I?"

"I'm sorry, I just can't think."

Merle nodded. "It's all right. I understand."

Dinah took a shallow breath, all she could manage. "How do you think Vardis felt about what she had done?"

"Ah. You want to me to tell you she must have suffered. But I can't say. How does the fire feel after it burns your hand? I think it just feels that your hand got in the way."

"Don't you think she had any human emotions at all?"

"I said you wouldn't want to hear the truth."

"And I said you were wrong." Dinah spoke as forcefully as she could, but it wasn't so. She didn't want the truth, she didn't want the story to be true.

"You know," Merle said, "I went to see you once."

"What do you mean?"

"Just before I was married. I went to Brooklyn, to the building your parents lived in. I stood outside for almost half an hour, trying to decide whether to do anything. Then I saw a woman coming out with a child. It was Rose Leone. Your mother, I should say. I hid and watched the two of you go up the street. You hung on to Rose's hand, chattering like a magpie. She took you to a playground a few blocks away. For a while I watched you playing on a jungle gym. You were about eight, I think. You fell and scraped your knee. Rose hugged and kissed you and cleaned the knee with her handkerchief. I decided I couldn't . . . I just went back to the city. I don't suppose you remember that day?"

"I'm afraid not. But I remember the playground. We went there a lot."

"And of course children are always scraping their knees."

"Yes."

"Dinah," Merle said meditatively. "It's not the kind of name Vardis would have liked."

"Maybe I'm not the kind of person she would have liked, either."

"That could be. Perhaps you have too much independence." Merle stood up, her silk suit rustling, and tucked her purse under her arm. "I'll go now."

Dinah knew there must be other things to say and ask, but her mind couldn't find them. She went to open the door. Standing that close to Merle, she saw that the creamy skin was free of makeup, and caught a whiff of lily-of-the-valley fragrance. "You saved my life," she said, wonderingly. "I can't just say thank you, and then good-bye."

"I'd like to ask one thing of you. Now that you have the truth, don't use it to hurt us. Just leave us alone. But of course . . . it's out of my hands." Merle looked down at them and sighed. "The one thing I never thought is that you would come back into our lives. But then, I never thought anything would be the way it is."

Dinah stood in the doorway, watching her walk to the elevator. The strange thing was the sense that came drifting back, in spite of Merle's elegant, erect bearing and firm step, the sense that something was crushing her.

Vardis onstage, face rapt, eyes and voice mesmerizing. Her hands rising. Long, beautiful fingers yearning and reaching for something . . . A bundle. Lifting it, preparing to hurl it down. . . .

The images played in Dinah's mind again and again.

I am the child of greatness. The daughter of Awe. The words rose from her memory like bile. How exalted she had felt when she left the Ashley town house, after Conrad had confirmed that she was Vardis's daughter.

Maybe she was being punished for the sin of hubris. Plain old Dinah Mitchell, with her ordinary name and her ordinary life, wanting reflected glory . . .

The part of her mind that needed to make sense of things stirred and said, Wait a minute. If Merle never told anybody, how did Conrad know? It's not credible that Vardis told him herself, so how did he . . .

But the question and the desire to answer it dissipated. She folded over, head on her arms and arms on her knees, not thinking anything, just feeling flattened. And mocked.

Finally she got up and began to walk around the living room in a long oval. The way Cary had done when he was talking about Vardis.

Cary, she thought. She hadn't asked Merle a thing about him, or about her childhood. In Czechoslovakia—like Cary's.

Did Cary know about trying to kill the child?

Not "the child"—Dinah Leone Mitchell. *Her.*

I tell you she was a killer, and some day you'll know I'm right.

No, Cary couldn't know about it. Not if Merle had never told anyone.

But wait. Maybe Merle was lying about that. And everything else. Yes—first she lied about killing Vardis. Then to make the confession more plausible, she invented a story about letting

Vardis get away with trying to murder her infant daughter. It must be a lie! There was no evidence, after all. No proof, no witness, not even someone to whom Merle had confided the story.

Then how did Merle know Rose and Dan Leone's names? And where they lived?

And her story explained the two birth certificates: one for the Leones' natural daughter, who was born in a Brooklyn hospital but died shortly—the certificate Dinah's mother had given her; and one Merle got from the Bronx hospital and mailed to them. The certificate hidden in the stocking bag.

If those things were true, then so were the other things Merle had said.

Dinah went into the bedroom. She took her parents' wedding picture from the frame of the dresser mirror: her father's face split in a grin, her mother's happy but solemn. She had always thought of herself as the child in relation to them. But suddenly she was the adult, and they were the ones who looked like children, innocent and trusting: We always did our best. We thought you loved us for it. How could you expect us to do something, or be something, that was outside our abilities and our comprehension?

"I'm sorry," she said to them. "I do love you." She sank onto the bed, cradled herself as if someone had kicked her, and buried her face in the pillow.

After a while she went into the bathroom to splash cold water on her eyes. In the kitchenette she refilled her teacup and rested her chin on its rim, trying to decide what to do now that she had the truth. It should go to Sam, she thought.

Sam. She had a sudden, sharp desire for his presence. It would have been soothing to tell him everything. To hear his reactions, bounce ideas off him, have him take her hands in his big paws and sympathize because her idol-mother had smashed into ugly pieces. But now it couldn't be soothing, just professional and awkward. Her hands, still cradling the cup, sank to the counter. Her watch showed it was only three hours since he had walked her home.

Tall and trim in his tennis whites, smiling while she joked about her backhand, he had suddenly asked, in a voice both too casual and too earnest, "Think we could do things like this on some kind of regular basis? See each other?"

She had walked on a bit and said, "You don't mean as just friends, do you?"

"No. I don't. Since the divorce I . . . You're the most attractive goddamn woman . . . Christ, I'm lousy at this. It's been twenty-five years since I asked a girl—I mean, a woman—for a date."

She had known she couldn't let silence wedge between them. As soon as she could phrase it, she had said, "I like being with you, Sam. I feel a lot of things for you. But you feel something more than I do. I'm . . . I wish . . . I'm sorry."

Too quickly he had said, "What the hell, Dinah, I understand. I figured it'd be that way." He hesitated. "Can I ask if you're involved with somebody else?"

As clearly as if he'd said the name, she knew whom he meant. Which would hurt him less, yes or no? Which was true? "I'm just . . . not really, Sam."

They had stood in front of the building, neither knowing quite how to leave. She had talked too much, telling him his friendship meant a lot to her, until, when she touched his arm and looked into his face, he had pulled back and said, "Don't apologize, Dinah, dammit. We each feel what we feel, and that's that."

She sighed, lifted her teacup again, and wished that things, a lot of things, could be different.

Ten minutes later she was still standing at the counter, staring into space with the tea cooling between her hands, when the apartment door opened.

A suitcase appeared, followed by Cassie, in jeans. She stopped when she saw Dinah. "Oh. Hi. I called just before lunch but you were out."

"Playing tennis."

Cassie grimaced and put the suitcase down. "It wasn't going to work."

"What wasn't?"

"The thing with the stage manager. Gorgeous on the outside but inside, not Mr. Nice."

"I'm sorry." Dinah heard herself add, "He sounds like my father."

"Yeah? Well, anyway, I decided there was no point in hanging around when— What do you mean, like your father? I never heard you talk about him that way."

"I mean my natural father."

"You found out who he is?"

"Yes."

"So?" For a moment Cassie looked her usual, belligerently friendly self. Then she added carefully, "I mean, if you want to tell me."

"Sure." But as she said it, Dinah knew she didn't want to tell Cass the whole story, although she needed to tell it to someone. It was lodged in her throat, demanding air. She put down her cup and said lightly, "My father was a tall, handsome blond going to college on the GI Bill. He had a summer fling with Vardis and backed away when she got pregnant."

"Refused to marry her, you mean?"

"I don't think it got that far. As soon as he heard, he disappeared."

"I see. A prince." Cassie pulled off her sweater and sat down. "And this was . . . you're thirty-one? Thirty-two years ago? Jesus. It was rough then, for unwed mothers. You didn't just walk around pregnant and then go showing the kid off. I remember hearing that one of my older cousins got pregnant during the war. The family went into shock, like she'd committed murder, and shipped her off someplace in the Midwest to hide till she had it. She gave the baby up for adoption and everybody pretended it never happened. But her grandfather—do you believe this?— refused to speak to her and cut her out of his will." Cassie shook her head. "So, tell me. Did Vardis give you up to avoid a scandal?"

"That was part of it." Dinah swallowed back the rest.

"How'd you learn all this?"

"From her sister-in-law. They were roommates at the time."

Cassie tucked up a leg. "So how do you feel?" she said in concern.

Dinah looked at her: untidy blond hair, intense brown eyes. Too casual about too many things, yet devoted to people and things she cared about. Were there so many people who cared about her, Dinah thought, who had shared some important part of her life, that she should fight with one of them? If Cassie slept around too much, that wasn't evil. Evil was wanting to kill your child.

"I'm glad you're back, Cassie," she said. "I need you around."

"Yeah, well, I need you too. I mean, here I was in bed with this stage manager, and I looked at him and thought, I don't even like this guy. How come I didn't find that out before we hit the sack? Maybe Dinah's got something. I mean, how much fun is sex if you're having it with a jerk?" Dinah laughed. "But don't get all excited. I mean, I'm not going to turn into a nun or anything."

"What a relief."

"Well!" Cassie clapped her hands. "How about some food? It's after five—we could go to Fat Wong's for sweet-and-sour pork while you tell me everything you learned from Vardis Wolf's sister-in-law."

Dinah considered it for a moment, but Cassie was not the one she needed now. "I'd like to, but I can't," she said. "I've got to go see somebody."

There was a guard in the lobby of the building, who said Mr. Mathias wasn't expecting any visitors. But finally he agreed to ring up and say she was there.

"OK," he reported when he hung up the phone. "Mr. Mathias say to come up. You take elevator back there."

It went up so slowly that she was aware of no motion, only the racing of her heart.

When the door opened, Cary stood there. She had forgotten how tall he was, how brown his eyes were, how thick his hair.

"Am I interrupting something?" she asked.

"Nothing that can't wait."

"I would have called first, but your number's unlisted."

"I should have given it to you. Come in." He started to reach for her arm but pulled back, and gestured to the open door across from the elevator. She went in, aware of him behind her.

It was after six o'clock, but the light was still bright, coming at her from windows on three sides. She walked around slowly. The furniture was contemporary and sparse. The room's real furnishings seemed to be the views from its many windows and the plants that formed living green curtains.

There was a large couch upholstered in pale Indian cotton. He'd been sitting there, reading some documents that lay on the coffee table. Piano music came at low volume from hidden speakers.

"Schubert?" she asked.

"Right. The B-flat Sonata."

She started to walk to the other end of the room but turned back. "I came to talk about something I learned. To tell you you were right."

He came around the couch, limping slightly. "I can't just look at you. I have to touch you." He put his hands on her forearms, but she resisted. "You don't want to be touched?"

"You know I do," she said, barely audible.

"But?"

"We should talk."

"Why? Am I going to learn things that will make me hate your voice? And your mouth? Am I going to say things that will turn those wonderful gray eyes hostile instead of—"

"Maybe," she said.

"Then, goddammit, let's at least have something to regret!"

Voices clamored in her mind—caution's, and her own, and then Sam's—but Cary's mouth closed over the sounds, and when his arms brought their bodies together, there was silence except for the Schubert sonata and some greedy noises that could have come from either of them, or both.

They sank onto the couch together. She had her hands in his hair, which was coarse, but when she felt him touch the skin of her back, she slid her fingers down, under the light sweater he wore, under a T-shirt; below the wiry curls of chest hair his skin was taut and smooth. It didn't matter that she still had doubts, because there was the pleasure of letting his hands brush them away. To feel desire for a man's body rising again was sweeter than she could have believed. She had come to him as a single, unbroken, unfeeling surface, but she was turning into a crystal with endless facets, each one able to feel the pressure of his lips in a slightly different way. A dozen places on her skin, then a hundred, needed his touch.

He pulled away from her, as if to ask a question. She couldn't think what it might be, but she said yes anyway.

He smiled and whispered, "Do you mind the light?" She shook her head. Looking oddly boyish, he pulled off his sweater and T-shirt. She didn't think she could wait the moments it would take until she could feel her breasts bare against his chest, and then all of his hard, tall body. Once she thought, dimly, that she was being too greedy, but his moans told her otherwise. And she didn't care anyway. She *was* greedy. Shuddering the moment he entered her, and again, and again, all of her reduced to a delicious progression of explosions.

When the blood receded from her ears, she heard him saying her name, against her neck. In the background there was still piano music, and evening light from many windows. She wished everything else would stay away—the room, the evening, and the world they were attached to.

But the sonata ended and the light grew a shade paler. She sat up.

Cary held on to her arm. "Don't say anything yet. Please. I want to take you up to see something."

It was so lovely—trees and shrubs and flowers silhouetted against the river and the sky—that words would have been superfluous. The best tribute was silence.

"For days I've been thinking of showing it to you," Cary said. The restlessness she had always seen in him was gone. They walked along a row of birches and delicate maples, to a rose garden, then to a greenhouse of orchids. "The computer is my gardener," he explained. "There are sensors on the leaves of certain plants that detect when their pores, in effect, close. That's a signal they need water. Other sensors check the humidity and the temperature, and some go right into the pots to check the alkalinity or acidity of the soil. All that information is fed into the computer, which is programmed to water or fertilize or adjust the pH whenever necessary. During the winter the ornamental tubs could freeze and crack, so there are automatic heating cables to keep the temperature just above freezing."

"You designed it all yourself?" Dinah asked.

"I finished the basic program about five years ago, but I keep tinkering to see if I can make it better yet."

"Are you going to market it?"

"I like the idea that it's just for me."

"But it must be terrifically expensive."

"When I want something badly enough," he said, "price is no object." He put a hand on the back of her neck.

She looked at him, and everything that had been pushed aside earlier came rushing back. She touched his face. "Are you ready to listen to me now?"

"It's so damn peaceful. Being here. Having you here. Do you really have to change it all?"

"Yes."

He sighed. "OK. Let's sit over there."

Against the low wall was an ornate wrought-iron bench, its design formed of a woman's profile and flowing head of hair. He leaned back into the bench and exhaled deeply. How close would he let her come to him? Dinah wondered. Harry had let her come very close.

"You don't know anything about how I was born and given up?" she asked.

"I didn't even know you existed." He smiled. "More's the pity. The day you went to see Con, when we talked afterwards and you showed me the birth certificate, that was the first I heard of any of it."

"Merle Rostov knew all about it. She came to see me today, and told me."

Tension slid over him like armor. "Merle went to see you? Why?"

"She hadn't been returning my calls, but suddenly she phoned and asked to come to my place. I think it was because I'd been to see her daughter."

"Ah." He gripped the arm of the bench. "And you got Merle to tell you what you wanted to know? Just like that?"

"Not just like that. But I think she wanted to tell me. To tell somebody, after all these years. I think it was a relief to her. Anyway . . . she told me. And I want to tell you."

She clasped her hands and began, looking not at him or the garden or the sky but at places and people so vivid in her mind that she seemed to have known them. And in a way she had, so maybe the memories did exist, stored within her in a wordless reservoir: the fifth-floor walk-up with a tub in the kitchen, the voice struggling to regain its prebirth glory, the couch she had lain beside in an orange crate, the pillow lifted above her and held there . . .

"Jesus," she heard Cary say, but she didn't look at him, just went on telling, about the walk toward the river, and the vacant, stinking lot, and looking up at a night sky and a bony face, and a brick.

Her hands were locked so tightly on her arms that they hurt.

She made them fall into her lap. A plane sailed overhead, tiny and high. She watched it until the jet noise faded, then told the rest: the arguments between Merle and Vardis, at the time and just before Vardis married Conrad.

When she finished, Cary was staring ahead, a muscle in his jaw swelling up into a knob. "I can't believe it," he said flatly.

"But you're the one who told me she was a killer! That's what I came to tell you—that you were right."

"I can't believe Merle didn't tell us. How could she keep it to herself? Jesus. But wait a minute, Con knew. Did she tell Con?" He wasn't looking at Dinah; the questions were not for her.

"Then you think Merle Rostov told me the truth?"

He turned to her in surprise.

"You didn't even question it for a moment?"

"It explains so many things," he said.

Dinah put her head in her hands. "I guess now I have to accept the other things you told me, too, and try to understand them. Like saying she needed to have power over other people." He was silent. "If you want power over people," she said, "I guess you're not looking at them as equals. So you can come to see them as dispensable."

"Look at history, Dinah. Look at every dictator who ever lived."

"But Vardis spoke out against dictatorships! Crusaded against them! Are you saying that was all an act?"

"No," he said slowly, "I'm positive it wasn't."

She lifted her head. "Then how could she—"

"I don't know how, Dinah. Maybe when we talk about people like her—extraordinary people—we can never really understand them. Maybe all we can do is observe what they are."

"But what *was* she? An artist who was also a killer?" The words wouldn't stay calm. Hurt and anger pushed them out. "All right, her career would have been harder with an illegitimate child. But . . . to try to kill it? How can I accept that?"

Cary dug his fingers into his thighs. "I suppose if she felt that her art was the overpoweringly important thing . . . if she thought it was her only way of, I don't know, of being in control, or important, or loved, or something like that . . . then nothing could be allowed to stand in its way. And the child . . . you . . . stood in the way."

Behind and below them a tug hooted on the river.

"I can't forget the story you told me," Dinah said. "About how she sang the *Kindertotenlieder* when it wasn't part of her repertoire or even ideal for her voice. Why would she do that? Why would she sing a lament for dead children unless she wanted to use her artistry to make some kind of atonement?"

"I don't know."

"And she never would sing *Medea*. Hannah Sebastian mentioned that once."

"And you think maybe it all means that she felt guilty for having tried to kill her own child?"

"You don't think so, do you?"

"I don't know what it means, Dinah. Honest to God, I don't."

The clouds over the river began to turn a deeper, more metallic blue.

"When you told me how she treated people in the Wolfpack," Dinah said, "I tried to use her talent to excuse her. Even what she did to Conrad—part of me was still saying, OK, it was wrong, but we're talking about Vardis Wolf, not just anybody." She added wonderingly, "And I'm still thinking that if she felt guilt and remorse over me, maybe she wasn't so terrible after all. I'm . . . My God."

"What's the matter?"

"I wasn't willing to draw the line at her being cruel to people, so I wind up wanting to excuse her for trying to murder *me*. One thing led to the other, didn't it?"

"I think maybe it always does," he said.

"If you let them get away with something, eventually you'll let them get away with . . . anything."

He reached for her hand.

She clung to his, but she had to pull away. "Maybe I'll never understand Vardis. But there's one thing I'm sure I know."

"What's that?"

"You didn't kill her."

He looked away.

"It was Merle Rostov. She had the strongest motives."

She waited but there was no answer, only the hard lines of his profile and the muscle in his jaw swelling and releasing, swelling and releasing.

"Cary, don't lie to me anymore. Please. Stop claiming you're the one who killed Vardis because I know you're not."

"You don't know anything," he said softly.

"I know who killed her, but that's not the biggest mystery. The biggest mystery is why all four of you are claiming you did it. Why is Hannah Sebastian willing to lie for the person who killed her idol? Why is Conrad Ashley willing to claim he killed his own wife, the artist he worshiped? What is Merle Rostov to you that you're willing to risk a murder charge for her?"

He rose abruptly. "The light is going. It's close to eight o'clock."

She looked up at him, remembering the scent of his body, the feel of his skin. "I should go," she said. "I've got papers to grade."

They walked in silence through the garden and down the stairs into the apartment. The couch, still rumpled, mocked them.

When they stopped at the door, he asked, "What are you going to do?"

"About what?"

"About who you think is guilty."

"I don't know. How can I turn Merle Rostov in? She saved my life, Cary. Don't I owe something . . . everything . . . to the woman who saved my life?"

His eyes grew darker. "Now you know what I feel."

"What do you mean? Cary, what does that mean?"

He shook his head, then lifted his right hand and touched her cheek.

She gripped his wrist. "Tell me what you meant!"

"I can't."

"Yes, you can! Tell me why you all say you killed Vardis. Tell me why *you* say it! Don't you know what you're doing to me? You ask me to believe you committed murder, and when I learn you're innocent, you still . . . You're cheating the law and you won't even tell me why! How do you expect me to feel about people who cheat the law? Who protect a murderer? I'm a cop's widow, remember? A cop who was . . . How can I feel this way about someone who . . ." Her throat closed; she had to stop.

"I can't tell you," he said.

She willed him to keep looking at her. She realized he wanted to cry. But that was another thing he couldn't do.

"I have to go," she said.

At home, she forced herself to correct papers because they had to be done and she couldn't stop being conscientious. If the world was falling apart—and it was—she would sit in the rubble doing what had to be done. Because that was the way she was, and you could only be what you were. Cassie had said, "You want to talk?" but had accepted her no and retreated into a book.

She worked doggedly, trying to make herself feel angry—over the mistakes or the spelling or her own failure to get better results or a system that allowed functional illiterates to go to college—or sorry for the students who wouldn't get a grade and would have to repeat the course if they wanted to stay in school. By eleven she had finished half the papers, and had felt nothing.

How could you stay in a career, she thought, that made you feel nothing?

She lifted her head, waiting for some inner rebellion, or at least confusion. But there was only relief. Strange how simple things could be, if they were right.

"Cass," she said, "I won't be doing this much longer. Grading papers."

"Great. How about I make some popcorn?"

"No, I mean I'm going to quit teaching."

"Well, Lord sound thy trumpets! How come? What made you decide?"

"I guess I just realized that you were right. It's not making me happy. And then . . . I planned it with Harry, you know, that I should be a teacher. I think maybe I've been living as if he was alive. Unwilling to let go of him or of anything we planned together."

"Ah, kid," Cass said, and was hugging her when the phone rang.

"I'll get it," she said. She ran into the bedroom to answer, sure it would be Cary.

"Dinah?" Sam said. And after a pause, "Are you all right?"

"Fine." She swung her head. "How are you, Sam?"

"Oh . . . kind of sorry about this afternoon. I didn't mean to put you on the spot like that, I just wanted to . . . Well, never mind. I just hope I didn't ruin a friendship. I'd still like us to get together once in a while. For old times' sake."

She could see him clearly: blue eyes intent, red hair lopping over one of them. She said, "I'll want to as long as you do, Sam."

He paused. "Did Merle Rostov show up this afternoon?"

"Yes." For once she was glad of the caution Sam's investigation forced on him. He would feel he couldn't probe for information she didn't volunteer. "I can't talk about it just now," she said. "I'll call you when I can. OK?"

"Sure," he said. She could see him frowning. "Sure."

She hung up, hating herself for cutting him off that way after hounding him from the beginning, getting him to tell her more than he should, involving him at each step of her own search. But she couldn't talk to him until she decided what to do about Merle.

And she couldn't decide that until she had found out everything.

CHAPTER
20

After her morning class she had tea at a donut shop on Broadway, instead of lunch, and went straight over to the East Seventies, to the Dolan Company.

The receptionist was cool and practiced. "Is Dr. Sebastian expecting you?"

"No. But I must see her. Tell her it's an important personal matter."

The woman's nails were so long that she had to hold her hands as if they were sterile, but somehow she managed to press a button on her intercom and pick up her phone. She turned back to Dinah with a glint of satisfaction. "Dr. Sebastian will be unable to see you."

"If she's busy, I can wait. As long as it takes."

"I'm afraid Dr. Sebastian will have no time at all for you today. She made that quite clear."

Dinah thought for a moment. There was no listing in the phone book for Hannah; if she waited outside the building at the end of the day, she could catch her then. Or follow her home and confront her there. Or she could try something else.

She smiled at the receptionist. "What a shame. I'll have to try to reach Dr. Sebastian at her apartment. I'm the daughter of an old friend of hers."

The woman looked bored.

Dinah started to the door. But halfway there, she staggered and crashed into one of the chairs. "Oh no!" she cried, and collapsed to the floor. "Oh, please . . . Help me!"

The receptionist came around the desk. "What's wrong?"

"It's my legs—please—some water to take my pills . . ."

"I'll call one of our doctors."

"Thank you. But my pills first— If I don't take them right away, the pain will— Please!"

The woman hesitated, then ran through the doors behind her desk.

As soon as she was out of sight, Dinah leaped up and raced through the same doors. The woman had gone to the left, so she went right.

In the center of the floor was a curved metal staircase. A man was coming up, reading a sheaf of papers. "Dr. Sebastian?" Dinah asked. Without looking up the man said, "Downstairs, third door on the right, past Tissue Culture."

The lower floor was the laboratory itself, a cool, pale world of glass and stainless steel. Dinah found the door and knocked sharply.

"What is it?"

Dinah said nothing.

"I'm busy now. Please come back later."

Dinah gripped the doorknob, turned it, and went in.

Hannah Sebastian, sitting at a desk, blinked in surprise, which her glasses magnified into fear. "But I said I couldn't see you."

Everything in the small office was tight with compulsive neatness, except Hannah herself. Her white-blond hair sagged from the rubber band that was supposed to hold it, her lab coat was buttoned crookedly, and her fingers played with the edges of a pile of papers. She looked like what Dinah hoped she would be —the weakest link of the four friends. The one most likely to break, because she had worshiped Vardis the most blindly.

Dinah said, "I'm sorry to come in on you this way, but I have to talk to you. I know you claim you killed Vardis Wolf. But I've learned the truth. I know who really did it."

In the pale skin below Hannah's left eye a vein jerked. "What do you mean?" she whispered. "What do you know?"

Dinah pushed aside the pity she felt. "I know that Merle Rostov killed Vardis Wolf. And I know why."

"Oh, no," Hannah said. "No."

Someone rapped imperiously on the door. A man called, "Dr. Sebastian."

Hannah didn't answer; she didn't even seem to have heard.

The door opened. The receptionist stood there, with a man who said, "Dr. Sebastian, I'm told this woman got in without permission. Shall I see that she leaves?"

The gentle, precise manner Hannah had once had reappeared for a moment, like a ghost. "No. It's all right."

"Are you sure? I know you haven't been feeling well lately, and I—"

"It's all right," Hannah repeated.

The door closed reluctantly. Hannah put two thin fingers up under her glasses, touched the jerking vein, and brought them down again.

"Merle Rostov came to see me yesterday," Dinah said. "She told me everything. I know you didn't kill Vardis, nor did Cary or Conrad. Merle did it."

Hannah shook her head violently. A loop of hair swung out of the rubber band and hung over her ear. "That's not possible. Merle wouldn't have lied to us. Never!"

Excitement and caution rose together in Dinah's throat. What was it that Merle had lied about?

She thought for a moment. Carefully she asked, "Did Merle tell you how I was born? Because she knows all about it. Oh, yes. She told me the story yesterday. How Vardis had an affair here in New York. Before you and the others left Cross of Glory." Hannah made a muffled protest. "Oh, yes, I know all about Cross of Glory. How the four of you and Vardis went there from the war."

"Merle wouldn't tell you that!"

"Are you sure? She told me about Vardis's affair, which she's kept a secret from all of you. If she could do that, she could lie to you about other things."

"No, she wouldn't. Mila . . . How could she say we had to save him if she was the one who did it herself? She wouldn't. Never! Why would she say we had to save *him?*"

Dinah's hands went icy with caution. "Save Conrad, you mean? But that was a lie."

"She said he confessed to killing Vardis! She said we had to use the Pact to save him!"

"But Merle is the one who killed Vardis. I swear it to you, in Vardis's name."

"No," Hannah whispered. "No. *Jeden za všechny a všichni za jednoho....* To kill Vardis and then use the Pact ... She said we were going to be all right ... She said it ..." Hannah began to make choking, retching sounds, as if she were being pulled inside out through her throat.

Dinah went around the desk to her. She touched the pale hair, then put her arms around Hannah. The woman's body was bony and frail and sexless, as if she were very old. Yet it seemed to Dinah that she was comforting a child.

Finally the choking sounds diminished.

Dinah said, "Let me get you some water."

Hannah sighed. "Please."

Dinah brought back three paper cups filled from a cooler down the hall. Hannah drank two without stopping. She laid her thin hands on the desk and stared at them as if they had no connection to her.

Dinah covered them with her own. "I know everything else," she said. "So I must know about the Pact, too. Mustn't I?"

Hannah sighed again.

There were no times before the Bad Times.

Ah, well, perhaps there were, but who could remember them?

Memory itself began with feeling hungry and afraid. Hunger was easier than fear because hunger was your own, lodged in your belly—gnawing as loud after meals as before them, because meals were nearly always the same and never enough. Soup of potatoes and carrots, simmered in the black pot on the cast-iron stove, with a taste of meat in it as faint as hope, and black bread that got grayer as time went on. Still, hunger was easier because you could understand it and know what would fix it. Fear was hard because it was everywhere, all the time, and there was no way to plug it up with soup and gray bread, even for a moment.

Some days the fear would squeeze Papa's and Mama's faces like a big hand. The two of them would whisper to each other, and the word *Germans* would hang in the air like the smell of rotting potatoes. The Germans, Hana knew, had caused both the fear and the hunger. She had seen two of them once. They had come banging on the door of the farmhouse, calling out "Police" and demanding to know, in strange accents, if any Jews were hiding inside. They had shoved in, smelling of metal and wool and sweat, and as they poked everywhere, even shining their flashlight into the stove, they talked of "Protektor" Heydrich. Hana knew who he was. After Germany took away parts of Bohemia and Moravia for itself, it called what was left a "Protektorate" and put the man named Heydrich in charge.

The two Germans hadn't stayed long, but the frightening thing was that they had laughed and smiled. If devils could smile, then God could cry. One of them had patted Hana's blond hair. Mama had gone as stiff as a broom, but the German had only smiled. Then they had taken the last of the chickens, laughing when Mama tried to protest. Papa told her never to open her mouth again to such people, she was lucky they hadn't killed her or done worse. And what if they had found out about Hana's older brother, who was with the underground?

Not long afterward Papa said that the underground had attacked "Protektor" Heydrich. They had leaped on his car with a bomb, and he had been wounded, taken to a Prague hospital. The enraged Germans were combing the countryside, looking for the assassins.

The next night when Papa came up to the house for supper, he opened the door, his face dark and heavy, and shoved two sacks in front of him. "Found them in the granary," he said to Mama. The sacks stirred and began to stand up. They had legs and arms. They were a girl about eleven and a boy maybe a year older than Hana, about seven. Straw clung to them and to clothes that were dirty but looked expensive. "They are Miroslava and Konrád," Papa said. "They say they have walked from Prague. Give them some supper."

The two ate in silence, hazel eyes staring out warily from faces that had the same bone structure, lips making no noise with the soup even though it went down as if they were starving. When they finished, the girl said, "Thank you very much." The boy added, "It was good," and smiled at Hana.

Papa asked, "Are you running away from Prague?" The girl nodded yes. "Because you are Jews?"

The girl looked at him, trying to size him up. When she spoke, you could tell she came from the city. "My father is Jewish, but we are not religious."

Papa looked at the wooden cross hanging on the far wall. "With us you do not need to lie about your religion."

"It's not a lie," the girl said. "We don't go to the synagogue. My father is an engineer. He builds bridges. One night he didn't come home. We didn't know where they had taken him. My mother tried to find out, but one day when we got home from school, she was gone herself, and none of the neighbors knew why or where. My brother and I stayed in the house for a month, but there wasn't enough food or money, and the streets were always full of police. So I decided we should sneak away and go to our cousins Karel and Matyáš, who live in Lidice. But there were always German soldiers on the road. We had to hide so many times that I lost the way. We've been walking for a long time. My brother is tired."

"I am all right," the boy said stoutly. He looked at Hana and smiled again. His teeth were very white and his smile made her want to go closer to him.

"Can you tell us how to get to Lidice?" the girl asked.

"It is not too far," Papa said. "In a week or so I can take you there. In the meantime you will stay here."

But he kept saying there were too many Germans on the roads to travel. One day he announced, "Heydrich has died. Now the Germans will . . ." He sighed.

Not long after that he came in with his face so hard that Hana shrank against the wall. "Lidice is gone," he said. Mama stared. "Yes, gone. All the men shot. All the women and children deported. Not a cat or a cow left. Everything burned to the ground. As if it never was." He swallowed hard and looked at the two children from Prague. "I am sorry." In a strange croak he added, "My mother was born in Lidice."

No one could speak. Mama put her apron over her face. At last the girl—her nickname was Mila—asked, "Why did it happen? Why is Lidice gone?"

"Reprisal. For Heydrich. The underground killed our 'Protektor,' so the Germans kill Lidice. One town in exchange for one man. Butchers!" Papa wiped his nose with his hand.

"Oh my God, Jan," Mama said. She went to Papa and they held

on to each other. Fear was as strong in the room as boiling
cabbage.

Mila took her brother's hand. "Would you like us to go now?"
Hana thought of the house without them. Mila so lively and
pretty, not just a peasant girl like her, but someone different and
exciting. And Konrád with his dreamy look that made you want
to crawl inside his head and share the dream. Behind her back
Hana crossed her fingers, on both hands.

Mama looked up at Papa, begging him, only you couldn't tell
for what.

"You cannot go now," he said. "You will stay and live with us."

"Forever?" asked Konrád.

"Until the war is over," Papa said. "That is forever enough.
But no one can know you are here. You must stay inside, as you
have been doing. If anyone comes, you must hide in the attic."

Sometimes Mila looked as if she thought they should leave
anyway, but Papa kept bringing news of more German reprisals because they couldn't find Heydrich's killers: over two hundred murdered besides those at Lidice. And when he said that
the Germans had destroyed another entire village, Levzsaky, in
the south, Mila seemed to accept that she and Konrád must re-
main.

In the other room of the house, next to the kitchen, were two
beds besides Papa and Mama's. Mila shared one with Hana, and
Konrád slept in the other, which belonged to Hana's brother,
who was away with the underground. It was good to curl against
Mila; she was like a second skin keeping out the fear. In bitter
weather Konrád crawled into the bed too, and the three of them
nested like spoons.

Once Mila said, "In Prague we each had our own bedroom, and
we had a piano in the parlor." But most of the time she didn't talk
about their life in Prague. She asked questions instead. She
wanted to know how everything was done: how Mama used
acorns to make coffee and flour, how the cow was kept alive,
where the seed stock was hidden. She asked a lot about the Germans, what they said and did, and would they have destroyed the
villages if they had found the people who killed Heydrich. Papa
answered as if she were an adult, even telling her about the
underground—how they had switched to guerrilla warfare and
were living mostly in the mountains. More than once he mut-

tered to Mama, "That Mila is a smart one." But he told her she thought about Lidice and Levzsaky too much.

Time went by. The soup got thinner, the bread grayer and stickier, and the weather warmer. It was harder for Konrád and Mila to stay in, especially when the birds and the sun came out just as if there were no war.

The last morning was like that: warm and sunny, the woods beckoning, the fear napping at the back of your mind.

Out of the dazzling blue sky Papa ran in to say there were Germans coming, quick, quick, up to the attic, yes, Hana, you too. The three of them were still clambering up when a car roared into the yard, the noise vibrating in their throats. In the attic was a big, humpbacked trunk. Mila shoved Konrád and Hana down into the moldy smell, threw a blanket over them, and shut the lid.

The smell was thick and choking, but the sounds were worse. Men's voices, angry. Crashes and thumps, as if everything in the house was being thrown on the floor. A voice that would have been Mama's except it was high and squawky like a chicken's and there weren't any chickens anymore. Anyway, it cut off in midair. A string of gunshots. The car roaring again, and then silence, as heavy and putrid as the blanket shoved in your mouth. Silence so long you had to whisper that you were going to pee, you couldn't help it, and Konrád whispered "Me too," and the water ran out hot with relief and shame, pee and tears together.

The smell in the trunk grew sharp. Days seemed to go by before the lid lifted and Mila said softly, "Come out." But it wasn't even night yet. The sun was just setting.

"Where did you hide?" Konrád asked her.

"In the rafters. I could see and hear everything."

Downstairs all the furniture was tossed about and the stuffing from the mattresses spilled out like guts on butchering day. In one corner of the kitchen, against a wall, there was a large, blanket-covered pile. From one end a heavy, familiar boot stuck out. "Don't look!" Mila said. She pulled the blanket down over the boot. That made something appear at the other end of the pile: a familiar blue-and-white kerchief. Hana's mouth formed syllables but could make no sound. Mila put her arms around her. "I'm sorry," she whispered. "I tried to cover them, but . . . Don't try to look, Hana. Please. Here, I know what you can do. The crucifix is still on the wall. You can put it with them." She brought it over. "Lay it on the blanket."

Hana did and turned around, bewildered, looking for the world she had always known.

"Now we must get ready to leave," Mila said.

"Where are we going?" Konrád asked.

"To hide. We can't stay here. I heard the Germans talk about your brother in the underground, Hana. That's why they came —reprisal. Hurry now, we must take what food and clothes we can carry."

That was how it began: three children, each carrying a bundle, creeping from a farmyard at twilight.

Before it ended, over two years went by.

At first, while the weather was warm, they managed fairly well. By day they stayed in the woods, among spruces they came to know so well they gave them names, like "Blue Beauty" and "Nine Hundred Needles." There was the frequent sound of gunfire between partisans and Germans, sometimes near, and of trucks roaring on the roads, so they hid either in the trees or, if it rained, under a shelter of branches and leaves. When it seemed safe, they hunted for nuts and berries and sweet grass, or found a pool of sun to sit in and talk: about life in Prague, for Konrád would speak about it even though Mila said little, or about why people were making the war happen, or about Hana's brother and how they might find him. After a while, Hana began to talk about Mama and Papa, too.

At night they wandered away from the woods, needing to move and to supplement their dwindling food reserves. Once they stole into a chicken coop and managed to grab four eggs before the squawking woke someone, but in the dash back to safety two of the eggs broke. Mila made Konrád and Hana eat the remaining two. "I am not hungry," she insisted, lying just as Mama would have done. Except for being so pretty, she was like Mama in other ways: going ahead to check things, taking charge of how and what they ate, making sure they washed every time they found a stream or a pond, putting her arms around them at night. "We are going to be all right," she said, so often that they all believed it.

"Aren't you afraid?" Hana once asked. "Of course," she said, "but I am older. I am twelve." At the time, that was a satisfactory explanation.

They had two blankets and a coat for each of them—with a knife Mila had cut down Mama's and Papa's coats for Konrád and herself—but when the weather turned cold, they started to shiver at night, no matter how closely they huddled. "We will have to find a place to live for a while," Mila said, so matter-of-factly that it seemed possible. They started traveling at night if the roads were quiet, trying to head south because Hana had a vague idea that's where her brother was. They skirted small villages and stole into stables and haystacks to sleep; they felt numb all over, from their icy feet up, except in their gnawing bellies. One frozen red dawn, when the crowing of cocks warned them to leave the granary they had found at the edge of a village, Konrád said he couldn't go on. Mila was arguing with him, in a whisper like angry straw, when the old woman found them.

She moved slowly on thick legs wrapped in rags, and she smelled like an unused cupboard, but she let them stay there in the granary under the hay and even gave them some old horse blankets. She gave them soup, too, and when Mila begged to wash, she let them all into her kitchen to bathe in a wooden tub. She studied their bodies, which had grown so thin they all stared at the sight of one another, and she carefully examined Konrád's penis, muttering to herself. Hana had to sit with one leg out of the tub; her shoe wouldn't come off; frostbite had swollen her foot. When they were clean, the old woman took a knife and made a nick in the doorjamb. "Once a month you will bathe. Each time I will make a mark, and we will know how long you are here." She gave them bread every morning and let them come into the kitchen to eat and sit by the stove. At night she would often spread newspapers on the table, comb lice out of her long gray hair, and squash them with her fingernails as they hit the paper.

Early one morning, when there were three nicks on the doorjamb, she came hobbling out to the granary and said they must leave at once, now, yes, now! "You cannot be here! The Germans are coming!" Her rheumy eyes drooled terror. The three of them flung their things into bundles and ran.

They were too late. Cars and trucks were roaring into the village, toward the square. Mila looked around wildly, saw a chicken coop in a courtyard, and pulled them all into it. By the grace of God it was empty, and they lay in the dust and feathers, watching through the slats as the Germans went from house to house, dragging people out and ordering them into the square. The men were separated from the women.

Hana understood little German, but Mila whispered, "They say someone who comes from the village blew up a railroad station, and if they do not find him, all the men will be killed." The women and children began to shout and sob. "No one is saying where the man is," Mila whispered. The Germans lined the men up and shot them. The air filled with horrible sounds: people screaming, dogs howling, even the birds seemed to go mad. You could not tell whether it was worse to shut your eyes, or to see.

The three of them lay clinging to one another in the chicken dirt. Their bodies seemed to be the only island of safety in a world of horror. "We are going to be all right," Mila whispered. If she could say it, Hana thought, then they would have to try to believe it. When it grew dark, they crept out of the coop and through the town, which was as quiet as if no one had ever lived there. They reached the edge of a small forest and lay together under a tree, staring back toward the village as if they could still see it.

After a long time Mila said, "It was reprisal. Like Lidice and Levzsaky. That is what the Germans do, but we must not let them do it to us. I have been thinking how we can stop it. We must be as if we are one person: Konrád-Mila-Hana. All one. If one is in trouble, all come to the rescue. If the Germans catch one of us, the others must come forward. So that two of us do not have to watch them kill one of us. And so the Germans will not kill innocent people. Do you understand me? We do everything together. We live together, and if they catch us, we are caught together, too. *Jeden za všechny a všichni za jednoho.* One for all and all for one. That is from a book I used to read in Prague, about three brave men who made a pact and did everything together. We will use their motto and be safe, as they were. Do you understand?" Konrád and Hana said they did. "Then swear," Mila said. As they all put their hands together and said the motto, Hana felt she had never loved anyone as much as Konrád and Mila, not even Mama and Papa and her brother, Frantisek. And she began to feel safer, for now they had a way to deal with the Germans.

They had lost all sense of where they were. Not even sure they were still in their own country, they simply traveled, hunting ceaselessly for food, stealing when they dared, otherwise living on dandelions—quite bitter—and other greens. By trial and error they learned how to catch a rabbit or squirrel occasionally— Konrád got quite good at it—but they didn't dare build a fire, so they ate little. However, Mila tied the skins together for clothing. Most of the fields they saw were badly neglected, and there were no beasts or fowl. Often they passed farms, or even whole villages, that had been burned. The countryside had a sad, charred look, and sometimes a burnt smell would hang in their noses.

Once they nearly stumbled into a clearing, and watched, frozen at its edge, while Germans lined up rows of Jews, shot them, and piled them into three large graves. Only one bullet was used per person, and some of the Jews lay moaning in the graves. Then peasants appeared with axes and began to chop off the fingers wearing rings and the feet wearing boots.

When Hana started choking, Mila put a hand over her mouth and whispered, over and over, "We are going to be all right."

Several days later they came on another scene: a painted gypsy wagon with its horses gone, a man and woman lying in oddly neat pools of their own blood. The woman's skirt was up over her head. She wore no panties. Mila pulled the skirt down; the dead face was twisted in a terrible expression. "Let's look in the cart," Mila said. "There may be food and things we can use."

They found a heavy shawl, a good knife, and a loaf of black bread, which they were tearing into like animals when they heard a noise from one corner of the wagon and saw they had found something else: a boy of perhaps three or four.

Wearing a red shirt and ragged little pants, he crouched behind a trunk, his large brown eyes wet with fear and incomprehension. Gripped by something stronger than hunger—the exultation of finding a living creature—they put down the bread and began to talk softly to him. It was Mila who finally coaxed him out. He took her hand. "We cannot leave him here," she said. "He must come with us." They looked in the trunk and found a coat for the boy, a man's felt hat, and some brightly colored necklaces they didn't take, whose glassy tinkle seemed to come from another world.

When they left, Mila tried to keep the boy away from the corpses beside the cart, but he ran over and started tugging on the dead woman's arm, his face twisting as if to match hers. Mila pulled him away gently. As they scurried off, he kept looking over his shoulder. That night in the woods, as the boy lay beside Mila, Konrád asked, "What shall we call him?" There was a long silence, except for the sound of airplanes, flying low in formation. "I am thinking," Mila said, "of our cousins Karel and Matyáš, in Lidice. Do you remember them?" Konrád said "Yes," but uncertainly. Mila said, "We will call him Karel Matyáš, to help us remember them."

Later she added, "It is a good omen. Because the three men in the book were joined by a fourth man." And she began to tell them stories from the book, as she sometimes did.

It was harder to travel with the boy, except in one way—they never had to worry that he would cry or make sounds to give them away. They all talked to him, especially Mila, who kept explaining that now he was one of four who all had to stand together, but he made no sounds at all. Not even when he had a dreadful blister on his foot, which Mila discovered and bandaged with straw. They began to fear the Germans had found some horrible way to cut out a person's voice.

Because Karel didn't cry, Hana felt she couldn't either—after all, she was older, by three years or so—but she wanted to sob most of the time with hunger.

Instead, she tried to steal something by herself.

It happened the night they crossed a meadow and miraculously found some cows with full teats. Hana knew how to milk them, sending steaming white lines into the felt hat Konrád held out. They passed it among them, drank voraciously before the milk could seep through, and filled the hat again and again. For hours afterward the milk moved around in their stomachs like a heavy bag of warm air. Hana finally threw all of hers up.

By the time they found a barn to hide in, she burned with the feeling that she had been cheated. Through a crack in the wall she stared up at the farmhouse and dreamed that a woman lived there who was fixing sweet dumplings filled with plum jam. The more she knew it wasn't so, the more desperately she had to see. She didn't think she could evade Mila's watchfulness, but Mila was exhausted from carrying Karel because of his blister and slept like a dead thing, clutching him. Konrád slept too, one hand curled on his eyes, the other holding the knife that was his responsibility. His mouth twitched, the way it always did in his sleep.

Hana moved soundlessly, as they had all learned to do.

The farmhouse kitchen was empty. No dumplings, no bread, no meat, none of the things she dreamed of ceaselessly. Only four potatoes in the sink. A sob escaped her. She took the potatoes and moved to the door.

Hands closed on her, and a farmer's hard red face glared in the dawn light. She couldn't understand his words until he switched to her language, with a heavy accent. "Thief! A little Jew thief, I'll bet, who dyes her hair blond!" Hana swung her head wildly, but his fingers dug into her arm like spikes. She dropped the potatoes. They thudded to the floor, and one of them split, enraging the man. "I will teach you to steal! I will take you to the Germans, little Jew thief!" He began shaking her so hard she felt her bones scraping inside her skin. Suddenly he let her go. She flopped to the floor, like the potatoes.

"And who are you?" he demanded. She followed his gaze: Mila and Konrád and Karel stood in the doorway.

"Excuse me, please," said Mila, "but I am also stealing your potatoes." She stepped inside and picked one of them from the floor.

"I am a thief," Konrád said, doing the same.

And while they all stared—Mila, Hana, Konrád, and the farmer—Karel picked up half the broken potato. His baby face broke into a defiant glare.

The farmer took a step backward and scratched his mottled bald head. Finally he said to the other three, "You were hiding?" They nodded. "Why did you not stay where you were?"

"Because we are all potato thieves," Mila said. "So you cannot punish her alone."

The farmer grunted and sank onto a chair. Perhaps he could not grasp that in the midst of war, when to be innocent was to suffer, anyone would step forward and claim guilt. Or perhaps the sight of their loyalty reminded him of a time when no man thought of taking another to the Germans, for he turned to Hana and asked, "These are your friends?" She nodded.

There was silence. Then he grunted again and said harshly,

"Put the potatoes back in the sink. And go, all of you. Far away! Go!"

They threw the potatoes and ran, back to the barn for their bundles and then on to the first cover they could find, where they huddled together, reliving what had happened and hugging Karel.

"Now you are truly one of us," Mila told him.

Konrád said, *"Jeden za všechny a všichni za jednoho."* They took one another's hands, and love flowed among them, each to the next to the next.

They moved on, first in one direction, then in its opposite. They stayed away from the roads, which were more and more crowded with people in carts piled with possessions, soldiers in various uniforms, scrawny men who looked like prisoners. Mila said something must be happening in the war, but they were afraid to ask anyone.

The weather was growing cold again, and their clothes were not only ragged and too small but filthy. They had all begun to itch and scratch, which brought Mila close to tears. "We have lice!" she wailed. Because they had all grown out of their shoes, they tied rags around their feet. It was the rags that caused Karel's accident. He wasn't used to them and tripped over a large root, twisting his leg so hard that sweat beads popped out all over his face. But he still didn't say anything or make a sound. While they freed him, he panted like a little dog. Mila said the leg probably was broken and they must try to straighten it. Karel fainted while she and Konrád worked on it. They made a splint from branches and tied it on with rabbit skins, but of course Karel couldn't walk, and he was getting too big to be carried. They had to find a place to stay for a while.

It seemed a miracle when they found the hole—a small pit gouged out of the earth that needed only a little digging for all of them to be able to fit inside. They made a cover of branches and grass, and each night either Konrád or Hana would stay with Karel while the other went with Mila to forage for food. But the hole grew cold and Karel grew weaker.

"We have to find somebody to help us," Mila said. "I will go looking, by myself, and come back for you as soon as I can."

"But we are together," Hana stammered. "Four-as-one. How can you leave?"

"Because we can't go together, Hanička. So you must be three-as-one until I come back." She held each of them for a moment and kissed them. "We are going to be all right," she said, then wrapped the gypsy shawl around her and left.

Three days went by, and she didn't return. Konrád and Hana kept reading the same thought in each other's eyes—what if the Germans had caught her?—but neither would say it, for fear saying would make it true. Instead they lay huddled with Karel, telling him she would be back soon, or, when it was quiet, they got out of the hole to relieve themselves and to stretch and walk. It was important to keep moving. By the fourth day their hoard of stolen potatoes and carrots was gone. That night Konrád had to go look for food, and when Hana was alone with Karel, a thought began gnawing at her, with the hunger. Suppose Mila had left them? Had found a place and was staying there without telling about the three of them, because people might take in one child but who would take four?

Konrád came back empty-handed. The next night, when he went out again, the fear that Mila had left them became a little animal, burrowing inside Hana with sharp teeth and making her sick. She lay beside Karel, cold and ready to die.

Voices pulled her out of her fog. When she saw Mila, she grabbed her with relief so sharpened by guilt that it hurt. Never again would she doubt Mila. Never, ever, as long as she lived.

Mila had Konrád with her, and also a strange man with a kind, crinkled face who kept shaking his head in disbelief. Hana had a flash of seeing them as he did—skinny, filthy things living in a hole in the ground—but it disappeared in joy when Mila said they were going to stay in his house. The man picked up Karel, and they all trudged after him, carrying the scraps of their belongings.

He was a priest, they learned. Mila had found him after hiding near his village to make sure it held no Germans and then watching his house for two more days before deciding to approach him. He gave them soup and bread—real black bread!—and soap. Their clothes seemed to have grown into their skins and had to be peeled off. He gave them his whole attic to sleep in. He would have brought a doctor to look at Karel's leg, except that Mila protested violently. "Poor child," he said, "has the war left you no trust at all?" He promised not to get the doctor, dressed

Karel's leg as best he could, and gave him some medicines that made him feel better.

Most miraculous of all, he had known Hana's brother. The news was bad, though: The Germans had killed Frantisek. But the priest told stories of how brave he had been and how he had never stopped working for freedom.

Karel's leg began to heal, and all of them began to look better. Their skin lost the red, bleary look that came from too much cold and too little food. The priest gave them some books and a few precious sheets of paper, so Mila could read and the rest of them could learn something of their letters. They were worried about missing their education. Even Karel, still too young for school, picked up their concern. The priest told them of the war and its progress: The Allies had come to help, the Red Army was pushing west to meet them, and, God be praised, it seemed the war would end, perhaps by summer.

So they couldn't believe it when the Germans came to the house.

There were three soldiers and an officer. In the middle of the night they crashed into the house, dragged the priest from his bed, and accused him of helping the Reich's enemies. "They know we are here!" Mila whispered. They all huddled over a crack in the attic floor, unable to accept what they saw or to move.

But Mila was wrong. The Germans were after a radio, which they found after smashing the bookcase, and some guns and ammunition they brought up from the cellar. They were about to leave, taking the priest, when the officer spotted the attic entrance. He barked at his men. Two soldiers climbed up, grabbed the four of them, and threw them down like so many rag dolls.

The priest said in German, "They know nothing about anything. They are my nieces and nephews. All good Catholics." His eyes tried to give them courage.

The officer smiled. "You keep your nieces and nephews in the attic? In rags? And one is blond, one is as dark as a gypsy, and the other two . . . ?" To Konrád he said, "Are you a good Catholic?"

Konrád hesitated. "Yes."

"Where were you baptized?"

"In Prague."

"What church?"

He hesitated too long. The officer said, "We will see how good a Catholic you are. Take down your pants."

The trousers, cut down from an old pair of the priest's, slid to the floor as if they had fainted.

The officer laughed. "The good Catholic has been circumcised."

There was no way to argue, nothing to do but stare at Konrád's shanks, which looked blue in the light and thin as slats, and to choke with how much you loved him. "Pull up your pants, Jew," the officer said. "You are coming with us. Get going!"

The soldiers moved toward him.

"Wait!" Mila cried, blocking their way. "Can't you see that we are brother and sister? That I am also Jewish? You must take me, too."

The officer looked startled, and a bit annoyed. He spoke to his soldiers so rapidly that Hana couldn't get the words.

She took a breath and said, as loudly as she could, "So am I."

"Hana," the priest whispered, "in God's name save yourself. You are Catholic, I know it! Tell them the truth."

For a moment Hana saw the kitchen of her old home, and Mila placing a cross on a pile covered by a blanket. A sudden, terrible sadness flew at her, but she clenched her fists. "I am Jewish."

The officer muttered, something about his daughter and how Hana looked like her. "Do not be foolish," he said to her.

"I am Jewish," she said fiercely.

"I am too," said a high voice they had never heard before, almost a squeak. They hardly realized it was a voice at all. It had come from Karel.

"You are a dirty gypsy," said one of the soldiers. He raised his hand and slapped Karel's face with the back of it. He must have worn some kind of ring, for blood welled up on Karel's cheek.

Karel staggered backward, but he clutched his cheek and said, "I am Jewish, too. We are all together, the same."

The four of them took one another's hands and stood facing the Germans.

The room was quiet, as if the world had stopped moving and couldn't start up again until the officer gave the signal. His face seemed to switch between anger and something Hana couldn't name. She thought of a doll she'd once had, whose expression would change from sad to happy if you pushed a wooden peg in its neck. She clung to Konrád's hand and looked at the German's neck, but nothing was there except a high coat collar and a flap of flesh hanging over it.

"So you tell me I am to take all of you or none of you?" he asked.

"Yes," Mila said. Together, the rest of them repeated it after her.

"In God's name," the priest said, "leave them alone. The war will soon be over, what would you do with these poor children?"

"Shut up," the officer said. "I know what to do with *you.*"

Hana knew his next words would tell whether they lived or died, but it was impossible to guess which; it was like shutting your eyes and pushing the peg in the doll's neck back and forth and not knowing which expression would be there when you opened your eyes.

The officer gave a short laugh. "I cannot waste time with children who are so stupid they ask to be killed." Then, as if he was angry with them for making him say it, he shoved Konrád roughly. They all fell to the floor with him.

"God bless you," the priest cried. But to the four of them or to the German? They could never be sure.

The door opened. A knife of cold air sliced through the room. The soldiers pushed the priest outside. Boots clattered. The door closed. A motor roared. Everyone was gone.

The four of them got to their feet. They hugged Karel, who made funny little yips in his newly found voice. They came together and stood there hugging and holding, four bodies making a single knot of flesh with one heart and one thought: They had saved one another.

It was a moment she could never forget. Nearly forty years later she could still feel the oneness, skin to skin, and the thrill running through their common blood because they had succeeded.

The memory of that moment got them through what followed. For weeks they stayed on in the priest's attic, waiting for the weather to warm up a bit, one of them always on guard in case anyone approached the house. Then they traveled for some time, trying to get back to countryside they knew while staying out of the way of something as terrifying as Germans—the Red Army. Moving west to meet its allies, it was stealing and plundering everything in its path, so that land already bare and scabbed from years of Nazi rule was being plucked raw by filthy, unshaven Red soldiers. Finally, when they thought they were nearing Prague, so Mila could seek some trace of her family, they learned they were many miles south. A patrol of American soldiers found them and took them to Major Dan, who was able to find out that Mila and Konrád's parents had died in a camp. . . .

Afterward the war itself was something to be reduced to nightmares in a safe bed and finally pushed into the dark of the mind. But the thing that had got them through the Bad Times—the embrace they shared, the embrace of the Pact—that was forever. Born of the war, it was bigger than the war. It had saved them even in their new lives. At Cross of Glory, when Konrád had been accused of stealing money, they had all come forward and claimed to have done it, and Mother Louise had been helpless. It would always be part of them because it symbolized their oneness, their readiness to give their lives for one another. . . . a sacred covenant in a world where so few things were sacred.

Dinah looked across the desk at the pale blue eyes, now shining. She wanted to do two things—put her arms around Hannah again, and shake her in disbelief. Instead she cleared her throat and watched while Hannah lifted the paper cup that was still full of water and drank, using both hands.

Finally she said, "I can't conceive of what you all went through. I guess that's why it's hard to believe your Pact could still have such a hold over you."

"Oh, how can I make you . . ." Hannah's fingers dug into her face. "If you had lived through it, through things you can't forget no matter how deep you bury them . . . if you knew what it was like to feel the others with you, their bodies against yours, to know you had nothing left of your world, no parents, no home, but you were not alone. . . . It's part of you, something you couldn't separate from yourself even if you wanted to."

"So it was stronger," Dinah asked gently, "than what you felt for Vardis Wolf?"

"Yes." Hannah crumpled into her chair. "Yes."

"And Mila—Merle—said you had to use the Pact to save Conrad?"

"She called us together. She said Conrad had confessed to killing Vardis but if we used the Pact, we could save him . . . No!" she cried. "I can't believe Merle lied to us! Why would she let us think Conrad killed Vardis?"

"Perhaps," Dinah said, even more gently, "she couldn't take the chance her daughter would learn for certain that she was the guilty one."

Hannah looked up. Her face twisted with the effort of throwing off Dinah's words but finally sagged in defeat.

Dinah touched her hands again. "I think I'd better leave, Dr. Sebastian. Will you be all right? Is there anything I can get you?"

"No," Hannah said tonelessly. "Nothing."

As Dinah reached the door, Hannah said, "Are you going to tell the police?"

"I . . . don't know what I'm going to do."

CHAPTER
21

She left the office building and stopped short, blinking in the shock of sunlight. How could it not be dark in the world, and cold? But the clock on the bank opposite read only three-ten, and Second Avenue was warm, bright, and loud with traffic.

She wandered into a coffee shop and ordered a sandwich. After a time there were crusts on her plate, but she had no memory of eating or of doing anything except staring into space and seeing four children, who became four adults into whose lives she had been thrust. Or had blundered.

Or was the blunder yet to come?

She took out the notebook in which she'd recorded everything and began listing the things she now understood. At the end she was left with some smaller questions and a glaring large one. She knew it could be answered only one way.

Fifteen minutes later she was once again walking toward the Ashley town house, remembering how she had approached it first, feeling like a fly in amber.

She didn't want to see Jenny. Fortunately, no one seemed to be home in the basement apartment. She walked up to the front door and rang. He had to be there, hiding from the other three, and from everybody else. If he didn't answer, she would holler up at his windows until he did.

But after several minutes of ringing, the door opened. Ashley looked out, a full glass in one hand, and registered her presence. "Ah, yes," he said.

"Hello. Were you expecting me to come back?"

"No," he said. "I don't expect anything."

"I came to ask you something."

He looked at her, a glaze of politeness in his eyes.

"Will you let me in?"

"Why not?" He led her across the gray marble floor into a large room dominated by a white baby grand. There was a vase of white roses on it. Some petals had fallen to the carpet and lay curled and brown. The windows were closed and the air seemed to hang in heavy veils. "Please," Ashley said, gesturing to a chair. But Dinah didn't want to sit if he didn't, so they both stood, as if she were a prospective buyer and he a strangely elegant caretaker.

"Vardis died in this room. Did you know that? Over there." He pointed with his glass.

"No, I didn't know." Dinah cleared her throat. "Mr. Ashley, I came to ask why you confessed to the police."

He stared at her, then at the place where he'd pointed. "I confessed because I was guilty."

"I've talked to the other three—Cary, Hannah, and Merle. I know your sister killed Vardis, and I know why."

His grip tightened on the glass, but he said nothing.

"And I know about the Pact."

He looked into the glass, then drank deeply from it.

Dinah's voice was gentle. "Hannah told me your sister invoked the Pact *after* you confessed. Yet your sister told the others they had to use the Pact to save you—she was letting them think you had done it, or at least that you were determined to be convicted for it. But *you* knew you hadn't done it, so why did you confess?" He said nothing. "Was it to save your sister? But if that was it, how did you know she was guilty?"

"She isn't."

"Please, Mr. Ashley. None of the rest of you have motives as strong as hers. She had three of them: what Vardis had done to you, the way she was alienating Jenny . . ." Dinah waited for his eyes to lift to hers. "And an old crime your sister had let her get away with: trying to kill me."

Until that moment she had thought she was sure of Merle's guilt. But she knew there must have still been doubts when the look on his face dispelled them: The liquor glaze on his eyes cracked, and pain seeped through.

He whispered, "How do you know Vardis tried to kill you?"

"Your sister told me."

"But if you know that . . ." He sank into a chair so heavily that liquid slopped over the glass onto his slacks. He stared helplessly at the stain.

"Would you like me to get a towel or something?"

"No," he said, as if needing help was the final indignity. When he put the glass down, one edge hit the table before the other.

Dinah waited a moment. "Did you know your sister was guilty because she told you?" He was silent. "Maybe I can work it out. After Merle poisoned Vardis with cyanide she got from . . . from Hannah at her lab, she came to see you and said—"

"Not from Hannah," he said dully.

"Where, then?"

"I knew she was going to do it."

"You mean she told you?"

He shifted in the chair. "She came to see Vardis. A while before the last tour. She hadn't been here in a long time. Maybe years. I was . . . out when she came." He hesitated. "Buying a bottle. Why hide that when I'm telling the rest? I came in quietly, so Vardis wouldn't ask where I'd been. She and Merle were arguing. Loudly. In here. I stayed in the foyer and listened. Merle was telling Vardis to leave Jenny alone. To stop taking her away from her own mother and ruining her life the way she had ruined mine." He lifted the glass, drained it, set it back. He was articulating carefully, retrieving words from slurring, occasionally missing one. "I'd never heard Merle so angry. Not in all our lives. She said if Vardis didn't leave Jenny alone, she'd kill her. 'You had a daughter of your own,' she said. 'Why didn't you keep her instead of trying to take mine?' I didn't think I could have heard right, but she said it again. But that time she said Vardis had left the daughter to die and she, Merle, had saved her. The wors-worst part was, Vardis didn't deny it. She was furious. She kept saying if Merle talked about it to anyone, she'd take Jenny away from her so fast and far that Merle would never see her again.

Then Merle repeated it: 'Leave Jen alone or I'll kill you. I'll find some way to kill you.' And I knew she meant it. I know her so well. I knew she meant it."

He reached for the glass again and saw it was empty. His face sagged. "I couldn't believe Vardis had had a child. I tried to ask her—not directly, just asking if she ever thought about her first years in New York, if she didn't want to talk about those days sometimes. . . . She never did. She said I lived in the past too much." He sighed and stared into space.

In a moment he shook his head. "Vardis didn't leave Jenny alone. She fussed over her more than ever. So I knew it was going to happen. I didn't know how, but I kept waiting for it." He clenched his hands.

"Why didn't you talk to your sister and try to stop her?"

The look Ashley gave her told Dinah she must have hit on his deepest agony. In some way, to some degree, he had wanted to be free of Vardis. And knew, perhaps, that he lacked the strength to free himself.

"So when it happened," she said, "you just assumed Merle had done it? Or did you speak to her?"

"When they said it was cy-cyanide, I remembered the tins of old weed killer up in her potting shed. She'd talked about them last winter. I called her and asked if they were still there. She didn't answer at first. Then she said, in the oddest voice, 'Most of them are.' So I knew. 'It'll be all right,' I said. And I hung up."

"Then you went to the police and confessed, to save her?"

"I was as guilty as Merle!" he cried. "I stood there and watched her . . . over there! She was writhing and twis-twisting, bending like a hairpin, it was horrible, but I just stood and watched and thought, It's happening, she's dying, Merle has done it, she's always the one who does things for us, I must try to save Vardis but I don't want— Oh God!" he cried. "I didn't try to save her until it was too late!"

There was no way to comfort him, nothing to say. But she couldn't leave him, either. You couldn't walk away from such suffering. At the other end of the room was a handsome carved cabinet. She went to it, found it contained what she suspected, and brought back a fifth of Scotch. He looked up, said "Thank you" like a child, and filled his glass.

She sat close to him. "Mr. Ashley, please don't torture yourself this way. The random poisoner's victims—some of them didn't survive either, yet I think most of them were taken to the hospital right away. So the chances you could have saved Vardis aren't very good." Dinah hesitated. "And I can understand why you might have stood there for a few minutes and had some, well, negative thoughts. Because Vardis had been rather cruel to you, hadn't she?"

"Who told you that?"

"Cary Mathias."

"Ah. Cary." He smiled, then drank. "Did you learn all about Vardis? Tell me what you learned. No, I insist. I've told you things. Now you should tell me."

Dinah flushed. "I gather she was brilliant and mesmerizing and sometimes generous, but also . . . egocentric and ruthless and cruel. She seemed to need to, well, dominate people. To have power over them."

"Perfectly true." He drank. "And what do you make of it all?"

"She was full of contradictions. I'm not sure I'll ever understand her."

"Why should you? Who are you to understand a woman like Vardis Wolf? Who am I? Or any of us? Do you think a woman like that can be reduced to some petty psy-psychological formula that could fit the cleaning woman too? She was a genius! How can the complexity of her genius, how can it be confined by any explanation we could come up with? With our minds so much smaller than hers? We can't even understand the mystery of her art—how can we try to explain the mystery of her character?"

It was hard to believe he was the same person who had met her at the door—this man suddenly flushed with animation, as if he had caught it like a fever. "Maybe we can't understand," Dinah said doggedly, "but I think we have to try. If Vardis Wolf treated you cruelly, if she tried to kill me, we have to—"

"What she did to us doesn't matter! Don't you understand? We don't matter. Nothing matters except her music!"

Dinah stayed a while longer, although there was little else to say to the pathetic, elegant man who was racked with guilt because he had desired to be free of what he worshiped.

·   ·   ·

By the time she found a cab and got to East Forty-sixth Street, it was ten of six.

Demeter, Inc., was still open, although the receptionist was getting ready to leave. Yes, Mr. Mathias was there, but he was on a long-distance call and would she please have a seat?

She waited in limbo, vaguely aware of software packages framed on the walls, computer magazines piled on the tables, people leaving and saying good night. She heard his voice, calling something about advertising rates, and then he was in the door of the reception area, a cigarette in one hand. He smiled, pleased but puzzled. She wanted to run to him, but clutched the arms of the chair. He stubbed out the cigarette in an ashtray by the door and came to her. He took her hand and led her through a large room full of desks and computers, into his office. He stood looking at her, holding her hand by three fingers.

She raised her other hand to touch the moon-scar on his right cheekbone. "You got this in a priest's house. When a Nazi soldier hit you with his ring."

She felt his muscles leap with tension. "Who told you?"

"Hannah."

He sucked in his breath. "Did she tell you everything?"

"Everything I needed. Except what I just learned from Conrad."

He released her hand and sank onto the edge of his desk. "You were too tenacious, too smart. I suppose I knew you'd find out."

"Didn't you hope I would?"

"I don't know. Maybe."

She took a chair close to him. "It's the most terrible story I ever heard, and the most beautiful. I love the way you love each other and want to protect each other. I want to hold you in my arms for what you lived through."

"But? There's a but, isn't there?"

"I just have to be sure I understand. Does that relationship supersede . . . everything else?"

"I'm not sure you can understand."

"Try. Please."

"It feels . . . as if I was born with this feeling about them. Because I was, I guess. My life began the day they found me. That's the day it would have ended otherwise. My first memory is of Mila—Merle—coaxing me to come with them. . . . Do you realize what she did? She shepherded three children, one of us almost a baby, through occupied territory when she was a child herself—twelve, thirteen years old. She kept us away from German patrols and Nazi sympathizers and the Red Army, she found food and shelter, she saw that we didn't become wild animals. She kept us *alive.*"

"I think what she did was magnificent."

"But?" he said softly.

"I just want to understand. Do you mean that for the rest of your life, anything she asks, you'll do it?"

He was quiet for a while, eyes far away. "I don't remember a lot of it. I was too young. But the way I'll always see her . . . It was one night, after she'd given the rest of us whatever food there was. She'd cut herself some bark off a tree. It made her sick, so we stopped to rest. I guess she'd been carrying me, because she was still holding me. It was dark but the moon came through some clouds. I looked up at her face, and it was . . . There was this silver light pouring over her, and she was beautiful, but her eyes were closed and she looked so drained and still, like the bodies we had seen. I thought the Germans had killed her. I touched her face, and it was so cold. . . . But she opened her eyes and looked at me. I suppose I looked terrified. Then I saw her face come back to life, as if she was forcing herself . . . I can't explain it, forcing herself not to be dead, because she had to take care of us. I could feel the effort it took, feel it in my own body. The others woke up and she said she was all right, we were going to be all right because we were four-as-one, and we all held on to each other. . . . Yes, I'll do anything she asks."

"Forever?" No answer. "Cary, the Pact was almost forty years ago. You were children. It wasn't even very logical, was it? To give yourselves up in order to avoid reprisals?"

"What logic is there in war? There's dying and there's living, that's all. The Pact let us live."

"Yes, but . . ." She winced. "Back then you used it to save your lives. Now you've been using it to cover up a murder."

"For the record, it was to save Con. I didn't think he'd really done it, though God knows he had reason. I thought we were protecting him from making some crazy gesture of self-immolation. And after I met you, after I knew how you felt, don't you think I clung to that?" He must have seen the leap of hope in her eyes. He must have seen it die when he added, "I did it because Merle asked me to. But I'd have done it if I thought she was the guilty one."

After a silence Dinah said, "She didn't tell you the truth about it, did she?"

"It doesn't matter," he said harshly.

"I can understand why she didn't. I suppose she'd planned that Vardis's death would be taken as another random poisoning. But then Conrad confessed, and everything changed. She couldn't let him pay for her action. But if she told the truth, she'd have no hope of keeping her daughter. And keeping Jenny was the reason she'd killed Vardis in the first place. What a terrible choice. No wonder she decided not to do either one, and used the Pact instead."

He said nothing.

"Did you . . . I thought maybe you'd talk to Merle last night, after I left."

"I did."

"Then you know I'm right?"

He lifted his head. His eyes looked as if they burned. "There's no physical evidence against her. Against anybody."

"I know that, Cary. But she committed murder."

"Think of all you wanted Vardis to get away with."

"I think I was wrong."

They looked at each other. Her body remembered his so well. Too well. She heard a sound, like a whimper, and realized it had come from her.

"My darling," he said.

She stared at him, willing his mind to open and let in her thoughts. They would travel through the dark of his eyes, into his brain, to the sightless place where his soul was, and he would understand them . . .

"Cary," she said, "I don't want her to go to jail for killing Vardis Wolf! I don't want her to suffer anymore, I don't want any of you to suffer. But if it was wrong to let Vardis get away with what she did, does that make it right to let . . . Oh God, I don't know what I want. Yes I do, but it's not possible. I don't want Merle in prison, and I don't want to sanction murder. Vardis died horribly, you know. Haven't you read in the papers what it was like for people who took the cyanide pain-reliever pills?"

It was a long time before he spoke. "I never said I liked what we're doing, Dinah."

"But you'll keep on with it."

He didn't answer; it hadn't been a question.

She looked down the years and saw the four of them, their friendship turning into a prison, locking them to one another, never allowing them the peace of separateness, forcing them to carry the burden of their common knowledge until, perhaps, one of them could no longer bear the weight.

"Cary, have you thought about the future? Can the four of you live with this . . . knowledge for the rest of your lives? Can she?"

"We've lived through worse." He gave a wry smile that tore at her.

She stood up, as tall as he because he still sat on the edge of the desk, and tried to speak matter-of-factly. "I know you wonder what I'm going to do. I could keep after Hannah and Conrad, because they're the weak ones, aren't they? Try to make them break down completely and rescind their confessions. Or I could work on Jenny, maybe convince her that in justice to Vardis, the police have to know the truth. She's the one person who could get Merle to tell it, isn't she?" His eyes had gone very black. "But I won't do any of those things. I couldn't make myself do them."

His eyes closed. The lids trembled.

"So now I'm part of it, too," she said. "Covering up for a murder. The one thing I'd have sworn I could never, ever do. It feels like a terrible betrayal. But how can I do anything else?"

"Oh Christ," he whispered. "I never wanted to tear you apart. I wanted to make you happy."

"I know that."

He opened his eyes. "I'm forty-three, give or take a year. I didn't think I'd ever find anyone like you."

"I'm half in love with you," she said.

"Only half?" He tried to smile. "I'll go all the way."

If only he wouldn't look at her that way, she thought. If only Vardis Wolf hadn't come into their lives, and twisted people from the paths they would have taken. "I understand how you feel about your friends, Cary. I even admire it. But I can never share the feeling because it's from a different world. Yet it's the most important thing to you. More important than I could ever be."

"Don't say that, Dinah."

"You asked me to believe you were a murderer."

"It's the only lie I told you. And it damn near killed me."

"And you'd *still* be telling me you're a murderer if I hadn't dug out the truth. Wouldn't you?"

"I . . . don't know," he said.

"I do. You'd tell me if Merle and the others agreed. But only if. You're not free to be one person. You're four-as-one, for life."

Finally he said, "But you did dig out the truth."

"So it would always be up to me to dig out the truth if your friends didn't want me to know it?"

"There isn't anything else to dig out," he said pleadingly. "You've got it all."

If only he wouldn't look at her that way. She turned from him and went to the window. "Don't you understand?" she cried. "How could I be with you, with any of you, and not keep remembering that I'd betrayed things that matter deeply to me? Even if I believe that what I did was right?"

Down on the street, cars and people moved as if life was perfectly normal. She wanted to shout at them to stay out of each other's way because no encounter was ever painless and some were agonizing.

Behind her, she heard Cary sigh. "It's because of your husband, isn't it?"

"No, it's not." The words came out before she understood their meaning; then it began to penetrate, and she stood there listening to what she had said and realizing, finally, that it was true.

Slowly she turned back to him. "It isn't just because of Harry. I thought it was, you know—that if I cared about bringing murderers to justice and not cheating the law, it was because of the way Harry felt, and what happened to him. That is part of it, of course. But now I know that those things matter to *me*. I know it because I could never leave you if they didn't."

He came to her and took her in his arms and they rocked together in pain and comforting.

Finally she stood back. She put her fingers into his coarse, thick hair. "Good-bye, Karel Matyáš," she said.

If only he wouldn't look at her that way.

On a day that felt like summer, she waited at the West Seventy-second Street entrance to Central Park, watching people on the benches. They looked peaceful, deep in communion with the sun. Farther in on the grass, a couple on a blanket was kissing with trancelike intensity. In the city, Dinah thought, you were always private, protected by strangers' anonymity.

Behind her she heard her name. She turned and Sam was there, smiling, his eyes very blue and warm. "Hi," she said a bit shakily.

"Hi." His shoulders lifted and fell back. "Hope you don't mind having lunch in the park. It's such a damn nice day that I thought we—"

"It was a great idea." Then she heard "Oh, Sam" come blurting out and found to her horror that she was flinging herself against his chest, the most comforting place in the world.

"Hey, hey," he said. She felt his hands settle on her back.

As soon as she had a grip on herself, she pulled away. "I'm sorry."

"Don't be. I'm not." He grinned, then sobered. "Are you OK?"

"Yes. Fine. Let's get some lunch and sit down."

They bought food from one of the carts at the entrance and walked in. Sam found a shaded bench, carefully sat a few feet away from her, and finished two hot dogs in six bites. A cluster of pigeons strutted toward them, heads jerking in the search for crumbs. Sam popped up the top of a soda. "Not hungry?"

"Not really." Dinah laid most of a pita sandwich down on its wrapping. "I think I'd just like to say what I have to say."

"Sure." Sam rolled up his hot dog wrappers and lobbed them into a trash can. The pigeons flapped up noisily and settled back to their search.

"Sam, I found out all the things I wanted to know."

"Congratulations," he said quietly.

"I learned that Vardis Wolf didn't want to keep me because she thought a child would interfere with her career. But she didn't give me up. She tried to kill me. Left me somewhere to die."

"Jesus," Sam said. A long breath hissed out between his teeth. "What a rotten thing to discover." She saw his hand lift to reach for hers, then sink back. "Does it make you sorry you tried to find out?"

"A little. But regret is pointless, now that I have the truth. You know, Sam, I thought that if I learned about Vardis Wolf, I'd learn something about myself, who I am and where I came from. And I did, but not the way I expected. Because I don't really have anything to do with Vardis Wolf. Oh, I got physical things from her, like gray eyes, and I guess some people would argue that I inherited an affinity for music. But searching for her made me focus on who *I* am: the self-made person who has nothing to do with her. I learned something about the things that matter to me." She leaned forward. "And one of them is for justice to be done in this situation. But what *is* justice here? I've stayed awake nights trying to figure it out."

"You don't have to decide things like that," Sam said. "That's what the courts are for. And us—we're here to see that things get into the courts."

She sat up straight. "Let me say the rest of what I came for."

"OK." She felt his attention fix on her like a laser beam.

"I don't know if I've made the right decision about what to tell you, but it's . . . the decision I've made." She clasped her hands. "Sam, I don't think there's any way to make those four people tell you the truth. At least no way I could imagine, or would want to be part of. They're unbreakable from the outside. If they ever do break, it's going to come from within themselves."

"Didn't you break them?"

"No. I just got them to tell me things. And I put two and two together, that's all."

"That's what a cop does, Dinah. Maybe you should be working with us."

She stared at him. "Be a cop, you mean?"

"Why not? You've done a hell of a good job here. You stuck to it, you had brains and guts. And if you found out everything you wanted to know . . ."

Neither of them spoke for a while.

Finally she said, "Sam, they went through the war together. As children. They survived because of each other."

"I see," he finally said. He took a long drink of his soda. "If you told that to Harry, what do you think he'd do about it?"

"I'd . . . I think he'd feel the way I do. That you can understand why they protect one another. Even sympathize with it."

"Yeah, I think that's what Harry would feel. But I asked you what he'd *do*. Drop the case?"

"I don't think he could."

"That's right. He'd still have an open homicide."

"So he'd have to keep trying to solve it."

"That's right. And so do I. I don't know how much time I'll have for it, or how much help, but I have to keep on. Talking to people, sifting through the confessions and my notes, going over everything. Three people are telling a lie, and it's hard to keep telling a lie and be consistent. Maybe somebody will make a mistake, say something that doesn't jibe with what they said before. Maybe they can be charged with hindering a prosecution."

They were silent again. The world went on around them, full of chatter and wings and food smells. The sun was caught in the trees overhead, and a nursemaid sat across from them, rocking a carriage with one foot.

"I take it," Sam said, "that you're not going to tell me who killed Wolf?"

It was the moment she had been dreading. She said nothing.

His unspoken thought was so loud that she bit her lip to keep from answering it. From asking whether justice hadn't already been done; whether any court could decree a worse punishment for Merle Rostov than losing the daughter she had killed to keep.

"Well," Sam said, "God knows you don't have to tell me. You don't have to tell me anything at all."

She clenched her hands. "When Vardis Wolf left me to die, one of them saved me. One of the four."

"Ah," he said, stretching the sound out, very long.

He put his hands over his eyes for a moment. "OK, Dinah," he said. "I know what you're telling me. I can even understand."

But? she thought wryly. There's a but, isn't there?

He stood up. "I better be getting back. Lot of stuff piled on my desk."

She looked at him and saw the change take place. The man who had met her at the entrance to the park had been trying to hide that he was still half in love with her. This man was pulling away from her. From now on, she knew, he'd always have mixed feelings about her. But maybe that was good; it might be better for him. Easier.

They walked back to the edge of the park.

"You're disappointed in me. Aren't you, Sam?"

He looked at her, his face both rumpled and tight. "I won't lie to you, Dinah. Yeah. I am. No, don't tell me you're sorry. I know you're sorry. So am I."

Why, she thought, why couldn't he be the man she had fallen in love with?

He squared his shoulders and said, "Well, I'll be in touch. Take care."

"You too, Sam."

Why did it hurt so much? she thought as he walked away. When she hadn't even wanted him to fall in love with her?

That night, alone in the apartment, she took some records from the shelf and put them on the turntable. She curled on the couch, holding one of the jackets. In the cover photo the face was lifted in ecstasy, the hair fell back, the streak of white slanted from the temple like a dagger.

> *Stand here, my friend, with me*
> *And help me look at death.*
> *That is where our flowers*
> *Sprang from the earth, to live in the sun,*
> *And that is the wall where they stand to die. . . .*

She tried to listen as if she had never heard it before. After all, it was just a voice. Pure and mournful, but just a voice. Like mountain air. Like a gravesong high in the mountains . . . She hardened herself against it. *Don't confuse the artist with the work of art.* Cary had told her that, in the beginning.

> *See the knives come, see the blood run,*
> *Watch the cutting of all our young flowers . . .*

The voice had pulled words like *freedom* and *justice* down from their grand height of abstraction and thrust them at her with the immediacy of an embrace. Would the words mean as much to her today if she hadn't learned their power from that voice?

After leaving Sam, she had done a strange thing. Fordham was so close, and she had found herself walking over, standing in front of the law school. Thinking about the whole system of criminal justice. Not about working on the force, like Sam and Harry, but . . . Stay in teaching for a few more years, to finance law school at night? It could be done. Anything could be done, if you decided to do it. If the idea kept edging into your mind, if the search for Vardis Wolf had not only answered questions about the past but had also been a search for the future.

The next record clicked into place on the turntable. The voice began to sing in Italian: *Addio del passato*, farewell to everything the dying woman had cherished; a voice of silver and pain, rising in supplication, asking God's pity and pardon for her sins . . .

What if that voice had never sung? What if a Dinah Mitchell, trying to serve justice, had known of its crimes and taken actions that might have stilled it? Should she have done such things?

Could she have done them?

The voice went on, rising, reaching for her heart.

ABOUT THE AUTHOR

KAY NOLTE SMITH left the Midwest for New York in the late 1950s to become an actress and writer. She worked in the theater, doing summer stock and off-Broadway plays, and wrote short stories, mostly mysteries. She is the author of *The Watcher* (1980), winner of the Edgar Award for best first novel. Her acting experience prompted her to write *Catching Fire* (1982) and then *Mindspell* (1983). Mrs. Smith has also written film, theater, and opera criticism for *Opera News*, *Vogue*, and many other publications. Her lifelong passion for opera inspired her to write *Elegy for a Soprano*. She lives in New Jersey with her husband, Phillip J. Smith.